DAMAGE
6/10

D0225894

Title Withdrawn

JAN 0 8 2007

The Collected Works of

Langston Hughes

Volume 8

The Later Simple Stories

Projected Volumes in the Collected Works

The Poems: 1921–1940

The Poems: 1941–1950

The Poems: 1951–1967

The Novels: *Not without Laughter*
and *Tambourines to Glory*

The Plays to 1942: *Mulatto* to *The Sun Do Move*

The Gospel Plays, Operas, and Other
Late Dramatic Work

The Early Simple Stories

The Later Simple Stories

Essays on Art, Race, Politics, and World Affairs

Fight for Freedom and Other Writings on Civil Rights

Works for Children and Young Adults: Poetry,
Fiction, and Other Writing

Works for Children and Young Adults: Biographies

Autobiography: *The Big Sea*

Autobiography: *I Wonder As I Wander*

The Short Stories

The Translations: Federico García Lorca, Nicolás Guillén,
and Jacques Roumain

An Annotated Bibliography of the
Works of Langston Hughes

Publication of

The Collected Works of Langston Hughes

has been generously assisted by

Landon and Sarah Rowland

and

Morton and Estelle Sosland

Editorial Board

Arnold Rampersad, Chair, Stanford University

Dolan Hubbard, Morgan State University
Leslie Catherine Sanders, York University
Steven C. Tracy, University of Massachusetts, Amherst

The Collected Works of

Langston Hughes

Volume 8

The Later Simple Stories

Edited with an Introduction
by Donna Akiba Sullivan Harper

University of Missouri Press
Columbia and London

Copyright © 2002 by Ramona Bass and Arnold Rampersad, Administrators of the Estate of
    Langston Hughes
Introduction copyright © 2002 by Donna Akiba Sullivan Harper
Chronology copyright © 2001 by Arnold Rampersad
University of Missouri Press, Columbia, Missouri 65201
Printed and bound in the United States of America
All rights reserved
5 4 3 2 1   06 05 04 03 02

Library of Congress Cataloging-in-Publication Data

Hughes, Langston, 1902–1967
    [Works. 2001]
    The collected works of Langston Hughes / edited with an introduction by
Donna Akiba Sullivan Harper
      p.   cm.
    Includes bibliographical references and indexes.
    ISBN 0-8262-1409-6 (v. 8 : alk. paper)
    1. African Americans—Literary collections.   I. Harper, Donna Akiba Sullivan.
II. Title.
PS3515 .U274   2001
818'.5209—dc21   00066601

⊗™This paper meets the requirements of the
American National Standard for Permanence of Paper
for Printed Library Materials, Z39.48, 1984.

Designer: Kristie Lee
Typesetter: BOOKCOMP, Inc.
Printer and binder: Thomson-Shore, Inc.
Typefaces: Galliard, Optima

Contents

Acknowledgments

The University of Missouri Press is grateful for assistance from the following individuals and institutions in locating and making available copies of the original editions used in the preparation of this edition: Anne Barker and June DeWeese, Ellis Library, University of Missouri–Columbia; Teresa Gipson, Miller Nichols Library, University of Missouri–Kansas City; Ruth Carruth and Patricia C. Willis, Beinecke Rare Book and Manuscript Library, Yale University; Ann Pathega, Washington University.

The *Collected Works* would not have been possible without the support and assistance of Patricia Powell, Chris Byrne, and Wendy Schmalz of Harold Ober Associates, representing the estate of Langston Hughes, and of Arnold Rampersad and Ramona Bass, co-executors of the estate of Langston Hughes.

Akiba Harper thanks God, whose grace enables her to do whatever she has accomplished.

Chronology
By Arnold Rampersad

1902 James Langston Hughes is born February 1 in Joplin, Missouri, to James Nathaniel Hughes, a stenographer for a mining company, and Carrie Mercer Langston Hughes, a former government clerk.

1903 After his father immigrates to Mexico, Langston's mother takes him to Lawrence, Kansas, the home of Mary Langston, her twice-widowed mother. Mary Langston's first husband, Lewis Sheridan Leary, died fighting alongside John Brown at Harpers Ferry. Her second, Hughes's grandfather, was Charles Langston, a former abolitionist, Republican politician, and businessman.

1907 After a failed attempt at a reconciliation in Mexico, Langston and his mother return to Lawrence.

1909 Langston starts school in Topeka, Kansas, where he lives for a while with his mother before returning to his grandmother's home in Lawrence.

1915 Following Mary Langston's death, Hughes leaves Lawrence for Lincoln, Illinois, where his mother lives with her second husband, Homer Clark, and Homer Clark's young son by another union, Gwyn "Kit" Clark.

1916 Langston, elected class poet, graduates from the eighth grade. Moves to Cleveland, Ohio, and starts at Central High School there.

1918 Publishes early poems and short stories in his school's monthly magazine.

1919 Spends the summer in Toluca, Mexico, with his father.

1920 Graduates from Central High as class poet and editor of the school annual. Returns to Mexico to live with his father.

1921 In June, Hughes publishes "The Negro Speaks of Rivers" in *Crisis* magazine. In September, sponsored by his father, he enrolls at Columbia University in New York. Meets W. E. B. Du Bois, Jessie Fauset, and Countee Cullen.

1922   Unhappy at Columbia, Hughes withdraws from school and breaks with his father.

1923   Sailing in June to western Africa on the crew of a freighter, he visits Senegal, the Gold Coast, Nigeria, the Congo, and other countries.

1924   Spends several months in Paris working in the kitchen of a night-club.

1925   Lives in Washington for a year with his mother. His poem "The Weary Blues" wins first prize in a contest sponsored by *Opportunity* magazine, which leads to a book contract with Knopf through Carl Van Vechten. Becomes friends with several other young artists of the Harlem Renaissance, including Zora Neale Hurston, Wallace Thurman, and Arna Bontemps.

1926   In January his first book, *The Weary Blues,* appears. He enrolls at historically black Lincoln University, Pennsylvania. In June, the *Nation* weekly magazine publishes his landmark essay "The Negro Artist and the Racial Mountain."

1927   Knopf publishes his second book of verse, *Fine Clothes to the Jew,* which is condemned in the black press. Hughes meets his powerful patron Mrs. Charlotte Osgood Mason. Travels in the South with Hurston, who is also taken up by Mrs. Mason.

1929   Hughes graduates from Lincoln University.

1930   Publishes his first novel, *Not without Laughter* (Knopf). Visits Cuba and meets fellow poet Nicolás Guillén. Hughes is dismissed by Mrs. Mason in a painful break made worse by false charges of dishonesty leveled by Hurston over their play *Mule Bone.*

1931   Demoralized, he travels to Haiti. Publishes work in the communist magazine *New Masses.* Supported by the Rosenwald Foundation, he tours the South taking his poetry to the people. In Alabama, he visits some of the Scottsboro Boys in prison. His brief collection of poems *Dear Lovely Death* is privately printed in Amenia, New York. Hughes and the illustrator Prentiss Taylor publish a verse pamphlet, *The Negro Mother.*

1932   With Taylor, he publishes *Scottsboro, Limited,* a short play and four poems. From Knopf comes *The Dream Keeper,* a book of previously published poems selected for young people. Later, Macmillan brings out *Popo and Fifina,* a children's story about Haiti written with Arna Bontemps, his closest friend. In June, Hughes sails to Russia in a band of twenty-two young African

Americans to make a film about race relations in the United States. After the project collapses, he lives for a year in the Soviet Union. Publishes his most radical verse, including "Good Morning Revolution" and "Goodbye Christ."

1933   Returns home at midyear via China and Japan. Supported by a patron, Noël Sullivan of San Francisco, Hughes spends a year in Carmel writing short stories.

1934   Knopf publishes his first short story collection, *The Ways of White Folks*. After labor unrest in California threatens his safety, he leaves for Mexico following news of his father's death.

1935   Spends several months in Mexico, mainly translating short stories by local leftist writers. Lives for some time with the photographer Henri Cartier-Bresson. Returning almost destitute to the United States, he joins his mother in Oberlin, Ohio. Visits New York for the Broadway production of his play *Mulatto* and clashes with its producer over changes in the script. Unhappy, he writes the poem "Let America Be America Again."

1936   Wins a Guggenheim Foundation fellowship for work on a novel but soon turns mainly to writing plays in association with the Karamu Theater in Cleveland. Karamu stages his farce *Little Ham* and his historical drama about Haiti, *Troubled Island*.

1937   Karamu stages *Joy to My Soul*, another comedy. In July, he visits Paris for the League of American Writers. He then travels to Spain, where he spends the rest of the year reporting on the civil war for the *Baltimore Afro-American*.

1938   In New York, Hughes founds the radical Harlem Suitcase Theater, which stages his agitprop play *Don't You Want to Be Free?* The leftist International Workers Order publishes *A New Song*, a pamphlet of radical verse. Karamu stages his play *Front Porch*. His mother dies.

1939   In Hollywood he writes the script for the movie *Way Down South*, which is criticized for stereotyping black life. Hughes goes for an extended stay in Carmel, California, again as the guest of Noël Sullivan.

1940   His autobiography *The Big Sea* appears (Knopf). He is picketed by a religious group for his poem "Goodbye Christ," which he publicly renounces.

1941   With a Rosenwald Fund fellowship for playwriting, he leaves California for Chicago, where he founds the Skyloft Players. Moves on to New York in December.

1942   Knopf publishes his book of verse *Shakespeare in Harlem*. The Skyloft Players stage his play *The Sun Do Move*. In the summer he resides at the Yaddo writers' and artists' colony, New York. Hughes also works as a writer in support of the war effort. In November he starts "Here to Yonder," a weekly column in the Chicago *Defender* newspaper.

1943   "Here to Yonder" introduces Jesse B. Semple, or Simple, a comic Harlem character who quickly becomes its most popular feature. Hughes publishes *Jim Crow's Last Stand* (Negro Publication Society of America), a pamphlet of verse about the struggle for civil rights.

1944   Comes under surveillance by the FBI because of his former radicalism.

1945   With Mercer Cook, translates and later publishes *Masters of the Dew* (Reynal and Hitchcock), a novel by Jacques Roumain of Haiti.

1947   His work as librettist with Kurt Weill and Elmer Rice on the Broadway musical play *Street Scene* brings Hughes a financial windfall. He vacations in Jamaica. Knopf publishes *Fields of Wonder*, his only book composed mainly of lyric poems on nonracial topics.

1948   Hughes is denounced (erroneously) as a communist in the U.S. Senate. He buys a townhouse in Harlem and moves in with his longtime friends Toy and Emerson Harper.

1949   Doubleday publishes *Poetry of the Negro, 1746–1949*, an anthology edited with Arna Bontemps. Also published are *One-Way Ticket* (Knopf), a book of poems, and *Cuba Libre: Poems of Nicolás Guillén* (Anderson and Ritchie), translated by Hughes and Ben Frederic Carruthers. Hughes teaches for three months at the University of Chicago Lab School for children. His opera about Haiti with William Grant Still, *Troubled Island*, is presented in New York.

1950   Another opera, *The Barrier*, with music by Jan Meyerowitz, is hailed in New York but later fails on Broadway. Simon and Schuster publishes *Simple Speaks His Mind*, the first of five books based on his newspaper columns.

1951   Hughes's book of poems about life in Harlem, *Montage of a Dream Deferred*, appears (Henry Holt).

1952   His second collection of short stories, *Laughing to Keep from Crying*, is published by Henry Holt. In its "First Book" series for children, Franklin Watts publishes Hughes's *The First Book of Negroes.*

1953 In March, forced to testify before Senator Joseph McCarthy's subcommittee on subversive activities, Hughes is exonerated after repudiating his past radicalism. *Simple Takes a Wife* appears.

1954 Mainly for young readers, he publishes *Famous American Negroes* (Dodd, Mead) and *The First Book of Rhythms.*

1955 Publishes *The First Book of Jazz* and finishes *Famous Negro Music Makers* (Dodd, Mead). In November, Simon and Schuster publishes *The Sweet Flypaper of Life,* a narrative of Harlem with photographs by Roy DeCarava.

1956 Hughes's second volume of autobiography, *I Wonder As I Wander* (Rinehart), appears, as well as *A Pictorial History of the Negro* (Crown), coedited with Milton Meltzer, and *The First Book of the West Indies.*

1957 *Esther,* an opera with composer Jan Meyerowitz, has its premiere in Illinois. Rinehart publishes *Simple Stakes a Claim* as a novel. Hughes's musical play *Simply Heavenly,* based on his Simple character, runs for several weeks off and then on Broadway. Hughes translates and publishes *Selected Poems of Gabriela Mistral* (Indiana University Press).

1958 *The Langston Hughes Reader* (George Braziller) appears, as well as *The Book of Negro Folklore* (Dodd, Mead), coedited with Arna Bontemps, and another juvenile, *Famous Negro Heroes of America* (Dodd, Mead). John Day publishes a short novel, *Tambourines to Glory,* based on a Hughes gospel musical play.

1959 Hughes's *Selected Poems* published (Knopf).

1960 *The First Book of Africa* appears, along with *An African Treasury: Articles, Essays, Stories, Poems by Black Africans,* edited by Hughes (Crown).

1961 Inducted into the National Institute of Arts and Letters. Knopf publishes his book-length poem *Ask Your Mama: 12 Moods for Jazz. The Best of Simple,* drawn from the columns, appears (Hill and Wang). Hughes writes his gospel musical plays *Black Nativity* and *The Prodigal Son.* He visits Africa again.

1962 Begins a weekly column for the *New York Post.* Attends a writers' conference in Uganda. Publishes *Fight for Freedom: The Story of the NAACP,* commissioned by the organization.

1963 His third collection of short stories, *Something in Common,* appears from Hill and Wang. Indiana University Press publishes

Five Plays by Langston Hughes, edited by Webster Smalley, as well as Hughes's anthology *Poems from Black Africa, Ethiopia, and Other Countries.*

1964   His musical play *Jericho–Jim Crow,* a tribute to the civil rights movement, is staged in Greenwich Village. Indiana University Press brings out his anthology *New Negro Poets: U.S.A.,* with a foreword by Gwendolyn Brooks.

1965   With novelists Paule Marshall and William Melvin Kelley, Hughes visits Europe for the U.S. State Department. His gospel play *The Prodigal Son* and his cantata with music by David Amram, *Let Us Remember,* are staged.

1966   After twenty-three years, Hughes ends his depiction of Simple in his Chicago *Defender* column. Publishes *The Book of Negro Humor* (Dodd, Mead). In a visit sponsored by the U.S. government, he is honored in Dakar, Senegal, at the First World Festival of Negro Arts.

1967   His *The Best Short Stories by Negro Writers: An Anthology from 1899 to the Present* (Little, Brown) includes the first published story by Alice Walker. On May 22, Hughes dies at New York Polyclinic Hospital in Manhattan from complications following prostate surgery. Later that year, two books appear: *The Panther and the Lash: Poems of Our Times* (Knopf) and, with Milton Meltzer, *Black Magic: A Pictorial History of the Negro in American Entertainment* (Prentice Hall).

The Collected Works of
Langston Hughes

Volume 8

The Later Simple Stories

Introduction

Langston Hughes established himself as a permanent figure in world literature by carrying out his own mission "to make a living from *the kind of writing I wanted to do.* . . . I wanted to write seriously and as well as I knew how about the Negro people, and make *that* kind of writing earn for me a living."[1] Most readers think first of poetry when they hear Hughes's name, and without question poetry is the hallmark of his career. Nevertheless, his efforts to earn a living as a writer led him to produce works in nearly every conceivable genre. While he wrote several volumes of short fiction, no other character has endured or has received the critical and popular acclaim of Jesse B. Semple, best known as "Simple."

Born in Virginia, Simple moved north to Baltimore, Maryland, as a young man. According to his "Remembrances," included in this volume, he moved to escape the repercussions of an irate parent's false accusations that he had fathered her daughter's child. When his marriage to his first wife, Isabel, failed, he left her and Baltimore.[2] He settled in Harlem, and his stories emerge mostly as conversations with a bar buddy who serves as narrator for the reader and as foil for Simple. This narrator originated as Langston Hughes himself when the character first appeared in the February 13, 1943, edition of the *Chicago Defender.* Hughes experimented occasionally in his weekly column, and "My Simple Minded Friend" first appeared only as an experiment, allowing Hughes to express the limited viewpoints of some blacks who had not traveled as extensively as he had. Readers loved Simple's viewpoint, however. In response to enthusiastic fan mail in praise of Simple, Hughes withdrew his own journalistic voice and his name; instead, he created a more erudite and more proper foil for Simple. Although seldom named, this foil came to be known as Ananias Boyd. With this foil, Simple discusses the women in his life, his boss, national politics, economics, and various fantasies. "You know I like to talk," says Simple in "Interview." Because the foil represents a different

1. *I Wonder As I Wander* (New York: Hill and Wang, 1964), 5.
2. See "Less than a Damn," in *The Collected Works of Langston Hughes, vol. 7, The Early Simple Stories,* 209.

background and a different perspective, his dialogues with Simple are often provocative.

The Early Simple Stories republishes the first two volumes that Hughes collected, *Simple Speaks His Mind* and *Simple Takes a Wife,* originally published in 1950 and 1953, respectively. Readers of these later stories would do well to know the characters introduced in the early stories, when Langston Hughes conscientiously translated his fictional Harlem everyman from newspaper columns to books. One needs the background of the early stories to understand Simple's youth, his failed first marriage to Isabel, his extended courtship of Joyce Lane, his frequent forays with good-time girl Zarita, his constant financial deficits, and his consistent frustration with the empty promises of "liberty and justice for all" in an America that never let him forget he was a Negro citizen—not a fully privileged U.S. citizen.

This volume, *The Later Simple Stories,* returns to print the third and fourth volumes of Simple stories, *Simple Stakes a Claim* (1957) and *Simple's Uncle Sam* (1965), along with some episodes Hughes did not include in any of his books. More than did the early stories, these later episodes rely on the historical and social context within which they were produced. The stories in this volume revive the genial Harlem everyman, Jesse B. Semple, and his more reserved and more cosmopolitan bar buddy, Boyd. Simple still utters some of his noteworthy and repeatable lines. For example, "Love is a many-splintered thing," he sings in "The Moon." Social climber Joyce Lane is now Mrs. Jesse B. Semple, and she has curbed Simple's budget for beer, if not his appetite. Simple has voluntarily minimized his flirtatious contacts with other women, happily and proudly claiming his wife as the only woman in his life. Thus, Zarita is occasionally mentioned but does not appear in the later stories collected by Hughes.

Readers will not miss Zarita, however, because the later stories introduce two unforgettable and powerful female characters, Simple's cousins Minnie and Lynn Clarisse. Minnie becomes a recurring character who eventually carries a few of her own episodes without interpretation from Simple. Cousin Minnie drops in on Jesse, having come north from Virginia to find freedom. As we learn in "Cousin Minnie Wins," she, like Simple, has left behind both the South and a failed relationship. She enjoys alcohol as much as does Simple, but she must preserve her honor while still accepting drinks from men at the bars. The stories allow us to observe both her skills of "self-protection" against men and her willingness to riot to defend her rights as a citizen.

Simple's cousin Lynn Clarisse, on the other hand, is featured as the titular character in only one episode, but she is mentioned in others and represents the well-educated black woman. Lynn Clarisse is the only character in whom the bar buddy Boyd ever appears to take a romantic interest. Educated at Fisk University, she enjoys literature, theater, and philosophy. More important, however, she takes a truly activist role in trying to ameliorate some of the racist woes that Minnie escapes from and Simple pontificates about. Unlike Simple's cousins F.D. and Minnie, Lynn Clarisse cannot remain in Harlem, because her conscience calls her back to do the work required to achieve voting rights for blacks in the South.

In the later stores, and especially in some of the episodes Hughes did not collect into books, Joyce Lane Semple emerges from her prim and upwardly mobile niche to display pride and knowledge about her African heritage. In "Africa's Daughters," for instance, she shows a diasporic consciousness that had certainly not been evident in her earlier associations with Mrs. Sadie Maxwell-Reeves and the Athenian Ladies Club that held the unforgettably embarrassing "Banquet in Honor."[3] Simple notes in "Roots and Trees" that women are taking "*action and more action.*" Even Simple himself displays the broader sensibilities that had been the original aim of Hughes's column. Ever conscious of race, Simple offers thought-provoking links between colored populations and the use of atomic weapons and even birth control measures in "Serious Talk about the Atom Bomb" and "Population Explosion." In one highly unusual episode, "Money and Mice," Simple refuses to bring race into his discussions of labor and animal rights. In "Simple Arithmetic," he reveals an increasingly impressive knowledge of black history. Clearly the Simple who bids us all "Hail and Farewell" from the *New York Post* on December 31, 1965, is no longer the naive and provincial fellow Langston Hughes introduced to the reading public on February 13, 1943, in the *Chicago Defender.*

Simple remains focused on race, however. He points out the shortcomings of his own people in addition to the flaws of the white and powerful. He observes that his Cousin Minnie has no business accepting a gift of a poodle ("Dog Days"), and he notes that cantankerous counter clerks "can spoil even soul food" ("Soul Food"). Readers will also see in several stories comments still overheard today in black communities. "Foreign colored folks carries more weight than us home-grown kind,"

3. Ibid., 74.

Simple laments in "Only Human." He also notes, "I am used to American whites getting the best go. But I just hate to see some old foreign whites come here and have the same break" ("Be Broad-Minded, Please"). Residents of black communities still complain about their own disadvantages in the face of perceived advantages given to international folks. On the other hand, the foil continues to help balance the picture. Similar to Thomas Sowell, the syndicated columnist and Stanford economist, or Ken Hambin, radio's "Black Avenger," the foil chastises Simple by telling him in "Face and Race": "It is so easy to blame all one's failures on race, . . . to whine *I can't do this, I can't do that* because I'm colored. That, I think, is one bad habit you have, friend—always bringing up race." Taken together, the foil and Simple represent divergent views about race and racism. Thus, they allow readers to think and to form their own opinions.

The stories first gathered in *Simple Stakes a Claim* and *Simple's Uncle Sam* reflect the times in which they were written, not just the fictional adventures and fantasies of the main characters. These circumstantial reflections are both an asset and a liability. *Simple Stakes a Claim* was published in 1957, and it reflects the troubled and troublesome period of the McCarthy trials and the Cold War. *Simple's Uncle Sam* appeared in 1965, and it captures the turbulent era when Black Americans asserted their rights, including their privilege to call themselves "Black" and wear their hair in natural styles. The nonviolent strategies of civil disobedience and the violent strategies of urban rioting had converged to amplify African American voices as they demanded justice. These dangerously political times did not lend themselves to humor—for Hughes or for anyone else.

Hughes's own history as a writer might explain the obvious erosion of aesthetic detachment in *Simple Stakes a Claim* and *Simple's Uncle Sam*. From the days of his earliest poetic efforts, the realities of his life weighed in to shape his works. His famous poem "The Negro Speaks of Rivers" emerged from his feelings about his parents' hostility toward each other. Many of his astonishing short stories in *The Ways of White Folks* reflect his complicated relationship with his own patron, Mrs. Charlotte Osgood Mason. The earliest Simple stories and the newspaper columns in which they first appeared provided Hughes a means of addressing blacks during the turbulent and politically complicated years of World War II, but those were years that had afforded him some measure of aesthetic detachment.

Hughes's personal detachment was dissolved by his own appearance before the Sen. Joseph McCarthy's Senate Permanent Sub-Committee on Investigations in 1953. Nearly everyone's detachment was eroded by the lynching of fourteen-year-old Emmett Till in Mississippi in 1955. Till's murder is mentioned in many of the stories from the 1957 collection, and the reality of that shocking crime casts a sober tone on the stories in which it is mentioned. Similarly, *Simple's Uncle Sam* never lets the reader forget the September 15, 1964, bombing of Sixteenth Street Baptist Church in Birmingham, Alabama. That act of terrorism took the lives of four young girls attending Sunday school. Both of these collections remind readers that daily life in the United States had been decorated with new signs bearing yellow, triform designs. These signs purportedly identified spaces then thought to be shelters from nuclear bombs. Children added bomb drills to their fire drills in schools, innocently practicing their face-shielding maneuvers. The threat of atomic bombs was very much a part of daily life after World War II ended, and the anxiety mounted during the Cold War and especially after the Cuban Missile Crisis. Thus, Langston Hughes was affected by the times as author, as ethnographer, and as participant-observer. The seriousness of the era crept into the later Simple stories to a degree that the politics of the 1940s had not overshadowed the earlier stories.

Readers may find it ironic that Hughes includes his *Chicago Defender* column from November 6, 1943, "Let's Laugh a Little," as part of the foreword to *Simple Stakes a Claim*.[4] After all, *Claim* clearly reveals the politically distrustful era in which it was published. Yet Hughes offers a strategy to conquer Dixiecrats, who remained active: "Since we have not been able to moralize them out of existence with indignant editorials, maybe we could laugh them to death with well-aimed ridicule," he suggests. The reader has to wonder, however, if the book accomplished the goals of the foreword. Although "Simple's Platform" amuses us with its digs at "politicianers," "Duty Is Not Snooty" becomes preachy rather than entertaining, and even the bar buddy fails to enter the dialogue with a meaningful alternate viewpoint. Boyd merely punctuates Simple's list of things that whites need to experience. One might chuckle just a bit, but the closing line is far more cynical than humorous. One doubts that such a story could "laugh them to death." Thus, despite his obvious awareness of the value of humor, Hughes relied more on sarcasm or pointed criticism than on humor in these later stories.

After he received his own copy of *Simple Stakes a Claim*, Carl Van Vechten commented to Hughes that the foreword "takes some of the

---

4. The other portion of the foreword was a tribute to the Negro press, "Nothing Like It," from the *Chicago Defender*, June 19, 1948.

sting away from the race talk with its constant insistence on the villainy of the white man." As a friend of Hughes and a patron of black creativity, Van Vechten certainly could not have felt that he deserved the sharp criticisms about racist white behaviors. Nevertheless, he wrote to Hughes, "white men innocent of misbehavior towards black brothers will read some pages with burning cheeks."[5] Van Vechten thought it was important that white readers feel embarrassed about the illogical and hurtful racist behaviors that Southern whites were inflicting upon blacks. Thus, while the book may not have had readers laughing, their emotional response may have been appropriate and important. Half a century later, in an era when affirmative action is scorned in some legal and social circles, that response may be even more important.

Perhaps before sitting down to read this volume of Simple stories, readers ought to review *Jet* magazine from the 1950s and early 1960s, to see the hideous and grotesque remains of Emmett Till. His mother insisted on an open casket, because she wanted the world to see what had been done to her son. Maybe readers should view the television series *Eyes on the Prize,* to see the marches, demonstrations, and violent retaliations that led to voting rights and desegregation in the South. Maybe readers should watch Spike Lee's film *Four Little Girls,* to see how the terrorist explosion by racist extremists in Birmingham ended four truly innocent lives. Perhaps readers should view or review such images to see why Simple—why Langston Hughes—was not laughing or making us laugh very much in these stories.

One explanation for a conspicuous departure in the later stories from the depth of character development in the early stories is that Simple had reached a stage of life that Hughes could only speculate about. Simple had married Joyce at the end of *Simple Takes a Wife,* but Hughes never married. He had friends who were married, including collaborator and Fisk University librarian Arna Bontemps and photographer Griffith J. Davis, who had rented a room in Hughes's brownstone. Nevertheless, it makes sense that Hughes struggled—and sometimes fumbled—trying to represent the domestic life of a married couple in a fictional series extending for a decade after the marriage. With every year of Simple's marriage, Langston Hughes was further removed from his valuable vantage point as participant-observer.

5. Carl Van Vechten to Langston Hughes, August 18. 1957, James Weldon Johnson collection, Langston Hughes correspondence, Yale Collection of American Literature, Beinecke Rare Book and Manuscript Library.

The additional stories included in this volume were never published in a book that Hughes assembled, but they were all published in *The Return of Simple*.[6] They cover nearly the entire chronological span of the Simple stories, from June 24, 1944, when Simple first meets Zarita ("On Women Who Drink You Up"), to December 31, 1965, when he bids farewell to the bar, his bar buddy, and his readers ("Hail and Farewell").

Although correspondence shows that Hughes selected for his books the Simple stories that seemed most likely to endure, one must wonder why he didn't believe his discussion in "Liberals Need a Mascot" would be perfectly clear and humorous for decades to follow. Likewise, all the adventures of Cousin Minnie seem timeless, especially her well-planned revenge against a two-timing lover in "Cousin Minnie Wins."

Some of the additional episodes are selected specifically because they *do* reflect the times in which they were created, particularly the emergence of the black pride movement, seldom associated with the Simple stories. Although in her early years Joyce appears to be "brainwashed," she changes her attitudes in the later stories. Even though Joyce insists that she will not don African robes to "pass for African," she spends time exploring black history in the Schomburg library and desires to attend a meeting in Africa. Her enthusiastic description of the conference articulates a diasporic consciousness and a woman-centered consciousness never before revealed in the Simple stories. In "Africa's Daughters," she explains to her husband the conference she hopes to attend.

> "I am talking about . . . an African conference of women, black . . . like me! From all over the world where there are black women—which is the U.S.A., also Cuba, Haiti, Jamaica, and Trinidad. Also Brazil . . . and all the West Indies, not to speak of Africa, full of beautiful black women! From everywhere the sisters of Africa are coming together next spring to meet to discuss how to get a good education for every child of every black woman. Also how to be sure husbands and fathers make a decent living anywhere in the world. Also that no woman has to be beholding to any man, white or black, for her living. And no woman needs to make her body a part of her job, like too many women have had to do in the past."

Langston Hughes is seldom recognized for penning such bold declarations of women's rights, especially within the Simple stories. Simple himself is justifiably labeled sexist because of many of his opinions, but

---

6. Edited by Donna Akiba Sullivan Harper and published by Hill and Wang in 1994.

the female characters who speak in these later and uncollected episodes help to balance the scales.

Even with the inclusion of the additional stories in this volume, not all of the Simple episodes have been collected. The editorial decision to allow some of the columns to remain buried in the archives results from an awareness that some of the Simple stories were hastily produced to meet journalistic deadlines. Thus, retrieving all of the stories might diminish the craft Hughes applied to his finished stories. The additional episodes gathered here are offered in light of all the stories Hughes did collect. These stories expand the roles and voices of women and increase the spectrum of local and global issues discussed by Simple.

Respectful of Hughes's own desire to keep an eye on the potential tastes of posterity, this volume rounds out the presentation of Jesse B. Semple and the various people in his world. He and his foil sometimes make us chuckle, but more important, they make us think. While these episodes often focus on particularities of the times, they also articulate broader truths that remain valuable. After all, as the foil tells Simple in "Jim Crow's Funeral," "the trouble is that the patterns of evil are not individual, they are social. They spread among a great many people. Electrocute one murderer today, but someone else is committing murder some other place at that very moment." Perhaps patterns of good are similarly social, and these Simple stories may help to spread among many people the will to engage in open dialogue and to work together for mutually beneficial aims. Through his newspaper columns and through these stories that emerged from the columns, Langston Hughes brought to the reading public some Simple solutions, and as the foil says in "Concernment," "Simplicity can sometimes be more devious than erudition."

A Note on the Text

For this edition of the third and fourth volumes of Simple stories, we have used the first editions of *Simple Stakes a Claim*, published by Rinehart and Company in 1957, and *Simple's Uncle Sam*, published by Hill and Wang in 1965. All spellings, capitalization, punctuation, and word compounding have been retained as they originally appeared, although obvious typographical errors have been corrected.

Most of the uncollected stories are from Langston Hughes's manuscripts preserved in the James Weldon Johnson Collection at the Beinecke Library at Yale University. The manuscripts generally had been revised for publication, but they had not actually been included in a book during Hughes's lifetime. Several of the uncollected stories had been published only in the *Chicago Defender* from 1944 to 1949 ("On Women Who Drunk You Up," June 24, 1944; "Simple and the High Prices," April 19, 1947; "Liberals Need a Mascot," May 21, 1949; "Serious Talk about the Atom Bomb," August 18, 1945; "Simple's Psychosis," May 18, 1946). These apparently were not revised and were simply left behind. Three episodes were from the *New York Post* in August and December 1965 ("Little Klanny," August 14, 1965; "Population Explosion," December 10, 1965; "Hail and Farewell," December 31, 1965). These were printed after Hughes had compiled his manuscript for *Simple's Uncle Sam*. All of the uncollected stories follow the texts published in *The Return of Simple* (New York: Hill and Wang, 1994).

Hughes sprinkled the names of his well-known contemporaries throughout his stories. Most of the sports figures, musicians, and others mentioned should be easily recognizable. A few less well known today have been identified in the notes.

Simple Stakes a Claim

(1957)

To Adele Glasgow

Simple originated in the *Chicago Defender.* The author and publisher are grateful to that newspaper for permission to reprint the material that first appeared in its pages.

Contents

Foreword: Let's Laugh a Little

My favorite reading is the Negro press. I know it should be the *Iliad,* the *Odyssey,* Shakespeare, or Tolstoy, but it isn't. It is the Negro press. Every week the Lord sends, if possible, in Harlem, I buy the *Courier,* the *Afro, Jet,* the *Amsterdam News,* and, of course, the *Defender* for which I write—so I can read myself. Also I buy whatever local colored papers there are in whatever city I may be when traveling. Whenever I find myself in a town where the colored papers are not available—like Carmel, California—I feel on weekends as though I were completely out of this world and have lost contact with my people. Abroad, the two things that I miss most are American ice cream and Negro newspapers.

In my time I have been all around the world and I assure you there is nothing printed in the world like the American Negro press. It is unique, intriguing, exciting, exalting, low-down and terrific. It is also tragic and terrible, brave, pathetic, funny and full of tears. It's me and my papa and mama and Adam Powell and Hazel Scott and Rev. Martin King, Eartha Kitt, and folks who are no blood relation of mine but are brothers and sisters in skin. It is also George S. Schuyler.

When I was a child, headlines in the colored papers used to scare the daylights out of me. I grew up in Kansas and for years I was afraid to go down South, thinking—as a result of the Negro press—that I might be lynched the minute I got off the train. Now the colored papers still help to keep me afraid of Southern white folks. Even on the days when white folks do not do anything bad to me, I read in the papers about what they have just done to others. Democracy as recorded in the Negro press certainly has a woeful record.

However, up to date, America's traditional freedom of speech finds one of its strongest examples in the Negro press. There the Negro race says just about anything it wishes to say concerning white folks, and democracy, too. *The Black Dispatch* of Oklahoma City, edited by Roscoe Dungee, has some of the longest, strongest, and most unique editorials against prejudice in the world.

Humor in headlines is also a unique contribution of certain of our race papers. The *Baltimore Afro-American* and the *Los Angeles Tribune* are particularly blessed with impish souls in the editorial rooms. (In the case of the *Tribune* I suspect it is Almena Lomax, who is the female Philip Wylie of Negro Journalism.) The leading editorial in a *Tribune*'s pre–Mother's Day issue once was, THE HAND THAT ROCKS THE CRADLE HAS GOT THE WORLD ALL LOUSED UP. Easterners have not yet forgotten an *Afro-American* news headline some years ago: GROOM HONEYMOONS WITH BEST MAN. Since then, the *Afro* has inserted many more laughs into its heads and even more into its news coverage.

But Negro newspapers do not intend to be funny—and usually they are not. For a race with so great a sense of humor, however, as that of the Negro people, it is strange that we have no primarily humorous publications. Since we have in our race a number of excellent cartoonists—some unsurpassed in America—and since we have several good writers capable of creating fun on paper, a humorous Negro monthly magazine should be a welcome addition to American cultural life and a happy success from the beginning. For cartoonists there are E. Simms Campbell, kingpin of *Esquire;* Ollie Harrington, creator of Bootsie; Mel Tapley of the *Amsterdam News;* plus a number of others.

Among writers of humor there is the inimitable Zora Neale Hurston, who is one of the most amusing and aggravating female scribes living. There is Evelyn Cunningham, Nat Williams and Ted Poston, also George S. Schuyler whose wry satire carries a punch as well as a laugh. There is Dan Burley, the Ring Lardner of the Negro race, and an old past master of Harlem jive talk. There is Arna Bontemps, who has a rare sense of humor when he chooses to put his mind to it. And from the entertainment world, Pearl Bailey, Willie Bryant, Nipsey Russell, Jackie Mabley, or Timmie Rogers could dictate a bit of hot cha for publication now and then. And maybe Gerri Major of the old *Tattler* might be persuaded to take up her sparkle as of yore.

I would love to write for a humorous Negro publication. The serious colored magazines like the *Crisis* or *Phylon* do not publish humor even if given to them *free*. These magazines evidently think the race problem is too deep for comic relief. Such earnestness is contrary to mass Negro thinking. Colored people are always laughing at some wry Jim Crow incident or absurd nuance of the color line. If Negroes took all the white world's daily boorishness to heart and wept over it as profoundly as our serious writers do, we would have been dead long ago.

Humor is a weapon, too, of no mean value against one's foes. In the Latin American countries, it is used socially. The humorous magazines there are often more dangerous to a crooked but ambitious politician than the most serious articles in the intellectual press. Think what colored people in the United States could do with a magazine devoted to satire and fun at the expense of the Dixiecrats. Since we have not been able to moralize them out of existence with indignant editorials, maybe we could laugh them to death with well-aimed ridicule.

The race problem in America is serious business, I admit. But must it *always* be written about seriously? So many weighty volumes, cheerless novels, sad tracts, and violent books have been written on race relations, that I would like to see some writers of both races write about our problems with black tongue in white cheek, or vice versa. Sometimes I try. Simple helps me.

Simple Stakes a Claim

Simple's Platform

"I am standing on my own," said Simple.

"Your own what?" I asked.

"My own two feet of space," said Simple. "The President can stand on the whole United States, because he is President. Ralph Bunche can stand on the United Nations. But I can only stand on what my two feet will cover when I am where I am at the time. So that is what I am standing on—me—where I is."

"In other words, your political platform is yourself. What you stand for is *you*?"

"Right," said Simple.

"Now that we have got that straight, what do you stand for?"

"*Equal Rights for All*," said Simple. "I also stand for *Africa for the Africans*."

"So do the Africans," I said. "But since you are not African, why stick your neck out for them?"

"Because my neck is black, too," said Simple. "Also, I stand for no more lynchings in Mississippi."

"Now you are getting nearer home."

"Mississippi ain't nowhere near Harlem," said Simple. "But I am tired of reading about killing Negroes, I am tired! So I stand for no more lynchings in Mississippi."

"I suggest you go to Mississippi and make your stand," I said.

"I am not running for office yet," said Simple.

"If you were in Mississippi, you would be running for something."

"For safety," stated Simple. "But once I got back to Harlem, I would again speak my platform: *Equal Rights, Africa for the Africans,* and *No More Lynchings.* I'll bet you I would get plenty of votes."

"What party banner do you intend to run under?" I asked.

"My own party, then I would not have to cut nobody in on my graft."

"Graft?" I said. "I thought you were an honest man."

"I would be a politicianer," said Simple.

"Politicians are not all grafters."

"I thought that's what *politicianer* meant," said Simple.

"You know better than that," I said. "If you are intending to run for public office, you should run on an *honest* ticket for an *honest* purpose."

"*Equal Rights, Africa for the Africans,* and *Nary Lynching More* is what I would be running on."

"Would you expect to achieve those results for the voters?"

"If I did not get them, I would raise sand whilst in office and before I got voted out for not getting them, everybody would know I had been in Washington, particularly white folks. I would leave my mark on politics forever . . . and I would be writ up in books, put down in history, and raised up on monuments. My name would go down with Booker T. Washington, George Washington and Dinah Washington. I would be one politicianer people would remember. Grandfathers would tell their children's children about how they voted for me, Jesse B.—how I won and lost, and how my head were bloody but unbowed. *Equal Rights, Africa for the—*"

"I know your platform by heart," I said. "But what *results* would you achieve?"

"Results?" repeated Simple. "Man, if everything a politicianer puts in his platform resulted in results, there would be no need to hold any more elections. Results has nothing to do with politics. It's the platform! I stand on my platform, not the results."

"I give up," I said.

"Not me," said Simple, "I will stand and run."

"You can't stand still, can you, and run at the same time?"

"A politicianer can," declared Simple.

Bang-up Big End

"I wonder how come they don't have lady pallbearers?" asked my friend.

"Lady pallbearers?"

"Yes," said Simple, "at funerals. I have never yet seen a lady carrying a coffin. Women do everything else these days from flying airplanes and driving taxis to fighting bulls. They might as well be pallbearers, too."

"Maybe it's because women are more emotional than men," I said. "They might break down from sorrow and drop the corpse."

"Whooping and hollering and fainting and falling out like they used to do at the old time funerals," said Simple, "has gone out of style now, leastwise in Harlem where the best undertakers has a nurse in attendance. If anybody faints at a funeral now, the nurses stick so much smelling salts up to your nose that you sneeze and come to right away. You better come to—else that ammonia will blow your wig off. They say undertakers' helpers get paid by the hour now, too. They are very busy people, also expensive, so they have no time for nobody holding up a funeral by fainting. And these modern educated ministers do not like their sermons interrupted by people screaming and yelling. Modern ministers is all Doctors of Divinities and such, so too cultured for hollering. But I remember a funeral I went to once down in Virginia where all the mourners delivered sermons, too, and talked and hollered louder than the preacher. And the widow of the deceased asked the dead man why did he leave her.

" 'Why did you leave me, Thomas?' she cried. 'Why?'

"She knew darned well the man drunk himself to death, also that she had put him out of the house more than once, and quit him twice. Yet there she was crying because he had relieved her of his burden once and for all. You could hardly hear the minister who was preaching the corpse to heaven instead of hell, so much racket did his wife and relatives keep up."

"Ways of grieving vary," I said. "In India, for example, the widow in some communities throws herself onto a flaming bier and perishes with her husband."

"Them widows must be right simple," said Simple.

"In some countries widows wear black all the rest of their lives after the husband dies."

"Which saves them cleaning bills," said Simple. "Dirt does not show on black."

"In Ireland they have wonderful wakes the night before a funeral and eat and drink all night."

"I wish I was in Ireland," said Simple. "I could really help drain a bottle."

"And in Haiti they play cards at the wake."

"No," said Simple, "*no cards!* I would not want to lose my money gambling, not even for my best friend. I would not play no cards at nobody's wake."

"In some parts of Asia, they bury the dead standing up."

"Which is better than being buried upside down," said Simple, "or cremated—burnt up before you gets to hell."

"Cremation is a sanitary process, I think. Besides, ashes takes up very little space. Just imagine all the acres and acres of land nowadays taken up by cemeteries. A person's ashes in a jar can be kept on the mantelpiece."

"What old mantelpiece? Where?" cried Simple. "Never no ashes of no deceased on my mantelpiece. Oh, no! When a person is dead and gone they should be where they belong, in the ground."

"Pure custom," I said. "In some countries folks are not buried in the ground at all. In certain primitive communities the dead are put on a mountaintop and left there. At sea you're dropped in the water. It's all according to what you are accustomed."

"Well, I have not been buried yet," said Simple, "but when the end comes and I am, I want to be decent buried, not dropped in no water, nor left on no mountain, neither burnt up. Also I want plenty of whooping and hollering and crying over me so the world will know I have been here and gone—a bang-up big end. I do not want no quiet funeral like white folks. I want people to hear my funeral through the windows. If not, I am liable to rise up in my coffin myself and holler and cry. I demand excitement when I leave this earth. Whoever inherits my insurance money, I want 'em to holler, moan, weep and cry for it. If they don't, I dead sure will come back and cut 'em out of my will. Negroes don't have much in this world, so we might as well have a good funeral."

Big Round World

"The other day a white man asked where is my home," said Simple. "I said, 'What do you mean, where is my home—as big and round as the world is? Do you mean where I live now? Or where I *did* live? Or where I was born?'

" 'I mean, where you *did* live,' the white man said.

" 'I did live every-which-a-where,' I told him.

" 'I mean, where was you born—North or South?' the white man said.

" 'I knowed that's what you mean,' I said, 'so why didn't you say so? I were born where you was born.'

" 'No, you weren't,' he declared, 'because I was born in Germany.'

" 'Some Negroes was born as far away as Africa,' I said.

" 'You weren't, were you?' he asked.

" 'Do I look like a Mau Mau?' I said.

" 'You look African, but you speak our language,' that white man told me.

" '*Your* language,' I hollered, 'and you was born in Germany! You are speaking *my* language.'

" 'Then you are an American?'

" 'I are,' I said.

" 'From what parts?' he kept on.

" 'All parts,' I said.

" 'North or South?' he asked me.

" 'I knowed you'd get down to that again,' I said. 'Why?'

" 'Curiosity,' he says.

" 'If I told you I was born in the South,' I said, 'you would believe me. But if I told you I was born in the North, you wouldn't. So I ain't going to say where I was born. I was just borned, that's all, and my middle name is Harlem.' That is what I told that white man. And that is all he found out about where I was borned," said Simple.

"Why did you make it so hard on him?" I asked. "I see no reason why you should not tell the man you were born in Virginia."

"Why should I tell him that? White folks think all Negroes should be born in the South," said Simple.

"There is nothing to be ashamed of about being born down South," I said.

"Neither about eating watermelon or singing spirituals," said Simple. "I like watermelon and I love 'Go Down, Moses,' but I do not like no white man to ask me do I like watermelon or can I sing spirituals."

"I would say you are racially supersensitive," I said. "I am not ashamed of where I was born."

"Where was you borned?" asked Simple.

"Out West," I said.

"West of Georgia?" asked Simple.

"No," I said, "west of the Mississippi."

"I knowed there was something Southern about it," said Simple.

"You are just like that white man," I said. "Just because I am colored, too, do I *have* to be born down South?"

"I expect you was," said Simple. "And even if you wasn't, if that white man was to see you, he would think you was. They think all of us are from down in 'Bam."

"So what? Why are you so sensitive about the place of your birth certificate?"

"What old birth certificate? Where I was born they didn't even have no birth certificates."

"Then you could claim any nationality," I said, "East Indian, West Indian, Egyptian, German."

"I could even claim to be French," said Simple.

"Yes," I said, "or Swiss."

"No, no!" said Simple. "Not Swiss! Somebody might put *chitterling* in front of it. And I am not from Chitterling-Swiss! No, I am not from Georgia! And I have not traveled much, but I have been a few places. And one thing I do know is that if you go around the world, in the end you get right back to where you started from—which is really going around in circles. I wish the world was flat so a man could travel straight on forever to different places and not come back to the same place."

"In that case it would have to stretch to infinity," I said, "since nothing is endless except eternity. There the spirit lives and grows forever."

"Suppose man was like the spirit," said Simple, "and not only lived forever but kept on growing, too. How long do you suppose my hair would get?"

"Don't ask foolish questions," I said.

"Negroes who claim to have Indian grandmas always swear their grandma's hair was so long she could set on it. My grandma did not have so much hair in this world. But, no doubt, in the spirit world that is changed, also her complexion, since they say that up there we shall be whiter than snow."

"That, I think, refers to the *spirit,* not the body. You change and grow in holiness, not in flesh."

"I would also like to grow in the flesh," said Simple. "I would like to be bigger than Joe Louis in the spirit world. In fact, I would like to be a giant, a great big black giant, so I could look down on Dixie and say, 'Don't you dare talk back to me!' I would like to have hands so big I could pick up Georgia in one and Mississippi in the other, and butt them together, bam! And say, 'Now you-all get rid of this prejudice stuff.' I would also like to slap Alabama on the backsides just once, and shake Florida so bad until her teeth would rattle and she would abolish separate schools.

"As I grew taller, I would look over the edge of the big round world and grab England and shake her till she turns the Mau Maus free, and any other black parts of the world in her possession. I would also reach down in South Africa and grab that man, Malan, and roll him in mulberry juice until he is as dark as me. Then I would say, 'Now see how *you* like to be segregated your own self. Apart your own hide!'

"As I keep on growing bigger and taller I'll lean over the earth and blow my breath on Australia and turn them all Chinese-yellow and Japanese-brown, so they won't have a lily-white Australia any more. Then some of them other folks from Asia can get in there where there is plenty of room and settle down, too. Right now I hear Australia is like Levittown—NO COLORED ADMITTED. I would not harm a hair of Australian heads. I would just maybe kink their hair up a little like mine. Oh, if I was a giant in the spirit world, I would really play around!"

"You have an imagination *par excellence,*" I said, "which is French for *great.*"

"Great is right," said Simple. "I would be the coolest, craziest, maddest, baddest giant in the universe. I would sneeze—and blow the Klu Klux Klan plumb out of Dixie. I would clap my hands—and mash Jim Crow like a mosquito. I would go to Washington and rename the town—the same name—but after Booker T., not after George, because by that time segregation would be plumb and completely gone in the capital of the U.S.A. and Sarah Vaughan would be singing like a bird in Constitution Hall. With me the great American giant, a few changes would be made. Of course, there would be some folks who would not like me, but they would be so small I would shake them off my shoe tops like ants.

I would take one step and be in California, another step to Honolulu, and one more to Japan, shaking a few ants off into the ocean each time I stepped. And wherever there was fighting and war, I would say, 'I don't care who started this battle, stop! But right now! Be at peace, so folks can settle down and plant something to eat again, particularly greens.' Then I would step on a little further to wherever else they are fighting and do the same. And anybody in this world who looked like they wanted to fight or drop atom bombs, I would snatch them up by their collars and say, 'Behave yourselves! Talk things out. Buy yourselves a glass of beer and argue. But he who fights will have *me* to lick!' Which I bet would calm them down, because I would be a real giant, the champeen, the Joe Louis of the universe, the cool kid of all time. This world would just be a marble in my pocket, that's all. I would not let nobody nick my marble with shells, bombs, nor rifle fire. I would say, 'Pay some attention to your religion, peoples, also to Father Divine, and shake hands. If you has no slogan of your own, take Father's, *Peace! It's truly wonderful!*' "

Duty Is Not Snooty

"I remember one time you told me that you thought that if white people who *say* they love Negroes really *do* love them, then they ought to live like Negroes live. Didn't you say that?"

"I did," said Simple, "especially when they go down South."

"That means then that our white friends should ride in Jim Crow cars, too?"

"It does," said Simple.

"Why?" I asked.

"To prove that they love me," said Simple, "otherwise, I do not believe them. White folks that love me and care about my race ought to sleep in colored hotels when they travel—which are mostly not built for sleeping. They also ought to eat in colored restaurants—which in small towns is generally greasy spoons.³ They should also wait an hour for a colored taxi in them places where white cabs won't haul Negroes. Also let my white friends what plan to stay in the South awhile, send their children to the colored not-yet-integrated school, which is most generally across the railroad track in a hovel. And when they get on the buses to come home, let them ride in the back of the buses. If the back seats for colored is crowded, then let them stand up, even if some of the white seats is empty—which colored dare not set in for fear of getting shot through the windows. When nice white folks got through with all that Jim Crow, from eating to sleeping to schools to Jim Crow cars, then we would see how they feel for real."

"If you are expecting our good white friends to go through all of that, then you are expecting them to be superhuman," I said.

"I ride in Jim Crow cars and I am not superhuman."

"You ride in them because you have to," I said.

"I believe in share and share alike," declared Simple. "Them white folks that really loves me should share them Jim Crow cars with me, and not be setting back up in the hindpart of the train all air-cooled and everything whilst I rides up by the engine in an old half-baggage car. Also, I want my white friends to experience a Jim Crow toilet. There is nothing like a COLORED toilet in a Southern train station! Half the time, no mirror, no paper towels, sometimes no sink even to wash your hands. They is separate, all right, but not equal. Let them try one, then them nice white folks, who are always asking me what more do I want since the Supreme Court decided I could vote, would understand what I want. I wants me a train-station toilet with everything in it everybody else has got."

"You know it is against local law for white people to use COLORED waiting rooms down South, or for colored people to use WHITE. Do you want decent white folks to get locked up just to prove they love you?"

"I'd get locked up for going in their waiting rooms, so why shouldn't they get locked up for going in mine? It ain't right for friends to be separated."

"What good would it do us for our white friends to get locked up?"

"It would teach them how dumb it is to have WHITE and COLORED signs all over Dixie."

"Liberal whites already agree that is stupid," I said.

"They would agree more if they experienced it," said Simple. "And if they got locked up a few times, them signs would come down! White folks do not put up with whatever they don't like. Just let a white man get turned down when he goes in a restaurant hungry. He will turn the joint out. If I get turned down, all they do is turn me out. White folks has got a theoretical knowledge of prejudice. I want them to have a real one. That is why I say when these nice white folks from up North goes down to Florida in the winter, let them go Jim Crow. When they get there let them stay at one of them colored hotels where they don't have no bell boys to wait on them hand and foot, also no valet service, and no nice room service for breakfast on a push wagon, and where the elevator is liable to be broke down, if they got one. Let them live colored for just *one* vacation. I bet they will not be so sweet-tempered then. They would not like it. They would be mad! It is not enough for white folks just to be nice and shake my hand and tell me I am equal. I know I am equal. What I want is to be *treated* equal. So maybe if the nice white folks really find out *what* it is like *not* to be treated equal—after they live Jim Crow themselves—I bet you, things will change! You know, white folks would not put up with Jim Crow—if they ever got Jim Crowed themselves. They don't really know what Jim Crow is. But it is their duty to find out, and duty cannot be snooty."

"Your flights of fancy are rather intriguing," I said, "but you know none of what you are saying is going to happen. Good people are not *that* good. To tell the truth, if I were white, no matter how much I loved Negroes, I doubt that I would submit myself to Jim Crow living conditions just to prove my love."

"Neither would I," said Simple.

"Then you would not be very good, either."

"No," said Simple, "but I would be white."

Great but Late

"Don't you think that it's great that the Supreme Court finally banned segregation in the public schools," I asked, "and has also decreed against Jim Crow on buses?"

"It's about time," said Simple.

"You don't sound very enthused," I said. "Of course, the time is long overdue. But now that it's done, it *is* something of which democracy can be proud."

"I don't see nothing to be proud of—just doing what they ought to do," said Simple. "If white folks was doing something extra, yes, then be proud. But Negroes have a right to go to decent schools just like everybody else, also to set on buses. So what's there to be proud of in that they are just now letting us? They ought to be ashamed of themselves for Jim Crowing us so long. I might have had a good education myself had it not of been for white folks. If they want something to be proud of, let them *pay* me for all the education I ain't got."

"You certainly expect a lot out of people," I said. "I thought you would be happy about the Court's historic decisions."

"I am happy," said Simple, "for all the colored kids still going to school and all the folks still in the South. But what about the folks as old as me who went to them ramshackle old beat-up shacks they had for colored schools down home all this time? Them schools should of *been* gone! I see nothing to be proud about in that they are just trying to start getting rid of them."

"Maybe 'proud' was the wrong word to use," I said.

"No, it wasn't," said Simple. "Them white folks downtown where I work are just as proud of themselves as they can be, talking about 'There now! You see what democracy can do! We are not so bad in this country after all.'

"'You are bad enough,' I said, 'waiting until I am mighty nigh forty years old to do something you should have done before I was born and which you do for Hungarians no sooner than they light on these shores. And now that you've done it for me, you are going around talking about how wonderful it is that colored children can run through brickbats to go to school with white children down South. What's so wonderful about that? They should have been going to school together all these years.'

"Whereupon, one of the white guys says to me that I am just an old sorehead. Whereupon, I says, 'What did *you* do to bring this change about? Did you give a thousand dollars to the N.A.A.C.P. to pay for all this Supreme Court business which cost way up in the millions when it should have been for nothing?'

"He says, 'I didn't know it cost all that money to pass a law.'

" 'Well, it did,' I says. 'Also it took a whole lot of arguing to persuade them judges to make up their minds to do right. That lawyer named Marshall near about spoke himself hoarse in the last ten years. I see nothing to be so proud about when it is so hard and so expensive for white folks to do right. And once you start doing right, the more you blow your own horn, the less good what you are doing sounds to me. There is nothing worse than a conceited Christian.'

" 'I am not a Christian, I am Jewish,' says the guy. 'And you must admit these Supreme Court decisions are a big step forward.'

" 'Sure, they are a step forward for people who was so far back,' I says. 'But to be proud of something, you have got to move *far* ahead. And they have not moved ahead of anything much down South. All they done is *start* to catch up—and they're putting that off until sometime in the future when they can work things out with all deliberate speed. It should have been worked out long ago when my grandma was a baby.'

" 'It's obvious you have no regard for historical determinations,' says the guy.

" 'That's just it,' I says, 'white folks have been determined to keep me down for so long, that now that they are turning me loose, it's just like when you have had your foot on a man's head. You finally take your foot off and say, *Ain't I wonderful! I took my foot off your head!* I'll be dogged if I see anything wonderful about that! You're still white—so I guess you think white makes right.'

" 'You are hard to discuss any subject with intelligently,' says the guy. Then he walked off, mad with me for not being proud of him for being proud of himself for keeping me out of decent schools all these years where I should of been going all the time until he let me in. But I see nothing for me to be proud of in going where I ought to have been. Do you?"

"Most decent people feel that great victories have been won," I said.

"Do you mean to say then that I ain't decent?" asked Simple.

"I don't know what to say about you," I said.

"Did I ask you to say anything?" asked Simple.

Bones, Bombs, Chicken Necks

"For the first time since I been married," said Simple, "Joyce has not spoke to me all day."

"Did you speak to her?" I asked.

"I tried," said Simple, "but she did not answer."

"What happened? What's the matter?" I asked.

"She's interfered with my habits," said Simple.

"What do you mean, interfered with your habits?"

"My pleasure, and my ways," said Simple.

"Well, tell me," I said, "if you are going to tell me."

"It were like this," Simple began. "After dinner, I were setting in my front window gnawing on a pork-chop bone, observing Harlem, and I had just got down to the juicy part, when Joyce says, 'Jesse B., why did you take that bone away from the table?'

"I say, 'Baby, to gnaw on.'

" 'But not in the front window,' says Joyce.

" 'It's my window,' I said.

" 'It's also mine,' says Joyce, 'and I do not wish bone-gnawing there in public for the world to see.'

" 'Not even in my own window?'

" 'Most especially in *our* own window,' says Joyce. 'What you are doing is real down-homish—leaning from the window with a meat bone in your hand. You are my husband and I do not wish everybody passing by the street to see you. Eat at the table, and stop eating when you get up. Do not, *please*, carry bones to the window.'

" 'Aw, Joyce,' I says.

" 'Aw, Joyce, nothing,' says she. 'You do not see me leaning from a window with a bone in my hand.'

" 'You're a lady,' I says.

" 'And I hope you are a gentleman,' says Joyce.

" 'People eat hot dogs in public in the Yankee Stadium,' I says, 'and corn on the cob at Coney Island. So why can't I gnaw a bone in my own house?'

" 'Inside the house, yes,' says Joyce. 'But, Jesse B., listen to me! Please do not gnaw that bone in the window! *Please*.'

"Which, when I saw she were so serious I asked her, 'Why?'" said Simple. "And you know what Joyce told me? 'Because Emily Post says "DON'T."'"

" 'Baby,' I says, 'Emily Post were white. Also, I expect, rich. That woman had plenty of time to gnaw her bones at the table. Me, I work. When I get home, I want to look out in the street before dark and see what is going on. Since I'm married, I don't get out much. At least, honey, let me *look* out.'

" 'Look out all you want to,' says Joyce, 'but not with a bone in your hand. That is most inelegant.'

" 'Inelegant, hell!' I says, and I sat right there. 'Just you try to get this here bone away from me.'

" 'I want Negroes to learn etiquette,' said Joyce. 'Bone-gnawing is *not* etiquette—at least, not in public.'

"I did not answer. And, don't you know, Joyce burst out crying. Do you reckon Joyce is pregnant? They tells me womens act crazy that way sometimes when they is in the family way. Why should Joyce care if I suck a pork-chop bone in the front window or not? We ain't got no back window. And I do not see why a man can't gnaw a bone and look out in the street at the same time. Nobody is looking up specially to see what I am doing. Nobody in the world cares if I gnaw a bone or not in my window—nobody but Joyce."

"Which should make you happy," I said, "that somebody cares when you commit a *faux pas*."

"What have I committed?" asked Simple.

"A *faux pas*," I said. "It really is not proper to sit in the window gnawing on a bone."

"Is it a crime?" asked Simple.

"It's not a crime," I said, "but it is a *faux pas*."

"It must be something *awful* for Joyce not to speak all day," said Simple. "Write that word down for me, so I can tell her I will not commit it again."

"*Faux pas* is a French phrase," I said.

"Then, now I know how to say 'gnawing a bone' in French," said Simple.

"*Faux pas*—boner," I said.

"Bone," said Simple, "and there's one other thing which the Lord made and put on this earth almost as good as a pork-chop bone—that is the neck of a chicken. One reason I very seldom like to eat in restaurants is because you seldom get a chicken neck. If they do serve a neck, it is not proper to eat it, so Joyce says, because you have to suck on the bones. Now, why is it not proper to suck a chicken neck in a restaurant?"

"Because it makes so much noise in public, and therefore is bad manners."

"Manners is sometimes mighty inconvenient," stated Simple.

"You may not care about manners," I said, "but your wife does. Certainly Joyce is a woman to be proud of. She tries to uphold the tone of the Harlem community. One reason why white people don't want Negroes in their neighborhoods is because they say we lower the tone of the community. Eating bones in the window just isn't done in high society."

"Who's in high society?" asked Simple. "Not me, and I don't want to be. White folks might not gnaw bones in windows, but they sure do some awful other things. They murders their mothers almost daily. I never read of so many children knocking off their parents as here of late—but you seldom read of a colored child doing such. White folks also Jim Crows colored people, which I do not think is good manners. I had rather they gnaw a bone than segregate us. White folks blows off atom bombs and burns up people, too. It looks like to me it would be better to gnaw a bone than to singe them Marshall Islanders all up, like them pictures last year showed after that big bomb test they had out in the Pacific. Them folks will never have no more hair on their heads, and them atomized Japanese fishermens never will have no more children. I think white folks would do better to set in their front windows and gnaw bones myself, even if they were not so high-tone. Bone-gnawing, to my mind, is better than bomb-bursting. Atom bombs is low-rating the tone of the whole world. When I gnaw my bone or suck my chicken neck, I am not hurting a human soul."

"You're hurting your wife if you make her feel bad," I said. "So for Joyce's sake, if not your own, you could suck your chicken necks and gnaw your pork-chop bones in private. In fact, consideration for others begins at home—which might in a sense explain the behavior of American white folks. They've gotten so accustomed to mistreating Negroes at home in the past that it is hard for them to care about what colored folks in Asia think. And if you keep on gnawing bones in spite of what Joyce thinks, after a while you will not care what anybody else thinks either. From your own selfishness in regard to your wife's wishes, it is only a step to being inconsiderate of everyone everywhere.

Consideration begins inside yourself first, right where you are, *at home.* Bones and bombs are not unrelated, pal. And certainly good manners are better than chicken necks or pork-chop bones."

"From whence did you get such wrong information about such good food?" asked Simple.

A Dog Named Trilby

"Once when I were a child in Virginia, I knowed an old white lady who had a dog named Trilby," said Simple. "Trilby were black with white feet, white around the eyes, and she walked sort of sideways so you did not know if she were going or coming. Trilby and that old lady was both very old and very mean—but Trilby was the meanest. Both were mean, but that dog had her beat.

"Well, another old lady who was colored, named Jenkins, lived just down the block two or three houses away from the white woman. It being a small town, everybody lived in houses. Some houses had yards front and back, and nearly everybody had porches. In summer they kept their doors open and the screens closed. But any dog could easy open a screen door and walk in and out of any house. Now, Trilby never paid no attention to the inside of old lady Jenkins' house until after Mrs. Jenkins' dog died. Before that time, Trilby would just play with the Jenkins' dog in the yard, but never go in the house. Trilby were not too mean to play with another dog, even if it belonged to colored folks. But with people Trilby only snarled, growled, also barked at every human, including me. Only at her madam, Trilby did not snarl—nor at that other dog belonging to Mrs. Jenkins. Seems like when Trilby was with that other dog she lost her meanness. Trilby loved that dog.

"Now, the old white lady what owned Trilby naturally did not associate with old Mrs. Jenkins, it being down South. Neither did she like her dog playing with a colored woman's dog. But dogs will be dogs, so she could not stop that. When she saw Trilby in Mrs. Jenkins' yard, though, she would always call her home.

" 'Here, Trilby! Here, Trilby! Here, Trilby!'

"Then that old white lady would give Trilby something good to eat to keep her home. Whereupon Trilby would grab her fine bone, lay behind her screen door, and growl at everyone who went by. Else that dog would run out and bark when she got tired of gnawing on her bone. Trilby never did gnaw on me, though, because I would have kicked that old mutt sky-high to a firecracker if she had. I loved dogs, but I did not like Trilby. Nobody liked Trilby except her owner and old lady Jenkins' dog. Them two dogs got along fine, both being ageable and shaggy and hair-balls—some kind of spitzes and poodles, part cur, one black, one white—the white lady's dog being the black one, and the colored dog being the white one.

"It were wintertime when the white dog died, and old Mrs. Jenkins were left dogless. Then Trilby did not have nobody to play with. Trilby's mean old lady-owner were glad that other dog had died. She did not like Mrs. Jenkins nohow. And with that other dog gone, she took for granted Trilby would stay home, not be playing in old lady Jenkins' yard come summer, nor romping on her porch with her dog. Now, she would not have to bribe Trilby into staying home with her. But such were not the case. Meanwhile, Trilby begun to lose her appetite that winter. Come spring she were a thin old rail of a black dog, with white circles around her eyes. Trilby looked like she were made up for Halloween. And she become meaner than ever, snapping and snarling at the mailman, the milkman, and also at me delivering papers. So I took to passing on the other side of the street.

"But that mean old white lady loved her mean old dog. The butcher said she even bought Trilby fresh calf's liver every day to build up her vitamins—which were unheard of in our town where dogs just ate scraps and bones from the table. Not Trilby—she had liver. But, as nice as that old lady treated her, Trilby showed her anatomy. Come spring, as soon as the door were opened, Trilby went down to Mrs. Jenkins' house, spite of the fact that Trilby's friend-dog was dead and there was nobody for her to romp and play with there. But, don't you know, that dog just opened Mrs. Jenkins' screen and nudged herself into the house—which were the *first* time she had been inside—and laid down on the rug where that other dog used to lay.

"Her old mistress would call her from up the street, 'Trilby! Trilby! Hey, Trilby!' But Trilby would not come. Finally the woman had to go right to that other house and holler from the sidewalk, 'You-all send my dog home.'

"No answer, so she had to go up to the door and knock to get results. Trilby caused them two old womens—one white and one colored—to exchange words for the first time in years. But what they said were not Christian on neither side. Trilby's madam had to drag her by the scruff of the neck. Next day, it being warm and the doors being open, Trilby were right back again, nudging at Mrs. Jenkins' screen door with her bony old nose. She went in, and settled down on the rug.

" 'Trilby! Trilby! Come here, Trilby!' called Miss White Lady.

"But Trilby did not budge. Trilby had adopted herself a new home in her old age—the run-down old house where her dog friend used to live which her mistress did not like. Every chance Trilby got, she were there. In fact, Trilby did not stay at home at all any more if she could help it. And every time that old white woman would come after her dog, them two old women would say words to each other folks never knowed they knew and which are not in the books. Finally, even I got sorry for that mean old white lady whose mean old dog did not want to come home.

" 'Trilby! Now, Trilby!' she begged.

"But she had to drag Trilby home each and every day. Then she would pet her, humor her, and dine her on fine fresh liver. She even bought Trilby a soft new rag rug to lay on. But as soon as the door were open, off went Trilby back to that other house.

" 'Trilby! Trilby! Please, Trilby!'

"She reached out her hand to pet her, but Trilby commenced to snarl at her mistress what had bought her that expensive liver. She growled, bared her teeth, and growled again each time that old lady come near. Then one day she snapped at her, and a little speck of blood come on that white lady's finger.

" 'Why, Trilby, you snapped at me! *Me,* what loves you! And you done bit the hand that fed you!'

"Well, that old woman did not live very long after that. She taken so low sick she could not come to drag Trilby home no more. And the day she died all by herself, Trilby were laying on that *other* rug in that *other* house inside that *other* door."

Enter Cousin Minnie

"Guess who has come to town now?" said Simple, pushing an empty beer glass back from the bar and frowning deeply.

"Who," I said, "has come?"

"Some new cousin name of Minnie," said Simple.

"Minnie? How does she look?" I inquired.

"Like the junior wrath of God," groaned Simple. "Yet, ugly as she is, last week she walks up to my door, all unknown to me, and rings my bell, and states, 'I am your Cousin Minnie.'

"I says, 'Whose Cousin Minnie?'

" 'Yours,' says she, out of the clear blue sky. 'Ain't you Jesse B. Semple?'

" 'I am,' says I. 'But *who* are you?'

" 'Your mother's brother's youngest child,' says she.

" 'How come I never heard of you before?' says I.

" 'Because I am an offshoot from the family,' says she.

" 'What shot you back at me?' I asked before I thought, because I really did not mean to insult the girl.

" 'Aunt Mamie down in Piedmont, Virginia, give me your number,' says she, 'because Mamie knowed I did not know nobody in New York, and she did not want me to be way up here in Harlem all alone. So I look up you—my one cousin in the world who knows what the North is all about. Jesse, I done come North.'

" 'Why did you wait so long?' says I. 'It is very late now to do any good for yourself. You almost as old as Aunt Mamie.'

"I do not know why I wanted to hurt that girl right off the bat, but she was so ugly she made me mad. Also, I think she were somewhat drunk. She looked like to me she might be most of the time drunk. Did you ever have any relatives what was drunk—or if they was not drunk, they looked drunk?"

"No," I said. "Not relatives. But I have known a few alcoholics. They can be difficult at times."

"That is just what Cousin Minnie is," said Simple, "difficult. Since I have come to know her, I finds that she is a goodhearted girl. But her heart is in a very weak body. Minnie is weak for licker. Just why Aunt

Mamie would give her my address in Harlem, big as Harlem is, I do not know, and me married to a woman like Joyce who hates the smell of whiskey, wine, or beer on *my* breath, let alone on a relative's who is distant to me. I says, 'Minnie, don't come around to my house drunk, please, neither come here high. I do not wish to be low-rated in my wife's sight. Joyce thinks my people is somebody.'

" 'I might have been somebody myself,' says Minnie, 'if your uncle had married my mama. But I'm a side child.'

" 'Don't say it,' I said. 'There's none such in our family! But you do look exactly like my Uncle Willie, who were nobody's picture for framing. Minnie, I can see the Semples' spitting image in your features. You sure resembles the family line. But where have you been all these years that I did not know you before?'

" 'They kept me hid. I was a secret child.'

" 'I wish you was a secret now, because I do not know what to do about a woman like you related to me. Why did you come to New York?'

" 'Because I have done got plumb tired of the South,' said Minnie. '*Ebony, Jet,* and the *Chicago Defender* all talks about how beautiful is the North, so I come up here to see. I am plumb tired of Jim Crow.'

" 'Give me your hand,' I said. I shook it. I were proud of her ambition.

" 'Have you got a little drink of any kind around?' says Minnie.

" 'If I had, I would have drunk it,' says I. 'All we keep in our icebox is milk and Kool-Aid.'

" 'Cousin Jess, can you lend me a dollar?' says Minnie.

" 'I do not keep money in the home, neither,' says I.

" 'Aunt Mamie said if I come to New York, you would help me,' said Minnie. 'If I ever needed help, I need it now, Cousin Jess.'

" 'In the middle of the week,' says I, 'even if it were payday, I could not be too generous.'

" 'Then have you got a place I can sleep here in your apartment with you-all?'

" 'God forbid!' said I. 'Don't you know folks in Harlem ain't got no place for relatives to sleep? This is a kitchenette.'

" 'Down South they say Harlem is heaven,' says Minnie. 'Yet you has nowhere for me to rest my head?'

" 'You know that old song,' said I, '*Rest Beyond the River?* In Harlem, we *all* got one more river to cross before we can rest. Set down and I will tell you about Harlem, Minnie, so you will be clear in mind. In fact, I will tell you about the North. Down South you're swimming in a river that's running to the sea where you might drown but, at least, you're swimming with the current. Up North we are swimming the other way, against the current, trying to reach dry land. I been here twenty years, Minnie, and I'm still in the water, if you get what I mean.'

" 'Ain't you got just a drop of something that ain't water in the house,' asks Minnie, 'to help me swim better?'

" 'Come on, girl, put on your coat,' I said, 'and I will take you out to a bar before my wife comes. I reckon we both need a drink to help us swim better. Let's go see if we can make it somehow or another to dry land right now. Come on, Minnie.'

"And we went. Whilst setting at the bar, I discovered that Minnie is really very partial to what comes in a bottle with a government seal on it."

"I can see where you're going to have a problem with your cousin," I said. "She seems to be an alcoholic."

"Which is a habit Minnie really cannot afford," said Simple, "especially since she always wants to borrow money. Now, you know and I know, money is usually the *last* thing I possess—and in that regard, I falls for no hypes. Setting there on that bar stool, 'Minnie,' I says, 'I give you my love, I give you my cousinship, I give you my welcome to Harlem, U.S.A., but I cannot give you money. You are up here in the free North now where you got to scuffle the best way you can.'

"But Minnie says, 'Jesse, I am a lady, and there are some things I do not do such as hustle.'

"I said, 'I did not mean that you should do wrong, neither did I use the word *hustle*. I said scuffle, which means, work, work, work.'

" 'That is one thing, Jess, I will do, work. But lend me a little something until I gets a job.'

" 'That's what the Relief and Welfare is for,' I says. 'Many a human has been here in Harlem ten years and has not got a job yet, not since they found the Relief Bureau. If you be's lucky enough to get a nice Relief Investigator, you can live awhile.'

" 'I want no handouts, city or otherwise,' says Minnie. 'Also, I really want no advice just now. What I need tonight is five dollars.'

" 'Cousin,' I said, 'if you asked me for the moon, I could reach up in the sky and snatch it down quicker than I could find five dollars. We is poor folks in Harlem.'

" 'Poor it do seem,' said Minnie. 'Why I used to could borrow five dollars most anytime down home in Virginia. You-all Negroes up North is real broke.'

" 'Say that again!' says I. 'And of all those that are brokest, I am among the most.'

" 'How do you keep your home together?' asked Minnie.

" 'By the budget,' says I, 'and Joyce controls that. I do not know a thing about a budget. In fact, I never saw a budget. My wife has got one—but she always loses it before the week is out. Else she keeps it in a Mason jar. Anyhow, I cannot go in the budget and get nothing out for you, not this late in the week, no way.'

" 'So I must suffer?' says Minnie.

" 'I fears 'tis so,' said I.

" 'By coming up North all alone,' moans Minnie, 'I have made my bed hard and therefore I got to sleep in it?'

" 'I hope you will not be rest-broken,' says I.

" 'When *just* five dollars would take the rocks out from under my pillow?' pleads Minnie.

" 'Girl, don't make it hard for me, too! Have mercy on your cousin. Or do you take me to be simple? Do you think you can beg me out of what I ain't got even if I had it?'

" 'I'll say no more,' says Minnie, 'except that I wanted freedom, which is why I come up North. You know, I do not like Jim Crow. I likes to drink in joints where people is integrated, like this one. Jesse, help me to stay up North in freedom.'

"Well, pal, that weakened me—that word *freedom!* Don't you know I let that old girl beg me out of five dollars—which I went home and borrowed from Joyce's budget, which never balances nohow, so I don't reckon freedom can throw it off much more than it always is. Minnie is a refugee from the South. America has always been good to refugees. Since Minnie has come to America, New York, Harlem, U.S.A., I just had to lend that girl five dollars. If I never get it back, I have made my contribution to freedom—freedom to be integrated anywhere, at any time, drunk or sober—which really ain't no hype."

Radioactive Red Caps

"How wonderful," I said, "that Negroes today are being rapidly integrated into every phase of American life from the Army and Navy to schools to industries—advancing, advancing!"

"I have not advanced one step," said Simple. "Still the same old job, same old salary, same old kitchenette, same old Harlem and the same old color."

"You are just one individual," I said. "I am speaking of our race in general. Look how many colleges have opened up to Negroes in the last ten years. Look at the change in restrictive covenants. You can live anywhere."

"You mean *try* to live anywhere."

"Look at the way you can ride unsegregated in interstate travel."

"And get throwed off the bus."

"Look at the ever greater number of Negroes in high places."

"Name me one making an atom bomb."

"That would be top-secret information," I said, "even if I knew. Anyway, you are arguing from supposition, not knowledge. How do you know what our top Negro scientists are doing?"

"I don't," said Simple. "But I bet if one was making an atom bomb, they would have his picture on the cover of *Jet* every other week like Eartha Kitt, just to make Negroes think the atom bomb is an integrated bomb. Then, next thing you know, some old Southern senator would up and move to have that Negro investigated for being subversive, because he would be mad that a Negro ever got anywhere near an atom bomb. Then that Negro would be removed from his job like Miss Annie Lee Moss, and have to hire a lawyer to get halfway back. Then they would put that whitewashed Negro to making plain little old-time ordinary bombs that can only kill a few folks at a time. You know and I know, they don't want no Negroes nowhere near no bomb that can kill a whole state full of folks like an atom bomb can. Just think what would happen to Mississippi. Wow!"

"Your thinking borders on the subversive," I warned. "Do you want to fight the Civil War over again?"

"Not without an atom bomb," said Simple. "If I was in Mississippi, I would be Jim Crowed out of bomb shelters, so I would need some kind of protection. By the time I got the N.A.A.C.P. to take my case to the Supreme Court, the war would be over, else I would be atomized."

"Absurd!" I said. "Bomb shelters will be for everybody."

"Not in Mississippi," said Simple. "Down there they will have some kind of voting test, else loyalty test, in which they will find some way of flunking Negroes out. You can't tell me them Dixiecrats are going to give Negroes free rein of bomb shelters. On the other hand, come to think of it, they might *have* to let us in to save their own skins, because I hear tell in the next war everything that ain't sheltered will be so charged with atoms a human can't touch it. Even the garbage is going to get radioactive when the bombs start falling. I read last week in the *News* that, in case of a bombing, it will be a problem as to where to put our garbage, because it will be radioactive up to a million years. So you sure can't keep garbage around. If you dump it in the sea, it will make the fish radioactive, too, like them Japanese tunas nobody could eat. I am wondering what the alley cats will eat—because if all the garbage is full of atomic rays, and the cats eat the garbage, and my wife pets a strange cat, Joyce will be radioactive, too. Then if I pet my wife, what will happen to me?"

"You are stretching the long arm of coincidence mighty far," I said. "What is more likely to happen is, if the bombs fall, you will be radioactive long before the garbage will."

"That will worry white folks," said Simple. "Just suppose all the Negroes down South got atomized, charged up like hot garbage, who would serve the white folks' tables, nurse their children, Red Cap their bags, and make up their Pullman berths? Just think! Suppose all the colored Red Caps carrying bags on the Southern Railroad was atom-charged! Suitcases would get atomized, too, and all that is packed in them. Every time a white man took out his toothbrush to wash his teeth on the train, his teeth would get atom-charged. How could he kiss his wife when he got home?"

"I believe you are charged now," I said.

"No," said Simple, "I am only thinking how awful this atom bomb can be! If one fell up North in Harlem and charged me, then I went downtown and punched that time clock where I work, the clock would be charged. Then a white fellow would come along behind me and punch the time clock, and he would be charged. Then both of us would be so full of atoms for the next million years, that at any time we would be liable to explode like firecrackers on the Fourth of July. And from us, everybody else in the plant would get charged. Atoms, they tell me, is catching. What I read in the *News* said that if you even look at an atom bomb going off, the rays are so strong your eyes will water the rest of your life, your blood will turn white, your hair turn gray, and your children will be born backwards. Your breakfast eggs will no longer be sunny-side up, but scrambled, giving off sparks—and people will give off sparks, too. If you walk down the street, every doorbell you pass will ring without your touching it. If you pick up a phone, whoever answers it will be atomized. So if you know somebody you don't like, for example, just phone them—and you can really fix them up! That's what they call a chain reaction. I am getting my chain ready now—the first person I am going to telephone is my former landlady! When she picks up the phone, I hope to atomize her like a Japanese tuna! She will drive a Geiger counter crazy after I say, 'Hello!' "

"My dear boy," I said, "what makes you think you, of all people, would be able to go around transferring atomic radiation to others? You would probably be annihilated yourself by the very first bomb blast."

"Me? Oh, no," said Simple. "Negroes are very hard to annihilate. I am a Negro—so I figure I would live to radiate and, believe me, once charged, I will take charge."

"In other words, come what may, you expect to survive the atom bomb?"

"If Negroes can survive white folks in Mississippi," said Simple, "we can survive anything."

Face and Race

"It is so easy to blame all one's failures on race," I said, "to whine *I can't do this, I can't do that* because I'm colored. That, I think, is one bad habit you have, friend—always bringing up race."

"I do," said Simple, "because that is what I am always coming face to face with—race. I look in the mirror in the morning to shave—and what do I see? Me, colored. I go to work and who do I see looking at me out of my boss's eyes? Me again. I ask for an advancement and I don't get it. Why? Because the union won't admit colored in the skilled department. So I keep on sweeping *under* the machines instead of working at one. My pay check is *me*. When I get ready to vote, the first thing I think about is how do the candidates stand on equal rights—meaning *me*. I look for *me* in everything them politicians say—they don't say much and they does less. I might want to move downtown near to where I work. Can I? They won't rent to colored folks in that part of New York. Who comes back to Harlem? *Me*. I want to get born in a nice private room at the hospital. Do I? No private rooms for colored. I want to get buried in a pretty lawn-mowed cemetery. Huh? We don't sell Negroes burial lots in this white resting place. Try Low Level Plots in Marshland, Jersey Flats, across the river. From birth to death my face—which is my race—stares me in the face."

"O.K., admitting all you say is true, don't you suppose race stared Dr. Bunche in the face, too? And Josephine Baker? And Adam Powell? And Joe Louis? But Joe Louis, Negro, licked the world's best fighters. Adam Powell, Negro, went to Congress. Josephine Baker, Negro, went dancing around the world. Ralph Bunche went to the United Nations. Suppose they had all just stood at a beer bar like you and moaned about race, race, race!"

"I ain't built like Joe—I'm a lightweight. I can't dance like Josephine —my feet's too big. I can't holler like Adam Powell, neither shake my hair like a lion's mane because I ain't got that much hair, nor have I a microphone in my mouth. Ralph Bunche is a smart man, colleged, with mother wit. I am not that smart and far from high educated. But when I work—which is all the time—the floors is clean for the men and the machines that makes the things that go all over the world with *U.S.A.*

stamped on them. A part of that U.S.A. is me. But I am the bottom part, on the floor, broom pusher. How come I can't work up to get off the floor and have my hand on a machine, too?

"Out of what little money I make, I bought tickets to all Joe's fights. Part of my wages helped Joe get that championship belt, and Mike Jacobs get wealthy, and the radios to get their broadcasts, and the moving pictures to make fight films—because I paid at the gate for the fight to go on. Part of my money went through the ticket window when Josephine Baker was singing and dancing down on Broadway. I took Joyce, so I bought *two* tickets. My tickets helped keep them lights bright over that theatre on the Great White Way. Each and every time Adam Powell goes to Congress, I vote him in. And they tell me American taxes helps keep the United Nations going. I pays taxes. They deducts taxes from my pay check each and every week. If I made more, they could deduct more. Why don't they let me make more then?

" 'You're black,' that's what they tell me. Only they don't say it out loud any more because it ain't democratic. They say it silent. But they keep me sweeping floors and wiping up grease and polishing machine bases, and 'maintaining.' I can run one of them machines backwards, but the union won't take me in, and the boss ain't ready to upgrade me, and nobody is ready to let my face pass my race. The other reason I talk about race is, it makes a good argument. I always gets a rise out of you. You are about the most *un-Negro* Negro I know. You ought to be a race leader. White folks would love you."

"I'm only trying to look on both sides of the question," I said.

"To do which, you have to straddle *both* sides of the fence. Me, I stand on one side and look on the other—and all I see over there is white. On my side, is me. Setting on the fence is you."

"I didn't build the fence," I said.

"Then tear it down," said Simple.

Two Sides Not Enough

"A man ought to have more than just two sides to sleep on," declared Simple. "Now if I get tired of sleeping on my left side, I have nothing to turn over on but my right side."

"You could sleep on your back," I advised.

"I snores on my back."

"Then why not try your stomach?"

"Sleeping on my stomach, I get a stiff neck—I always have to keep my head turned toward one side or the other, else I smothers. I do not like to sleep on my stomach."

"The right side, or the left side, are certainly enough sides for most people to sleep on. I don't know what your trouble is. But, after all, there are two sides to every question."

"That's just what I am talking about," said Simple. "Two sides are not enough. I'm tired of sleeping on either my left side, or on my right side, so I wish I had two or three more sides to change off on. Also, if I sleep on my left side, I am facing my wife, then I have to turn over to see the clock in the morning to find out what time it is. If I sleep on my right side, I am facing the window so the light wakes me up before it is time to get up. If I sleep on my back, I snores, and disturbs my wife. And my stomach is out for sleeping, due to reasons which I mentioned. In the merchant marine, sailors are always talking about the port side and the starboard side of a ship. A human should have not only a left side and a right side, but also a port side and a starboard side."

"That's what left and right mean in nautical terms," I said. "You know as well as I do that a ship has only two sides."

"Then ships are bad off as a human," said Simple. "All a boat can do when a storm comes up, is like I do when I sleep—toss from side to side."

"Maybe you eat too heavy a dinner," I said, "or drink too much coffee."

"No, I am not troubled in no digestion at night," said Simple. "But there is one thing that I do not like in the morning—waking up to face the same old one-eyed egg Joyce has fried for breakfast. What I wish is that there was different kinds of eggs, not just white eggs with a yellow eye. There ought to be blue eggs with a brown eye, and brown eggs with a blue eye, also red eggs with green eyes."

"If you ever woke up and saw a red egg with a green eye on your plate, you would think you had a hang-over."

"I would," said Simple. "But eggs *is* monotonous! No matter which side you turn an egg on, daddy-o, it is still an egg—hard on one side and soft on the other. Or, if you turn it over, it's hard on both sides. Once an egg gets in the frying pan, it has only two sides, too. And if you burn the bottom side, it comes out just like the race problem, black and white, black and white."

"I thought you'd get around to race before you got through. You can't discuss any subject at all without bringing in color. God help you! And in reducing everything to two sides, as usual, you oversimplify."

"What does I do?"

"I say your semantics make things too simple."

"My which?"

"Your verbiage."

"My what?"

"Your words, man, your words."

"Oh," said Simple. "Well, anyhow, to get back to eggs—which is a simple word. For breakfast I wish some other birds besides chickens laid eggs for eating, with a different kind of flavor than just a hen flavor. Whatever you are talking about with your *see-antics*, Jack, at my age a man gets tired of the same kind of eggs each and every day—just like you get tired of the race problem. I would like to have an egg some morning that tastes like a pork chop."

"In that case, why don't you have pork chops for breakfast instead of eggs?"

"Because there is never no pork chops in my icebox in the morning."

"There would be if you would put them there the night before."

"No," said Simple, "I would eat them up the night before—which is always the trouble with the morning after—you have practically nothing left from the night before—except the race problem."

Great Day

"I got me a plan of action for right here. Do you know what I am going to do some one of these days when I get rich?"

"No," I said.

"I am going downtown in New York to one of them fine white integrated restaurants and order me the right half of the left breast of a young squab, a side order of hummingbird's tongues, six quarts of champagne, and a Corona-Corona. When I get through eating I will sign for the check like rich folks do, not pay then and there. When you're integrated, you don't have to pay for things on the line, you know. Your credit is good. Fact is, that's what integration means—*in the money, in great,* real great, son."

"That is not what the dictionary says *integration* means. The dictionary says it means 'united into a whole, combined, fused.' "

"It *will* take a fuse to unite some peoples."

"The dictionary does not say how integration will be achieved. It just tells us what it means."

"I'm telling you how it will be achieved," said Simple, "with a fuse, else a blowtorch."

"In other words, in your opinion, prejudice must be melted down?"

"Burnt out," said Simple. "Not just melted down, but *burnt up*. You know if I went downtown to one of these fine white integrated restaurants in New York and set down beside the governor from Mississippi in town on a visit, I would have to go to the Supreme Court to hold my integrated seat. And I would not wish to be bothered, disturbed from my meal. But until prejudice is burnt out and burnt up, I would expect to be disturbed if somebody from Mississippi was eating there. If they saw me, black, with the left half of the right breast of a young squab on my plate and a glass of ten-dollar champagne in my hand, that would be too much, too much, too much! To tell the truth, I doubt if I could stand it myself."

"Have you ever tasted champagne?"

"No," said Simple. "I never did."

"I doubt if you would like it," I said. "It tastes like rather tart soda water."

"I would drink it, anyhow, just to spite them folks from Mississippi. I would set at that table with that nice white tablecloth and drink three bottles, just out of spite."

"Then you would be drunk," I said.

"Don't worry, I would not bother nobody, unless they bothered me. Of course, better not nobody look at me cross-eyed, neither. I know my rights in a public place up North. Besides, like I told you, I will be rich then, so I'm liable to have my lawyer with me. Rich peoples give lawyers what they calls a 'retaining fee.' Therefore I would retain my lawyer with me all the time, especially when integrating."

"You're making a mighty lot of drama out of simply having a meal in a downtown restaurant. Why make a production of it, even in your mind? I hope you're not like these Negroes who always go in a public place with a chip on your shoulder."

"I carry no chip on my shoulder," said Simple, "but sometimes there is a doubt in my mind. It is so hard for white folks to act right. So it pays to be prepared. When I get a place to integrate, and set down and order me a integrated dinner, I do not want to have to call up the N.A.A.C.P. before I can eat it. All I want to do is have a Great Day."

With All Deliberate Speed

"I see that in some states, the governors still say they will abolish the public-school system before they allow Negro children to mix with whites."

"I dug some such stuff in the papers, too," said Simple, putting his beer glass on the bar. "But it is not what the governors *say*, it is what them Southern white people *do*. Some of them Dixieland governors have been damning race-mixing ever since time begun, allowing as how God made everybody separate. Then, after nightfall, them governors themselves start mixing as hard as they can. Why, I went to school with a governor's son who were colored on his mother's side. Them governors talk against intermarriage, but don't say a word about intermating, which amounts to practically the same thing—and there is many a yellow Negro to prove it. You are kinder light-complexioned yourself."

"We are speaking of education," I said, "not mating. Are you trying to slip me in the dozens?"

"I did not say nothing about your mama," said Simple. "Your family might have got light *way back yonder*."

"Let's not go into it," I said. "What we all must be concerned about now is integration of the schools. All right-thinking Americans wish to see it work out smoothly."

"Smooth it will never be," said Simple, "since most Americans don't think right, and they do not think right because they have been thinking wrong too long."

"It is the democratic hope that all of us can be taught to think right," I said.

"Hope on," said Simple.

"I shall. Democracy grows in an ever-widening arc. Once the stone is dropped in the water—in this case the Supreme Court decision regarding the schools—the circles of decency begin to spread and the healing waters to lap the shores of prejudice and wash away the sands of intolerance."

"That sounds fine," said Simple.

"There will, of course, have to be an adjustment period," I continued, "but in due time, now that the legal barriers are broken, the schools of this nation will be integrated, even in Mississippi."

"That adjustment period is what is going to be a bodiddling—especially in Mississippi," said Simple. "And that first day will be a lulu! It is going to take a brave child to walk into a white school that morning. Some will go tipping in, but flying out."

"What do you mean?" I asked.

"I mean colored children will go in all polite and nice and behaving themselves, and they will come flying out before they get time to say, 'Excuse me!' If you have never lived in the South, you do not know how unceremonious some of them white folks down there can be. They do not have all these fine manners you read about in *Gone With the Wind*, and they do not pay no attention to the law if they don't want to."

"You, my dear friend, have been up North in Harlem so long you are, no doubt, talking about certain aspects of the South as you knew it fifteen or twenty years ago. From what I read now, the South has changed, and is changing ever more rapidly every day."

"Which paper have you been reading?" asked Simple.

"*The New York Times*," I told him.

"That one I do not very often see," said Simple. "And if I did, I would not believe a word of it. As for me being up in Harlem fifteen or twenty years, I intend to be up here fifteen or twenty more before I go back down home. My children will go to school right here where it don't take no Supreme Court to get them in, and where I won't have to go to school with them every day whilst they are getting adjusted. If I was down home and had a child and he was about to go to a white school, I know I would have to go with him—and I do not have time to take off from work to go to school with no child. But if we was down South, I would go! I would also enter."

"Do you think all the colored parents in the deep South are going to have to go to school right along with their children?"

"They better," said Simple. "They also better have flying feet or shooting arms when they go."

"You're looking on the dark side, as always," I said, "always looking for the worst."

"Until *all deliberate speed* catches up with a snail! But it's them white folks down there that need educating more than us. However, I would hate to tell them Dixiecrats who their teachers are going to be."

"Who?" I asked.

"Nasser, Nehru and Chou," said Simple.

"Why, those Asiatics are not even Christian!" I said.

"Ain't they?" asked Simple. "Them white folks in Mississippi *are* Christians, so they say, but they don't act like it. Southern Christians behave like they never heard of Christ. Such Christians is really not fit to be teachers to nobody. No wonder the white kids down South don't know how to act, being taught by such teachers. But them Egyptians and Indians and Africans, also Chinese, are going to teach Mr. Charlie something in due time. Just wait."

"How long?" I asked.

"*With all deliberate speed,*" said Simple. "Meanwhile, let them down home Kluxers and White Citizens Councilors keep on disgracing themselves in the sight of the world. God knows a new day is dawning when they will be cut down to size."

"Do you think the peoples of Africa and the East are going to declare war on America?"

"I hope not," said Simple, "because I do not want to get shot myself."

"Then what do you think is going to happen?"

"I think they are just going to make Dulles and Talmadge and Uncle Sam and the Governor of Mississippi so mad they will choke to death trying to think of something to say. You see, the American white man is not used to colored folks paying him *no* attention. Someday when colored Egypt and dark India and black Africa, egged on by China, just ignore him, and do not pay him *no mind at all,* the white man is going to get so bugged he will go to pieces, start trembling and shaking, frothing at the mouth, and be so dizzy in the head that he will fall down and faint in front of them schools from which he has barred Negroes out. Then the Negroes will just walk on in school and set down and start studying."

"You are dreaming up a real fantasy," I said.

"It will be no dream to them down-home crackers—it will be a night-mare," said Simple. "Southern white folks are living in a dream world already—dreaming how smart and clever and better than me they are. Which, I say, let them dream, because they are perched up on a high, tall building of deceit. When they look down and start dreaming that they are falling, and screaming like Talmadge in their dream, that will be when their dream will turn into a nightmare. Then when they fall ker-plunk on the ground—with the colored kids stepping politely over them going to school—that will be the day they have, for real, done fell out of bed. Then they will call me to help them up, but I will be too busy getting my arithmetic."

"I see you don't believe in returning good for evil."

"I do," said Simple, "but *with all deliberate speed*. I would let them Southerners lay there a few years on the cold, cold ground and get used to moderation. I would not go to no extremes to pick them up, since Eisenhowser has done spoke out against extremes. I would say, 'These things take time. Let the people of good will of both races work it out, meanwhile you lay in the mud.' "

"Out of the confusion of your parable, I gather that you visualize the Southern white man prone—but the Southern Negro, hale, hearty, and fit to tell him off. All this, you say, will come about through a combination of forces overseas."

"Black, yellow and brown forces," said Simple, "and not by fighting—just by being sassy. A Southern white man would rather be shot than sassed by somebody he thinks is lower than himself. He classes Indians, Egyptians and Chinese mighty near as low-down as he does Negroes. So if them foreign countries keep on sassing Mr. Charlie, Mr. Charlie is just going to get so upset he can't take it, and blow his own top. When his top is blowed and his wig is gone, that is when colored folks—who are not worried about no Suez Canal, Formosa, or Pakistan—that is when my race will just march on in school and take up their studies with a clear mind. Me, I will go back to school, too, to begin where the white folks left off, and try to learn something about behaving myself. Out of their own books, I will try to learn something good."

"But when the Southerners have recovered from their nightmares and fainting spells—or whatever spells you imagine you have wished on them—what will happen then?"

"The N.A.A.C.P. will have done carried my case to the Supreme Court, as usual," said Simple, "and won again. So I'll just set in school and sing *with all deliberate speed*, 'I Shall Not Be Moved,' and I would ask the white folks outside to join in the chorus. After which I would invite them crackers into the schools to learn something, too, because today they are just pure-D ignorant, that's all."

Puerto Ricans

I was rushing past the newsstand at 125th and Lenox on the way to work this morning when I bought a comic book to read in the subway. When I got on the train and opened it, that book were in some kind of foreign language. I said to the guy beside me, "What's this?"

He said, "*Español!*"

I said, "What?"

He said, "Spanish—for Puerto Ricans."

I said, "Puerto Ricans? Are you one?"

He said, "*Sí,* are you one, too?"

I said, "I am not! I am just plain old American."

He said, "You—*Negro* American."

I said, "You look just like me, don't you? Who's the darkest, me or you?"

He said, "You, darkest."

I said, "I admit I have an edge on almost anybody. But you are colored, too, daddy-o, don't forget, Puerto Rican or not."

He said, "In my country, no."

"In *my* country, yes," I said. "Here in the U.S.A. you, me—all *colored* folks—are colored."

He said, "*No entiendo.* Don't understand."

I said, "I don't blame you. I wouldn't understand color either if I could talk Spanish. Here, take this comic book in your language which, me—*no entiendo.*"

So I gave him my comic book and went on to work. On the way I kept thinking about what a difference a foreign language makes. Just speak something else and you don't have to be colored in this here U.S.A.—at least, not as colored as me, born and raised here, and 102 per cent American. The Puerto Ricans come up here from the islands and start living all over New York, Chicago, anywhere, where an ordinary American-speaking Negro can't get a foothold, much less a room or an apartment—and the last place a Puerto Rican wants to live is Harlem, because that is colored. So they live uptown, downtown, all around town, the Bronx, Brooklyn, anywhere but with me, unless they can't help it. And do I blame them? I do not! Nobody loves Jim Crow but an idiot, and I am Jim Crowed.

Español! Now that is a language which, if you speak it, will take *some* of the black off of you if you are colored. Just say, *Si,* and folks will think you are a foreigner, instead of only a plain old ordinary colored American Negro. Don't you remember a few years ago reading about that Negro who put on a turban and went all over the South speaking pig Latin and staying at the best hotels? They thought he was an A-rab, and he wasn't nothing but a Negro. Why does a language, be it pig Latin or Spanish, make all that much difference?

I have been in this country speaking English all my life, daddy-o, yet and still if I walk in some of them rich restaurants downtown, they look at me like I was a varmint. But let somebody darker than me come in there speaking Spanish or French or Afangulo and the headwaiter will bow plumb down to the ground. I wonder why my mama did not bear me in Cuba instead of in Virginia? Had she did so, I would walk right up to the White Sulphur Springs Hotel now and engage me a room, dark though I be, and there would not be a white man in Dixie say a word. But just let *me* enter and say in English, "I would like a reservation."

The desk clerk would say to me, "Negro, are you crazy?"

I would say, "No, I am not crazy. I am just American."

He would say, "American though you be, you will never sleep in here. This hotel is for white folks."

Then I would say, "You ought to be ashamed of yourself, drawing the color line in Virginia where Thomas Jefferson was born in this day and age of such great democracy."

Whereupon he would call the manager who would say, "You better get out of here before I have you arrested for disturbing the peace."

I would say, "What kind of peace are you talking about? That is the trouble with you white folks, always wanting peace, and I ain't got no privileges. You are always keeping the best of everything for yourself. All the peace is on your side."

Then the old head desk clerk would say, "Get out of here before I call the law." And the manager would reach for the phone.

Whereupon I would pull my Spanish on him. I would say, "*No entiendo.*"

Then they would both get all red in the face and say, "Oh, I beg your pardon! Are you Spanish?"

But by that time I would be mad, so I would say, "I will not accept a room here." And walk stalking out. I would say, "Where I cannot spend my money if I speak American, I will *not* if I speak Spanish. You white folks act right simple. Good-bye!" I would leave them with their mouths wide open. "*Adios!*"

Then, if I was an artist, I would put all that into a comic book. I wonder why somebody don't make comic books out of the funny way white folks in America behave—talking democracy out of one side of their mouth and, "Negro, stay in your place," out of the other. I wish I could draw, I would make me such a book. I would start a whole series of comics which I bet would sell a million copies—*Jess Simple's Jim Crow Jive,* would be the title. I would make my books in both English and Spanish so the Puerto Ricans could laugh, too. Because it must tickle them to see what a little foreignness will do. Just be foreign—then you don't have to be colored.

Depression in the Cards

"I really think another depression is coming back," said Simple.

"Why do you say that?" I asked.

"I see it in the cards," said Simple. "House-rent parties is returning to Harlem in a big way. I have collected me a whole cigar box full of house-rent party cards this winter, and still getting them. Look at these in my pocket now. Here's one that says:

> "HOP, MISTER BUNNY,
> SKIP, MISTER BEAR!
> IF YOU DON'T DIG THIS PARTY
> YOU AIN'T NOWHERE.
> AROUND THE CORNER
> AND UP ONE STAIR,
> HEY STED, JIM DADDY,
> THE ROCKING'S THERE!

"And last night when I stopped by this bar for my Friday beer, a fellow come handing me this card which says:

> "WITH DIM LIGHTS ON
> AND SHADES PULLED TIGHT,
> LET'S CLOWN ON DOWN
> TILL BROAD DAYLIGHT—
> AT A SOCIAL GIVEN BY SNOOKS AND AMY
> FRIDAY NIGHT—TEN—UNTIL!

"I asked Joyce did she want to go. Joyce said, 'With all the nice friends we got, why would you wish to be going to a party at somebody's house you don't even know?'

"I says, 'House-rent parties is fun, girl. Has you ever been to one?'

"Joyce said she has not and, what is more, is not going to none. She said I better not go neither. So I reckon I won't. But look here at this card which I have still got in my pocket from last week:

> "DON'T MOVE TO THE
> OUTSKIRTS OF TOWN.

JUST DROP AROUND
AND MEET A NEW BROWN
AT SUSIE SEALEY'S DO-RIGHT PARTY
SATURDAY NIGHT! TOO TIGHT! 50¢

"Naturally, I did not show that card to Joyce."

"Did you go to the party?" I asked.

"I were tempted," said Simple, "but I did not yield. And here is one sounds kinder good for next weekend. Do you want to come with me?"

"Where's it going to be?"

"Way up town, 154th Street, in the brown-sugar part of Sugar Hill. Listen to these poetries at the top of this card:

"NOT TOO SLOW
AND NOT TOO FAST
BUT A REAL GOOD TIME
WHILE THE DANCING LAST—
GIVEN BY PRETTY POLLY & SUNSHINE LENNIE—
PLENTY TO EAT, DRINK, AND BE MERRY WITH.
ENTRY: ONE SIMOLEON

"Don't you think we ought to go?"

"Well, maybe we should take it in," I said. "I haven't been to a house-rent party since the depression days of bathtub gin and wood alcohol."

"Now they serves Long Island corn," said Simple. "Supposed to be from the hills of West Virginia, but they make it right across the river in Brooklyn. It tastes like corn whiskey, though. You know, they can make anything in New York City."

"I rather hate to see bootlegging and pay-parties coming back," I said.

"Why?" asked Simple. "Sometimes you can have more fun at a pay-party than you do at a free one. At a free party to which you is invited, you has to behave yourself. At a paid one, you can clown down. Listen at this card:

"WE'LL HAVE OODLES OF GIRLS,
TALL, SLIPPERY AND SLIM.
THEY CAN DO THE MOMBO
TILL IT'S TOO BAD, JIM!

"And who will mombo right along with them is me, daddy-o! I know there'll be a kid setting back in the corner with a Calypso drum. You can smell the pigs' feet from the kitchen to the parlor, and hear folks laughing clean down on the first floor."

"Or screaming, 'Bloody Murder!' if a fight breaks out," I interposed.

"Negroes do not fight so much like they used to in the old days," said Simple, "not even at house-rent parties. Of course, now, if somebody puts it down too strong on somebody else's old lady—Help! But I do not goof off like that myself with strange women. I respect other men's property, pay-party or not. I do not like excitements. Now this card about the party tonight is pure mischief:

> "ONE LIGHT'S BLUE AND
> THE OTHER LIGHT'S RED.
> YOU CAN STAY ALL NIGHT
> BUT YOU CAN'T GO TO BED
> AT TALL SLIM MAMIE'S PARLOR SOCIAL
> WHERE AIN'T NO DEPRESSION—
> JUST A LITTLE RECESSION!
> SO PAY AS YOU GO!

"Should I go," asked Simple, "or not?"

"No," I said.

"If everybody said no, poor Mamie could not pay her rent. I believe I will run by for a few minutes and spend a dollar. I might need help myself someday should I throw a party. Who knows?"

The Atomic Age

"White folks always seems to be worried so about intermarriage," said Simple. "Why I do not know. All a white girl has to do to keep from marrying a Negro is to say, '*No.*'"

"That problem really has a simple answer," I agreed.

"Nobody can make a woman marry a man, white or colored, so the answer is just a plain and simple, '*No.*' But me, I got a great many other things to worry about besides intermarriage. And I already got a wife on my hands, chocolate-brown and sweet-all-reet, so intermarriage is no problem to me, not Jesse B., at all. What I am worried about is the times to come."

"The times to come?"

"You know what the cotton gin did to the Negro race in times past, don't you?"

"No," I said. "What?"

"When the cotton gin were invented, I read once in a book that nine million Negroes were throwed out of work," said Simple. "All them big husky and little tineechy ones, too, that stripped the fields from North Carolina to Texas, had to weigh in their sacks and go to town looking for jobs. That is why Harlem is so full of all kinds of Negroes now, the overflow from Richmond, Atlanta, Charlotte and points South, which cities were already full before they left the fields. Now a machine can do the work of forty mens. Which is why I dreads what is coming for colored folks tomorrow."

"What do you mean, coming?" I demanded.

"The Atomic Age," said Simple, "when they start using atoms for peace. I read in the papers where the President done issued a statement that it won't be long now."

"Long till what?"

"Till them atoms will be doing the work of men. They gonna stop making bombs in the United States and start making all kinds of little old small machines for peace that will do more work than a thousand big machines like we got now. And all you will have to put in them new baby machines will be just a little old grain of an atom. A handful of mens can run them. They won't need hardly anybody much no more to work. So

69

who do you think will be the *first* to be throwed out of work? Negroes!"

"You're always looking on the dark side," I said.

"I am dark," said Simple, "and you know as well as I do, when the atom comes in, Negroes go out. 'Last to be hired, first to be fired.' And, man, such another firing as there will be when the atom comes to power! Imagine taking one little old grain of atom, about the size of a pinhead, and heating a great big whole apartment house. Won't need nobody to shovel coal in no furnace, neither deliver coal, neither mine it then. What are Negroes gonna do that mines coal, shovels coal, drives coal trucks, and stoke furnaces, huh? You don't think they are going to hire all them colored folks, just to lift a pinhead atom into a cup-sized furnace? You know they ain't! That will be skilled labor—and one white man can do that. So far as I know, they don't let no Negroes touch atoms nohow, nowhere, no place. Leastwise, I have not read about none in this U.S.A. and I have not seen the picture of nary a colored atom scientist being investigated by no Congress committees. The atom belongs to white folks. I have not seen a Negro with an atom nowhere in his possession, not even a speck of an atom, not even atom dust. Have you? Have you ever met any black atom makers? Do you know any colored man with an atom? So all I can think is, when the Atom Age do come in, Negroes will be so far behind the atom ball it ain't funny. We are going to be S.O.L., *but good!*"

"My dear fellow," I said, "the Atom Age is intended to benefit all of mankind enormously. People will only have to work a few hours a day."

"*White people*," said Simple, "because Negroes will not be working *at all*. They will be laid off."

"You take a most pessimistic view of everything. We're American citizens, too. So we should benefit equally."

"*Should* and *would* is two entirely different things," said Simple. "When the big boss starts cutting down, who does he cut down first? Me! And when that atom starts doing the cutting, watch out, Jack, if you're black! You're gone! Why? Because an atom does not even make ashes, so they won't need nobody to clean up after it like they do from coal. An atom does not make soot, so they won't need no soot wipers. An atom don't weigh an ounce and it's no bigger than a pinhead so they won't need no lifters to lift it, nor haulers to haul it, nor shovelers to shovel it. So what will there be for a black man to do when they start using atoms for peace?"

"I am flabbergasted. If what you say is true, what will we do?"

"I know what I will do," said Simple. "I will get on Relief. I will let the government take care of me. I will say, 'You-all made this pinhead atom. I had nothing to do with it. *But God made me.* Now you-all take care of *me* until God gets ready to take me to His bosom.'"

"But suppose the government refuses to take care of you. What will you do then?"

"Raise so much sand that they would be glad to look after me, my wife, my relatives and also my in-laws. They would not want no parts of me when I got through with that Relief Office. I would sound off like Bikini. I would blast like Louis Armstrong's trumpet. I would make them relief people think I had a loudspeaker in my throat like Adam Powell. I would also claim discrimination."

"In other words, you would be a trouble maker?"

"If I can't be an atom maker," said Simple. "Anyhow, if peace don't work, and war comes it's gonna be who's first on the draw with that atom bomb—because who draws last is lost."

"Both sides in a war will probably be lost," I replied, "and you included, just standing on the side lines."

"I would not be lost if I had a bomb," said Simple, "because I dead sure would throw mine first."

"Your nation has atom bombs, and you are a part of the U.S.A., so those bombs are being stock-piled for *your* protection by *your* government."

"Then I wish my government would use one of them bombs in Mississippi," said Simple. "Trouble is, if a bomb went off in Mississippi, it might mess me up even up North. One of them atom clouds might just drift right on over New York. Then what?"

"Then what is right!" I said. "What would you do in case of an atom-bomb raid?"

"Phone the liquor store to deliver me a fifth quick, tip the delivery boy, and set down to enjoy my last few moments on earth," said Simple.

Minnie Again

"You know I wish my Cousin Minnie would leave New York and go on back down home to Virginia where she come from," allowed Simple. "Even if she did come North looking for freedom, Harlem is too much for her."

"Why? What's happened now?" I asked.

"Last week Minnie got behind in her rent and was about to be evicted from the house where she rooms at," said Simple. "So she come calling *me* up from a pay phone to ask me am I going to let her get put out in the street."

"What did you say?"

"I told Minnie I has nothing to do with the matter, being as I'm neither her landlord, her husband, her father, nor her brother. I am just an off-cousin—not even by marriage."

"Minnie said, 'Jess, I did not waste my time and my dime to call you up to listen to no such talk as that concerning our cousinship, which is by blood, if not by law. I needs me some money.'

"Now, I hate to get too plain-spoken with anybody, least of all a woman. But I had to tell Minnie what I thought she was. After which I told her what I thought she wasn't—which is that she ain't right bright. Minnie ought to could look at me by now and tell I never have no money. I also told Minnie that she is not stable, as the Relief folks says, because to my knowledge Minnie has had four jobs in three weeks and kept none of them.

" 'Furthermore, Minnie,' I says, 'you are not sober. I can tell right now the way you talk on this phone you are not sober. Tomorrow, you will have a hang-over, and cannot go to work again, even if you have a job. Don't bother me about money,' I said and I started to hang up. But before I got the hook from my ear, Minnie called me a name which no man can take on the phone. In fact, Minnie were so indignant she called me *out of my name*. So I was forced to reply. Just then Central said, 'Five cents more, please,' which Minnie did not have. So our conversation were cut off on an unpleasant note with the last word being Minnie's. Boy, did you ever have a begging relative?"

"Who hasn't had such kinfolks?" I asked.

"Just when Joyce and me get a phone in our room, after being married almost two years without a phone of our own, who should come to New York and start phoning us but Cousin Minnie! I got a good mind to take my phone out of its socket."

"Then Minnie would probably come to your house and worry you in person," I said.

"Not if my wife put the evil eye on her," said Simple. "Joyce is a good girl, but she can look *so-ooo-oo-o* mean at times that even me, her lawful wedded husband, am scared to look back at her. Joyce can keep Minnie out of our house. Only reason she has not done so up to now is because Joyce tries to treat the woman right since Minnie is my kinfolks. But Minnie is driving kinship in the ground. Minnie loves money more than she does me, else she would not bug me with that word so much. From the first time I laid eyes on Cousin Minnie she needed money. First, money to stay in town after she got here, then money to buy something to eat (which is what she calls drink), then money to pay for a job at the employment office, then money to get out to her new job in the subway, then money to get another job after she quit the first job because the lady who hired her did not like frozen food, and Minnie said she did not intend to shell no fresh peas when peas come already shelled frozen. Now Minnie wants money to keep from getting put out in the street because she is three weeks behind on her rent. Minnie thinks I am a Relief Station, else God—and I ain't nothing but a man, a working man, and a colored man at that. Do you believe Minnie's in her right mind?"

"I think she is simply uninformed as to our habitual state of impecunity in Harlem," I said. "Many newly arrived immigrants from the South think all New Yorkers are rich. They don't realize that most of us live from day to day, from hand to mouth."

"I have tried to break that sad news to Minnie," said Simple, "but it does not seem to penetrate. I have put my hand in my pocket and turned it inside out to show her that my pockets are empty. I have told Minnie that my wife and me runs on a budget and that the budget runs out before the week does. But I want to tell you one thing, cousin or not, the next time Minnie asks me for money, I am going to sic Joyce on her, and I bet you Minnie will understand then!"

"Why would you bring Joyce into your family affairs?" I asked.

"Joyce is my loving wife," said Simple, "and from her I hides only a few secrets. You know it is nice to have a nice wife. And, so far, Joyce treats all my relatives polite. When Joyce first met Cousin Minnie, newly come to our town from Virginia, to tell the truth I thought my wife might snob Minnie. But Joyce did not snob her. My wife is as nice to Cousin Minnie as if Minnie was cultured—which Minnie is not. In fact, as you know, Minnie drinks. But Minnie had sense enough to come to my house last night almost sober. But she come, as usual, with a purpose. The first thing Minnie said last night was 'Jess, I been caught in the toils of the law.'

"I said, 'Minnie, don't toil me up in no law, because I will have nothing to do with what you been doing. What have you done?'

" 'Well,' said Cousin Minnie, 'I were caught in an after-hours spot when it got raided Saturday, and they took everybody down, including me.'

" 'What was a lady like you doing out so late in a speak-easy?' I inquired.

" 'Ain't you never been out late yourself?' said Minnie.

" 'I admit I were.'

" 'And in an after-hours spot?' asked Minnie.

" 'I have been in such,' I said, 'but I did not allow myself to get caught. Nobody has caught me in a speak-easy, except folks like me that was in there themselves, and they were not polices.'

" 'You been lucky,' says Minnie. 'I been caught two or three times in raids—twice in Virginia where they catch so many Negroes they let us all off easy. But up here in the North, I been remaindered for a hearing. And it is not prejudice, because that joint was integrated. There was white folks in the place, too, drinking, and they got remaindered also. Remaindered means I might have to pay a fine, and I has no money, which is why I turn to you, Jess, my only cousin in New York City.'

" 'I wish you was no relation to me,' I says, 'because I has no money, neither, and I hate to turn a relative down.'

" 'If you are just temporarily out of cash,' says Minnie, 'can't you borrow some?'

" 'My credit is not good,' I said. 'And were I borrowing for myself, it would be hard. For you, that is another story. Minnie, I don't hardly know you, even if you do be Uncle Willie's child. We was not raised up together at no time!'

"As easy as I can, I says, 'I has no money, never have had no money and if you looking to borrow what money I get, *I never will have none.* Do you not remember our Aunt Lucy who used to say, "Neither a borrower nor a lender be?" That was her motto. It is also mine.'

" 'That,' says Minnie, 'is a very old corny motto. You ain't hep to the jive. The new motto now is, Beg, borrow, and ball till you get it all—a bird in the hand ain't nothing but a man.'

" 'I ain't coming on that,' I said. 'You sound like a woman I used to know named Zarita in my far-distant past. But, Minnie, I'm a married man now. I need my money for my home.'

" 'For lack of five simoleons you would let me maybe go to jail, your own blood-cousin, here all alone by herself in Harlem where I don't know nobody. The reason I were in that joint that got raided was, I was trying to get acquainted. I met a right nice colored man in there who bought me a drink and seemed really interested in me until we all got hauled down to the Precinct. Then I asked that man if he would help me to get out. He said, "Baby, I got to get myself out, I can't be bothered with you." Peoples is hardhearted in New York City. You are hardhearted, too, Jesse B. Semple.'

" 'Hard as that rock in the St. Louis Blues that were cast into the sea! Minnie, I regrets this is what big-town life does to peoples. Girl, you had ought to stayed down yonder where you was in Virginia.'

" 'I'll say no more,' said Minnie. 'Have you got some beer in the icebox?'

" 'Not with me around the house,' I says. About that time, Joyce come back out of the kitchenette where she was peeling potatoes and says, 'Miss Minnie, could I offer you a nice fresh glass of Kool-Aid?'

"So you know what Minnie says? She says, 'Thank you, I never drinks a drop of no kind of ade, neither nothing else clear colored, such as water. I thank you just the same, Cousin-in-law, married as you is to my favorite cousin, Jesse B., I thank you just the same. And good night.'

"The very word Kool-Aid run Minnie out of the house. When she left Joyce laughed and said, 'I knowed that would get rid of her—Kool-Aid! I would never let Minnie drink up that nice cold can of beer I just bought for you on my ways home from work out of our budget.'

" 'Joyce, I don't know which I love the most,' I said, 'you or your budget!' "

Sketch for TV

"I have composed a little sketch," said Simple, "which I will now play for you for TV. Excuse me for playing both parts, but I am short on actors today, therefore I will take all two roles both myself. Imagine this bar to be the Mason-Dixon line. Yonder where the bottles is, is North. Their side where I am is South.

"Title: *Jump Steady!*
"Action: *Terrific!*
"Place: *Down Home.*
"Time: *Saturday night.*
"Scenery: *Chitterling Switch, Georgia.*

"Let's go! I will now narrate: Talmadge is asleep. There is *one* block in this town where Negroes hang out, one pool hall, one beer parlor, one barbecue joint, and one general store where our folks are allowed to trade. The town's one cop is walking up and down that one colored business block with his stick in his hand. A boy is standing on the corner looking bad just because he is black. The cop is white. The boy is colored. On mike! . . . Lights! . . . Camera! . . . Action! . . . Enter Cop.

" 'Boy, why didn't you jump like you oughta when you saw me coming?' says the cop.

" 'I didn't see you coming, mister, sir,' sirs the Bad Black Boy.

" 'Then jump now,' says the Bad Southern Cop. 'Also bend your head down so I can beat it.'

" 'Please, mister, sir,' sirs the Bad Black Boy, 'I might need my head tomorrow to think with.'

" 'Then turn your hiney around,' says the Bad Southern Cop, 'and let me whale it.'

" 'Aw, please, mister, sir,' sirs the Bad Black Boy, 'I'm liable to need my hind to set down on.'

" 'Then,' says the Bad Southern Cop, 'I will hit you on your shins. What you say you want is equality, ain't it?'

" 'Yes, sir.'

" 'Then you got equality—because I hit white folks on the shins, too. Wham!'

" 'Then hit me again and make me equal,' says the Bad Black Boy. 'Still and yet, I don't see what you're hitting anybody for.'

" 'You committing a crime, ain't you?'

" 'What crime, sir?'

" 'Walking around with a chip on your shoulder, that's what.'

" 'Boss, I ain't got no chip on my shoulder.'

" 'Are you disputing me, boy, and I'm white?'

" 'No, sir! But where is the chip?'

" 'Every time you look at me, I can see a chip, boy. You want to walk around like me, all free and everything. Don't want to ride the Jim Crow car no more. Don't want to say *yes, sir—yes, m'am* to white folks. Don't want to stay in your place. That's the chip you got on your shoulder. I'm giving you a break—I'm just gonna bust you 'cross your shins tonight, instead of 'cross your head.'

" 'But I don't want to be busted nowhere, mister, sir. I ain't done a thing.'

" 'You born black, ain't you? So what more do you need to do? And you tired of staying in your place, ain't you? And you don't jump when you see me coming, do you? Then take that! And this! And that! And don't holler!'

" 'Aw-ow-ow-OOO-oooo!'

" 'I said, "Don't holler."'

" 'Boss, I got to holler, you hurting me.'

" 'I'm supposed to hurten you. Don't holler!'

" 'Yeow-ow-ow-ow-oooooow!'

" 'Don't you like it?'

" 'No sir.'

" 'You don't?'

" 'Yes, sir!'

" 'Then stay off the corners! It looks bad to see you colored boys lounging around on a Saturday night whilst white folks are clerking and working.'

" 'I would be working, too, boss, if you'd give me a job.'

" 'We ain't giving you nothing. All I got to do is beat your head! Otherwise, how am I gonna keep you in your place?'

" 'Boss, you sound just like Hitler did, sir!'

" 'Like who?'

" 'Hitler!'

" 'Folks, y'all heard him! Everybody heard what he said! Boy, I'm gonna take you to jail.'

" 'Charged with what, mister, sir?'

" 'Treason, black boy! Treason! That's what!' "

Sex in Front

"Time was when we did not have any colored magazines. Now we got so many, I don't know which one to buy," said Simple. "Colored magazines on the newsstands all over town, and white folks buying them, too. Nowadays they got *Ebony.* They got *Color.* They got *Jet.* They got *Sepia.* They got *Copper.* They got *Tan,* the *Negro Review, African Opinion, Hue, Brown,* and *Bronze.* I am going to start me one called, *Black.*"

"Why *Black?*" I asked.

"Because that is the only magazine we have not got," said Simple. "They done used all the other colors up. So mine will be *Black.*"

"*Ebony* means *black.* So does *Jet.* Therefore, you will not be starting anything new."

"Except that mine will really be *Black,*" said Simple. "There is no reason why there should not be a magazine named after the black man. They already got the tan man, the sepia man, the brown man, *Color,* and also *Hue.*"

"What would you put in your magazine?" I asked.

"Pictures, like the rest of them," said Simple, "also a little writing. The writing would be about, 'How I Got This Way.' Also 'Am I a Black Man, a Negro, or an Afro-American?' Or 'Does a Rose By Any Other Name Stay the Same?' Also 'Our Indians: The Blackfoot Tribe' which would have Indian pictures."

"What about sex?" I asked. "You have to have sex to put on the cover."

"I would have plenty of sex," said Simple. " 'Sex Galore—and More' would be one of my first pieces. Also I would run a series which would go through the whole list, like this: 'Ebony Sex,' 'Colored Sex,' 'Jet Sex,' 'Sepia Sex,' 'Tan Sex,' 'Brown Sex,' and 'Black Sex.' "

"Then, when you ran out, what would you do?" I asked.

"Start going backwards," said Simple, "and running the same things over under another name, like the rest of them magazines does. Facts is, I might even change the name of my magazine then to *Black Sex,* which would run the rest dead off the newsstands. I would sell one million copies each and every time *Black Sex* came out. Then I would take the money I made and start another magazine."

"And what would you call that one?"

"*Passing*," said Simple. "We do not have a magazine yet called *Passing*."

"What would you put in *Passing*?"

"Articles about 'How I Passed for Sepia,' 'How I Passed for Tan,' and 'How I Passed for White.' Then I would start another series about races: 'How I Passed for an Indian for Twenty Years,' 'How I Passed for an Arab,' 'How I Passed for Italian Without Knowing the Language.' Also I would start a short course on 'Ten Ways To Pass,' 'How To Pass Naturally,' and 'How To Bypass Passing.' I would have myself a magazine such another as you have never seen the like in America. It also would sell one million copies each time it came out."

"Without sex?" I asked.

" 'Can Sex Pass?' would be my *first* article," said Simple. "In the second issue, I would have on the cover in big letters, 'Sex Seized in Passing.' In the third issue I would have, 'Please Pass the Sex' in red headlines. Also on the cover there would be a picture of a pretty girl passing. Underneath would be writ, 'Is She White or Colored?' Then I would run an article on 'Can White People Pass for Black?' Oh, I would have myself a magazine that everybody would buy, white and black, and black and white, also brown, tan and sepia folks. I would print it in Spanish, too, so the Puerto Ricans could buy it. And my first article would be 'Puerto Rican Sex.' "

"Great day in the morning!" I said. "When you are making all that money from your magazines, just full of sex, what will you do with so much dough?"

"Give it to the other sex," said Simple. "But I hope you don't take me serious. My wife better not catch me starting no magazine by the name of *Black Sex*. Joyce has got too much race pride for that. Just the other day she said, from the looks of our magazine covers, when white folks see them on the newsstands they must think Negroes do not know a thing about sex—because every time you see a colored magazine it has got some simple old question about sex writ all over the cover of it, right on the front, such as 'Does Weather Affect Sex?'

"Joyce says she is getting ashamed these days to read some of the colored magazines in the subway on the way to work because white folks will think she is reading a sexylogical magazine. Such magazines is too sensational. Not being much of a reading man, the girls in them are pretty, which I enjoys. But the articles I scans do not tell me nothing

I do not know, or have not heard. I can answer all them questions on the covers myself."

"You are a grown man," I said, "so naturally you've been around."

"I has," said Simple, "and I learned from life, not books, from womens, not magazines. And I has nothing against sex, just as I has nothing against beer. But if they gonna put sex in a magazine which goes into schools and homes and all over, including subways where white folks ride, they don't just have to put it on the cover."

"You believe in being secretive about sex, heh? Putting it on the *inside* of a magazine, but not on the outside."

"I believe in having some kind of shame like Joyce," said Simple, "especially where our race is concerned. 'White Sex in Black Arms,' 'Sex in Jail,' 'Sex on the Mountain,' then 'Sex After Operations' and 'Sex Before Meals,' or 'Sex in a Wheel Chair'—now what kind of titles is them to put on the cover of a nice magazine? Especially when grandma, the kids, Joyce, and everybody wants to read it. If I was a married man with seven-eight-nine-years-old kids around, I would not bring no 'White Sex in Black Arms' into my home. And Joyce says she hates to see folks looking at her reading about 'Sex Before Meals' on a bus.

"Joyce said, 'What is happening in Africa is interesting, too, besides sex. And what goes on in Washington about integration. Also what Negro invented what invention last month—all that is good and inspiring to know. But I am not interested in "Can Men Make Love Over Eighty?" or "Do Weak Minds Have Strong Backs?" or "Are White Males Lousy Lovers?" Them things I do not think should be exposed to the public in big letters on the cover of a magazine, and I am getting tired of it. In fact, I am going back to buying white magazines like *Time* else *Look* to read on the way to work. I am tired of hiding my magazine behind my pocketbook in the street cars and such places. Somebody sees me reading a colored magazine with "Twenty Ways To Hold a Man" all over it and they will think I am a loose woman. Then is my face red?'

"I said, 'Darling, I do not believe your face will be red.'

"Joyce thought I meant she did not have no shame—which made her mad—but what I really meant was she is not exactly the blushing type. I said, 'Baby, I know you is a fine girl. You know I know that. And I know you don't like being seen with no reading matter such as "Ninety-Nine Nice Ways To Be Naughty," whilst on the back cover is a long-lashed hussy with her head down so her eyes will swim up, "Bedroom Orbs Bag Bachelors." And inside is the photo of a gal whose bosoms is too big for her brassieres, headed "Singing Sexation." But there can't be many more of them kind of articles from now on because our magazines have near about covered all the sex I ever heard of already. They done writ about black sex, white sex, Chinese sex, midget sex, third sex, "Can a Dog and Woman Mate?", fourth sex, "How Hot Is a Hottentot?" Also "What Do Pretty Women See in Pimps?" '

"I do not know why they asks so many such questions on the covers of colored magazines—and such brazen bold questions. White folks who see them questions on the newsstands must think Negroes don't know a thing about sex."

Out-loud Silent

"When you smell smoke there's due to be fire," said Simple. "And when you see sawdust, the mill can't be far away."

"Just what you mean by all this, I do not know," I said.

"I mean with Negroes setting in the front seats of buses down South, something is bound to happen," said Simple. "Montgomery, Birmingham, Miami, Tallahassee—every bus seat must be a hot seat. Wood do burn!"

"Speaking of sawdust," I said, "the mills of the gods grind slowly."

"But grind some mills do," said Simple, "and not just sawdust. Some mills also grind muscle, bone, flesh, and soul."

"Which is exactly what I was commenting on," I answered.

"You are an off-beat commentator," said Simple, "and I do not always know what you mean. You can be a puzzlement. Sometimes with me I think you are, sometimes not."

"True," I said, "sometimes *yes*, sometimes *no* in regard to you. You are not a man with whom I can always agree."

"I cannot always agree with myself," said Simple. "And when I talk back to myself, sometimes, I talk too loud."

"Out loud?"

"I ain't that old yet," said Simple. "I do not go around talking really *out loud* to myself. What I do is I talks silent in my own brain—*out-loud silent*—and sometimes I say, 'Jesse B., listen! You are getting old enough to know better. Now, at times you do do better, but not better enough. Jesse B., you got a long ways to go, and you didn't start from so far back that you are not due to be a lot further along. If you had not stopped so often to enjoy your damn self so much on the way, Jesse B., just think! You might own your own house in Harlem now and not be dependent on no landlord, neither landlady for a place to lay your head, and Joyce's.' "

"True," I said.

"Now, take Joyce, my wife, who is a good woman—I owes her a better living than I am making. She tells me so herself every day. I get mad to hear it, but it is the truth. Joyce deserves the best. What I give her is the best she can *make* of it, but not the *best*. Take our kitchenette. We got a bed that folds up and makes like a couch, so our place won't look like a bedroom when company comes. A man and wife, white or colored, should not have to fold up their bed every morning when they get up, particularly on Sundays. You might want to jump in it again—and there it is all folded up in case company comes. Dog-gone company, I say! But a woman does not take that position. A woman, no matter what she is doing, wants to have things looking well if company comes. Women get all flustered. I say just let company knock until you get the bed folded up. You can be sure there's no white folks coming visiting—and most colored folks live just like us in New York. But Joyce says it looks like by now we could at least afford a house with a bedroom. She is right. If I had not spent so much time in so many barrooms before marriage, I could have a bedroom after marriage. Oh, well, daddy-o, such a lot of beer has gone over the bar that there is no use crying over spilt milk in a kitchenette. Me, I cry not, but sometimes I recalls. And the beer were good!"

"But the memory is bitter," I commented.

"Not too bitter," declared Simple. "The trouble about remembering the past is that so many *wrong* things were *so* good. It is hard to regret what were FINE! It is also hard to kick yourself in the behind for what you got a kick out of doing. There is no kicks in kicks for kicks, nor sense neither. If I kicked my gizzard out now, it will not bring back one glass of the beer that has gone through my gullet, nor restore nary wasted dime to my pocket. I regrets I has no regrets—but honestly I has none, not even when I think silent. But I agrees with that book I read on how to get ahead in the world—the time to start is NOW, daddy-o-boy, not then. THEN is dust that the wind has blowed away. Yesterday is leaves on old trees that too many winters has caught. Tomorrow is almost all that is, since today is nearly gone by the time you get started, and tomorrow is nearly here now. The two connects so close together, today and tomorrow. So close, so close! But what I really love is tomorrow.

" 'But what if tomorrow never comes?' says Joyce.

" 'Aw, baby,' says I, 'then couldn't we leave our bed down *just* for today—and, in case tomorrow comes, make it up then?' "

Color on the Brain

"The reason why so many people go crazy these days and start talking to themselves is because they got so much to worry about," said Simple. "Me, for instance."

"What are you worried about, friend?" I asked.

"About the fact that with white people, their left hand don't always know what their right hand doeth."

"Meaning by that, what?" I asked.

"Meaning that their right hand, which is really the hand that is trying to do right—by which I mean the Supreme Court—has done decreed the end of Jim Crow. But most white folks down South is nowhere near ready to go to school with me, let alone set on a bus seat with Negroes. In fact, their left hands do not know what their right hand doeth—just like I said."

"You're talking about race again," I stated. "Race, race, race! The race problem is always on your mind."

"Being a race man, yes," said Simple. "Till the day I die—since I will be black until I am buried—race problems will be on my mind. How can they help but be? White folks forces me to it."

"There is such a thing as being above the struggle," I said, "as ignoring the petty things of this world."

"Petty means what?" asked Simple.

"Little," I said.

"Then I cannot be that small," declared Simple, "because my problems is big. Facts is, my problem is *ME*. I am colored, Afro-American, black, sepia, jet, ebony, whatever you want to call me. Until I am right in this world, and this world is right by me, I got to talk about my problems. Is there anything wrong with that? The Hungarians howl about their problems, so do the Israelis, likewise the Egyptians, also everybody else in the United Nations. Talk, talk, talk, is all I hear from the U.N. every time I turn my radio on. Me, I have no U.N., and Harlem is not represented there. I am not a nation. I am supposed to be a part of the U.S.A., and somebody named Lodge is supposed to represent me, but I have not yet read in nobody's newspapers where Lodge has said one thing about these all-black schools in Harlem that are ninety-nine years old, nor about them all-black schools in Georgia that has classes only when cotton don't need picking. That is what I mean about the left hand and the right. Our white folks can talk so big in the U.N. and do so poor on their own end—which is the U.S.A., America, also Harlem."

"Be careful," I said, "you'll commit treason. Then you'll never get a passport to go abroad."

"What old abroad?" said Simple. "I do not want to go to no abroad. In America I stakes my claim, and the only frontier I want to cross is that one called Jim Crow. The only place I want a passport to is Freedom right here. And the only soil I am yearning and longing to set foot on is the soil of Equality, which I have never yet seen. It must be somewhere across the Jordan in Beulah Land."

"In other words, you figure you have got to die to be equal to the whites?"

"The Bible says, 'This world and another one,'" said Simple, "and in the other world, I am due to be whiter than snow—whiter than Mr. Eisenhowser and Mr. Nixon put together."

"You think only in terms of black and white," I said. "Can't you ever get rid of your color phobia? With you, I am beginning to think, it is a poison like hydrophobia, a complex, a psychosis. You are psychotic."

"If you have to call me names," said Simple, "please call me something I can understand."

"You are a racial isolationist," I said, "a nationalist, a black chauvinist."

"You got one thing right," said Simple, "I am black. And, being black, right now I have got Egypt on the brain."

"Egypt?" I said. "Why Egypt?"

"Because them peoples are colored, too. Look at Nasser. He's about the color of Larry Doby or Don Newcombe."[1]

"Judging from his pictures," I said, "I'd take him definitely to be a colored man."

"He could not pass for white South of Washington," said Simple. "You know, I was looking in the geography atlas today for a map of Africa to see where Egypt was, and where do you reckon they had the map of Africa?"

"Where?"

"In the back of the book," said Simple, "the very last map. Why do you suppose white folks put everything black in the back? Even a map, which just goes to prove that old toast were not far wrong:

If you're white you're right.
If you're yellow you're mellow.
If you're brown, stick around.
But black—get back!

There is a lot of truth in them old toasts. But, daddy-o, I got a feeling from listening to the news on the radio these days that our white folks is getting frantic, not just about Alabama and Mississippi, but Egypt and India and Africa, too, and that they are beginning to think that maybe once ain't forever, two not always twice—if you roll long enough, there's bound to be a change in the dice.

"There is going to be more and more white folks walking the streets talking to themselves and going out of their minds than there already is, if they don't stop worrying about colored folks around the world from Harlem to South Carolina to the Suez Canal—which they want to snatch and put in their pocket. If I was Nasser, I wouldn't even argue with white folks. Like once down South a cracker asked me, 'Can a Negra get sunburnt?' "

"I said, 'Skin is skin. I ain't been skinned yet.' "

"But he wasn't satisfied. He had to ask me another question, 'Can a Negra blush?' "

"This I did not answer, so he repeated hisself, 'I say, can a Negra blush?' "

"I said, 'Can a white man hush?' "

"His mouth flew open. So I repeated myself, 'I said, can a white man hush?' "

"You know that old Dixiecrat got so red in the face that he did what he was asking me could I do—*blushed!* And all I asked him was, couldn't he hush. That man had color on the brain."

New Kind of Dozens

"These white folks and their investigating committees is getting frantic, ain't they?" said Simple. "They are even playing the dozens with each other—except that it is not your mother's morals any more, it's her politics. And white folks do not even know what the dozens is—which means talking bad, sex-like, about somebody else's mama. But they started playing them a year or two ago when they would not give that white boy his commission in the Navy when he graduated on account of his mother was a Communist. Do you remember?"

"Sure, I remember," I said.

"When it come time for Landy to graduate from that Merchant Marines School, all the head man said was, 'Your mama!' And he did not get his commission on graduation day. If that ain't the dozens, I don't know what is."

"You are reading something into the case that was not there," I said. "White people, as you say, have no knowledge of the dozens."

"But they play them right on," said Simple, "except that their kind of dozens don't have nothing to do with your mama in bed. Theirs is about your mama being *red*. I am glad my mother down in Virginia did not know nothing about no Communists. Virginia is overrun with crackers, not Communists. If my mama had ever met a Communist in her youthhood, I might lose my little half-a-loaf job in New York today for associating with my mama at the age of four. I'm telling you, white folks' dozens go a long way back. But they better not talk about my mama. If ever they do, they will have to face me. My mama borned me."

"I'm sure she did," I said, "otherwise I would not know how you got here."

"Are you slipping me in the dozens?" asked Simple.

"What are you trying to insinuate?"

"Who are you trying to put in sin?"

"You are certainly a suspicious Negro," I said.

"Then don't mention my mother," said Simple.

"Did I call your mother a Communist?" I demanded. "I bet, just as you said, there wasn't a colored Communist in Virginia when you were a child. Your mother could get a passport without any trouble—then or now, I am sure."

"If she was living," said Simple. "But my mother has got her passport to glory, passed all investigations, signed the holy loyalty oath, run Gabriel's gantlet, been sworn in by St. Peter, and is now setting on the right hand of the Chief Security Officer. My mama is in there, Jack!"

"I hope so," I said.

"What do you mean, you hope so?" asked Simple. "You don't think my mama is in hell?"

"I didn't say it," I said.

"You better not," said Simple. "If you do, I'll be forced to play the white folks' dozens with you. And they take their dozens serious. They don't fool around with just your mama, they fools around with your job."

"Do you mean to say you would put your job above your mother?"

"My mother stopped feeding me when I were nine years old," said Simple. "Now she's in heaven—but my job is right here on earth."

"You are in no danger of being fired, are you?" I asked. "I didn't know you had access to security matters—or anything else private."

"The only thing private I got access to is the MEN'S ROOM," said Simple.

Vicious Circle

"Housing, so I hear, is a vicious circle," declared Simple. "If the first colored family did not move into a white neighborhood, the second one couldn't. But as soon as one Negro moves in, here comes another one. After a while, so they tell me, we're right back where we started from—in a slum."

"What do you mean, slum? All colored neighborhoods are not slums."

"I thought that's what slums meant—*colored*," said Simple.

"You did not."

"Yes, I did, too. Folks are always yowling about *colored* slums."

"Whatever got you on this subject, anyhow?"

"Mrs. Sadie Maxwell-Reeves, Joyce's club lady friend," said Simple. "She has done moved into a high-class white neighborhood. But no sooner than she got there hardly, than another colored family moved in—which made her mad. Now, six more houses in the block have been sold to colored. Mrs. Maxwell-Reeves is beginning to think that she had just as well have stayed in Harlem and not tried to get outside the circle. Which I reckon she had, because she says it won't be no time now before the candy store on the corner is turned into a bar, and the jukebox will be playing 'Jelly! Jelly! Jelly!' "

"Surely Mrs. Reeves does not object to living next door to Negroes does she, being colored herself?"

"She shouldn't, but I am afraid she do. She's been telling Joyce for a year that she was moving out into a nice white neighborhood in the suburbans. She has moved. But by this time next year, she'll find herself in a nice *colored* neighborhood. Only Mrs. Maxwell-Reeves is afraid it won't be so nice by then—when all her own peoples gets out there. She says we is caught in a vicious circle. I asked Joyce who's to blame. Who started that neighborhood to turning colored? Answer: Mrs. Maxwell-Reeves herself! If she hadn't broke the ice and overpaid the price to move in, that block would still have been white. But when them white folks looked out the window and saw Sadie Maxwell-Reeves they started packing to leave. Real-estate prices went way up the next day. The agents saw Negroes coming, so they charged double to even inspect a house.

Still Negroes buy, no matter how high. Now, Mrs. Maxwell-Reeves is no longer by herself."

"What do you mean, by herself?" I asked. "Negroes in white neighborhoods are not by themselves."

"They are colored, though, ain't they?" said Simple.

"Isolationist," I said. "Self-segregationist! What do you want Negroes to do, never expand, never spread out?"

"Spread out all they like," said Simple. "But don't get mad if some other Negro spreads out with you. If Mrs. Maxwell-Reeves wants the whole white neighborhood to herself, with no other colored in it, then she ought to buy the *whole* neighborhood, the whole suburbans, not just one house. Mrs. Reeves got mad because when she moved in the block, here come some more colored folks moving in. Now one house has already got a ROOMS FOR RENT sign up, so she told Joyce. 'Roomers run down property,' says Mrs. Reeves. Which they do. Me, myself, to tell the truth, if I had a house, I would not want a roomer in it."

"You were a roomer yourself for years," I said, "before you got married."

"I know it," said Simple, "but now only until Joyce and me can find ourselves an apartment. I want to get as far away from roomers as I can—just once in life. Roomers dips into a man's business. They eye your wife—the mens do. Sometimes even a female tempts *me* myself, if she's pretty. Joyce has done warned me about that chick on the third floor where we room now."

"Then you can sympathize with Mrs. Maxwell-Reeves' position," I said. "Rooming houses do lower the tone of a residential section, over-populate an area, and cause it to cease to be exclusive. But often, Negroes who buy in exclusive neighborhoods have to have roomers to help them pay off the mortgage and keep up the high taxes. Not everyone is as well off as Mrs. Reeves."

"Mrs. Maxwell-Reeves is so well off she never did have no roomers even in Harlem, Joyce says. Just a whole house to herself! Some Negroes *is* rich."

"That is why she wishes to be exclusive," I said.

"Then she will have to move again," said Simple. "She paid the price to break the ice to get colored folks into that neighborhood first—now it is no longer exclusive—and when it gets crowded, it won't be suburban. So I guess she will just have to move again."

"Yet, if she does, the same thing may happen."

"That is what Mrs. Maxwell-Reeves calls a vicious circle," said Simple, "when Negroes move in. Listen, daddy-o, are Negroes vicious?"

"Do *you* think Negroes are vicious?"

"No," said Simple, "it must be the circle."

Jim Crow's Funeral

"I wish there was some way of dying without dying," said Simple, "of getting rid of the bad things that afflicts mens, keeping the good—and still being alive. For instant, my old Aunt Lucy had arthritis, which made her kind of snappy at times, but she was a good soul, one of the best. Now if the *arthritis* would have just died, instead of her, that would have been like it should be. Look at President Roosevelt—if what ailed him could have died, but not *him* the world might have been different today."

"In other words," I said, "you mean if the ills of the flesh could pass on, but not the good people who have them, it would be a fine thing. Your fallacy there is that not *all* people are good to begin with. Some are ill—and evil, too."

"It is the bad in them that I wish would die," said Simple. "If I were a judge I would not put nobody to death. I would just sentence the bad in them to die."

"Unfortunately, mankind has devised no sure-fire way to separate the evil from man, or man from evil. The theory of capital punishment is that if the *whole* man is put to death, the evil will go with him—his particular evil, that is. It is a kind of legal assassination. But the trouble is that the patterns of evil are not individual, they are social. They spread among a great many people. Electrocute one murderer today, but someone else is committing murder some other place at that very moment. Killing a man doesn't kill the form of the crime. It just kills him. What we need to do is get at the basic roots of evil, just as a physician tries to get at the roots of disease."

"That is what I mean," said Simple. "It is the sick root that should go, not the whole green tree."

"Of course, there are arguments on both sides," I said. "Sometimes the illness has spread from the root to the whole green tree, as you put it. So the leaves are no longer green, but withered and dry, and the branches have no sap in them, in which case some say you might as well cut the tree down."

"I really started out talking about people being sick, not trees, not murder, not evil. Just plain old backache, headache, stomach-ache sick—

which is what removes more people from this world than an electric chair. I am wishing, for instant, that I will never get nothing that will make me sick enough to die."

"In that case, you would just die of old age. Everybody dies of something."

"I do not want to catch old age, either," said Simple.

"Old age catches everyone sooner or later. No human is immortal on this earth. You were not meant to stay here forever."

"I'd *like* to stay here," said Simple.

"For what purpose?"

"To live to see the day when I would not have to hire a lawyer to go to the Supreme Court to eat in a restaurant in Virginia. I would like to live to see the day when I could eat anywhere in the U.S.A."

"That may not be long," I said.

"It will be longer than it takes for some germ to mow me down," said Simple. "If Jim Crow was only human, maybe Jim Crow would get sick, catch pneumonia, get knotted up with arthritis, have gallstones, a strain, t.b., cancer, else a bad heart—and die. I would not mind seeing Jim Crow die. If necessary, *put* to death. In fact, I would pay for Jim Crow's funeral—even send flowers. If the family requested, I would even rise and preach his funeral. Yes, I would! I would say, 'Jim Crow, Jim Crow, the Lord has taken you away! Thank God, Jim Crow, you will never again drink from no *white* water fountain while I go dry. Never again, Jim Crow, will you set up in front of the buses from Washington to New Orleans while I rides back over the wheels. Never again will you, Jim Crow, laying here dead, rise up and call me out of my name, *nigger*. I got you in my power now, and I will preach you to your grave.

" 'You did not know a Negro was going to preach your funeral, did you, Jim Crow? Well, I is! Me, Jesse B. Semple, was made in the image of God from time eternal from the clay of the infinite into whom was breathed the Breath of Life *just to preach your funeral,* Jim Crow, and to consign you to the dust where you may rot in peace until the world stops spinning around in the universe and comes to a halt so all-of-a-sudden-hell-fired-quick that it will fling you, me and everybody through the A.M. and the P.M. of Judgment *wham* to the foot of the throne of God! God will say, *Jim Crow! Jim Crow! Get away! Hie yourself hence! Make haste—and take your place in hell!*

" 'I'm sorry, but that is what God will say, Jim Crow. So I might as well say it first.

" 'It gives me great pleasure, Jim Crow, to close your funeral with these words—as the top is shut on your casket and the hearse pulls up outside the door—and Talmadge, Eastland, and Byrnes wipe their weeping eyes—and every coach on the Southern Railroad is draped in mourning—as the Confederate flag is at half-mast—and the D.A.R. has fainted—*Jim Crow, you go to hell!* ' "

Again Cousin Minnie

"You see that little old joker down at the end of the bar?" asked Simple, pointing with his beer. "Well, that Negro's been in jail so much he ought to belong to the Bail-Bond-of-the-Month Club."

"What's his claim to fame?" I requested.

"He's a numbers writer," said Simple. "But he's also got political influence. The cops take him down, but next thing you know, he's back walking the streets again. And fight! That little cat can fight, man, anybody! Hard as nails! I do believe he would fight his own papa."

"It's too bad he can't turn his energies to better purpose," I said, "such as the field of race relations where militancy is needed."

"He would be a Mau Mau," said Simple. "Was he in Montgomery, he would turn Rev. King's love feast upside down—and the buses, too. 'Love thy neighbor as thy self,' would not mean a thing to him. He do not love colored folks, let alone white. All that man loves is to fight. But the womens like him. See them girls all around him now down there at the end of the bar? When my Cousin Minnie was in this bar last, she asked me who he was and could I introduce her to him. I told her, not me! She would have to meet that man at her own risk, I said, and if she got hurt in the process, don't come running to me for help because I would not want to be mixed up in the rumble. But I told her last week:

"There is many a slop
'Twixt the lip and the chop."

"You are liable to get gravy on your chin before you get the pork chop in."

"What in the world do you mean by that?" I asked.

"Cousin Minnie," said Simple, "is still slipping and slopping around in them Lenox Avenue bars looking for a chump with a pot of gold. I told Minnie when she first come here that the rainbow with the pot of gold at its end arches right on over New York City. It must terminate somewhere out in the Atlantic Ocean, because it sure do not end in Harlem.

"Minnie said, 'Oh, as many rich old Negroes as there are around here, particularly West Indians, I am bound to find me a man with beaucoup loot and a Cadillac to boot. I never was a woman to play myself cheap.'

"Minnie has now been in Harlem a right smart while, and she is still trying to borrow five or ten dollars from me ever so often. But not if my wife knows it. Relatives or no relatives, Joyce does her best to balance me and the budget, and if I lent Minnie money every time she asks for it, nobody's budget would work out right."

"I gather your Cousin Minnie did not find her pot of gold as yet in New York," I said.

"No," said Simple, "but she thought she had found a rainbow. Minnie come telling me last month about some well-to-do old Negro she had met who had eyes for her like crazy, even spending seven or eight dollars to take her to Frank's for dinner, to the Palm Café for drinks, and to Small's to hear music. Then if she still was not ready to go home, down to that after-hours spot where they used to have the golden key and where drinks is a dollar a throw, even plain sodas with a cube of ice, and where the chicks are fine. I told Minnie she better keep that old geezer out of that speak-easy, else he might latch onto one of them pretty models and put her down.

"Minnie said, 'All that glitters ain't got what I got. I knows how to handle this old goat, myself. I am going to propose to him that we get married.' And don't you know, Minnie did. She proposed to the man herself."

"What did the man say?" I asked.

"That is where the slip came," said Simple. "But there was no use in Minnie's crying—because she proposed to the man. He did not propose to her, so there was no breach of promise nor promises breached. Just a clop betwixt the lip and the chop, that's all! That old man told Minnie, said, 'Daughter, I been married four times, and I think it will be a long time before I try it again.'

"Minnie said, 'But what about all your houses you owns over in Brooklyn and Corona, and them six lots full of potatoes out in Long Island? Where will they be? Who's gonna benefit from all that when you gone?'

"That old Negro told Minnie, 'Don't worry about when I'm gone because, barring poison, I will be here awhile. And it takes all them potatoes on all them lots to feed my children I got, without taking on another wife. Wife Number 1 was O.K., and Wife Number 2 did do.

Wife Number 3 quit me, and Wife Number 4 ain't no more. And all of them cost me money's mammy. But with what dough I got left, I intends to look out for myself. No jive, as long as I am alive, there will be no Number 5.'

"Whereupon Minnie hollered, 'Why, you old rat, you! You got one foot in the grave and the other one on the brink. I don't want you, nohow. I will put you down, and now—soon as you pay for this steak.' They was setting in Frank's when the blowup came and everybody in society heard what Minnie said. You read about it in *Jet* last week, didn't you? Only *Jet* did not mention no names. It just said an elderly Harlem real-estate man were embarrassed by a loud-mouthed, mad, brownskin woman. That were my Cousin Minnie. *Jet* did not repeat what Minnie said. She said, 'You are just a rat, that's all, an old rat!'

"But that man were not phased. He just told Minnie real quietlike, whilst he chewed on his diet, 'You are kinder old yourself—and an old ship can always leave a sinking rat.'"

Cellophane Bandannas

"Something tells me that Uncle Tommy has come again," said Simple, "but this time with a cellophane bandanna on his head. Since you can see his haircut through it, some folks don't even know he's got a bandanna on. But Tom can't fool me, not as long as I am colored."

"Whom are you talking about?" I asked.

"Some of these high-brow, educated, political double-talkers of the Negro race who, every election time, keep trying to flimflam and bamboozle me into voting for some of these low-brow white folks of both parties whose pictures I can just look at and tell they are cracker-minded, no good, and prejudiced from the back of their tongues on down, no matter what they say in their speeches. They lie every time they open their mouths."

"They're politicians, aren't they?"

"Also white, and the truth ain't in 'em," said Simple. "If I can see they're fakes, I know Dr. Butts can, and Prof. Golittle, Attorney Jimjams, and Rev. J. Coddington Simms, Ph.D. D.D. X.Z. from Yale, also Dr. Tom Cat. Colored though they be, they cannot fool me. How much do you reckon a cellophane bandanna costs?"

"In terms of money, I don't know," I said. "The men you mention are all pretty well off, so the price wouldn't matter to them. But it's their honor I worry about."

"That they wear like a loose garment," said Simple, "and I expect they keep two or three extra cellophane headrags in the pockets of their cars, so when they let the convertible down, their hair won't blow in their eyes, also it won't fall in their plates when they go to these interracial dinners at the Waldorf."

"Few of our politicians wear their hair that long," I said.

"I am not talking about the moss on their heads," said Simple, "but the moss on their ideas. Some of them Negro leaders are living way back in the year B.C."

"What do you mean, B.C.?" I asked.

"Before Cadillacs," said Simple. "Also Before Coming."

"Before Coming?"

"Coming North," said Simple. "You can take some Negroes out of the

South, but you can't take the South out of some Negroes. A Southern speech in a Northern accent is still a handkerchief-headed speech to me—and a bandanna is a bandanna even when you can see through it. Back in Booker T. Washington's day Negroes did not have cellophane bandannas. Then they were red with white dots. And in Uncle Tom's day they was any old rag that a Negro could get on his head. But nowadays bandannas is pure clear transparent so the bald head can show through. If the head was transparent, too, you could see that they don't have no brains inside."

"Be careful," I said, "in speaking of people of prominence. They must have some brains to get where they are."

"They got tough hides and whitleather souls," said Simple. "They got selfish hearts and double-talking mouths. They got money-making hands and grasping fingers. They will deal with the colored race with their right hand and the white race with their left, and drop me in the middle. And whichever party wins, some of them Negroes after election will get appointed to a ten-thousand-dollar-a-year office—and I will still be working at my same old job."

"As argumentative as you are," I said, "and as full of real loud opinions as a glass of beer makes you, why don't you go into politics yourself and quit bellyaching about your leaders?"

"Because I am not a politicianer," said Simple, "also I am hotheaded. I could not stand no bandanna on my head, cellophane or otherwise, because my brains would get overheated. My mind might explode. And if I did, no telling what I might say to these white folks."

"White folks, white folks, white folks! Everything you talk about is in terms of white folks," I said. "Don't you know this is a multiracial country, an interracial country made up of all kinds of people?"

"I am not talking about what the U.S.A. is made up of," said Simple. "I am talking about who runs this country. I am talking about who makes them cellophane bandannas they sell—even given out free—to any joker who can flimflam me. Negroes don't own no factories to make nothing, not even a cellophane bandanna. Do they? Huh? Do they? You know and I know they don't. But that man down there at the end of the bar has got a bandanna on right now. And one trouble with him is, he's got too much education to know how to use it. His predilect is for the intellect. He has been standing in this bar for two hours over a ten-cent glass of beer arguing about what is going to happen to Hungary where he has *never* been, when he ought to be talking about what is going to happen to Harlem where he is."

"Isolationist!" I said. "Hungary is a powder keg that might upset the world."

"These high rents in Harlem upset me," declared Simple, "also the lack of apartments. Here I been married almost a year and can't find no place to live yet at no kind of price. And if you do hear about an apartment, you have to buy it in order to rent it—which only racketeers can afford. Also, with meat as high as it is these days, if prices don't come down soon, I'll be so thin I'll have to stand up twice on a sunny day to cast a shadow once."

"Of course, my good man, local problems are important," I said, "but so are international ones."

"I want to deal with the local ones first," said Simple, "otherwise, I won't be living to deal with no others. But that man who is colleged, is always talking about someplace away far-off, like Hindu-China. Now he's done got all hot under the collar about Hungary. Why don't he come down to earth and get on Lenox Avenue?"

"You talk as though Negroes should not be concerned with international issues. Besides, that gentleman is a friend of yours, isn't he? Why don't you bring him down to earth?"

"Shaw!" said Simple. "Changing some folks is like trying to boil a shoat in a coffeepot. Besides, I am not my brother's keeper."

"No wonder you aren't interested in Hungary," I said, "when you are not even interested in your bar-buddies."

"I do not know anybody way over there in Hungary. If Uncle Sam would just stop worrying about Hungary and start spending half of that money in Harlem, instead of on Hungarians, we could tear down all these crowded old houses and build new ones—then I would have a place to live. We could tear down all these little old ugly schools—and there wouldn't need to be three shifts a day for our children. We could have more garbage trucks to collect the garbage so the streets wouldn't look like pigpens. And we could clean up all them dumps along the river front and make parks for the kids to play. Why, we could even tear down this bar—and make it over to look just like the Stork Club."

"You have gone from the sublime to the ridiculous now," I said.

"I have gone from Hungary to Harlem, that's all," said Simple, "which you and that joker at the end of the bar would both understand if you would take off your cellophane bandannas."

Negroes and Vacations

"I do not know why it is that vacations tire Negroes out," said Simple, "but they do. Negroes go on a vacation and come back so tired they can't hardly get to work. In fact, sometimes they have to take an extra week off to recover from their vacation. Vacations rest up white folks, *but they almost kill Negroes.* Somebody ought to find out the reason for this."

"You probably have some theories on it," I said, "or you wouldn't have brought the subject up."

"My theory is that Negroes play too hard. They always play like they're never going to get a chance to play again. If they do not have but one week's vacation, they try to crowd seven weeks of fun, fading, and fast living into *seven days.* If Negroes go to Saratoga they try to have a ball at *all* the night clubs, drink at *all* the bars, pass by *all* the springs, fade the dice on *every* table, and jive *every* cute little chick on Congress Street. That is why a Negro comes back from Saratoga—which is supposed to be a healthy place—completely broke down.

"If a Negro goes to Oak Bluffs—which is in style now—he tries to play society jam-up, sit in on every bridge or canasta game there is, play poker with every doctor and dentist, dance all night, then swim and dive all day, too. It is too much for him. He cannot make his job when he returns.

"If he goes to Atlantic City, the chorus girls in the Paradise and the Harlem will drive him mad, whether he knows them or not, they are so pretty, and they know so many places to go, until his tongue hangs out trying to keep up with the cuties. If he goes to Asbury Park, he's liable to sun-tan himself to death and come back so peeled and blistered he cannot get no rest because there is no part of his body he can lay on. So how can he go to work?

"And don't let a Negro go to Europe! Just talking about his trip when he gets back will keep him tired for months to come. The memory of Paris for a summer is enough to tire anybody out for the winter. A Negro that goes to Paris should have the whole winter off to rest."

"How do you know?" I said. "You've never been to Paris."

"No, but I have met some of these big-time sports who have, and they was too tired to sport around when they got back. Couldn't do nothing but sleep. It do not seem to make any difference where a Negro goes on his vacation, though, when that Negro comes back he is tireder than when he went. I never saw it fail. Why do you reckon?"

"Some kind of desperation is involved, I believe," I said. "Vacations for Negroes are hard to come by. Sometimes you have never had one before in your life, so when you get it, naturally you run it in the ground. Sometimes you take your only savings to have some real fun on a vacation. Figuring you might not have another one for a long time, you do that one up brown. Negroes are not rich like white folks who can take a spring vacation in the Carolinas, a summer vacation in Maine, an autumn vacation in Virginia, and a winter vacation in Florida. When you take three or four vacations a year, you get used to them. So you don't have to make every minute count. But when you only get a vacation once in a coon's age, you try to enjoy yourself all around the clock. Therefore, one has to rest when one returns. Don't you agree?"

"Must be," said Simple. "I know the last time I had a vacation, it took me a month to catch up on my rest when I got back home. I could not just lay down in bed for three or four hours and sleep quick like I usually do. I found myself going to bed with the chickens at eight-nine o'clock, and getting up twelve hours later still sleepy. This year I did not go on no vacation, and I feel twice as good as I did last summer when I went away. I just stayed right in Harlem this summer and drank beer. If I had gone to Atlantic City or Idlewild or Asbury Park or Saratoga, I would have also drunk licker. I would have courted and sported. I would have tried my luck on all the different kinds of games from galloping dominoes to the wheel of fortune. And I would have been broke, busted, disgusted, rest-broken and sleepy on my return. I am beginning to believe that the best vacation is right at home—especially when you are married."

"That is because you have no self-control," I said.

"Ain't there some kind of saying about, 'When in Rome, do as the Romans do'?" asked Simple. "Well, on a vacation, everybody is roaming. Me, too. And it sure do tire you out."

Only Human

"I was just reading in a New York paper that the world is two-thirds colored and only one-third white," said Simple.

"I guess that is correct," I said, "because all of Africa and Asia are colored, and they are pretty big continents. China, Japan, India, Ethiopia, and Nigeria are all colored countries with millions of people, so the world probably is two-thirds colored."

"I wish the world would get even more colored," said Simple.

"You always were a race man," I said, "so I am not surprised at your wish. But why?"

"Because the more colored the rest of the world is, the better our white folks here at home in the U.S.A. will treat us," said Simple. "From the way the papers sound, also the radio, it seems white folks are beginning to get a little scared of colored folks in the rest of the world. So, I figure, the more colored folks there are elsewhere, the more scared our white folks at home will get. Colored folks in China and India and places like that carry more weight than colored folks do here. Just let Nehru say ten words about Egypt, and it is a big headline in a New York paper. But me, I can holler my head off about a lynching in Mississippi and nobody pays me the least mind. Yet I live here in America. Why do you reckon that is?"

"You, my dear fellow," I said, "are only a plain American citizen. Nehru is the head of a great government, India."

"Yes," said Simple, "but India is thousands of miles away across land and sea, whereas right here and right now in the U.S.A. is me, and twice as dark as Nehru. I think when I speak, somebody ought to pay me some attention, too. Do I have to be an Indian to raise my voice and be heard? And all this Foreign Aid I read about Congress is giving. How come I can't get a few billion dollars, too, to build some houses right here in Harlem where I can't find an apartment for love nor money? I'm a grown man and married—I need a roof over my head that ain't a kitchenette. And instead of sending tanks to Saudi Arabia, how come they can't build a few more buses and streetcars and subway cars in New York so when I leave Harlem to go to work, I can set down awhile instead of being so crowded I have to stand on one foot because there ain't even room to put the other foot down? How come we got to send away so much Foreign Aid when there is so much to be done at home—which is where charity begins?"

"America is trying to set an example," I said.

"Example!" cried Simple. "How come we got to set an example for the rest of the world when the example we done set at home don't do a bit of good in Mississippi, neither Alabama nor Georgia nor South Carolina, neither my home which is Virginia? They want to put colored folks in jail for not riding Jim Crow buses in Montgomery, but there was no jail for that Indian from Nehru's country who didn't want to eat in a Jim Crow dining room in Texas last year. Him they put on the front page of *The New York Times* and wrote a big editorial of apologies. I have yet to see any white paper apologizing to Miss Lucy for them students that tried to kill her on the campus of the University of Alabama because she wanted to go to school.[2] I'm telling you, foreign colored folks carries more weight than us home-grown kind. When I get borned again, I'm gonna be born in India."

"That is a very remote possibility," I said. "It is hardly likely you will be born again."

"I might," said Simple, "and when it comes to pass—like the song says—'I'll understand it better by and by.' But right now, sometimes I wonder, with all the problems on it, who made this earth—and me?"

"In other words, you mean the human race."

"Yes," said Simple, "why is the human race what they is? Why is some folks slue-footed, some knock-kneed, some blockheaded, some black, and some white? If everybody was the same color, they would get along so much better. I love my race. But I do wish my feet pointed straight instead of sideways, also that I were not slightly bowlegged. But even that is better than being knock-kneed. And, thank God, I do not have freckles—or if I do, I'm too dark for freckles to show. Also, why did nature make some folks meriney?"

"Inscrutable are the ways of nature," I remarked.

"Screwed up and unscrewable," said Simple. "Treat me to a beer while I tell you that in Africa they got pygmies three feet tall, and in Arkansas they got white folks that eat mud."

"Dirt dobbers, they call them," I said, beckoning the bartender.

"Yes," said Simple. "And they tell me Italians eat snails."

"They do."

"There is some strange things in this world, which makes me wonder. For instant, why do the human race like to fight so much? Russia, Russia,

Russia, Communism, Communism, Communism is all you can hear these days! It looks like our white folks want to fight all of them. Now, why? We just got through one war not long ago, yet they want to start another one! Ever since I were a wee small boy, I been hearing about Russia. Russia must of been here a long time. It looks like our white folks would be used to Russia being in the world by now. But come to think of it, Negroes have been here much longer, and they ain't used to us yet. We been in America ten times as long as some of these foreigners that come here. But they get used to foreigners quicker. Even a Russian can move into a housing project and nobody throws rocks through his windows like they do through our windows. A Pole, a Hungarian, a German, a Turk, anyone can come over here and eat in any restaurant from New Orleans to Newark. But just let me peep in, and it's liable to be, 'We don't serve colored.' Puerto Ricans and Spanish come here and rent an apartment anyplace in town the minute they get off the plane. Me, I go outside of Harlem and see a FOR RENT sign and go in and ask about it, 'Sorry, but this is a white building.' As long as I have been in this U.S.A., they are not used to me being here yet! No wonder Americans can't get used to Russians being in the world, too. Americans is not very adjustable to different kinds of folks, I don't believe."

"Human beings *in general* are not very adjustable to each other. If they were, there would not have been throughout history so many wars."

"I am adjustable to white folks," said Simple. "I do not throw rocks through their windows. I do not Jim Crow them. I do not tell them they cannot live next door to me. I do not treat them like varmints."

"Why don't you?"

"Because I can't," said Simple.

"You mean, you would if you could?" I asked.

"I'm only human," said Simple.

Name in Print

"Just look at the front pages of the newspapers," said Simple, spreading his nightly copy of the *Daily News* out on the bar. "There is never hardly any colored names anywhere. Most headlines is all about white folks."

"That is not true today," I said. "Many headlines are about Negroes, Chinese, Indians and other colored folks like ourselves."

"Most on the inside pages," said Simple, blowing foam from his beer. "But I am talking about front-page news. The only time colored folks is front-page news is when there's been a race riot or a lynching or a boycott and a whole lot of us have been butchered up or arrested. Then they announce it."

"You," I said, "have a race phobia. You see prejudice where there is none, and Jim Crow where it doesn't exist. How can you be constructive front-page news if you don't *make* front-page news?"

"How can I make front-page news in a white paper if I am not white?" asked Simple. "Or else I have to be Ralph Bunche or Eartha Kitt. That is why I am glad we have got colored papers like the *Afro, Defender, Courier* and *Color,* so I can be news, too."

"I presume that when you say 'I' you mean the racial I—Negroes. You are not talking about yourself."

"Of course I am not talking about myself," said Simple, draining his glass. "I have never been nowhere near news except when I was in the Harlem Riots. Then the papers did not mention me by name. They just said 'mob.' I were a part of the mob. When the Mayor's Committee report come out, they said I were 'frustrated.' Which is true, I were. It is very hard for a Negro like me to get his name in the news, the reason being that white folks do not let us nowhere near news in the first place. For example, take all these graft investigations that's been going on in Brooklyn and New York every other week, unions and docks, cops and bookies, and million-dollar handouts. Do you read about any Negroes being mixed up in them, getting even a hundred dollars of them millions, or being called up before the grand jury? You do not. White folks are just rolling in graft! But where are the Negroes? Nowhere near the news. Irish names, Italian names, Jewish names, all kinds of names in the headlines every time Judge Liebowitz opens his mouth. Do you read any colored names? The grand jury don't even bother to investigate Harlem. There has never been a million dollars' worth of graft in Harlem in all the years since the Indians sold Manhattan for a handful of beads. Indians and Negroes don't get nowhere near graft, neither into much news. Find me some Negro news in tonight's *News*."

"I would hardly wish to get into the papers if I had to make news by way of graft," I said. "There is nothing about graft of which any race can be proud."

"Our race could do right well with some of that big money, though," said Simple, signaling the barman for another beer. "But it does not have to be graft, in unions or out. I am just using that as an example. Take anything else on the front pages. Take flying saucers in the sky. Everybody but a Negro has seen one. If a Negro did see a flying saucer, I bet the papers wouldn't report it. They probably don't even let flying saucers fly over Harlem, just to keep Negroes from seeing them. This morning in the subway I read where Carl Krubelewski had seen a flying saucer, also Ralph Curio saw one. And way up in Massachusetts a while back, Henry Armpriester seen one. Have you ever read about Roosevelt Johnson or Ralph Butler or Carl Jenkins or anybody that sounded like a Negro seeing one? I did not. Has a flying saucer ever passed over Lenox Avenue? Nary one! Not even Daddy Grace has glimpsed one, neither Mother Horne, nor Adam Powell. Negroes can't get on the front page no kind of way. We can't even see a flying saucer."

"It would probably scare the wits out of you, if you did see one," I said, "so you might not live to read your name in the papers."

"I could read my name from the other world then," said Simple, "and be just as proud. Me, Jesse B. Semple—my name in print for once—killed by looking at a flying saucer."

Golfing and Goofing

"Man, I am tired of working like a Negro all day in order to live like white folks at night. What I want's a part-time job with *full-time* pay," said Simple. "Sometimes I wish I could pass for white. But to tell the truth, if I *was* light enough to pass for white, I would be scared my next door neighbor might also be colored *passing* for white. There are so many light colored people these days. I know a colored man across the street from me who is white."

"How do you know he is colored then?"

"Because he is Baptist," said Simple. "He lives in Harlem, likes chitterlings, and was born in Yamakraw. But his skin is white, his hair is light, his eyes is gray, and if he wanted to, he could pass—like lots of Negroes. If I was a white man these days I would be afraid the family next door to me was passing for white."

"Do you mean to say that if you were white, you would be prejudiced, and would not want any colored neighbors?"

"Of course I would be prejudiced," said Simple. "How could I help myself? I would be raised up that way and not know no better."

"I do not understand your reasoning."

"That's because you're colored."

"We're both colored, so I believe you are talking illogically."

"I'm talking from experience."

"You have never been white," I said.

"No, but sometimes I wish I could pass for white. At least I could get a good job. I am tired of working so hard."

"I think you must be so tired you have brainfog," I said. "Why don't you go to Florida on a vacation—as Truman used to do when the cares of state got him down?"

"Truman is the only man I ever seen swimming with his glasses on," said Simple. "But since he is not President no more Truman does not go swimming in Florida, for which I am glad. Just like I wish Eisenhowser would not go golfing in Georgia. Florida and Georgia is both Jim Crow states, therefore un-American. Eisenhowser loves Georgia. He is about the most golfingest, goofingest President I ever seen."

"Why do you say goofing?" I said. "Do you consider it a mistake, with all the burdens a President has, for him to take care of his health, to get out in the open air a little?"

"He gets out more than a little," said Simple. "And every time he turns around, he is going to Georgia, of all places! I wish he would not go down there to goof."

"To *golf,* you mean."

"I think it is a mistake to go to Georgia, which is why I say *goof. Goof* means mistake," explained Simple.

"Georgia is still a part of the United States," I said.

"Is it?" asked Simple. "I thought it were a part of Dixie."

"You're goofing off yourself. You know as well as I do, Georgia is in the U.S.A."

"In the Free World?" asked Simple.

"Supposed to be," I said.

"You're weakening! *Supposed* is right!" said Simple. "In Georgia I am not even free to go in the MEN'S ROOM in the train station, unless it has a sign on it COLORED. And the COLORED MEN'S ROOM do not have no facilities. In the Free World I think every MEN'S ROOM should have facilities. Also, you know what Georgia said when the Supreme Court opened up the schools to everybody's children? Georgia said it would shut the schools up! If I was the President, I would not play golf in a state like that. I would bring my golf clubs to some place North of Dixie, where I could play with Sugar Ray Robinson if I wanted to. They would not allow Sugar Ray on that golf course down in Georgia where the President plays, unless Sugar were a caddy—and Sugar is too slick-headed for that."

"Why on earth are you so worried about where the President plays golf?" I demanded.

"I do not think it is good for a man's health to play golf outside the Free World, that's why," said Simple. "It would upset my nerves to be playing golf someplace where ten million other citizens in my country could not play."

"If you are referring to Negro citizens, our number is sixteen million."

"I were not counting children," said Simple, "neither most womens."

"Well, if you want to boil it down that way," I said, "you could reduce the figure still further. Not many Negroes play golf."

"Well, Negroes that do play should be able to play wherever the President plays," said Simple. "And you know, and I know, where white folks play golf in Georgia a Negro better not light, unless he lights to work. Therefore, since Eisenhowser is President of white and colored, he has got no business playing golf in Georgia—where they do not even want me to vote if the Dixiecrats can help it. There is plenty of open air up North."

"*Cold* air in the wintertime," I said, "and golf is an outdoor sport."

"Also a rich man's sport," said Simple. "I have always heard tell the Republican Party is a rich man's party. But I also heard tell it were Abraham Lincoln's party. Right? I'll bet you Lincoln would not have been caught dead playing golf in Georgia."

"Lincoln," I said, "was not a golfing man."

"Nor a goofing one, either," said Simple.

Reason and Right

"Well, sir," said Simple, "did you see in the paper where they canceled that Brotherhood Week program down in Florida because a colored minister and a white minister was to speak together on the same program, and the choirs was to be mixed?"

"No," I said. "What happened?"

"They canceled it 'in the interest of brotherhood'! I'm telling you, white folks is something, particularly in Florida—barring out Negro Republicans from their own party dinner, barring Lena Horne out of that hotel at Miami Beach, and then canceling their Brotherhood Week programs—so they can have brotherhood!"

"That later action," I said, "certainly sounds like a contradiction in terms."

"It is a contradiction," said Simple. "White folks at times can certainly be contrary. That is no way to behave in our democratic day and age. If a white minister and a colored minister can't even preach together, and white choirs and colored choirs can't sing together, how in God's name are Christians ever going to *get* together? The paper says the old folks— the white old folks—even gave the children notes to take to school, saying they didn't want to be no part of a Brotherhood program with colored folks on it. Them white parents put ugly ideas into their children who might act right if they was let alone. Don't the Bible say, 'Unless ye become as little children . . . ,' which my Aunt Lucy always said meant *pure* as childrens are, unless which 'ye cannot enter into the kingdom of heaven'? I do not see how Florida folks are ever going to get into the kingdom."

"I don't either, unless they are born again."

"Well, if they are born again, they ought to be born old—and grow backwards, from old age to youth. Then maybe they would get smarter as they grow younger—like children are smart—because now as folks get older they get dumber. It would be nice anyhow for everybody to be born seventy years old, bald-headed with false teeth, then grow backwards into children, getting younger and younger, instead of older and older. By the time a Southern white man had growed backwards in age to be ten years old, he might by then be nice and pure and good like a child. Growing backwards, by the time he got to be a baby, he would not have to suffer and die. He could just go on back where he came from and wouldn't even know it, since a baby don't know here from yonder. So, at that age, dying wouldn't mean a thing."

"A fantastic idea," I said.

"But a good one," said Simple. "In fact, for anybody, white or colored, to be born old and grow young would be good, instead of like it is now, being born young and growing old. Just think, if I was growing younger every day instead of older, what I would have to look forward to! In reverse, I could look backwards to when I was forty and had drunk too much licker, smoked too many cigarettes, suffered too much rheumatism, had too many toothaches, too many hangovers, and too much backache. But I could say, 'All that is going, going, gone now. I'm getting younger everyday. I can look forward to not drinking at all soon because I'll be under age, sneezing if I inhale a cigarette, and never having toothache, backache, or any other kind of ache—not being married. I can look forward to being a boy again with nothing to worry about in the way of wives, even undivorcing myself from my first wife without having to pay a cent, just by growing backwards. Even growing out of owing you the five dollars which I do now—by growing backwards past all my debts. Oh, it would be wonderful to grow backwards instead of forwards, pal, younger instead of older.'

"For white folks, it would really be something, growing in reverse. Them old prejudiced crackers could outgrow all their prejudices just by growing backwards to childhood, before they knew any difference in color. They could grow right back to brotherhood, too, even in Florida. Then just think how wonderful it would be in Miami! White folks and colored folks all sun-tanning on the same beach together, children singing in the same choir in the same church, all integrated, with a fine young five-year-old minister, white, saying, 'It's truly wonderful!' And me, colored and four years old, saying, 'Thank you, father!' And over in Atlanta, Georgia, Talmadge, just two years old, making a speech, saying, 'We're all brothers—everybody, white and black—not just during Brotherhood Week, but every week.' To which I would say, 'Amen!' Then all of America would soon be a young nation again, like they was before they forgot what brotherhood means. I say, let's grow backwards."

"By growing backwards, you think we might solve the problems of race. But how do you feel about juvenile delinquency?"

"We old folks, white or black, *do* behave better than the young ones nowadays, don't we? We damn sure do! Take for example, when I was young," said Simple, "kids used to fight with their fists, wrestle and run, and maybe at a distance, throw stones. At the worst, the very worst, if you was *real* bad, a boy might draw a knife—but seldom use it. Nowadays, these teen-agers and children, too, shoot—and shoot to kill. Why do you reckon that is?"

"When we were young," I said, "wars were fought with rifles. Nowadays, wars are fought with atom bombs. Fighting has moved ahead for the worse."

"When I was young," said Simple, "if I got caught smoking just a plain old Piedmont cigarette, I were whipped. Nowadays, cigarettes ain't nothing. Kids smoke reefers and blow the smoke in their mama's face. Why you reckon that is?"

"When you were young," I said, "grownups were having a wild time if they went on a beer party and got home at midnight. Nowadays, if they don't have Scotch, bourbon, gin and vodka, it's a tame shindig. And midnight is just about the time to start. Everybody's gotten wilder since your generation."

"I were twenty-five years old," said Simple, "before I ever saw a dirty picture. Now, I read in the papers where they sell them naked in the schoolyards."

"When you were young," I said, "people hid *True Confessions* so their grandmothers wouldn't see it around the house. But that was before the days when grandmas read Mickey Spillane, and comic books are on every newsstand."

"Comics was really comic when I was a kid," said Simple. "You know 'Mutt and Jeff' and 'Bringing Up Father' and 'The Katzenjammer Kids.' Now the comics ain't even funny no more. They are all crime and stuff, and monsters and crazy people and spies and such. No wonder kids have stopped trying to be cute and are trying to be criminal. And the movies used to be all about pie-throwers and love and vampires and Chicago gangsters who got shot in the end. Now, it's not just gangsters shooting up the show. Everybody carries a gun in pictures nowadays. This must be the Gun Age. I thought people had to have a license to carry a gun. But I never see nobody pull out a license in the movies. They just pull out a gun. *Bam!* And somebody is dead! I seed six killings in one picture the last time I went to a movie. Same on TV. Same on the radio. A show is not a show without one killing at the beginning, two in the middle, and three on the end. Can you blame children? Kids think life ain't worth living, I reckon, if they ain't shooting."

"Certainly our entertainment media are full of violence," I said. "But after all, it's make-believe. I think even youngsters realize it is not real."

"It's so exciting, they want to make it real," said Simple.

"So you believe life imitates art? Personally, I think it is the other way around. The radio, TV and the movies are so violent nowadays because life itself has gotten so violent. Or maybe it's just a vicious circle."

"At least, thank God," said Simple, "it ain't just Negroes in the circle. Everybody is shooting and killing now. We are the least of it. On radio you never hear a Negro kill nobody, just white folks killing. And the biggest and best crimes on TV are committed by whites."

"No one race has a monopoly on crime. So why bring color in at all?"

"Because I am colored," said Simple. "My peoples was colored and my children will be colored. So why not bring in color?"

"To a sociological problem like crime," I said, "I consider color irrelevant."

"If I was an elephant, I would bring in elephants," said Simple. "Was I a lion, I would bring in lions. Beings I'm a Negro, I bring in Negroes. I do not want to be segregated, not even in crime, neither in life, the movies, nor on TV. I wants my rights—to which I stakes a claim."

"Violence and crime are wrong," I said. "Do you want the right to be wrong?"

"I want every right there is," yelled Simple. "Then I can pick out the right to be right. A man has to have the right to be *wrong* in order to have the right to be *right*, don't he?"

"Your logic defies reason," I said.

"Then you take reason, but give me right," said Simple. "Meanwhile, I intends to grow younger."

Mississippi Fists

" 'Fight or forget it,' that is what I said," said Simple. " 'I do not want to hear any more words. Put up or shut up.' "

"Why did you lay down such a rough ultimatum?" I asked.

"Because that Negro at the bar were bugging me," said Simple, "talking about Mississippi ain't no worse than Virginia. Virginia is my home state."

"Southerners like you always stick up for their home state," I said, "no matter how bad it may be."

"Bad?" cried Simple. "Who said Virginia is bad?"

"It's a Jim Crow state," I said.

"Jim Crow it might be," countered Simple, "but Virginia does not lynch children. Nobody fourteen years old like Emmett Till has ever been lynched in Virginia."

"So far as *you* know," I cut in.

"Or so far as anybody else knows, either," said Simple. "Neither does Virginia shoot a Negro for trying to vote like they shot that colored minister down in Mississippi and killed another man stone dead for registering. In Mississippi a Negro dare not vote. We votes in Virginia. So don't let nobody come telling me *my* state is as bad as Mississippi."

"But I see you are living in New York, not Virginia," I said.

"Naturally," said Simple. "I have left Virginia behind me. In Mississippi, I have never been, have no intentions of going, and if I had had the unfortune to be born in Mississippi, I would of left there much sooner than I left Virginia—which were as soon as I got big enough to wear long pants. None of them Jim Crow states is worth as much as the left-hand corner of 125th and Lenox Avenue. All of them states put together, from Virginia to Florida and Florida to Texas, I would not trade for one barstool in New York. Anybody can have the South that wants it, not me."

"Why do so many Negroes stay down South?" I wondered.

"Why does a pig stay in his pen?" asked Simple. "Answer—because his slop is there."

"Some Negroes, like doctors and undertakers, make money in the South," I said. "But sharecroppers and ordinary folks just barely make a living—and a precarious one at that—under conditions of terror in a state like Mississippi. Those are the Negroes I wonder about. Why do they stay?"

"They must be simple," said Simple. "I did not stay."

"You are an exception, but there are still eight or ten million colored folks in Dixie. That's why they call it the Black Belt."

"The Bible says, 'Turn the other cheek,'" said Simple, "but from the looks of that picture of the dead Till boy in the papers, they punched him in both cheeks—and he were nothing but a child. They also shot him through the head, kicked and beat him. Then they weighed him down with a cotton-gin wheel and threw him in the river like as if he were a dog. And he weren't but fourteen years old and could not fight back. I say Negroes that is older, if they intend to stay in Mississippi and stay black, they had better learn how to keep from being throwed in the river, too."

"If you were there, how would you go about protecting yourself?"

"In the first place, I would not be there," said Simple. "Neither would I send my child down there on a vacation. But if I ever found myself in Mississippi, Lord help me, I would know it was a nightmare! I would pick up my bed and walk. 'Get to Cairo, make St. Louis by myself,' it says in 'The St. Louis Blues.' But I would not stop in St. Louis. Too far South! I would at least get on to Chicago—which is where that poor little Till boy lived, but never did get back to. 'Such as ye do unto the least of these, ye do it unto Me,' says the Bible. Me! ME—I can feel them fists in MY own face right now, and them white men's kicks here in the middle of ME right now, and their big old, hairy old hands around MY throat so I cannot cry out loud, and that rope tied onto ME with that heavy old iron wheel from the cotton gin pulling ME down in that muddy old, dirty old, stinking, sluggish old river full of mud and cold, and there ain't no mud like Mississippi mud—filthy—and there ain't no fist like the hard fist of a man that would hit a child BAM! In the face hard like they hit that boy, and there ain't no heart as hard as the heart that would do a thing like that to any mother's son living! There ain't nobody so cruel in all the world as them men in Mississippi, and I do not want to talk about it any more, so do not ask me what I would do if I was there, nor how I would protect myself because I might be forced to show you, and you would get hurt. So don't ask me, I said! Don't ask me."

Minnie One More Time

"Do you know what?" asked Simple.

"No, what?" I said.

"Cousin Minnie's knees is farther apart than necessary. In other words, she is bowlegged as she can be. In fact, so bowlegged she could not catch a pig."

"Say not so!" I said.

"Minnie is also homely, squat, shot, beat and what not," said Simple, "yet there is something about that chick that mens admires. To tell the truth, if Minnie were not my cousin by blood—as well as by fooling around—I might kinder like her myself. Minnie is not pretty, but she is something else not pretty—which is I do not know how to explain by sight—but which must be good."

"Never having laid eyes on your Cousin Minnie, I can't imagine what you are talking about in exact terms, but I think I understand. Minnie is an ugly woman who has pretty points, a homely dame who hypes men, a sad sack who signals back when it comes to the Male Code, not the Morse Code. Am I right?"

"No more righter could you be than in what you say about Minnie! There is something about Minnie that carries her through this world without work. That broad has not worked three weeks in six months, yet she lives, drinks and enjoys life. How does she do it? Answer—some chump called a man lays it on the line for Minnie. To look at her, you would never think that Minnie could attract a chimpanzee, let alone a chump. But she do. Now, me, I have to work for a living. Does Minnie? I'm ugly. But Minnie's uglier. Still and yet, when Minnie flashes that big old smile of hers on some simple-minded man on payday—his payday is her heyday. Minnie can cover her rent for a month—and the chump is out of his week's salary. And does Minnie care about the square? She does not! Not Minnie! She'll let the poor man go home so broke he don't have a nickel for church on Sunday morning. I told Minnie someday some man is going to give her a good old New York head-whipping if she don't watch out.

"Minnie said, 'Don't you believe it. I can take care of myself,' which I do believe she can. Anyway, I am glad Minnie is getting some acquaintanceship in Harlem and knows somebody else besides me, because when Minnie first come North she like to almost worried me to death coming around every other day or so to borrow a dollar, or borrow five, or something. Now that girl knows so many folks, she borrows from me less often. I am not afraid to answer the bell at my house no more as I used to be, for fear it might be Minnie. A begging relative can be a nuisance.

"I told Minnie once, 'Girl, you got to learn to stand on your own two feet in Harlem, because up here in the free North it is every soul for himself. Even if you are too bowlegged to catch a shoat, you better catch a number or something and get yourself some money.'

"Minnie said, 'I am going to catch a man. But until I do, Jess, I depends on you for help. You are my very first cousin.'

" 'As often as you run to me, your first cousin, for money,' I said, 'I must be your last cousin, too.'

" 'You know I ain't got nary another relative in New York, Jess Semple, besides you. And if I had, I would be too proud to ask them for anything. I asks you because you be's my favorite cousin, also you come North in search of freedom, too. You got brains.'

" 'Thank you for the compliments,' I says. 'But I really cannot afford to pay for none. Minnie, I cannot lend you even a dime tonight.'

" 'Then make it a quarter,' says Minnie."

"Has Minnie ever offered to pay you back any of the money you lent her when she first got up here from Virginia?" I asked.

"Minnie believes it is more blessed to give than to receive—providing the man is the giver. No, Minnie has not yet offered to pay me back anything, and I am too much of a gentleman to ask her. But some day I am liable to get high and say, 'Minnie, I hate to insult your ladyhood, but I need my money which I have lent you in the past.' Not that I will expect to get it, for I learned long ago never to put my trust in relatives."

"Not all relatives are like your Cousin Minnie," I said.

"Thank God for that!" cried Simple. "Minnie takes after me—she's a lickertarian. But in drinking, I cannot keep up with her. Miss Minnie claims she is drowning her sorrows since she arrived in Harlem. Well, they sure ought to be well drowned by now! That woman can go, Joe!"

"You should be the last one to condemn her. I've known you to be quite intoxicated in your heyday."

"My heyday is over," said Simple. "This is my stay-home day—now that I'm a married man. But Minnie! She can drink a poor boy friend under the table and not bat an eye—still be setting on her stool sober as an owl. Last Saturday night I watched a stevedore trying to get Minnie drunk so he could make his point. That man's whole week's salary went into Minnie—and she still sat there unhugged, unkissed and untouched. She has done got hep to big city ways now, too. Minnie don't just drink plain whiskey no more when she is being treated. She orders Scotch—which is ninety cents a throw. It do not take a working man long to unbalance his budget at that rate, before even the weekend is over, let alone before next week's expenses begin. A wise man would at least save something out for subway fare and for facing the landlady. But many a joker in this world is not wise, do you know that? Facts is, I can remember when I had so little sense myself as to let chicks like Zarita drink me up. But Minnie is another story. You know, she come around to my house Sunday whilst Joyce was at church."

"Wanting money again?" I asked.

"Not this time," said Simple. "This time she wanted some kind of jive protection from her latest boy friend who threatened to knock her on her anatomy."

"Why?"

"Minnie says she does not know why," said Simple, "but I think I know. Minnie has done asked that man for money one time too many, and he knows she does not do anything with money but pour it over a bar. Minnie has been in Harlem, New York, mighty near all winter and has not got herself a warm coat yet. Coming from a mild climate like the South, she is liable to catch her death of pneumonia and go into a decline. Yet to tell the truth, Minnie has not even had a cold. Licker is good for something, as I know myself. It is good for cold."

"Then you cannot blame Minnie for wanting to keep warm," I said.

"No," said Simple, "but she cannot wear licker when she goes out. I like to see my kinfolks dressed up, not looking like Gabriel's off ox when they strolls the avenue. Minnie is no beauty, so she needs clothes to set off what she ain't got. I know I used to drink considerable before I got married, but I do not like to see a woman drink much—unless she is some old gal I am trying to make a quick point with—and then licker is on my side. But Minnie makes bars a habit. No wonder her boy friend has got to the place where he is about to draw back and teach her a lesson. And if Minnie thinks I am going to get mixed up in that rumble, she is wrong. No, not I!"

"You mean to say, you would not protect your cousin from force and violence on the part of a man?" I asked.

"In the first place, Minnie is not my full cousin. In the second place, I did not know she was in the world until she showed up here in Harlem claiming cousinship. In the third place, I do not know what Minnie might have done to provoke that man. Minnie might have done more than you or me can imagine. Women can drive a man sometimes to force and violence."

"In my opinion," I said, "there is no excuse for a man to hit a frail helpless woman, and do you mean to tell me you did not go to her rescue Sunday?"

"No."

"Well, have you heard what happened since? Aren't you worried? Today is Wednesday and Minnie might be annihilated by now."

"I saw Minnie in Paddy's Bar last night, solid as ever, setting on a stool spending somebody's good money. I did not linger, being married, but just got a quick beer and whilst I was drinking my beer, I asked Minnie how she were.

"Minnie said, 'Fine! Fine as wine and twice as mellow.'

"I said, 'What about the boy friend?'

"Minnie said, 'Oh, that old Negro is in bed asleep. The only times he comes out is Saturday night, which is the time he wants to ascertain his prerogative to fuss and fight. That is why I came to you Sunday for protection. Saturday night in Harlem ain't no different from Saturday night in Virginia, which is everywhere the night for mens to get rambunctious. But I never did like to be threatened with no force nor violence. Of course, one of the nice things about this man is that he will tell you in front what he is liable to do. Some mens just haul off and hit you.'

" 'Suppose that was to happen to you?' I asked Minnie.

" 'Cousin Jess, I would phone you to come and go my bail, because I would be in jail, and the man would be in Paradise,' said Minnie.

" 'Then why come running to me Sunday for protection since you can take care of yourself?' I asked her.

" 'Because I hates, if threatened, not to be a lady,' said Minnie. 'But if ever some man was to hit me, Jesse B., I would wear my ladyhood like a loose garment, with my sleeves rolled up. Bad man or no bad man, as sure as I am setting on my anatomy this evening, I would be setting on it tomorrow, too. When push comes to shove, Jesse B., I am one woman who can take care of myself, married or unmarried. Listen, I learned long ago that when a man slaps a woman, that is the time for a woman to make a stand—the very first time she gets slapped. If she don't, the next thing you know, that man will hit her and knock her down. If she lets him get away with that, next thing, he will kick her—slap her first, kick her, then stomp her. Next thing, he'll cut her. If a man gets away with cutting a woman and she don't stop him, he will shoot her. Yes, he will! If a woman lets a man slap her in the beginning, he is liable to shoot her in the end. I say, stop him when he first raises his hand! My advice to all women is to raise theirs, too! Raise your hand, women! Protect yourself—then you won't have to bury yourself later! That's my theory.' "

"Then you won't have to worry about your Cousin Minnie's physical well-being while she is in New York," I said.

"I don't," said Simple. "To tell the truth, I would be scared of that woman myself were she not related to me."

Simple Stashes Back

"When I stash back on my hind legs and really speak my mind," said Simple, "white folks better beware of what they are liable to hear."

"What do you mean, stash back?" I asked.

"I mean rear back and tell them off," said Simple. "I always did have bench legs, so I can stash back farther than you can."

"I believe you are double-jointed at the knees," I said, "since you can bend your legs almost as far backwards as you can forward."

"I got ball-bearing joints," said Simple, "so when I get ready to sound off, Jack, I really stashes back."

"But most of the sounding off you do is done in Harlem with not a white man in earshot, unless it is some Italian bar owner who has been selling you liquor for years—and bar owners are so used to Negroes sounding off that they pay you no mind."

"I wish I was in the United Nations," said Simple, "so the world could hear what I have to say. When I would rise in the Assembly and step to the podium, I would take my text from the word *Mississippi*—which is spelled M-i-s-s-i-s-s-i-p-p-i—and I would go right down the line from there, starting with *M*. I would say, 'Gentlemens of the United Nations and delegates, including Russians, the word *Mississippi* starts with an *M* which stands for *Murder*, which is what they have done there to Negroes for years just for being colored, with nobody sent to jail, let alone electrocuted. Mississippi murder did not just begin with little Emmett Till a few summers ago, nor with Rev. Lee who wanted to vote at Belzoni. It goes way back to slavery days when they whipped Negroes to death, and freedom days when the Klan drug us behind horses till we died, and on up to now when they shoot you for belonging to the N.A.A.C.P., so this evening I begin my talk with the word *murder*, and the first letter comes from Mississippi—not from behind nobody's Iron Curtain, but from M-i-s-s-i-s-s-i-p-p-i.

"I now continues with the next letter which is *I*—which means me. I, colored, am not even worth two hoots in hell in Mississippi, so therefore I myself do not give two hoots in hell about Mississippi. But I take that word for a text this evening just to let the world know how I feel. Wait!

Correction! Strike *me* from the record. What that first *I* really means is *igaroot* from *ignoramus*—*I* for *igaroot*.

"*S* is the next letter, which stands for several things. Mississippi ain't from none of them, neither from double *S*, which is followed by an *I* meaning *imps*—imps of Satan—which is what Mississippians is. In spite of the fact that they claim to be Christians, they is devils. *I* is followed by double *S* again—s-s—which means I will not Soft Soap you into believing Mississippi is a part of the Free World because it is not. Mississippi is not from *Sugar,* neither from *Salt,* period! And it do not take a double *S* to spell what it is from neither. And I hope all you translators setting here at the United Nations with earphones to your ears translating into all foreign languages, has got an *S* in your language to spell what I mean that Mississippi ain't from.

"Let us continue with the next *I* after the double *S*. That *I* means *Idiots*—which some folks must be to behave the way they do in Mississippi. Now I will go on to the *P*—which is what I plan to do as soon as I reach heaven, attach my wings, and learn to fly. As soon as I get to be an angel, that *very* first day, I will fly over Mississippi and I will *P* all over the state. After which I will double the *P,* as it is in the spelling. Excuse the expression, but right over Jackson, which is the state capital, I will *P-P*. As I fly, I hope none of them Dixiecrats has time to get their umbrellas up.

"Now I come to the final letter which is *I*—*I* meaning *me*—who will spell as I fly, M-i-s-s-i-s-s—*yes*—*I-P-P-i*!"

An Auto-Obituary

"I will now obituarize myself," said Simple at the bar. "I will cast flowers on my own grave before I am dead. And I will tell people how good I were, in case nobody else has the same feeling. Even if you are good in this life, when you are gone, most people think it is a good riddance. So, before I become dust to dust and ashes to ashes, I will light my own light—and not hide it under no bushel. My light will be lit now."

"I believe you are well lit already," I said.

"I have not had a drink today," said Simple, "except these beers in this bar."

"Then what gives you this flow of morbid thoughts?" I asked. "And why is death so prevalent this evening in your conversation? You do not look like a man who is about to die."

"Cold weather has got me," said Simple. "I swear, when I went out to work this morning, I thought I would freeze to death. This cold wave is nothing to play with. Hawkins is talking like the rent man does on the fifteenth, when you should have paid your rent on the first. I have not done nothing to the weather, so I do not know why the weather should be so hard on me. But I am so ashy in that mirror I look like ashes, and so cold I feel like ice. That's why I'm talking about death this evening—because if I do die of cold, I want some FINE words said over my body—which is why I think I had better say them myself right now, then I know they will be said, because my wife may not have enough money to pay the minister to state what I want stated. I wants to be praised to the skies, even if I do go to hell."

"Such a desire is understandable," I said, "so go ahead, preach."

"I wants myself," said Simple, "a sermon preached by a good minister something like this: 'Jesse B. Semple, born in Virginia, married twice for better or for worse—the first time for worse, the last time for good. Jesse B. Semple, he were a good man. He were raised good, lived good, did good, and died good.'

"Whereupon, in my coffin, I would say, 'Rev, you have lied good. Keep on!'

"And my old minister would preach on: 'Jesse B. Semple deserves to rest in peace, deserves to pass on over to the other shores where there is light eternal, where darkness never comes, and where he will receive a crown upon his noble head, that head that thought such noble thoughts, that head that never studied evil in this world, that head that never harbored harm—that head, that head, oh, that head of Jesse B. Semple that receiveth his crown. And slippers! Golden slippers on his feet with heelplates of silver to make music up and down the golden streets. Oh, Jesse B. Semple, walking on the golden streets, hailing a celestial cab to go whirling through eternal space down the Milky Way to see can he find some old friends in the far-off parts of heaven! Angel after angel passes and he does not know any of them. He does not know this angel, nor that angel. But here, oh, here at last is an angel that knows him.'

" 'Rev! Rev!' I would whisper from my coffin, 'You will have to tell me the angel's name, because I don't recollect who it is. I think all my friends must have gone to hell.'

"Rev would preach on: ''Tis an angel from your youthhood, Semple, a young angel you grew up with, but whom you cannot recognize since this angel died before the age of sin, but is now whiter than snow, as all are here in heaven. No matter how dark on earth you may be, in heaven you are whiter than snow, Jesse B. Semple, whiter than snow!'

" 'Aw, now Rev,' I would say, 'with me you do not need to go that far.'

"But old Rev would keep on, because that sermon would be getting good to him by now: 'Though your sins be as scarlet, in heaven, I say, Jesse B. Semple, old earthly Semple, down-home Semple is whiter than snow. White! White! White! White! Oh, yes, you are whiter than snow!'

" 'Then, Rev,' I would have to holler, 'I would not know my own self in the mirror, were I to look.'

" 'In God's mirror all are white,' says Rev, 'white wings, white robe, white face, white neck, white shoulders, white hips, white soul! Oh, precious soul of Jesse B., worth more than words can tell! Worth more than tongues can fabulate, worth more than speech can spatulate, than throat can throttle, than human mind can manipulate! This soul, this Jess B. of a soul! This simple soul, this Semple! Gone to glory, gone to his great reward of milk and honey, manna and time unending, and the fruit of the tree of eternity.'

" 'Rev,' I would be forced to say laying there in my coffin thirsty, 'your words are as dry as popcorn and rice. You have mentioned neither beer nor wine—and I am *paying* you to preach this sermon.'

" 'The juice! Sweet, sweet juice of the wine! Juice, juice, juice,' Rev would say. 'Oh, yes, Jess Semple is partaking today of the juice of the vine, and the fruit of the tree, and the manna of time unending, and the milk and honey of the streets of gold, and the wine of the vine of timeless space in that blessed place beneath his crown of gold, wrapped in the white robes of his purity, with white wings flapping, and his immortal soul winging its way through immortal space into that eternal place where time shall be no more, and he shall rest in peace forever and forever, ever and forever—for Semple were born good! He were raised good! He lived good, did good, and lied—I mean, *died*—good. Amen!' "

Four-Way Celebrations

"Now that Negro History Week and Lincoln's Birthday is about here," said Simple, "I wonder when White History Week is coming?"

"White History Week?" I exclaimed. "I never heard of it."

"Neither have I," said Simple, "but there ought to be a White History Week. White folks have so many more things to celebrate than we do."

"For instance?" I asked.

"For instance," said Simple, "the day they bought the first Negroes off that slave ship in Jamestown and started us out working for nothing in this here country, and have been trying to keep us working for nothing, or little of nothing, ever since—that is one date they sure could celebrate in White History Week."

"They would hardly wish to celebrate so celebrated a mistake," I said, "since Negroes have been a headache to them from that time on."

"Well, they could celebrate as a part of White History Week all them three hundred years white folks lived off of Negro labor," said Simple, "when they had slaves, planting, plowing and hoeing for nothing, and living off what we made. I should think they could have a big celebration remembering that. The year 1619 was when the first slaves came; 1719, Negroes were still in slavery; 1819, the same, and 1919, not much better, because it took a long time to work up to decent wages, even after the Civil War was over. For three hundred years white folks was working Negroes for nothing. If I was white, I sure would celebrate all them good years. Wouldn't you?"

"I suppose I would," I said, "but hardly with pride."

"No," said Simple, "with money—made out of black sweat. I ain't never had nobody planting, plowing, hoeing, cooking, washing and ironing for me for nothing, never in my natural life. Not even a wife I paid good money to marry would do it. If ever it was to happen to me even for a day, I would celebrate. But white folks have had Negroes working for them on short rations since the year *o-n-e*, one, and no lie. This work was and is worth millions of dollars—all that back pay they owe us—which, if they wanted to be decent, they could use to wipe out Joe Louis's income taxes, and not miss a thing. If I was them, I would do some good little deed like canceling Joe's taxes during White History Week.

"That week I would also unveil a monument to Jim Crow whom white folks have honored for so long. I would let all the Dixiecrats come and lay a wreath at Jim Crow's feet whilst 'Dixie' would be played on every radio. In every school during White History Week there would be a Jim Crow Day in which white children could play like they was colored and did not have any advantages at all and nothing to look forward to but pure segregation. This would all be pretending, like colored children play democracy during Negro History Week in Mississippi. Oh, if I was white, I would have more fun in White History Week!"

"Nothing you say sounds funny to me," I said.

"Laugh anyhow," said Simple. "If you do not laugh, you might get mad, and if you get mad, that is no good for brotherhood. Brotherhood Week comes right after Negro History Week, don't it? Well, after White History Week, I would have Sisterhood Week, and dedicate it to the Protection of White Womanhood. That holy week I would celebrate all the lynchings of Negroes that took place since the Civil War in the name of pure white womanhood. I would dedicate a TV show to lynching, and show black bodies swinging on Southern trees in the name of rape never done, and show Negroes burned at the stake because some white woman dreamed she saw a colored man in her sleep. Also I would show little young boys like Emmett Till, killed because some white man thought the kid had looked sidewise at a white woman. Oh, I would have a big natural TV show on Sepians Sacrificed for Sisterhood. In the show I would get Harry Belafonte to play a Negro lynched in color—Harry on color TV lynched for looking at a white woman. Of course, he would get paid real good, because he is a good actor.

"I would have lots of White History Week celebrations on TV, too. All week long I would have big speakers like Eastland and Talmadge who would tell how they are determined to keep White History Week white because the Negroes have Negro History Week and so do not need no part of White History Week, unless they are paid to play a part—like I would pay Harry to look cross-eyed at a white woman. I would also pay Louis—good old Satchmo—to blow his horn whilst the bombs is blowing up the dance hall. Then I would hire Nat King Cole to sing again in Birmingham and act out how he was knocked down by white folks on the stage but did not even get mad about it. Such sweet singing Negroes I would honor on White History Week because nobody can sing like a Negro. Just as Negro History Week honors a few good white folks, so White History Week should honor a few good black folks.

"White History Week I would end, not with speeches and songs, but with an outdoor demonstration of healthy, happy, hard-hitting Americanism by the head of our nation, President Eisenhowser. I would present him teeing off at Augusta, down in Georgia. Every TV screen in the country would show our great President knocking a golf ball all the way from Georgia to Alabama—Go, Jim Daddy!—right into Reverend King's Montgomery backyard. A flying golf ball from the President of the U.S.A. would be my choice to end White History Week. Amen! Benediction! I mean, Benediction first—then Amen! After which—Period."

Be Broad-minded, Please!

"I hate to say it," declared Simple, "but any Hungarian refugee can come over here with transportation free, and get a good job in a bank or store or someplace where I can't even look behind the counter, a few weeks after he gets here. And I say it *ain't, is not,* and *never will be* right for such to happen. I'm an American."

"But," I said, "you cannot blame the Hungarian refugees for the American racial pattern, so try to be broad-minded. It happens that Hungarians are white—so naturally they have a head start on you, colored."

"But I am a citizen," said Simple.

"In some ways," I said, "but not fully. If you were a full citizen, there would be no need of the N.A.A.C.P. running to the Supreme Court all the time to try to consolidate your citizenship. You are a COLORED citizen."

"Which means Hungarian refugees is more citizens than I am," yelled Simple. "I declare that is not right. My father were here before me, also my grandfather before him, and I do not know how much farther back than that was my people. But I do know colored folks have been in this here U.S.A. a long time. Still and yet, you mean to tell me a Hungarian what has been here a half hour is worth more than me?"

"I am colored just like you," I said, "so why are you hollering at me? Did I create this condition?"

"You take it too calm," said Simple. "You must be an Uncle Tom."

"Do not call me out of my name," I said. "I see no use to get excited about obvious facts. Everybody knows that any white refugee can expect a better job in America than the average Negro."

"In other words, white is right, Hungarian or not," said Simple. "I am used to American whites getting the best go. But I just hate to see some old foreign whites come here and have the same break."

"I regret you have not only a white bias, but an antiforeign bias, as well."

"Don't regret for my sake," said Simple. "I can take care of my own regrets. Them foreigners come here and it don't take them two months to learn to call me dirty names. In a year they are living in some city housing project or somewhere like Levittown where I can't live. If I dare to move in after going to court and getting an edict, they throw rocks through my windows and put bombs under my doorsteps—and they can't even speak English good yet. Still, you are trying to make out that I should not even talk about them dirty dogs?"

"You should not talk about them as foreigners," I said. "Simply look upon them as bigoted human beings, whatever their background. Both native Americans and foreign immigrants have, in some instances, very bad social qualities. But, on the other hand, many foreign-born Americans have been great friends of the Negro, just as have many native-born Americans. All I am trying to say is, don't be antiforeign, just because some refugees are antinegro. If it happens they get better jobs than you, since they are white, don't blame the foreigners. Blame our own Jim Crow system, and try to help correct it, but not by knocking foreigners. If you were white and offered a good job, you would take it, wouldn't you—Hungarian or not?"

"If I was a Hungarian," said Simple, "I would make revolts in Hungary just to get free passage to America and find a job—because from all I can read, Hungary ain't from hunger, is it? Over here in America, we got fresh meat, smoked meat, frozen meat, and black meat—meaning me. They can lord it over my dark carcass every day. Sure, if I was a Hungarian, I would rush to America, settle here, and refuse to send my children to school with Negroes. Just to show how much I rate as white, I would demand my Hungarian right. I would be so American nobody could tell me from a Ku Kluxer or a Citizens Councilor. I would be so white I would be wrong to be right! Oh, were I a refugee, I would go to live in Levittown or Trumbell Park, or some other place where native Negroes could not light—which would prove I was 120 per cent American if any committee ever wanted to investigate me. It must be hard not to prove you are red, if you come from a red country like Hungary. But I would prove it by not living with either colored folks or Jews. I would also prove it by learning to say NIGGER as fast as I could. This I would learn to say even before I learned to sing 'The Star-Spangled Banner' or read the Constitution. Anyhow, a Hungarian does not have to read no Constitution or go through all them voting tests they put Negroes through down South. No, all a Hungarian needs is just to be white to get ahead—and even to vote before he can speak good English. So, naturally, if I was a Hungarian, I would learn real quick all them things and take advantage of them. I would not be backwards if I was Hungarian and white. But since I am neither one, being just plain black old me, with you I disagree, daddy-o. I am not broad-minded! Until I gets all the rights a Hungarian refugee has in the U.S.A., I intend to be anti-any-rights-for-any-whites whose whiteness puts them ahead of me—me, *American* since Old Glory blowed, but yet Jim Crowed! How broad-minded must a man's mind be to put up with that? I ask you! Huh?"

Grammar and Goodness

"I have writ a poem," said Simple.

"Again?" I exclaimed. "The last time you showed me a poem of yours, it was too long, also not too good."

"This one is better," said Simple. "Joyce had a hand in it, also my friend, Boyd, who is colleged. So I want you to hear it."

"I know you are determined to read it to me, so go ahead."

"It is about that minister down in Montgomery who committed a miracle."

"What miracle?" I asked.

"Getting Negroes to stick together," declared Simple.

"I presume you are speaking of Rev. King," I said.

"I am," said Simple. "He is the man, and this is my poem. Listen fluently now! This poem is writ like a letter. It is addressed to the White Citizens Councilors of Alabama and all their members, and this is how it goes:

> Dear Citizens Councilors:
> In line of what my folks
> Say in Montgomery,
> In line of what they
> Teaching about love,
> When I reach out *my* hand,
> White folks, will YOU take it?
> Or will you cut it off
> And make a nub?
> Since God put it in
> My heart to love you,
> If I love you
> Like I really could,
> If I say, 'Brother,
> I forgive you,'
> I wonder, would it
> Do YOU any good?
> Since slavery-time, long gone,
> You been calling me

All kinds of names,
Pushing me down.
I been swimming with my
Head deep under water—
And you wished I would
Stay under till I drowned.
Well, I did not!
I'm still swimming!
Now you mad because
I won't ride in the
Back end of your bus.
When I answer, 'Anyhow,
I'm gonna love you,'
Still and yet, today,
You want to make a fuss.
Now, listen, white folks:
In line with Rev. King
Down in Montgomery—
Also because the Bible
Says I must—
In spite of bombs and buses,
I'm gonna love you.
I say, I'm gonna LOVE you—
White folks, OR BUST!"

"You never wrote a poem that logical all by yourself in life," I said.

"I know I didn't," admitted Simple. "But I am getting ready to write another one now. This time I am going to write a poem about Jim Crow up North, and it is going to start something like this:

In the North
The Jim Crow line
Ain't clear—
But it's here!
From New York to Chicago,
Points past and
In between,
Jim Crow is mean!
Even though integrated,
With Democracy
Jim Crow is *not* mated.
Up North Jim Crow
Wears an angel's grin—

But still he sin.
I swear he do!
Don't you?

"I agree that the sentiment of your poem is correct," I said. "But I cannot vouch for the grammar."

"If I get the sense right," answered Simple, "the grammar can take care of itself. There are plenty of Jim Crowers who speak grammar, but do evil. I have not had enough schooling to put words together right— but I know some white folks who have went to school forty years and do not DO right. I figure it is better to *do* right than to write right, is it not?"

"You have something there," I said. "So keep on making up your poems, if you want to. At least, they rhyme."

"They make sense, too, don't they?" asked Simple.

"I think they do," I answered.

"They does," said Simple.

"They do," I corrected.

"They sure does," said Simple.

Chips on the Shoulder

"Take that chip off your shoulder," I said.

"I will not," said Simple. "And suppose I did? There's always some chip to weigh a colored shoulder down. I remove this one, white folks will put another chip up there tomorrow. All you have to do is read the newspapers—Montgomery, Clinton, Miami, New Orleans, Citizens Councilors, John Kasper,[3] the Ku Klux Klan, the New York School Board! Man, each and all of them is piling chips on my shoulder daily. So many chips I have to shift from the left to the right shoulder."

"You live in such a limited world," I said. "Broaden your horizons—get away from race."

"With my face?" asked Simple. "Dark as I be, you can't mean me? Or do you?"

"Suppose an Italian-American did not think about anything but Italy," I said.

"He'd still be Joe Di Maggio," said Simple, "or Costello."

"Suppose an Irish-American did not pay any attention to anything but Ireland."

"He'd still be a cop or a politicianer."

"Suppose the Jews were interested in nothing but Israel."

"My groceryman would still be in business in Harlem," said Simple. "So why can't I be interested in the Negro race without somebody like you calling my time? And you are as colored as me, too."

"But you have me beat on racialness," I said. "You talk about almost nothing but the race problem day in, night out."

"And women," said Simple.

"For a married man, you let your mind stray too often," I said.

"For a friend, you criticize too much," declared Simple. " 'Take the mote out of your own eye before you start to take the chip off of my shoulder.' That's what the Bible says."

"You're misquoting now," I said. "It does not."

"I growed up on the Bible," declared Simple, "and sometimes I live by it, too. My Aunt Lucy were a Bible lover. In fact, it were her Rock. And I still respects its word. The Bible says take the mote out of your own eye before you start talking about me. I might not be snow-white, but you are not snow-white yourself—and I am not talking about complexion in neither case."

"Forget and forgive then," I said. "Let's change the subject."

"What shall we talk about?" asked Simple. "How there ain't no white children hardly in Harlem schools? How we don't have integration up North, let alone down South?"

"You're picking up that chip again," I said.

"I don't have to *pick* it up, it falls from above. My head is beat with chips right now this evening, right here in this bar where I come for a quickie. If I had not run into you, man, I would be home in my bed by now enjoying my wife's dreams. Buy me a beer, buddy-boy-baby-daddy-o, old kid."

"I will not," I said. "You buy me one."

"I runs on a budget since I been married," explained Simple, "and my budget does not include beers for *myself,* let alone you. Of course, meet me on payday before I contributes to the budget, and I will see you go. Today is not payday. Come on, let's order up."

"Who—let's?"

"You—let's. Else no let's. Then the conversation is ended right now. I will take my chips and go home."

"Good night."

"But not before we have one for the road."

"See if your chips will pay for a beer."

"Man, you know this Italian bartender ain't interested in Negroes."

Jazz, Jive and Jam

"It being Negro History Week," said Simple, "Joyce took me to a pay lecture to hear some Negro hysterian—"

"Historian," I corrected.

"Hysterian speak," continued Simple, "and he laid our Negro race low. He said we was misbred, misread, and misled, also losing our time good-timing. Instead of time-taking and money-making, we are jazz-shaking. Oh, he enjoyed his self at the expense of the colored race—and him black as me. He really delivered a lecture—in which, no doubt, there is some truth."

"Constructive criticism, I gather—a sort of tearing down in order to build up."

"He tore us down good," said Simple. "Joyce come out saying to me, her husband, that he had really got my number. I said, 'Baby, he did not miss you, neither.' But Joyce did not consider herself included in the bad things he said.

"She come telling me on the way home by subway, 'Jess Semple, I have been pursuing culture since my childhood. But you, when I first met you, all you did was drape yourself over some beer bar and argue with the barflies. The higher things of life do not come out of a licker trough.'

"I replied, 'But, Joyce, how come culture has got to be so dry?'

"She answers me back, 'How come your gullet has got to be so wet? You are sitting in this subway right now looking like you would like to have a beer.'

" 'Solid!' I said. 'I would. How did you guess it?'

" 'Married to you for three years, I can read your mind,' said Joyce. 'We'll buy a couple of cans to take home. I might even drink one myself.'

" 'Joyce, baby,' I said, 'in that case, let's buy three cans.'

"Joyce says, 'Remember the budget, Jess.'

"I says, 'Honey, you done busted the budget going to that lecture program which cost One Dollar a head, also we put some small change in the collection to help Negroes get ahead.'

" 'Small change?' says Joyce, 'I put a dollar.'

" 'Then our budget is busted real good,' I said, 'so we might as well dent it some more. Let's get six cans of beer.'

" 'All right,' says Joyce, 'go ahead, drink yourself to the dogs—instead of saving for that house we want to buy!'

" 'Six cans of beer would not pay for even the bottom front step,' I said. 'But they would lift my spirits this evening. That Negro high-speaking doctor done tore my spirits down. I did not know before that the colored race was so misled, misread, and misbred. According to him there is hardly a pure black man left. But I was setting in the back, so I guess he did not see me.'

" 'Had you not had to go to sleep in the big chair after dinner,' says Joyce, 'we would have been there on time and had seats up front.'

" 'I were near enough to that joker,' I said. 'Loud as he could holler, we did not need to set no closer. And he certainly were nothing to look at!'

" 'Very few educated men look like Harry Belafonte,' said Joyce.

" 'I am glad I am handsome instead of wise,' I said. But Joyce did not crack a smile. She had that lecture on her mind.

" 'Dr. Conboy is smart,' says Joyce. 'Did you hear him quoting Aristotle?'

" 'Who were Harry Stottle?' I asked.

" 'Some people are not even misread,' said Joyce. 'Aristotle was a Greek philosopher like Socrates, a great man of ancient times.'

" 'He must of been before Booker T. Washington then,' I said, 'because, to tell the truth, I has not heard of him at all. But tonight being *Negro* History Week, how come Dr. Conboy has to quote some Greek?'

" 'There were black Greeks,' said Joyce. 'Did you not hear him say that Negroes have played a part in all history, throughout all time, from Eden to now?'

" 'Do you reckon Eve was brownskin?' I requested.

" 'I do not know about Eve,' said Joyce, 'but Cleopatra was of the colored race, and the Bible says Sheba, beloved of Solomon, was black but comely.'

" 'I wonder would she come to me?' I says.

" 'Solomon also found Cleopatra comely. He was a king,' says Joyce.

" 'And I am Jesse B. Semple,' I said.

"But by that time the subway had got to our stop. At the store Joyce broke the budget again, opened up her pocket purse, and bought us six cans of beer. So it were a good evening. It ended well—except that I ain't for going to any more meetings—especially interracial meetings."

"Come now! Don't you want to improve race relations?"

"Sure," said Simple, "but in my opinion, jazz, jive and jam would be better for race relations than all this high-flown gab, gaff and gas the orators put out. All this talking that white folks do at meetings, and big Negroes, too, about how to get along together—just a little jam session would have everybody getting along fine without having to listen to so many speeches. Why, last month Joyce took me to a Race Relations Seminar which her club and twenty other clubs gave, and man, it lasted three days! It started on a Friday night and it were not over until Sunday afternoon. They had sessions' mammy! Joyce is a fiend for culture."

"And you sat through all that?"

"I did not set," said Simple. "I stood. I walked in and walked out. I smoked on the corner and snuck two drinks at the bar. But I had to wait for Joyce, and I thought them speeches would never get over! My wife were a delegate from her club, so she had to stay, although I think Joyce got tired her own self. But she would not admit it. Joyce said, 'Dr. Hillary Thingabod was certainly brilliant, were he not?'

"I said, 'He were not.'

"Joyce said, 'What did you want the man to say?'

"I said, 'I wish he had sung, instead of *said*. That program needed some music to keep folks awake.'

"Joyce said, 'Our forum was not intended for a musical. It was intended to see how we can work out integration.'

"I said, 'With a jazz band, they could work out integration in ten minutes. Everybody would have been dancing together like they do at the Savoy—colored and white—or down on the East Side at them Casinos on a Friday night where jam holds forth—and we would have been integrated.'

"Joyce said, 'This was a serious seminar, aiming at facts, not fun.'

" 'Baby,' I said, 'what is more facts than acts? Jazz makes people get into action, move! Didn't nobody move in that hall where you were—except to jerk their head up when they went to sleep, to keep anybody from seeing that they was nodding. Why, that chairman, Mrs. Maxwell-Reeves almost lost her glasses off her nose, she jerked her head up so quick one time when that man you say was so brilliant were speaking!'

" 'Jess Semple, that is not so!' yelled Joyce. 'Mrs. Maxwell-Reeves were just lost in thought. And if you think you saw *me* sleeping—'

" 'You was too busy trying to look around and see where I was,' I said. 'Thank God, I did not have to set up there like you with the delegation. I would not be a delegate to no such gab-fest for nothing on earth.'

" 'I thought you was so interested in saving the race!' said Joyce. 'Next time I will not ask you to accompany me to no cultural events, Jesse B., because I can see you do not appreciate them. That were a discussion of ways and means. And you are talking about jazz bands!'

" 'There's more ways than one to skin a cat,' I said. 'A jazz band like Duke's or Hamp's or Basie's sure would of helped that meeting. At least on Saturday afternoon, they could have used a little music to put some pep into the proceedings. Now, just say for instant, baby, they was to open with jazz and close with jam—and do the talking in between. Start out, for example, with "The St. Louis Blues," which is a kind of colored national anthem. That would put every human in a good humor. Then play, "Why Don't You Do Right?" which could be addressed to white folks. They could pat their feet to that. Then for a third number before introducing the speaker, let some guest star like Pearl Bailey sing "There'll Be Some Changes Made"—which, as I understand it, were the theme of the meeting, anyhow—and all the Negroes could say, *Amen!*

" 'Joyce, I wish you would let me plan them interracial seminaries next time. After the music, let the speechmaking roll for a while—with maybe a calypso between speeches. Then, along about five o'clock, bring on the jam session, extra-special. Start serving tea to "Tea For Two," played real cool. Whilst drinking tea and dancing, the race relationers could relate, the integraters could integrate, and the desegregators desegregate. Joyce, you would not have to beg for a crowd to come out and support your efforts then. Jam—and the hall would be jammed! Even I would stick around, and not be outside sneaking a smoke, or trying to figure how I can get to the bar before the resolutions are voted on. *Resolved:* that we solve the race problem! Strike up the band! Hit it, men! Aw, play that thing! "How High the Moon!" How high! Wheee-ee-e!' "

"What did Joyce say to that?" I demanded.

"Joyce just thought I was high," said Simple.

Simple's Uncle Sam

(1965)

To my long-time friends,
Henri and Eli Cartier-Bresson

The author thanks the Associated Negro Press International, the *New York Post*, the *Chicago Defender*, and the *Saturday Review* for permission to reprint these Simple stories.

Contents

Simple's Uncle Sam

Census

"I have had so many hardships in this life," said Simple, "that it is a wonder I'll live until I die. I was born young, black, voteless, poor, and hungry, in a state where white folks did not even put Negroes on the census. My daddy said he were never counted in his life by the United States government. And nobody could find a birth certificate for me nowhere. It were not until I come to Harlem that one day a census taker dropped around to my house and asked me where were I born and why, also my age and if I was still living. I said, 'Yes, I am here, in spite of all.'

" 'All of what?' asked the census taker. 'Give me the data.'

" 'All my corns and bunions, for one,' I said. 'I were borned with corns. Most colored peoples get corns so young, they must be inherited. As for bunions, they seem to come natural, we stands on our feet so much. These feet of mine have stood in everything from soup lines to the draft board. They have supported everything from a packing trunk to a hongry woman. My feet have walked ten thousand miles running errands for white folks and another ten thousand trying to keep up with colored. My feet have stood before altars, at crap tables, bars, graves, kitchen doors, welfare windows, and social security railings. Be sure and include my feet on that census you are taking,' I told that man.

"Then I went on to tell him how my feet have helped to keep the American shoe industry going, due to the money I have spent on my feet. 'I have wore out seven hundred pairs of shoes, eighty-nine tennis shoes, forty-four summer sandals, and two hundred and two loafers. The socks my feet have bought could build a knitting mill. The razor blades I have used cutting away my corns could pay for a razor plant. Oh, my feet have helped to make America rich, and I am still standing on them.

" 'I stepped on a rusty nail once, and mighty near had lockjaw. And from my feet up, so many other things have happened to me, since, it is a wonder I made it through this world. In my time, I have been cut, stabbed, run over, hit by a car, tromped by a horse, robbed, fooled, deceived, double-crossed, dealt seconds, and mighty near blackmailed— but I am still here! I have been laid off, fired and not rehired, Jim Crowed, segregated, insulted, eliminated, locked in, locked out, locked up, left holding the bag, and denied relief. I have been caught in the rain, caught in jails, caught short with my rent, and caught with the wrong woman—but I am still here!

" 'My mama should have named me Job instead of Jesse B. Semple. I have been underfed, underpaid, undernourished, and everything but undertaken—yet I am still here. The only thing I am afraid of now—is that I will die before my time. So man, put me on your census now this year, because I may not be here when the next census comes around.'

"The census man said, 'What do you expect to die of—complaining?'

" 'No,' I said, 'I expect to ugly away.' At which I thought the man would laugh. Instead you know he nodded his head, and wrote it down. He were white and did not know I was making a joke. Do you reckon that man really thought I am homely?"

Swinging High

"A meat ball by any other name is still a meat ball just the same," said Simple. "My wife, Joyce, is a fiend for foreign foods. Almost every time she drags me downtown to a show, she wants to go eat in some new kind of restaurant, Spanish, French, Greek, or who knows what? Last night we had something writ on the menu in a Philippine restaurant in big letters as BOLA-BOLAS. They returned out to be nothing but meat balls."

"*Bola* probably means 'ball' in their language," I said. "But I am like Joyce. I sort of go for foreign foods, too—something different once in a while, you know."

"Me, I like plain old down-home victuals, soul food with corn bread," said Simple, "spare ribs, pork chops, and things like that. Ham hock, string beans, salt pork and cabbage."

"All good foods," I said, "but for a change, why not try chicken curry and rootie next time you take Joyce out."

"What is that?" asked Simple.

"An East Indian dish, chicken stewed in curry sauce."

"I am not West Indian nor East," said Simple.

"You don't have to be foreign to like foreign food," I said.

"Left to me, I would go to Jenny Lou's up yonder on Seventh Avenue across from Small's Paradise. Jenny Lou's is where all the down-home folks eat when they is visiting Harlem. They knows good home-like food a mile away by the way it smells."

"A restaurant is not supposed to smell," I said. "The scent of cooking is supposed to be kept in the kitchen."

"Jenny Lou's kitchen is in the dining room," said Simple. "When I were a single man, I et there often. Them low prices suited my pocket."

"How about Frank's?" I asked. "Now Negro-owned."

"That's where Joyce takes her society friends like Mrs. Maxwell-Reeves," said Simple. "The menu is as big as newspaper. So many things on it, it is hard to know what to pick out. I like to just say 'pork chops' and be done with it. I don't want soup, neither salad. And who wants rice pudding for dessert? Leave off them things, also olives. Just give me pork chops."

"Is that all?"

"I'll take the gravy," Simple said.

"Pork chops, bread, and gravy," I shook my head. "As *country* as you can be!"

"If that is what you call *country*," said Simple, "still gimme pork chops. Pork chops and fried apples maybe, if they is on the menu. I love fried apples, and my Uncle Tige had an apple tree in his back yard. When I was a little small boy, I used to set in a rope swing behind my Uncle Tige's house. The swing were attached to that apple tree which were a very old apple tree, and big for an apple tree, and a good tree for a swing for boys and girls. It were nice to set in this swing when I was yet a wee small boy and be pushed by the bigger children because I was still too small for my feet to touch the ground, and I did not know how to pump myself up into the air. Later I could. Later I could stand up in that swing and pump myself way up into the air, almost as high as the limb on which the swing were tied. Oh, I remember very well that swing and that apple tree when I were a child.

"It looks to me life is like a swing," continued Simple. "When young, somebody else must push you because your feet are too short to touch the ground and start the swing in motion. But later you go for yourself. By and by, you can stand up and swing high, swing high, way high up, and you are on your own. How wonderful it is to stand up in the swing, pumping all by yourself! But suppose the rope was to break, the tree limb snap off when you have pumped yourself up so high? Suppose it does? You will be the one to fall, nobody else, just you yourself. Yes, life is like a swing! But in spite of all and everything, it is good to swing. Oh, yes! The swing of life is wonderful, but if you are a colored swinger, you have to have a stout heart, pump hard, and hold tight to get even a few feet above the ground. And be careful that your neighbor next door, white, has not cut your rope, so that just when you are swinging highest, it will break and throw you to the ground. 'Look at that Negro swinging! But he done fell!' they say. But someday we gonna swing right up to the very top of the tree and not fall. Yes, someday we will."

"Integrated, I hope," I said.

"Yes, integrated, I reckon," said Simple. "But some folks is getting so wrapped up in this integration thing, white and colored, that I do believe some of them is going stone-cold crazy. You see how here in New York peoples is talking to themselves on busses and in the subways, whirling around in the middle of the street, mumbling and grumbling all by themselves to nobody on park benches, dumping garbage on bridges, slicing up subway seats with knives and nail files, running out of gas on crowded highways on purpose and liable to get smashed up in traffic jams. Oh, I do not know what has come over the human race—like that nice young white minister in Cleveland laying down *behind* a rolling bulldozer, *not* in front of it—where the driver could see him and maybe stop in time before the man got crushed to death. He were protesting Jim Crow—but sometimes the protest is worse than the Crow."

"That earnest white man, no doubt, was trying to call attention to the urgency of the civil rights," I said. "He wanted to keep the movement on the front pages of the newspapers."

"It has been on the front pages of the newspapers for ten years," said Simple, "and if everybody does not know by now something needs to be done about civil rights, they will never know. After so many Freedom Rides and sit-ins and picketings and head bustings and police dogs and bombings and little children blowed up, and teenagers in jail by the thousands up to now, and big headlines across the newspapers, colored and white, why did that good white minister in Cleveland with his glasses on have to lay down *behind* a bulldozer?"

"I gather there are some things you would not do for a cause," I said.

"I would not lay down behind a bulldozer going backwards. How would my dying help anything—and my wife, Joyce, would be left a widow? It is not that I might be dying in a good cause, but let me die on my own two feet, knowing where, when, and why, and maybe making a speech telling off the world—not in a wreck because somebody has stalled a car whilst traffic is speeding. To me that is crazy! Whoever drives them stalled cars might be smashed up and killed too."

"They would consider themselves martyrs," I said.

"They should not make a martyr out of me in another car who do not even know them," said Simple. "Let me make a martyr out of myself, if I want to, but don't make me one under other peoples' cars. I do not want to be a martyr on nobody else's time. And don't roll no bulldozer over me unless I am standing in front, not behind it when it rolls. If I have got to look death in the face ahead of time, at least let me know who is driving. Also don't take me by surprise before I have paid my next year's dues to the NAACP. Anyhow, a car or a bulldozer is a dangerous thing to fool around with, as is any kind of moving machinery. You remember that old joke about the washerwoman who bent over too far and got both her breasts caught in the wringer? There is such a thing as bending over too far—even to get your clothes clean. Certainly there is plenty of dirty linen in this U.S.A., but I do not advise nobody to get their breast caught in a wringer. Machines do not have no sense."

"A cynic might say the same thing about martyrs," I said. "Except sometimes it takes an awful lot of sense to have no sense."

"Maybe you are right," said Simple, "just like it takes a mighty lot of pumping to swing high in the swing of life."

Contest

"They are always holding Beauty Contests all over America," said Simple. "Why don't nobody ever hold an Ugly Contest?"

"An Ugly Contest!" I cried. "For what reason?"

"For the same reasons folks hold a Beauty Contest," said Simple, "for fun. There are so many ugly womens in this world, it would be fun to see which one wins."

"Beauty is as beauty does," I reminded him, "not how it looks."

"Oh, no!" declared Simple. "Beauty is as beauty looks. You can't tell me an ugly chick, be she ever so nice, is going to *look* pretty, not even if she goes to church every day and three times on Sunday. She may look holy, but she cannot look pretty if her mama did not born her so."

"The Lord made everyone in God's image," I said.

"Don't bamboozle me like that," said Simple. "If God is bowlegged, sway-backed, merinery, and buck-toothed, skippy! That I do not believe. But some womens is all of them things—and wear slacks besides. There are more homely womens in the world than there are pretty womens. So it would be easy to hold an Ugly Contest every week-end. And at the end of the year I would have an Elimination Contest for the Ugliest Young Woman on Earth. I bet whoever won that Grand Prize would get all kinds of Hollywood, TV, radio, and movie contracts, not to mention a week at the Apollo."

"The winner might get all those things," I said, "but the poor girl would have a hard time finding a husband after so much 'ugly' publicity."

"With all the money that Ugly Champion would be making, she could not keep the men away from her," said Simple. "Facts is, if I was single, as much loot as the most famous ugly woman in the world would be making, I would marry her myself just to spend some of her cash. Ugly is as ugly does, and if that woman did me good, I would not care what she looked like. Then if she uglied away into paradise, died in due time, and willed me her fortunes, my memories of her would be beautiful. No rich woman can get too ugly to find a husband. Money talks."

"Perish the thought," I said, "that the winner of the Ugly Contest would have to pay a man to marry her. Poor girl! That would be a hollow triumph indeed for all her trophies and her scrolls. But tell me,

since Beauty Contests have rules, you know, by which beauty is judged—
measurements of busts, waists, hips, and thighs, tint of complexion and
tone of hair—what rules would you set up for judging an Ugly Contest?"

"Busts the flattest, hips the barrelest, legs the thinnest, and the rest of
it, come what may," said Simple. "Also I would give a prize for the tight-
est slacks on the biggest haunches, the highest heels on the longest feet,
and the hair with the most colors in it. Just a two-tone hair job or a wig
would not get nowhere in my contest. I would give a prize to the head of
hair with a red streak, a yellow streak, a green streak, and a purple streak
in it—and only then if it had an orange horsetail as well. Oh, my ugly
woman winner would be a mad Myrtle without a girdle, I'm telling you!
She would look like King Kong's daughter plus the niece of Balaam's off-
ox. To win my contest, she would have to be a homely heifer, indeed.

"But I would give her a great big prize, then put her under contract for
all personal appearances on stage, screen, or at Rockland Palace. I would
charge one thousand dollars-a-day commission for the public to look at
her—the Homeliest Woman in the Whole World. The Ugly Champion
of the Universe! If ever she went up in a spaceship, she would scare
the Man in the Moon to death before she had a chance to meet him.
Miss Ugly would be so ugly she would be proud of herself, and her
mama before her would be proud of her, as would her daddy when he
learned how famous his daughter had got to be—pictured endorsing
every filter-tipped cigarette, singing commercials for toothpaste, and
posing for beer.

"Seriously, I believe I will start such a contest, get me maybe a thousand entries, hire a big hall, Count Basie's Band, and have me an Ugly
Parade instead of a Beauty Parade, appoint Nipsey Russell and Jackie
Moms Mabley as judges, and take a big pile of money. Besides, such a
contest would make me famous, too—as the only man in the world with
nerve enough to call a *whole lot* of women ugly! 'Jesse B. Semple, pro-
moter of the Ugly Contest!' And if I found a woman uglier than I am a
man, more homely than me, I would give her a special prize myself. A
gold beer mug with my picture on it, engraved:

To You From Me
Your Ugly Daddy
Jesse B. Semple
Congratulations

Empty Houses

"Once when I was a wee small child in Virginia," said Simple, "I was walking down the street one real hot day when a white man patted me on the head and give me a dime.

"He said, 'Looks like you could stand an ice-cream cone,' to which I said, 'Yes, sir.'

"That cone I bought sure was good. I were staying with some of my mother's distant kinsfolks at the time and when I went home and told them I had bought an ice-cream cone they said, 'Where did you get the money?'

"I said, 'A white man give me a dime.'

"They said, 'What was you doing out in the street begging for a dime?'

"I explained to them that I had not begged, but they said, 'Don't lie to me, boy. Nobody is gonna walk up to you and just give you a dime without you asking for it.' So I got a whipping for lying.

"They could not understand that there is some few people in the world who do good without being asked. It were a hot day, I were a little boy, and ice-cream cones are always good. And that man just looked at me and thought I would like one—which I did. That is one reason why I do not hate all white folks today because some white folks will do good without being asked or hauled up before the Supreme Court to have a law promulgated against them.

"Not everybody has to be begged to do good, or subpeanoed into it. Why, a cat in the bar the other night I hardly knowed offered me a beer, and when I said, 'Man, I'm sorry, but I am kinder short tonight and cannot buy you one back,' he said, 'Aw, forget it!' He bought me the beer anyway.

"Some folks think that everything in life has to balance up, turn out equal. If you buy a man a drink, he has to buy you one back. If you get invited to a party, then you have to give a party, too, and invite whoever invited you. My wife, Joyce, is like that—which makes folks end up having to give parties they do not want to give, and going to a lot of parties to which they do not want to go. Tit for tat—I give you this, you give me that. But me, I am not that way. If I was to give somebody I liked a million dollars, I would not expect them to give me a million dollars back. I would give a million like it warn't nothing. But even if you give a million and don't give it free-hearted, it is like nothing. Do you get what I am trying to say?"

"You are dealing in very high figures," I said, "so it sounds complicated. Nevertheless, since you have been standing at this bar for the last half-hour with an empty glass, I will give you a beer."

"I accept," said Simple. "Thank you."

"Don't mention it," I said. "It's nothing."

"Nothing is everything," said Simple, "when it comes from the heart. But even a glass of beer, when it don't come from the heart tastes like nothing. You know, I told you before, I were a passed-around child, so I know when something tastes like nothing. Even a Sunday dinner can taste like nothing, and if you are a little small child, you wonder why.

"One Sunday when I was little down in Virginia, even before they nicknamed me Simple, I went looking in the rain that dusk-like evening for something I did not know what, somewhere I did not know where. Seems like I was looking for somebody, I did not know who, because I had just come out of a house full of peoples but they was lonesome to me, and I was lonesome to them. Nobody put me out of no house that day, and they had give me plenty to eat, but I just went off in the rain by myself walking down the street looking. I went down a street with big rich fine houses setting on lawns under trees where poor folks did not live nor colored. And I thought nobody lonesome like me ever lived there, which maybe was wrong. I were only a little small child and I did not know then that rich folks sometimes might be lonesome, too, in a house full of loneliness even when their big fine house is full of peoples.

"Sundays my aunt sent me to Sunday School and I looked at Jesus who were white on a Sunday School card, and at Moses who were white, and Mary Mother of God also white, and I were lonesome in that colored Baptist Church in Virginia with Sunday School cards that were white— and me not the color of nobody I knew with white relatives. Jesus was the color of the white folks that black folks worked for in our town. Jesus had long straight hair that hung down to the neck of His robes, and I wondered what kind of drawers Jesus wore under His robes. All the men on them Sunday School cards had on robes, and I wondered if they wore underneath pants or what. I also wondered why Bible peoples wore their hair so long. Also, how did an angel with such long wings, ever set down? On the Sunday School cards the angels were always standing up, else flying. These such thoughts I thought setting in Sunday School, until the old lady teacher said, 'Now let's all sing, "Jesus loves me, that

I know, because the Bible tells me so.'" We also sang 'Jesus Wants Me for a Sunbeam.' Then she said, 'Let us pray.'

"I pictured in my mind a white God listening to me praying. And I wondered if he cared anything about a little colored boy's prayers, or did he just listen to the peoples in the big fine houses with the porches and lawns and trees and the pretty lamps with big shades in their windows at night. Did he listen to me setting in Sunday School wondering what kind of drawers Jesus wore? Anyway, I was walking that day in the rain. And I was thinking about my old aunt who was not really my aunt, but who was my father's stepfather's sister and who took me in and took care of me while my mother was away somewhere. I were a passed-around child. While my mother was not there and my father was not there and they was separated, I were left with whoever would take care of me when they was not there.

"Nobody was mean to me, and I do not know why I had that left-out feeling, but I did, I guess because nobody ever said, 'You're mine,' and I did not really belong to nobody. When I got big and grown up, I took for my theme song in my early manhood years that old record of Billie Holiday's which says, 'God bless the child that's got his own.' If I had a child, be he or she girl or boy, I would make sure I kept that child with me and it were my own and I were its own. I would make sure it did not want to go back home, even when it came dinnertime and you was hungry.

"Since I married my second wife, Joyce, I do not have that left-lonesome feeling so much any more. But it took me a long time to find somebody you want to come home to where the house does not feel empty even with somebody in it. It is bad for a full-grown man to come home to somebody who is not there, even if they have got dinner ready. For a little small child, it is worse—that nobody-home-that-belongs-to-you feeling. Even if the house is fun of peoples, it is not enough for them to just be there.

"If they do not have a little love for whoever lives in the house with them, it is a empty house. If you have somebody else living in the house with you, be it man, woman, or child, relative or friend, adopted or just taken in, even if it is just a roomer paying rent—even if you give them no money nor a piece of bread and not anything—if you got a little love for whoever it is, it will *not* be a empty house. But if nobody cares, it is an empty house. I have lived in so many empty houses full of peoples, I do not want to live in a crowded empty house no more."

The Blues

"I do not know why so many young folks these days and times do not like the blues," said Simple. "They like Rock and Roll, and Rock and Roll ain't nothing much but a whole lot of blues with sometimes a Boogie beat mixed in. Rock and Roll is seventy-two-and-one-half percent blues. But it don't have so many different kinds of expressions as does the blues! The blues can be real sad, else real mad, else real glad, and funny, too, all at the same time. I ought to know. Me, I growed up with the blues. Facts is, I heard so many blues when I were a child until my shadow was blue. And when I were a young man, and left Virginia and runned away to Baltimore, behind me came the shadow of the blues. Oh, if I was a singer man, I could sing me some blues! But I never was much on voice. Still and yet I can holler:

> The blues ain't nothing
> But a good woman on your mind.
> I say, blues ain't nothing
> But a good woman on your mind.
> But your potatoes is gone
> When the frost has killed the vine.
> If you see Corinna,
> Tell her to hurry home.
> Simple ain't had no loving
> Since Corinna's been gone.
> Blues, blues, blues, please
> Do not come my way.
> Gimme something else, Lord,
> Besides the blues all day!

"Do you remember that one?" asked Simple.

" 'Caledonia' sounds something like it," I said.

"Sure do," said Simple. "Corinna and Caledonia must have been sisters. So many blues is about womens.

> Did you ever see a
> One-eyed woman cry?
> She can cry so good just

Out of that one old eye.
I was raised in Texas,
Schooled in Tennessee.
Can't no little bitty woman
Make a fool out of me.

And from that you go into one that Old Blind Lemon used to sing:

I got so many womens I
Cannot call their name.
Some of them is crossed-eyed
But they see me just the same.
Blues, blues, blues,
Blues, how-do-you-do?
I would be blue but
I got a mojo in my shoe."

God's Other Side

"Some Negroes think that all one has to do to solve the problems in this world is to be white," I said, "but I never understood how they can feel that way. There are white unemployed, just as there are black unemployed. There are white illiterates, just as there are blacks who can hardly read or write. The mere absence of color would hardly make this world a paradise. Whites get sick the same as Negroes. Whites grow old. Whites go crazy."

"Some of us in Harlem do not have sense enough to go crazy," said Simple. "Some Negroes do not worry about a thing. But me, well, Jim Crow bugs me."

"Bigotry disturbs me, too," I said, "but prejudice and segregation alone do not constitute the root of *all* evil. There are many nonracial elements common to humanity as a whole that create problems from the cradle to the grave regardless of race, creed, color, or previous condition of servitude."

"But when you add a black face to all that," said Simple, "you have problem's mammy. White folks may be unemployed in this American country, but they get the first chance at the first jobs that open up. Besides, they get seniority. Maybe some white folks cannot read or write, but if they want to go to Ole Miss to learn to read or write, they can go without the President calling up the United States Army to protect them. Sure, white folks gets sick, but they don't have to creep in the back door of the hospital down South for treatment like we does. And when they get old, white folks have got more well-off sons and daughters to take care of them than colored folks have. Most old white folks when they get sick can suffer in comfort, and when they die they can get buried without going in debt. Colored folks, most in generally, do not have it so easy. I know because I am one."

"You let yourself be unduly disturbed by your skin," I said. "Sometimes I think you are marked by color—just as some children are born with birthmarks."

"My birthmark is all over me," said Simple.

"Then your only salvation is to be born again."

"And washed whiter than snow," declared Simple. "Imagine all my relatives setting up in heaven washed whiter than snow. I wonder would I know my grandpa were I to see him in paradise? Grandpa Semple crowned in Glory with white wings, white robe, white skin, and golden slippers on his feet! Oh, Grandpa, when the chariot swings low to carry me up to the Golden Gate, Grandpa, as I enter will you identify yourself —just in case I do not know you, white and winged in your golden shoes? I might be sort of turned around in heaven, Grandpa."

"What on earth makes you think you are going to heaven?" I asked.

"Because I have already been in Harlem," said Simple.

"How often do you go to church?" I asked.

"As often as my wife drags me," said Simple. "The last two times I was there the minister preached from the text, 'And I shall sit on the right hand of the Son of God.' Me, half asleep, I heard that much from the sermon. And it set me to wondering why it is nobody ever wants to set on the *left*-hand side of God? All my life, from a little small child in Virginia right on up to Harlem, in church I have been hearing of people setting on the right-hand side of God, never on the left. Now, why is that?"

"When a guest comes to dine, you always seat him or her on your right—that is the main guest sits there," I said. "The right-hand side is the place of honor, granted always to the lady, or the oldest, or the most distinguished person present. The right side is the place of honor."

"I would be glad to set on any old side," said Simple, "were I lucky enough to get into the Kingdom. Besides, if everybody is setting on the right-hand side of God that says they are going to set there, that right-hand side of God would be really crowded. One million Negroes and two million white folks must be setting already on the right. How is there going to be room on that side for anybody else?"

"In the Kingdom there is infinite room, whichever side is chosen," I said.

"No matter how much room there is," said Simple, "that right side of the Throne is crowded by now. I see no harm in setting on the left. God must turn His head that way once in a while, too."

"I suppose He does," I said. "But if you have your choice, why not sit on the right?"

"Just because everybody else is setting there," said Simple. "I would like to be different, and set on the left-hand side all by myself. I expect I would get a little more of God's attention that way—because when He turned around toward me, nobody would be there but me. On His right-hand side, like I said, would be setting untold millions. And all of them folks would be asking for something. God's right ear must be so full of prayers, He can hardly hear himself think. Now me, on the left-hand side, I would not ask for nothing much, were I to get to heaven. And if I did ask for anything, I would whisper soft-like, 'Lord, here is me!'

"Were the Lord to grant me an answer, and say, 'Negro, what do you want?' I would say, 'Nothing much, Lord. And if you be's too busy on your right-hand side to attend to me now, I can wait. I tried to leave my business on earth pretty well attended to—but just in case my wife, Joyce, needs anything, look after her, Lord. I love that girl. Also my Cousin Minnie—protect her from too much harm in them Lenox Avenue bars which she do love beyond the call of duty. Also my junior nephew, F. D., that I helped to raise when he first come to Harlem in his teens, who is out of the Army and married now, show F. D. how to get along with his wife and be a good young man, and not pattern himself too much after me, who were frail as to being an example for anybody.

" 'The peoples that I love, Lord, is the only ones I whispers into Your left ear about. If I was on Your right side, which is crowded with all the saints who ever got to Glory, me who ain't much, might have to holler from afar off for You to hear me at all. Me, who never was nobody, am glad just to be setting on Your left side, Lord—me, Jesse B. Semple, on the left-hand side of the Son of God! And I wants to whisper just *one* thing to You, God—I hope You loves the ones I love, too.' "

Color Problems

"Two things I would hate to be in Harlem right now is a light-skin Negro and a black cop," said Simple. "If it is true what the downtown papers said about some Black Blood Brotherhood out to kill all white folks, how can a near-white Negro the complexion of Adam Powell be sure that the Brotherhood might not make a mistake and kill him too?"

"What a thought!" I cried.

"Yes," said Simple. "And as to the colored polices in these days and times with civil rights at the boiling point, if a Negro cop tries to arrest somebody doing wrong to get his rights, that cop is liable to be taken as a traitor to his race, to integration, freedom and also equality. Yes, sir! In fact, any colored cop who has to arrest a civil rights demonstrator these days must feel bad, because I know that cop wants his rights the same as any other Negro. I would feel bad, too, would'n you?"

"Indeed, the position of the colored policemen in the civil rights battle must be difficult," I said. "I saw a photograph in the papers of a colored policeman in a Southern town arresting some colored teen-agers who were picketing a white movie theatre to which that colored policeman himself could not buy a ticket. I wonder what would you do if you were a Negro policeman in such a case!"

"I would refuse to make an arrest," said Simple. "I would not be a traitor to my race just in order to be a cop. In most Southern towns which have Negroes on the police forces, colored polices do not dare to arrest a white person. Colored cops is limited to making colored arrests."

"The police force, whatever the nationality of its individuals, should be color-blind," I said.

"What is and what *should be* is two different things," said Simple. "Harlem is so full of white cops with white faces and white viewpoints that when some of them see me, they see red because I am *not* white. So when a black cop sees me, he should not look through white eyes. I am his brother—even when I am walking on a picket line and do not move fast enough to satisfy the police commissioner. Colored cops should know why I do not move any faster—because I have been so slow in getting my rights to belong to that white union I am picketing which bars me from earning a living even on a project built by the city with my tax money. A colored cop ought not to be so quick to arrest me when that cop's own son cannot get into the union, either. That cop knows his tax money and mine is being spent to build government buildings where colored plumbers cannot even install a toilet."

"I admit the dilemma of Negro police in the face of the civil rights struggle is tough. In fact, they face a *double* dilemma."

"I would not like to be a colored cop in the face of no such double," said Simple. "It would break my heart to have to arrest my own teen-age son or his friends, or to arrest these young white students who is fighting and picketing and marching with us for civil rights. Fact is, I would not arrest any of them."

"Are you advocating disobedience to law on the part of Negro policemen?"

"When the law is not on the side of civil rights, then the law is not right, it's white," said Simple. "And if I was a light-complexioned Negro—instead of being dark as I am—I would be afraid some of these kids in Harlem that the papers is calling American Mau Maus might take *me* as being white. And these mixed couples living in Harlem, colored mens married to white womens, and white mens married to colored womens? Suppose Sammy Davis lived in Harlem or Lena Horne—and both of them are married white? I met a light-skin Negro friend of mine, a man, the other night who looks white. Some dark Negro he did not even know said to him in a bar, 'What are you doing up here in Harlem?'

"The light-skin man said, 'I was born in Harlem, and I live in Harlem, and I am as black as you.'

"The dark fellow said, 'You better show it then, and get a sun tan.'

"My friend said that for the first time in his life, he was scared of his own people. He said Adam Powell better come back home from Washington and make a speech about how black Negroes should not bother light Negroes in Harlem, since we is *all* blood brothers. Do you reckon them stories in the papers was true about the Blood Brothers being out to do white folks in?"

"Newspaper headlines make things seem many times worse than they are in reality," I said. "But whites in Harlem are apprehensive, that's sure. It's regrettable."

"Maybe that old saying, 'A dark man shall see dark days,' ought to be changed to include dark cops, *light* Negroes, and white mens. Me, I am glad I am neither," said Simple.

The Moon

"Love is a many-splintered thing," sang Simple, standing at the bar. "If my heart had rings in it like a tree log, you could tell how many loves I have had—I mean of the heart not the body. I used to fall in love with movie stars when I were a young boy, and you know I could not get near no movie star, they being white and way up yonder on the screen and me in a Jim Crow balcony down in Virginia. When I come to Baltimore as a young man, setting in a Jim Crow theatre on Pennsylvania Avenue, the first colored movie star I fell in love with was Nina Mae McKinney, who was showing herself off in a picture called *Hallelujah,* which were fine. Nina Mae were so beautiful she made my heart ache. Then I fell in love with Isabel, who became my first wife, and I forgot about movie stars. Isabel kept my nose to the grindstone, so I did not have neither time or money to go to movies.

"With Isabel it was always *buy* this, *buy* that, *buy* a icebox, *buy* a toaster, *buy* a washing machine which runs by electricity so I don't have to wash by hand, *buy* me a fur coat, *buy* me a boxer-dog. Isabel sure could want more things than you could shake a stick at. And when I was bought out, I was put out. Thank God, my present wife, Joyce, is not a *buy-me* girl, neither a *gimme* woman. Joyce works, too. We puts our money together, what she makes and what I make, and run on a budget. It's me who has to say 'gimme' to my wife now to even get beer money from that budget. We are saving to buy a house. But Joyce wants to go to the suburbans. I wants to stay in Harlem. So there's a conflict."

"And who will win?" I inquired.

"My wife," said Simple, "but not without a struggle. I can see myself now shoveling snow and cutting lawns so far from Harlem I can't even smell a pig's foot. Me, I do not want to go to *no* suburbans, not even Brooklyn. But Joyce wants to integrate. She says America has got two cultures, which should not be divided as they now is, so let's leave Harlem."

"Don't you agree that Joyce is right?"

"*White is right,*" said Simple, "so I have always heard. But I never did believe it. White folks do so much wrong! Not only do they mistreat me, but they mistreats themselves. Right now, all they got their minds on is shooting off rockets and sending up atom bombs and poisoning the air and fighting wars and Jim Crowing the universe."

"Why do you say 'Jim Crowing the universe'?"

"Because I have not heard tell of no Negro astronaughts nowhere in space yet. This is serious, because if one of them white Southerners gets to the moon first, COLORED NOT ADMITTED signs will go up all over heaven as sure as God made little green apples, and Dixiecrats will be asking the man in the moon, 'Do you want your daughter to marry a Nigra?' Meanwhile, the NAACP will have to go to the Supreme Court, as usual, to get an edict for Negroes to even set foot on the moon. By that time, Roy Wilkins will be too old to make the trip, and me too."

"But perhaps the Freedom Riders will go into orbit on their own," I said. "Or Harlem might vote Adam Powell into the Moon Congress."

"One thing I know," said Simple, "is that Martin Luther King will *pray* himself up there. The moon must be a halfway stop on the way to Glory and King will probably be arrested. I wonder if them Southerners will take police dogs to the moon?"

"You are a great one for fantasy," I said, "maybe stemming from your movie-going days."

"Which is when I first discovered that love is a many-splintered thing," sighed Simple.

Domesticated

"My Cousin Minnie, beings as she is temporarily alone again, tells me she is looking for a boy friend these days who means business," said Simple. "And what Minnie means by *business* is when she asks a man, 'Baby, can you pay my rent? That kitchenette of mine costs me $155 a month, which is without gas—so he who lives there must share.' That's what Minnie says."

"Economics plays a large part in love in Harlem these days," I agreed. "He who would woo, must shell out, too."

"Which is one reason I do not stray at all since I been married," said Simple. "I cannot afford it. My budget do not allow for me living with nobody but my wife, or drinking with nobody but myself, and playing more than one number a day, combinated. I am a man. Minnie is a lady. I takes care of myself. Minnie needs taking care of. I do not blame my boon cousin for asking what a man's finances are before she chooses a permanent friend. To get a good woman, any man must pay, and my Cousin Minnie is not to be sneezed at. Brains run in the Semple family."

"Your Cousin Minnie ought to make some man a good wife," I said.

"In the far distant future, when she gets tired of setting on bar stools," Simple replied. "Right now, let Minnie play the field. She's still young. If she picks a winning horse, she can always get hitched before the season ends. If the man is a sometimer, she can let him go and wipe the slate clean to chalk up new bets."

"It is too bad love and money have to be so mixed up," I said, "especially for a woman."

"Landlords are not interested in love—just money. They wants their rent each and every month," said Simple. "When a man and a woman are both working, they can share the rent. But Minnie is the type that likes to set down on a man. That is her way of 'making him a home,' as she puts it. She claims that if she goes out and works, too, the home is nothing but an empty shell. Minnie has got the same ideas as a rich white lady."

"I don't blame her," I said, "if she can get away with it. But most colored men hardly make enough to take care of themselves, let alone a family—which is one of the regrettable facts of Negro economics. Yet Minnie has the right idea. A woman should be a wife, not a work horse."

"She should have a man's dinner ready when he comes home," said Simple. "It is hard for a man to love a woman on an empty stomach."

"You are the old-fashioned type," I said. "You want your wife to work outside the home, and inside it too."

"I wants my dinner at night."

"Then you ought to hire a cook."

"I married one," said Simple. "Joyce has to eat the same as me. Since women have to cook for themselves, they might as well cook for their man too."

"Also, you expect your wife to keep the house clean?"

"Joyce swears she cannot live in filth, for which I am grateful," said Simple, "as I never was one for house cleaning, myself. I might sweep a little on Sunday. And lately Joyce has bulldozed me into scrubbing the linoleum. I also last week washed the front windows."

"Gradually getting domesticated," I said. "I am glad Joyce can get something out of you on Sundays, as late as you stay up sporting around on Saturday."

"Late?" said Simple. "I go home at closing time. I must love Joyce, as much as I have changed since I got married. Comes midnight no matter where I am, I think about my wife."

"You are probably scared she is thinking about you," I said.

"How did you guess it?" asked Simple. "I am going home right now before Joyce gets ready to raise sand. If you see my Cousin Minnie, tell her Jess Semple has been here and gone. Good night!"

Bomb Shelters

"It is wise to keep one eye open," said Simple, "even when you are asleep."

"To what are you referring now?" I asked, leaning on the bar as Simple gazed (with a hint my way) at his empty glass.

"The trickeration going on in this world," said Simple.

"What trickeration?" I inquired.

"Atom bomb shelters," said Simple. "Our landlord last week came talking to me about he was going to have to raise our rent in order to build us a bomb shelter in the back yard. Now you know, Harlem landlords have no intentions of building no bomb shelters for their roomers. With 50–11 people living in each and every rooming house, even if the law required it, how could landlords build enough shelters for every roomer? And if roomers built their own shelters—me and Joyce living in a kitchenette, for instance—suppose we build a bomb shelter in the landlord's back yard. How would we keep the other roomers out in case of a raid? Them people on the ground floor would beat us to our shelter before we could get downstairs. They has an ageable grandmother in their family downstairs.

"Now, what kind of a gentleman would I be if I said, 'Grandma, you cannot go in my shelter'? How would I sound saying to an old lady, 'If you come in, *I* have to stay out. This mail-order shelter I got is only assembled for my wife and me?' How would that sound? But them mail-order shelters is only big enough for two.

"Of course, I could always put it up to Joyce, who tells me I must be a gentleman, come what may. With the atom sirens sounding, standing at the door of my shelter, I would say, 'Joyce, you are my wife. Does you wish me or Grandma to accompany you inside this shelter? Should I give way to a nice old lady and stand outside and meet my death, or go underground with you and leave somebody else's grandma out? You have told me in the past, "Ladies first. Be a gentleman." What do you say now, Joyce?'

"Of course, Joyce might be real noble and say, 'Age before beauty.'

"Then I would say, 'Joyce, I know you do not mean I should go in.'

"Whereupon Joyce would say, 'This is no time for joking, Jess Semple!'

"So I would say, 'I will be a gentleman then, Joyce, and let Grandma go down in the shelter with you—although she is no relation to us.'

"I can just see Joyce turning as pale as her complexion will permit, at the thought of losing me, burnt to an atom, outside the door.

"But by then Grandma would take my arm and say, 'Son, you know I cannot go in that shelter without my grandchildren, Martha Mae, Ellen, and Johnny-Baby here.'

"Sure enough, if I looked back there would stand all them little ones in Grandma's family, scared as they could be, out there in the middle of the night at the door of *my* atom bomb shelter, clutching onto Grandma. Behind them would stand also their mother and father.

"Then one of the young ones would start crying, 'I don't want to go in that cave without my mama.'

"I would say, 'This shelter was built for two, honey. Your grandma, three children, and your mama makes five—not counting my wife, Joyce. Who can figure that out?'

"Whereupon, the big old Negro what fathered all them children— but neglected to build them a shelter—would say, 'Don't *nobody* count Papa?'

"I would yell, 'No, I do not count Papa. Before I would let you in my shelter, I would fight you. You have seen me in the corner bar ninety-nine times and have not treated me to a beer yet.'

" 'Do you want to make something out of it?' he would say, balling up his fists.

" 'I'll fight you barehanded,' I would say.

"But Joyce would scream, 'Jess Semple! With death staring you in the face, do you want to make a commotion?'

" 'I do,' I would say, taking off my coat. 'I'll fight him here and now.'

"But just at that moment, believe it or not, the all-clear signal would sound, the sirens would stop, and the radios would start blaring, 'Danger is past.' The warning must have been a false alarm. Grandma and that family downstairs would all go trooping back into the house.

"Joyce would throw her arms around my neck and say, 'Thank God, you're saved, Jess Semple! But let's tear that shelter down tomorrow. I could not go in there and leave them children and Grandma outside. Neither could I leave you outside, baby, Jess darling, my life!'

" 'Nor could I leave you,' I would say, hugging her in my arms as close as white on rice.

" 'So let's just tear our shelter down,' Joyce would say. 'If the bomb does come, let's just *all die* neighborly.' Then Joyce and me would go back in the house—our problem solved. Anyhow, we could not go in a shelter and leave Grandma outside."

Gospel Singers

"It looks," said Simple, "like the churches are buying up half the old movie theatres in Harlem and turning them into temples. Lenox Avenue, Seventh Avenue, Amsterdam, all up and down, it is getting so you can't tell a theatre from a church any more. Now the ministers have got their name up in lights out front just like movie actors. Have you noticed?"

"I have," I said. "I guess television is driving the neighborhood movie houses out of business."

"Yes, and churches are taking over," said Simple. "The church will be here when the movies are gone, that's a sure thing. But old-time store-front churches are going out of style. From now on, it looks like you will have to call them *movie-front* churches—except that the box office has turned into a collection plate, and the choir is swinging gospel songs. Money is being made, just one collection after another."

"You are not opposed to churches taking up collections, like other institutions, are you? They have to pay rent, light, heat, plus ministers' fees."

"I am not opposed," said Simple, "not when they put on a good show."

" 'Show' is hardly the word to use in reference to religion," I said. "Do you think so?"

"That is the way some of churches advertise their gospel singers these days," said Simple. "I seed a poster outside a church last night, Sister Mamie Lightfoot and Her Gospel Show, and they were charging one dollar to come in, also programs cost a quarter, and you had to buy one to pass the door."

"Did you go in?"

"I did, and it were fine! Four large ladies in sky-blue robes sung 'On My Journey Now,' sung it and swung it, real gone, with a jazz piano behind them that sounded like a cross between Dorothy Donegan and Count Basie. Them four sisters started slow, then worked it up, and worked it up, and worked it up until they came on like gang busters, led by Sister Lightfoot. Then they started walking up and down the aisle from the pulpit to the rear, making out like they really was on their journey to the Promised Land—and the church fell in. They did the last part over about seventeen times. Folks leaped, jumped, hollered, and shouted, and started marching too. Then they took up a collection for the benefit of Sister Lightfoot. The plates were overflowing. I put in a dollar myself."

"You mean after you had already paid a dollar at the door?"

"I were so moved that I did not mind contributing again," said Simple. "Besides there were a young Negro there named McKissick who rocked the rafters. That boy can stone sing a song! To tell the truth, gospel singers these days put more into a song than lots of night club stars hanging onto a microphone looking like they are on their last legs. Besides, you can hear a gospel singer two blocks off, singing and swinging, even without a mike. In the past I have heard Mahalia, the Ward Singers, Sallie Martin, Princess Steward, Elder Beek, James Cleveland, the Dixie Humming Birds, the Davis Sisters, also the Martin Singers, and I am telling you, the music that these people put down cannot be beat. It moves the spirit—and it moves the feet. It is gone, man, solid gone! Which is why I has no objections to paying at the door, then shelling out some more when I get inside even if they do invest most of it in automobiles.

"As good as them gospel peoples sing, why should they not ride on rubber—of any kind they want from Cadillacs to Jaguars. Why, I saw a quartet of five come driving up to a church in Harlem once, and each one of them singers in the quartet was driving a different kind of car, and each car were *fine*! Them five boys got out of them five fine cars and went into the church and started singing 'If I Can Just Make It In,' meaning into the Kingdom. They also sung, 'I Cannot Get There By Myself,' and everybody said, 'Help 'em Jesus! Help 'em!' Which the congregation did by contributing a dollar, or a dollar and a half. Them boys took home a bushel of money.

"Another song I like is 'Move On Up a Little Higher,' also 'Precious Lord, Take My Hand.' Don't you? Some of them large colored sisters can really sing such songs. We have some *great* gospel singers in this land. They are working in the vineyards of the Lord and digging in His gold mines. Why, some gospel singers these days are making so much money that when you hear them crying, 'I Cannot Bear My Burden Alone,' what they really mean is, 'Help me get my cross to my Cadillac.' Which is O.K. by me, as long as they keep on singing like they do. Good singers deserve their just rewards, both in this world and in the other one. Yes, they do!"

"You are really a gospel *aficionado*," I said.

"Whatever that means, I do like gospel. But take my wife, Joyce, she is not too much moved by it, although she appreciates Mahalia. Joyce goes for opera—which sounds like a lot of squalls and squawks to me."

"What operas?" I asked.

"Any opera," said Simple. "But what I am meaning now is them that Joyce listens to on the radio. My wife is the most opera-listening woman I know. Me, I do not care much for it."

"Probably because you do not understand opera," I said.

"They are all in Italian," said Simple, "and Joyce do not understand Italian neither, yet she loves opera."

"Your wife appreciates the music," I said, "and she probably takes the time and trouble to read the story of *Carmen* or *Tosca* or *Aïda* or what not. Culture may not always be appreciated without preparation. Perhaps if you were to read the libretto of an opera and know its story, you would understand it better."

"But why is all operas in Italian?"

"They are not all in Italian. Wagner's operas are in German, Bizet's in French, Mussorgsky's in Russian, and Menotti's in English," I said.

"Even when operas are in English, they *sound* like they are in Italian," said Simple. "Once I went with Joyce to Carnegie Hall to hear a colored opera presented by Madam Dawson and writ by a famous colored composer, and it sounded to me like it were sung in Yiddish. All the singers were colored. The programs said the opera were in English, so I know it was not Italian. But if you have ever pushed a cart like me down in the garment center with Jewish peoples, you have heard Yiddish. You know it is a language you cannot understand. Since I could not understand this opera, I asked Joyce did she reckon all them colored singers had Jewish singing teachers?

"Joyce said, 'Sh-sss-ss-s! Why do you ask such an absurd question?'

"I said, 'Because I do not understand a word!'

"Joyce said, 'But what tone! What projection! Do you not hear that bel canto?'

"I said, 'Hell, no! I can't oh!' Which made Joyce mad, oh! She began to tell me that she did not see why I had to show my ignorance right there in Carnegie Hall. She said I should not be talking during an aria, anyhow, and that Madam Dawson had put on a fine production.

"I said, 'Everybody sure looks fine down on that stage, most particularly that chick in the low-cut gown with the broach over her navel. She looks sharp!'

" 'She is singing flat,' said Joyce, 'and is the least good in the company!'

" 'I had rather look at her than at that big fat lady singing "Great Google Moogle!" ' I said.

" 'She is not singing "Great Google Moogle," ' cried Joyce. 'She is chanting "Great God of Mercy," crying to a voodoo god to save her lover from death.'

" 'I am glad you told me what it is all about,' I said. But by that time Joyce had turned her back as far as she could on me in them seats we had paid $5.50 per each for to hear that opera. Joyce were listening fluently—maybe she do enjoy that kind of music. But me I don't understand it! I prefers gospel."

"Just because you don't understand a thing, do not make fun of it too harshly, or be too critical of others for liking it. Tastes differ. You go for beer, some go for Bach, some for Goldoni, and some for gospel. As for opera, thousands of people like it. You happen not to be in that number. Yet, if I remember correctly, when Marian Anderson first sang with the Metropolitan Opera you were one of those cheering the loudest, right here at this bar."

"Right!" said Simple. "Right *here* at this bar, not at the opera. Bravo, Marian! Sing, woman, sing! Bartender, set me up a beer. And now that Marian Anderson has retired and put opera and concerts down, I hope she takes up gospel. She could make a million dollars as a gospel singer."

"Don't be ridiculous," I said.

"When was money ever ridiculous?" asked Simple.

Nothing but a Dog

"I once had a no-good husband—went off and left me. Didn't leave me nothing but a dog," Cousin Minnie said to Simple as they sat stool by stool at the bar. "Dog's name were Cargo. He were a black dog, had one white eye. My husband were in the Merchant Marines on a coal vessel sailing out of Norfolk at that time. He brought that little old black mutt back from Trinidad or somewhere. Since that little old hound looked like a load of coal hisself, so black, he named him Cargo.

"Cargo were something! Too affectionate for his own good, that dog. He loved me, but he like to drove me crazy, running off and stuff. He traipsed all over town like his master, and never got runned over. That dog knew a red light from a green one as well as I did. Cargo loved people, but hated dogs. This I never did understand. If I was a dog, I think I would like other dogs. But Cargo's hair bristled. He looked like a walking clothesbrush when he saw one. And he were evil.

"One time Cargo bit a white lady's dog down the street, and got bit in return. They fit, fought, and fit, barked, growled, howled, and bit. Both dogs were right smart chewed up.

"That old white lady come running down to my place and says, 'Your dog bit mine.'

"I said, 'It also seems like your dog bit mine.'

"She said, 'Your dog has no business biting my dog.'

"I said, 'Your dog has got no business biting Cargo.'

"She looked at me. I looked at her. She said, 'Don't be impudent with me.'

"I said, 'Don't you be impudent, neither, madam. I don't know you, and I never seen your dog. What proof you got that my dog bit your dog? Cargo *is* bit—look at his ear. But who bit him, and who exactly he bit, I do not know.'

" 'Do you dispute my word?' asked Old White Lady. 'I say your black dog bit mine.'

" 'Don't you call my dog black,' said I.

" 'Well it is black,' said the lady.

" 'So am I,' I said, 'but don't call me out of my name.'

" 'What is your name?' says Old White Lady, 'because I see where I am going to have to take you to court.'

"I started to tell her, 'Take your mama to court!' But she wouldn't understand, so I just said, 'Did *I* bite your dog?'

" 'Your dog has no license,' says she. 'I will have the Pound come and remove your dog from this street. He's a menace. What was your dog doing in my yard attacking my dog?'

" 'What are you doing at my door yelling at me? I am not a dog. Speak civil, else don't speak to me at all. Cargo, stop rubbing against that lady's leg. She's liable to bite you. Cargo, set down. Madam, I am sorry if my dog bit your dog!'

" 'I am no madam,' yells the lady, indignant-like.

" 'What is you?' I asked.

" 'My name is Mrs. Bertha—'

" 'Mine is Minnie,' I cut her off. 'So, Bertha, time's up. You go home to your dog and leave me with mine. Good-by!' I shut the door.

" 'I want redress,' said Bertha.

" 'Redress, huh! Colored folks dress—and white folks redress. Cargo, set down! You ain't nothing but a dog.' "

Roots and Trees

"My wife is an intellect," said Simple, "and that club she belongs to is always pursuiting culture. Nothing wrong, except that it takes so much time. Joyce was setting up in the library all last Saturday reading up on that old problem of how to solve the question of 'you can take a Negro out of the country but you can't take the country out of the Negro'—which I say is a lie. Harlem has certainly taken the country out of me. When I first come to the Big Apple, I did not know beans from bull foot. But look at me today—hip, slick, cool, and no fool."

"You manage to hold your own in New York," I said.

"A foothold is all I need," said Simple, "and my hands will hang on. I been hanging on in New York for a right smart while, and intend to stay. I will not return to the country, North or South. No backwoods for me. I am a big-city man myself. My roots is here."

"In other words, urbanized."

"That's a word I heard Joyce use," said Simple. "What her club is studying is how to make the un-urbanized Negro do right and stop throwing garbage out the window, sweeping trash in the street, fussing on the stoop, and cussing on the corner. Joyce says her club is making that a project. To which I said, 'Joyce, I think you-all have bit off more than a ladies' club can chew.'

"To which Joyce answers, 'Well, you men are doing little or nothing about it. What club do you belong to, Jesse B. Semple, that is trying to remedy the disgraceful conditions of adult delinquency here in Harlem? I am not talking about children, but grown delinquent men.'

"I said, 'Baby, do not look at me in that tone of voice. You know I carries myself right, drunk or sober.'

"To which Joyce says, 'To act right yourself is not enough. You must also help others to act right. We are all our brother's keeper—and cousin's, too.'

"I knowed Joyce was referring to my Cousin Minnie, who sometimes do not act like a lady. But I ignored Joyce's last remark. I said, 'Darling, you know I belong to the NAACP, and I would join the Elks if my budget would let me.'

" 'Our club,' says Joyce, 'is an auxiliary of the Urban League, and our president, Mrs. Sadie Maxwell-Reeves, is an officer in the Harlem branch of the League, which has done much to help transpose the rural Negro to big-city ways, the Southern customs to Northern manners.'

" 'Then that is where I should send my Cousin Minnie,' says I, 'to your club—to see if you-all can't take some of that down-home loudness out of her mouth. Minnie would be a right nice woman if she were not so loud.'

" 'Minnie also needs a job adjustment,' said Joyce.

" 'A job—period!' says I, 'but the kind of job where she does not have to go on time.'

" 'There are no such jobs in an urban community,' says Joyce. 'In the city, folks work by clocks, not by how they feel when they get up in the morning.'

" 'That I learned early,' I agreed. 'Before I married you and sobered up, Joyce, I learned to go to work on time, hangover or no hangover, else be fired. Northern white folks is harder on a late Negro than they are down South.'

" 'That is because the whole South runs late,' said Joyce. 'But up here in the free North—'

" 'A man ain't free to be late,' I said, cutting her off.

"But once Joyce latches onto a subject, there is no cutting her off. Joyce said, 'Jesse B., I want you to help me form a Block Club.'

" 'A what?' says I.

" 'A club to keep this block clean.'

" 'Baby,' I said, 'it would take more than a club. It would take artillery, tanks, and the state militia!'

" 'I am not joking,' said Joyce. 'Just theory and no action gets society nowhere, so Sadie Maxwell-Reeves said in her talk at the All-State Women's Convention last month, where she were the only colored woman to appear at the windup session. The message she brought back to us here in Harlem was, *action and more action.* Jess Semple, we women are marching into action. And you men are going to help us.'

" 'Joyce, baby,' I knowed I had better ask, 'what do you want me to do?'

" 'Help us take away their country ways and prepare them for big-city days.'

" 'In plain words,' I said, 'to live in the city, get with the nitty-gritty, wise up and be witty.'

"Joyce did not even smile. All she said was, 'Jess, don't be silly.' So I pulled a long face, too. Now you know I got to try to do what Joyce wants me to do. Next thing you know, Joyce will be president of our Block Club, and *I* am going to help her."

"Amen!" I said.

"Joyce says Harlem has got to let down our roots where we are," said Simple, "and let our trees grow tall. I wonder where is the tallest tree in the world, anyhow?"

"I have seen some pretty tall trees among the redwoods in California," I said, "and some very tall palms in Africa."

"But there has to be some tree on earth somewhere that is taller than any other tree anywhere," said Simple, "maybe just a tiny smidgen taller, say a quarter of an inch, or maybe only an eighth of an inch, but that little tiny bit extra of a fraction of an inch would make it the tallest tree, taller than any other tree in the world. And it could be proud. I wonder where that tree is? Probably in Africa—and, if so, the black race can be proud of having the tallest tree in the world."

"Nonsense," I said. "How can any race be proud of something it did not create? You know that song that so many singers moo and croon and bawl over about 'only God can make a tree'? How can a man be proud of a tree that just grew?"

"Well, at least he did not cut it down," said Simple. "Say, what do you think it would be like to be married to the tallest woman in the world? A little short woman is hard enough to keep in harness. And even a medium-size woman like my wife, Joyce, I am sometimes afraid to tackle. But the tallest woman in the world, unless she was married to one of the Globe Trotters, would be something for a man to handle. It is funny how God lets some folks grow so tall like Wilt Chamberlin, and others grow so short like Sammy Davis, and me so in-between with neither shortness nor tallness. Nobody makes admiration over me no kind of way—except my wife. Sharp-tempered as she can be sometimes, there is other times when Joyce says to me, 'Baby, you are the sweetest man on earth!' And she looks at me with them sweet, wonderful admiring eyes of hers; then I feel like the tallest tree in the world—that tree that is maybe just one little one-eighth of an inch taller than any other tree anywhere in the world. Me, I am that tree. Oh, friend, the power of a sweet kind word to keep you tall."

For President

"What is this the big shots are saying about us Negroes being cool because there might be a Negro President in the year 2011 in the U.S.A., huh? If I am going to run for President, I want to run now—because by 2011 I would be *too* cool.

"One time at the Apollo Theatre in Harlem I heard Jackie Moms Mabley talking about the good old days. She said, 'What good old days? I was there. There wasn't no good old days.' I agrees with her. First thing I remember in my youthhood was Depression. Everybody was on Relief that could get on Relief. But if you was colored down South, you had a hard time getting on Relief, even getting in a CCC Camp were you a teen-age boy. Them things was for white. If you be black—be hungry. Be black don't look for help from the Government. Be black just stay black and die. What good old days? When?

"Then come the war. Suppose you wanted to wear one of them pretty Navy uniforms, or fly in the sky. You better be white—else cook or scrub in the Navy, and not fly in no sky. No Negroes in the Air Force. Not then. Suppose you want to give your blood to the Red Cross. Un-uh! No black blood accepted. When they finally did, they put it in black cans. And just try to work in a war plant down South. What good old days?

"Also in war days, try to get on a train down South to go somewhere else. The one COLORED coach was always crowded when it come through your town. 'No more room for Nigras,' the conductor would cry. The good old days? When? They didn't want you in the South and they didn't want to let you out.

"You finally got up North. You sleep six in a room. Work on the docks loading ammunition, with the union not sure it wants you or don't. Ride that long subway to Harlem. Everything so high uptown it uses up all your money in no time. What good old days? Can't even be a clerk in your own butcher shop where you trade in Harlem, or a bartender in the bar where you spend your money. Good old days? When? Where?

"Now they come talking about a cooling-off period. Were I any cooler, I would be dead. How long must I wait? Like the blues says, 'Can I get it now, or must I hesitate?' I am still looking for the good old days and they don't come yet.

"Now they tell me I got to wait forty or fifty years to be President. I do not want to wait that long. I want to be President now, because I wishes to decree Alabama, Georgia, Mississippi, and Louisiana out of the Union. I wishes to give them states to the Devil, because it would take fire and brimstone to straighten them out. I would save only the dogs down there because dogs is nothing but dumb animals and I do not believe in sending dogs to hell.

"The Negroes in them states ought to know Judgment Day is coming —so let them make their peace, get away, or else. If they else, let it be like them Freedom Riders. Else in a big way!

"As to cooling off? Me? Cool off from what? I never held nothing hot. Who has got the guns and dogs and billy clubs and ballots in the South? Who does the lynchings and beatings and mobbings and name-calling? Whose blood rushes to they heads when they see a black face? Who gets hot under the collar when the Supreme Court edicts an edict that don't stick? Who calls every black man *red* that wants a piece of white bread? Suppose I was to run for President? Who would need to cool off most? Not me! Not mine! Not Mose, not Corinna, not Rev. Martin Luther King, neither Rev. Shuttlesworth.[1] Them black mens is cool, already coo-oo-ol, coooooooool, Jack, cool! You be cool too, Mr. President. Don't go putting no ideas in my head about running for President. I just might do it *now*. I am Simple."

Atomic Dream

"Man, I had the awfullest dream last night," said Simple.

"What did you dream?" I asked.

"I drempt that in the next war a white woman was running toward an atom bomb shelter, and some Negroes right behind her ran over her and tromped her. The rest of the white folks started to fight the Negroes, but the Negroes ran over them and tromped them, too. When the bomb fell, the shelter was full of Negroes. Why do you reckon I drempt that?"

"You were just acting out your aggressions, as the psychiatrists say, in dreams."

"Doing which?" asked Simple.

"Getting rid of your hostilities," I said, "working out your own evil by way of a dream. Where did this fantasy of yours take place, North or South?"

"You know it was up North," said Simple. "There wouldn't be no Negroes running over no white woman—by accident or otherwise—down South. In fact, the South would probably have no bomb shelters for Negroes in the next war, anyhow. If they did, it would be a little old Jim Crow shelter in Uncle Tommy's back yard meant just for handkerchief heads. The Freedom Riders would have to ride awhile to get in out of the fallout."

"Do you mean to tell me the white South would be so inhumane as to build public bomb shelters with signs up WHITE ONLY, and none for Negroes? What kind of people live in Dixie?"

"You go down there and see," said Simple. "You Northern Negroes do not know what Jackson or Birmingham is like. It is a bo-biddling! But lemme finish telling you about my dream. When I got down in that bomb shelter, who should be down there but Lena Horne singing the 'Wee Small Hours' blues. Lena was standing on top of an air cooler belting it out like she does at the Waldorf. 'In the wee small hours when the one you love is gone.' And the rest of the Negroes was standing around whooping and hollering just as if they was on Lenox Avenue in the Old Colony Bar and Grill. About that time a minister stood up and said, 'Ain't you-all got no respect for death? You should be kneeling and praying instead of singing and shouting the blues!' But nobody heard him, so he sat down again and started patting his foot himself."

"Where was your wife?" I asked.

"She was completely left out of that dream," said Simple.

"Further proof that you are in need of psychiatry, leaving your wife out in a time like that."

"It were only a dream," said Simple. "In real life, I would have kept Joyce with me, bomb or no bomb. But that night in my dream Joyce were not there. She was dreaming her own dreams on the other side of the bed. Me and Lena, we was singing the blues and waiting for the bomb to fall. By and by it fell—BAM! It blowed me down. And I woke up screaming! My dream had turned into a nightmare.

"Joyce just rolled over kind of sleepy-like and said, 'Jess, what is the matter with you, high again? What time did you come home?'

"I said, 'Baby, don't bother me with them kind of questions. I have just been caught in the fallout.'

" 'What fallout?' says Joyce.

" 'Out of bed,' I said."

Lost Wife

"That man down at the other end of the bar is named Efney," said Simple, "which is a funny name for a man. And he has got a bad deal. Efney's got five children. But no sooner did the oldest one of them get in high school, than his wife had to up and die on him. So Efney brings his old girl friend home to help take care of his children, some of them being only four-five-six years old. But Efney's girl friend is a bar stool girl. Besides she has two children of her own she brought along to Efney's house—which makes seven mouths for him to feed besides him and her. Efney now has his hands full."

"I'll say he has," I affirmed. "Seven children is enough for any man."

"Especially when his wages is less than he would get if all nine of them was to go on welfare. It is better for a man with a big family to be out of work these days than it is for him to work. On relief him and his children get more and bigger checks. Efney's girl friend is still on welfare. Even though she is living with Efney, she keeps her old address and some clothes there, so she can continue to get the checks. The welfare is a wonderful thing for people with more children than they want to take care of. They sure is lucky, since them that gets on welfare need not never get a job."

"Lucky in idleness? I don't agree. Something is wrong with a system where it is more profitable for people *not* to work than it is to work."

"Wrong to *you*," said Simple, "but not to them. Only trouble is Efney's girl friend does not give Efney any money to help feed herself nor her children.

"She says, 'I'm young, so that old Negro is due to take care of me and mine in style. It's me who is doing him a favor, passing my time at his house when I also got my own. He is lucky to latch onto a good-looking pullet like me.' That is what Carlota is going around the bars telling Efney's friends. And his friends is saying, 'That's right,' and wishing they could latch onto Carlota themselves. A friend often ceases to be a friend where womens is involved. I once knew a man's best friend who took his wife away."

"Such cases are not rare," I said. "You are a lucky man. You and Joyce have been married several years now with no sign of a riff, no sign of breaking up."

"The only thing we breaks is our budget," said Simple, "and that not often. But last week I did want some beer to go with the chitterlings Joyce cooks, so she let me have a dollar which she did not mark down on the budget.

"I said, 'Joyce, why do you keep track of all our money so carefully on that budget chart? When it is gone, it is just gone. But if you are going to keep track of everything, why don't you put this beer dollar down?'

"Joyce said, 'I do not want *beer* to show on the budget. That is ex-office.'

"I said, 'Not to me, baby.'

" 'We will never get to buy that house we want in the suburbs,' Joyce says, 'if you keep bursting the budget to buy beer.'

" 'Baby,' I says, 'let's buy a house in Harlem.'

" 'Harlem will soon be nothing but projects and welfare homes,' says Joyce. 'I want to get out where there is leaves and grass and birds. If you loved me, Jess Semple, you would agree with my ambitions.'

"Any time Joyce calls me by my full name, Jess Semple, I know she is serious. So I replies, 'I love you, Joyce, therefore I agrees with your ambitions. But right now, while you set the table, I am going to get my beer.'

" 'Every can of beer is one brick less in the foundations of our future,' says Joyce.

" 'The future of our foundations is you, my wife, my love, my all,' I said. 'Here, take this dollar, put it back in our budget.'

" 'Jesse, go and get your beer,' said Joyce. 'Our future is together. If you need a little beer to cement our bricks, go get it.' Whereupon we kissed. I pity Efney down yonder at the end of the bar who has lost his wife."

Self-Protection

"We crowned him king of kings," said Simple, "not to mention lord of lords. When my Cousin Minnie hit that man with a beer bottle, he were conked and crowned both all at once. Minnie raised a knot on his head bigger than the Koorinoor Diamond which, I hear, were the biggest diamond ever to be set in a crown."

"Why did your cousin attack the poor fellow in so positive a manner?" I asked.

"That man evidently did not know my Cousin Minnie very well, in spite of the fact he were her steady boy friend since last Thanksgivings," said Simple. "I could see trouble coming before the holidays. In the first place, that man did not buy Cousin Minnie what she wanted for Christmas, which were a fur stole. 'I did not ask him for a fur coat,' said Minnie, 'just a stole—and he did not even get that. Come explaining that his funds was short.'

"Well, I knew Minnie were not happy. Still and yet, it being the season of Peace on Earth, she put up with the joker. She even took him out sporting New Year's Eve on her own money. But, Minnie told me, he got so high before the bells tolled that he wanted to send *her* home. He wanted to stay out and run the streets all the night without being bothered with his old lady. Minnie allowed as how that would never do, not with her money that she had lent him to celebrate in his pocket. Whereupon, one word led to another, so he upped his hand at Minnie. Howsoever, Minnie acted like a lady and backed away. She said, 'Daddy, do not show your color in the Mill Ritz Bar. Let's not end the Old Year on a low note!'

"But Rombow were drunk. He must not have read that sign up over the bar which says WE GROW OLD SO QUICK, BUT GROW WISE SO SLOW. When Rombow upped his hand at Cousin Minnie, he did not use common sense. Minnie is a woman not afraid of man, beast, or devil. She is also no respecter of persons. Minnie were just respecting Rombow because they were out in public, it were New Year's Eve, and the bells had not yet tolled. She also at times tried to be a lady, and she did not wish to end the Old Year on a low note. Minnie said again, 'Rombow, I done spoke nice now, but listen I can raise my voice, too.'

" 'You better not raise it at me,' says Rombow.

"Whereupon, Minnie said, 'What?' so loud everybody in the bar heard her, in spite of all the noise going on plus Ray Charles on the juke box. 'What did you say?' says Minnie.

" 'If you can't hear my voice,' says Rombow, 'you can sure feel my hand!' Whiz! He thought he were fast, but Minnie was faster. When Rombow went to slap her, Minnie squatted. The blow went over her head. When Minnie come up, the nearest beer bottle were in her hand. With this Minnie christened, crowned, and conked Rombow all at once.

"Minnie said, 'If you want to be a king, Rom, I will crown you.' She did. A knot sprung out on Rombow's head the size of a hen's egg. But neither the bottle nor his head broke. However, what little sense he had must have been knocked from his head to his feet, because his feet had sense enough to carry him backwards fast, out of Minnie's way, and when he fell, he fell against the juke box. Rombow were stunned, shook up, shocked, and unconscious.

" 'You must be out of your mind,' said Minnie.

"He were, because when he came to, the bells had tolled. Minnie were surrounded by friends drinking to her health, and everybody had yelled *Happy New Year* so much that they were hoarse.

"It was about that time that I come into the bar, having taken Joyce home from Watch Meeting. I spied my Cousin Minnie and she told me her tale. I said, 'Coz, I should have been here to protect you.'

" 'There is as much difference between *should* and *is,* as between last year and this,' says Minnie. '*Should* has gone down the drain, but *is* is here. I am able to protect myself. Happy New Year to you!' "

Haircuts and Paris

"If I had ever been to Paris," said Simple, "I would like to go there one more time once."

"Since you have never been in Paris, how do you know you would?" I asked.

"I know I would, because a friend of mine just came back to New York and told me all about it," said Simple. "He is as dark as me, real colored in complexion, and he said in Paris for the first time in his life, he felt like a *man*."

"I do not see why a Negro has to go all the way to Paris to feel like a man," I said.

"Some do and some don't need to go," said Simple. "Me, I feel like a man anywhere in this American country, because I feel like a man *inside* myself. But some folks are not made like that. Some black men do not feel like men when they are surrounded by white folks who look at them like as if blackness was bad manners or something. It is not bad manners to be black, any more than it is good manners to be white. God made both of us. But white folks in the U.S.A. has got the upper hand—the whip hand—which they have had since the days of slavery. White folks still have a million and one ways of keeping a Negro from feeling like a man—especially if he is a weak Negro like my friend what went to Paris and stayed a year and for the first time said he felt like a man. Me, in Paris, I would feel like *two* men. That is why I want to go, and return, then go again."

"Once you got to Paris, why would you come back?" I asked.

"To get some corn bread and pigs' feet and greens," said Simple, "which is what my friend said he missed so much in Paris. Also to see Jackie Mabley and Pigmeat Markham and Nipsey Russell at the Apollo, and to hear the Caravans sing gospel songs one more time. Then I would return to Paris and stay another year. My friend says the wonderful thing about Europe is that a Negro can get his hair cut anywhere. That is certainly not true in the U.S.A., where a Negro has to look for a *colored* barbershop—in spite of the Civil Rights Bill—just like in most towns down South he still has to look for a *colored* restaurant in which to eat, a *colored* hospital in which to die, and a *colored* undertaker to get buried by, also a *colored* cemetery to be buried in. They has no such jackassery in Europe."

"What?" I said.

"White folks are not jackasses in Europe," said Simple. "In Europe they accepts colored peoples as human beings. Therefore Negroes can get their hair cut anywhere in any barbershop in Paris, France, or Rome, Italy, or Madrid, Spain. Also Negroes can get shaved. Here in the United States to get shaved, a white barber is liable to cut a colored man's throat instead of trimming his beard. It would take a brave black man to set down in a white barbershop in Memphis, Jackson, Tougaloo, Birmingham, Atlanta, or anywhere else down South. With all the love he has got in his heart, I have never read in no newspaper yet where Rev. Martin Luther King has gone into a white barbershop down South and said, 'I love you, barber. Cut my hair.' Martin Luther King has got more sense than that. He knows prayer might not prevail in no white barbershop in Jackson, Birmingham, Atlanta, or Selma. Or in Boston, either."

"You are right," I said. "My dentist's son, colored, attends college in a small town in Ohio where there is no colored barbershop. This young student has to travel forty miles to Toledo to get his hair cut. The white barbershops near the college will not serve him. They politely claim they do not know how to cut colored hair."

"If white Americans can learn how to fly past Venus, go in orbit and make telestars, it looks like to me white barbers in Ohio could learn how to cut colored hair," said Simple. "But since they also might cut my throat, I prefer to go to Paris, get my hair cut there, then come home for corn bread, and return to Paris again. Even here in Harlem, I thank God for Paris barbers. Amen!"

Adventure

"Adventure is a great thing," said Simple, "which should be in everybody's life. According to the Late Late Show on TV, in the old days when Americans headed West in covered wagons, they was almost sure to run into adventure—at the very least a battle with the Red Skins. Nowadays, if you want to run into adventure, go to Alabama or Mississippi where you can battle with the White Skins."

" 'Go West, young man, go West,' is what they used to say," I said. " '*Pioneers, oh, pioneers!*' cried Whitman."

" 'Go South, young man, go South,' is what I would say today," declared Simple. "If I had a son I wanted to make a man out of, I would send him to Jackson, Mississippi, or Selma, Alabama—and not in a covered wagon, but on a bus. Especially if he was a white boy, I would say, 'Go, son, go, and return to your father's house when you have conquered. The White Skins is on the rampage below the Mason-Dixon line, defying the government, denying free Americans their rights. Go see what you can do about it. Go face the enemy.' "

"You would send your son into the maelstrom of Dixie to get his head beaten by a white cracker or his legs bitten by police dogs?"

"For freedom's sake—and adventure—I might even go South myself," said Simple, "if I was white. I think it is more important for white folks to have them kind of adventures than it is for colored. Negroes have been fighting one way or another all our lives—but it is somewhat new to whites. Until lately, they did not even know what a COLORED ONLY sign meant. White folks have always thought they could go anywhere in the world they wanted to go. They are just now finding out that they cannot go into a COLORED WAITING ROOM in the Jim Crow South. They cannot even go into a WHITE WAITING ROOM if they are with colored folks. They never knew before that if you want adventure, all you have to do is cross the color line in the South."

"Then, according to you," I said, "the Wild West can't hold a candle to the Savage South any more."

"Not even on TV," said Simple. "The Savage South has got the Wild West beat a mile. In the old days adventures was beyond the Great Divide. Today they is below the Color Line. Such adventures is much better than the Late Late Show with Hollywood Indians. But in the South, nobody gets scalped. They just get cold cocked. Of course, them robes the Klan sports around in is not as pretty as the feathers Indians used to wear, but they is more scary. And though a Klan holler is not as loud as a Indian war whoop, the Klan is just as sneaky. In cars, not on horseback, they comes under cover of night. If the young people of the North really want excitement, let them go face the Klan and stand up to it.

" 'That is why the South will make a man of you, my son,' I would say. 'Go South, baby, go South. Let a fiery cross singe the beard off your beatnik chin. Let Mississippi make a man out of you.' "

"Don't you think white adults as well as white youth should be exposed to this thing?" I asked.

"Of course," said Simple. "If the white young folks go as Freedom Riders, let the white old folks go as sight-seers—because no sooner than they got down there, they would be Freedom Riders anyhow. If I owned one of these white travel bureaus arranging sight-seeing tours next summer to Niagara Falls, Yellowstone Park, the Grand Canyon, and Pike's Peak, I would also start advertising sight-seeing tours to Montgomery with the National Guard as guides, to Jackson with leather leggings as protection against police dogs, to the Mississippi Prison Farms with picnic lunches supplied by Howard Johnson's, and to the Governor's Mansion with a magnolia for all the ladies taking the tour—and a night in jail without extra charge.

"Negroes would be guaranteed as passengers on all tours, so that there would be sure adventures for everybody. My ads would read:

SPECIAL RATES FOR A WEEK-END IN A TYPICAL MISSISSIPPI JAIL.
Get arrested now, pay later. Bail money not included. Have the time of your lives living the life of your times among the Dixie White Skins. Excitement guaranteed. For full details contact the Savage South Tours, Inc., Jesse B. Semple, your host, wishing you hell."

Minnie's Hype

"When an emergency becomes a habit, that is carrying emergencies too far," said Simple over a glass of brew.

"What emergency are you speaking of now?"

"Borrowing money," said Simple.

"Is your Cousin Minnie annoying you again?"

"*Worrying* me would be a better way of putting it," said Simple. "But if I did not like Minnie, I would not be worried. People you like that are worrisome are the most worrisome kind of all. The one thing wrong with my Cousin Minnie is that she wants to live off of everybody else. Minnie is big, strong, healthy, and bold, so why should she have to make a habit of borrowing from me every time she sees me in this bar? And I am married, too."

"Doesn't Minnie have a job?"

"Not if she can help it," said Simple. "She does not believe in *live and let live*—earning her own living and letting other people earn theirs. She wants them to earn *her* living too. That I refuse to do. She is only an off-cousin of mine, anyhow—not by marriage."

"Blood is thicker than marriage."

"True," said Simple. "But if all who are not married denied their kinship, few people would be related in this world. To some folks a marriage license is too much trouble to purchase. And sometimes they can't wait that long. I do not hold her parents' doings against Minnie, nohow. She came into this world about the same time I did down in Virginia. I played with Minnie as a child. Everybody says she is my cousin, and I take for granted she is. Still and yet, she do not have to borrow from me every time she turns around. I am no bank. When Minnie came up here to Harlem looking for freedom, she must have thought Freedom was *my* name. I told her in the beginning I was not named Freedom, my home is not the North, and my wife did not love in-laws—even if Minnie is an out-law."

"Go ahead and lend your cousin a couple of bucks," I said. "It won't hurt you."

"I do not have it," said Simple. "Besides Minnie wants twenty dollars to pay her rent."

"Oh," I said.

"Oh, is right," said Simple. "Minnie could easy have paid her rent last week with what she spent getting a blonde streak put in her hair after it were denaturalized."

"Do you begrudge a woman her beauty rites?"

"When it is the man that has to pay for them," said Simple.

Yachts

"Sometimes I read in the papers about these peoples with yachtses," said Simple.

"Yachts," I said.

"Yachtses," said Simple.

"*Yachts*," I repeated.

"Anyhow, I would like to own one of them ships," said Simple. "Peoples with their own boats can sail the seas whichever way they want to, and guide their compasses where-so-ever they wishes. It must be wonderful. Nobody can tell you to go thisaway or thataway or whatever way to South America or North. Oh, I wish I was rich and had a yacht. I would sail away from Harlem any time I had a mind to."

"What about your wife?" I said.

"I would sail away if she even looked at me cross-eyed and said, 'Boo!' Womens quarrels too much. If Joyce even said, 'Why don't you hang up your clothes?' I would sail away. No more listening to a whole lot of yap-yap-yap—until I got ready to come back."

"What woman do you think would put up with a gone-away husband most of the time?" I asked.

"I would come sailing back up the Harlem River to Harlem once in a while," said Simple. "When I did, the lights would light up on Lenox Avenue, the radios all would play jump music, and the TVs would show first-run features in my honor. I would be back home. Joyce would kiss me at the door, then run to the stove to cook me the kind of dinner I like, and then—oh, then she would be mine all over again. There is nothing like absence to make the heart grow fonder—so they say, especially a woman's. But I do not believe I will test it."

"No?"

"No! If I had a yacht I would just take Joyce with me. I would not go sailing away all by myself. No."

"The possibility of your getting a yacht and sailing away is so remote, it is hardly likely you will have to face such an eventuality."

"Eventually, Joyce wants a home in the suburbans," said Simple. "She cares nothing for boats. Joyce wants wall-to-wall carpets and a chandelier. That is why Joyce keeps skimming our budget every week to put money in the Carver Bank to buy a house. But houses is so high these days, and mortgages so long to pay off, that I tell her by the time we get the house paid for I will be too old to even mow the lawn. After years of shoveling snow around a house, I would be broke down, anyhow. I prefers to stay here in Harlem in a nice warm apartment where the super shovels the snow, and the janitor sweeps the sidewalks and tends the furnace. All I do is pay the rent. But Joyce declares she wants to own a piece of land all her *own* before she goes to Glory and I go to hell. Joyce wants a little spot of grass, a house with a porch and a porch swing to set and rock in the cool of the evening and hear the crickets chirping in the dark.

"Me, Boyd, I prefer a bar booth; after dark I like a juke box blaring, and lights, lights, lights. I always did like lots of lights, don't know why, lots of people, don't know why, and sometimes a lot of noise. If I had a yacht, I would fill it up with friends. My boat would not only roll but it would rock with music all day long, jump with dancing all night long, smell with pots of food cooking in the galley, biscuits baking in the oven. At all hours there would be lights strung up along the decks, beautiful lights, and on each and every mast flags flying. Every time my boat whistle blowed, it would blow in the key of B-flat, which is the key of the blues.

"Then I would remember the lights shining on Lenox Avenue and how sometimes there might be a flag flying outside the Theresa, maybe on the Fourth of July, or like when Castro was staying there, and I would get homesick for 125th Street. On my fine yacht out yonder on some strange sea where the flying fishes play, I would turn my boat around and head home, yes, I would—*right then and there*—head home to Harlem, U.S.A. Why, I don't know, but I would."

Ladyhood

"When the man on the next stool last night asked my Cousin Minnie how old she were," said Simple, "she told him, 'Oh, about eleventeen! A man should not ask a lady's age,' she said, 'no more than he should ask if she has a wig on—which I do not tonight. Every strand is my own hair.'

" 'Can you do the Monkey?' asked the man.

" 'Backforwards and forwards,' said Minnie, 'including the Jerk.'

"Whereupon, the man put a quarter in the juke box and him and Minnie performed, until the bartender pointed at the sign No DANCING and made them stop because it had been five minutes since they had last bought a drink, and the barman's point and purpose is to keep his licker moving."

"I don't see how the bar makes much off of you then," I said to Simple. "But where is your Cousin Minnie tonight?"

"Home resting up until Friday—when the studs get paid," said Simple. "Minnie do not come out on quiet nights. She knows I do not treat relatives—except on Christmas—so she need not look to me to quench her thirst. To be a girl-cousin, Minnie can drink awhile, Jack, yet I have never seen her stagger, let alone reel. Minnie goes out of any bar under her own steam, no matter how many Scotches and sodas she has put away. You have to give it to Minnie—that chick carries her licker well and protects her ladyhood, too. Minnie knows she is a lone woman in this big city—except for me, her Cousin Jess."

"Your Cousin Minnie seems quite self-reliant."

"She is used to making her way in the world, if that is what you mean," said Simple. "If necessary, Minnie will even work to keep her head above water. But not if any other kind of lifeboat or lifeguard is in sight. To be a big woman, Minnie can look so little and lost and lone and helpless sometimes, setting on a bar stool with nothing but a little glass of Scotch when what she really craves is a double, that almost any strange man will take pity on her and say, 'Baby, I beg your pardon, perhaps you would accept some refreshments on me.'

"If he makes a polite approach, Minnie will turn her head to one side, somewhat down, and reply, 'With utmost pleasure—if you introduced yourself. But I do not drink with no man I do not know.'

" 'My name is So-and-so-and-so,' says the stud.

"Whereupon, Minnie says her name is Minnette, and that she were a Johnson before her mother married her third stepfather. Then, says Minnie, she took the name of Ashmore. But sometimes Minnie forgets which stepfather's name she took—*Butler* or *Ashmore*—which makes no difference because by then she has ordered a double Scotch on the man and their friendship is cemented. Minnie do not spend another dime of her own money that evening. My Cousin Minnie has a way with men, Boyd. She makes chumps out of them so sweet-like. It might take a man several months to find out Minnie can be big, bad, bold, and boisterous if she wants to. If a man goes too far with Minnie, she can raise her voice and embarrass him proper. Ray Charles can be screaming on the TV and Bill Doggett yelling on the juke box both at once, but you can still hear Minnie in the bar above all that noise telling some old joker, 'Don't let your licker go to your head, daddy, because if you do, I'll blow you off your feet. You done barked up the wrong tree, insulting me. Bartender, tell this man to vacate my person.'

"But by that time it is nearly closing, and the man has spent all his money anyhow. If he makes no argument, Minnie will calm down and say real ladylike, as she rises to leave—alone—'Good night.'

"But if the man raises his voice and asserts his manhood, it is not good night that Minnie says to that cat as she goes out the door. Oh, no, it is not good night. It is a word that begins with a letter I do not like to mention. Minnie knows more bad words than I do. To tell the truth, sometimes I think my Cousin Minnie is a disgrace to the race."

"Why?" I asked.

"Because, in protecting her ladyhood, Minnie does not always act like a lady. I told you about the time she hit that man with a beer bottle New Year's Eve, did I not?"

"You did. So?"

"It would have been more politer—and cheaper, too—had Minnie hit him with something that did not contain good alcohol," said Simple. "Or if she had screamed and throwed a glass. But Minnie did not scream. She just up and knocked the man out with a bottle. Should not a lady settle things in a more gentler manner? Maybe even faint first?"

"Your concept of the word 'lady' evidently comes from remote romantic sources," I said. "Gentle ladies in the days of antiquity never had to face the problems Minnie has to face. In fact, the whole conventional concept of the word 'lady' is tied up with wealth, high standing, and a sheltered life for women. Minnie has to face the world everyday, in fact, do battle with it."

"True," said Simple, "to remain a lady, Minnie often has to fight. It is not always easy for a colored lady to keep her ladyhood."

"You are bringing up race again," I said. "But this time I think you put your finger on the crux of the argument."

"The crust of the argument is that Minnie believes in peace so much she will fight for it," said Simple. "When Minnie wants the right to be let alone, she means to *be let alone*. Yet she will lead a man on, let him spend his whole wages on Scotch, beer, or wine—it depending on how much wages he has got as to which class she puts him in. Then when the man wants to bother Minnie, she does not wish to be bothered. That is what leads to trouble. I have told my cousin that mens were not made to be taken advantage of. But ever since Eve, that is what womens have done. I reckon I cannot change Minnie."

"Men do not have to let women run away with their senses," I said.

"No," said Simple, "but they do. There was a time when a woman could twist me, as much sense as I got, around her little finger. In fact, at one time Zarita had me all balled up in her little tiny fist. But that were before I met Joyce, my wife, who now has got me tied to her apron strings."

"Not very tightly," I said, "as often as I see you here in Paddy's Bar."

"Before I got married, I used to be in here every night the Lord sent," said Simple. "Now I am only in here every other night—or so."

"Or so, is right," I said.

"But I do not drink like I once did," claimed Simple. "Neither do I stray. My eyes might roam, but I stay home. I have got a good home, pal, which I mean to keep. What I wish is that my Cousin Minnie would settle down and make herself a good marriage, too. Minnie has been in Harlem long enough to get the country out of her hair now, and Virginia out of her system. Yet Minnie is in this bar more often than me. She is getting to be a settled woman now, so she ought to settle down—and not on a bar stool neither. A lady should not hang out in places which are shady. I have told Minnie she is liable to get hurt sometimes, the way she does her boy friends. A man can put up with so much, but Minnie sometimes piles it on."

"From all you have told me about Minnie, she can protect herself," I said.

"At the expense of her ladyhood," said Simple. "A woman should not put herself in a position where she has to fight her way out."

"You never forced a woman into such a position yourself?" I asked.

"Being a man, naturally, I have sometimes tried to make my point—and over-made it," admitted Simple. "My first wife, Isabel, once attacked me so ferocious, the neighbors had to help me get out of the house. That were in Baltimore. Since I come to New York, I have got more sense. Yet there is some chumps in Harlem who take one look at any woman, including Minnie, and their senses desert them. What is it about womens that makes a man lose his mind?"

"You answer that, if you can."

"I reckon it must be their ladyhood," declared Simple.

Coffee Break

"My boss is white," said Simple.

"Most bosses are," I said.

"And being white and curious, my boss keeps asking me just what does THE Negro want. Yesterday, he tackled me during the coffee break, talking about THE Negro. He always says 'THE Negro,' as if there was not 50-11 different kinds of Negroes in the U.S.A.," complained Simple. "My boss says, 'Now that you-all have got the Civil Rights Bill and the Supreme Court, Adam Powell in Congress, Ralph Bunche in the United Nations, and Leontyne Price singing in the Metropolitan Opera, plus Dr. Martin Luther King getting the Nobel Prize, what more do you want? I am asking you, just what does THE Negro want?'

" 'I am not THE Negro,' I says. 'I am *me*.'

" 'Well,' says my boss, 'You represent THE Negro.'

" 'I do not,' I says. 'I represent my own self.'

" 'Ralph Bunche represents you, then,' says my boss, 'and Thurgood Marshall and Martin Luther King. Do they not?'

" 'I am proud to be represented by such men, if you say they represent me,' I said. 'But all them men you name are *way* up there, and they do not drink beer in my bar. I have never seen a single one of them mens on Lenox Avenue in my natural life. So far as I know, they do not even live in Harlem. I cannot find them in the telephone book. They all got private numbers. But since you say they represent THE Negro, why do you not ask them what THE Negro wants?'

" 'I cannot get to them,' says my boss.

" 'Neither can I,' I says, 'so we both is in the same boat.'

" 'Well then, to come nearer home,' says my boss, 'Roy Wilkins fights your battles, also James Farmer.'

" 'They do not drink in my bar, neither,' I said.

" 'Don't Wilkins and Farmer live in Harlem?' he asked.

" 'Not to my knowledge,' I said. 'And I bet they have not been to the Apollo since Jackie Mabley cracked the first joke.'

" 'I do not know him,' said my boss, 'but I see Nipsey Russell and Bill Cosby on TV.'

" 'Jackie Mabley is no *him*,' I said. 'She is a *she*—better known as Moms.'

" 'Oh,' said my boss.

" 'And Moms Mabley has a story on one of her records about Little Cindy Ella and the magic slippers going to the junior Prom at Ole Miss which tells all about what THE Negro wants.'

" 'What's its conclusion?' asked my boss.

" 'When the clock strikes midnight, Little Cindy Ella is dancing with the President of the Ku Klux Klan, says Moms, but at the stroke of twelve, Cindy Ella turns back to her natural self, black, and her blonde wig turns to a stocking cap—and her trial comes up next week.'

" 'A symbolic tale,' says my boss, 'meaning, I take it, that THE Negro is in jail. But you are not in jail.'

" 'That's what you think,' I said.

" 'Anyhow, you claim you are not THE Negro,' said my boss.

" 'I am not,' I said. 'I am *this* Negro.'

" 'Then what do *you* want?' asked my boss.

" 'To get out of jail,' I said.

" 'What jail?'

" 'The jail you got me in.'

" 'Me?' yells my boss. 'I have not got you in jail. Why, boy, I like you. I am a liberal. I voted for Kennedy. And this time for Johnson. I believe in integration. Now that you got it, though, what more do you want?'

" 'Reintegration,' I said.

" 'Meaning by that, what?'

" 'That you be integrated with *me*, not me with you.'

" 'Do you mean that I come and live in Harlem?' asked my boss. 'Never!'

" 'I live in Harlem,' I said.

" 'You are adjusted to it,' said my boss. 'But there is so much crime in Harlem.'

" 'There are no two-hundred-thousand-dollar bank robberies, though,' I said, 'of which there was three lately *elsewhere*—all done by white folks, and nary one in Harlem. The biggest and best crime is outside of Harlem. We never has no half-million-dollar jewelry robberies, no missing star sapphires. You better come uptown with me and reintegrate.'

" 'Negroes are the ones who want to be integrated,' said my boss.

" 'And white folks are the ones who do *not* want to be,' I said.

" 'Up to a point, we do,' said my boss.

" 'That is what THE Negro wants,' I said, 'to remove that *point*.'

" 'The coffee break is over,' said my boss."

Lynn Clarisse

"How nice to be respectably dirty," said Simple's cousin, Lynn Clarisse, who had one of those double names like many girls, colored and noncolored, have down South. "How nice," she said "to be able to read *Another Country* and *The Carpetbaggers* and John Burroughs and Henry Miller and *The Messenger,* even *City of Night* and *Last Exit to Brooklyn* without blushing—because everybody else is reading them. There are lots of things in those books I know, of course, since I am full-grown and adult. But there are more things I don't know, at least not from experience."

"Let's experience a few," I said—testing her out, of course.

"We can't even get started on the spur of the moment, Mr. Boyd," she said, coming right back with an answer without blushing. No stammering. She wasn't a bit "country."

"You must have gone to a sophisticated college," I said. "Was it white, black, or integrated?"

"Fisk, as I know *you know* I told you," she said.

"Yes, you did," I remembered, "last night when Simple took me by his house to meet you. How come you have a cousin like Simple?"

"He's in the family," said Lynn Clarisse, "and is one relative who happens to be down with it. I love that cat, and I love his Harlem."

"I do, too," I said. "He told me you were colleged. But I sort of expected a girl whose mind did not go beyond the classroom, you know, conventional."

"There are no limits to where the mind or body goes," said Lynn Clarisse. "My body has been on Freedom Rides. See that scar where an Alabama cop tried to break my neck with his billy club. He just broke my shoulder, but it left a scar on my neck where his club burst the skin open. It might sound pretentious to say it, but while my body was in Alabama that night, my mind was on Sartre and Genet."

"Are you really colored?" I asked, just playing, of course.

"Are you blind?" she replied. She laughed. I laughed. "I am darker than dark brownskin." But the mystery was not solved. She had never been North before, Lynn Clarisse. So, how come so suave, so bright, so—well?

"Maybe you don't know it," she said, "but we do have libraries in Nashville, too. Integrated just like New York. And Fisk, a colored college, you know, only slightly integrated, has one of the best libraries in the country, and a librarian who helps students choose good books. We have a browsing room where some can browse, and others can sleep, whisper sweet nothings, or just clean their fingernails—sort of nice place. As for reading books, even far-out books, even beatnik books, fine. Only there are not enough books for me down South, which is one reason I came to New York. Or maybe I came to see books in action. Slow motion, though, so don't rush me, Mr. Boyd."

"I'm too flabbergasted," I said. "I can't believe you are Jesse B. Semple's cousin."

"Flesh and blood," she replied. "And he brought me in this café, which is the nicest one, so he says, on 125th Street. You know he's up there at the bar, so if you still don't believe I'm his cousin, call him and ask him."

"Let's not bother Simple this moment," I said. "We're cozy back here in this booth. Say, Lynn Clarisse, have you seen any plays in New York?"

"Not yet."

"Could I take you to see some? What do you want to see?"

"Anything with my people in it," said Lynn Clarisse, "the Sammy Davis musical, Ruby Dee in Shakespeare, Gilbert Price, Diana Sands, a LeRoi Jones play if any are running, *Othello*."

"You are a race woman for true," I said.

"I've got to keep up with my own culture," said Lynn Clarisse. "Those plays will hardly be touring down South."

"I thought you were going to stay up North awhile?"

"A few weeks. Then I'm going back South. We've got things to do."

"More Freedom Rides?"

"Voter Registration."

"I'll miss you when you leave."

"Come down South," said Lynn Clarisse.

"We've got things to do in Harlem, too," I said.

"And me, I have got something to do right now," interrupted Simple at the edge of our booth. "I have got to go home."

"All married men should be home by midnight," I said, motioning him away.

"Also all young ladies who come out in the evening with their cousins in Harlem," added Lynn Clarisse. "So good night, Mr. Boyd."

"You are both going and leave me all alone in this bar?" I asked.

"With 50-odd Negroes and the white proprietor, you'll have company," said Simple. "I will even order you a beer on me and drop a quarter in the juke box before I depart, so you can listen to Nina Simone.
Good night, old boy."

"Good night, my erstwhile friend."

"Good night, Mr. Boyd," said Lynn Clarisse.

"Good night!"

Interview

"Sometimes the *New York Times* looks almost like the Harlem *Amsterdam News*," said Simple. "There is so much Negro news some days from front to back in the *Times* that it seems like a colored paper. My wife, Joyce, says she reads the *Times* because it contains all the news that is fit to print. But for me it do not have as many pictures as the *Daily News*. Also it is hard to make out in the *Times* what the winning number is. For them that places bets on the numbers each and every day, and several times a day, that is important. Now, I am not much of a gambling man myself. But practically all my neighbors plays the numbers."

"I thought numbers was illegal in New York," I said.

"Ha-ha! If it wasn't for the numbers, half the people in Harlem would be earning no spending change at all, and Adam Powell would never have got on the front pages of the papers for being sued over how they say he called that widow lady a bag-woman.

"If the *New York Times* would just print the lead numbers, also the final number up there on its front page in that top left-hand box underneath 'All the News That's Fit to Print,' that paper might outsell the *Daily News* in Harlem—because even in the *News* the numbers is hard to unscramble for them that do not know how. Numbers might as well be printed out plain in the New York papers. If playing numbers is a sin, since sin is so open, why should it be hidden? If a man can bet at the race track, or play bingo in church, why should he not play the numbers in the barbershop, in his car, or, if you are a lady, in your beauty shop or laundromat?"

"Folks do play numbers in all those places," I said, "so why ask unnecessary questions?"

"Just to make conversation," grinned Simple. "You know I like to talk."

"I know," I said. "But you used to talk about civil rights."

"Yes," said Simple. "So many statements have been made, so many words have been said, so many reports rendered, surveys surveyed, Freedom Rides rode, and speeches spoke, sit-ins sat, that I do not know what else to say that is polite. What I were to say now would not be fit to print."

"Do you expect to be quoted by the *Times*?" I laughed.

"Not hardly," said Simple. "My name is not Roy Wilkins, neither Rev. King. I am also not this famous writer whose name is Baldwin. And no white reporter has caught me on a Harlem corner yet to get a candid interview from me, just a man in the street, because I do not spend my time on corners. When white folks look in this bar and find it full of Negroes, they most in generally do not come in, not even to see me. So I have not been interviewed."

"Suppose you were caught some night on a corner and interviewed by a white reporter from a downtown paper, what would you say?"

"An interview means express your views, does it not?"

"I think so," I said.

"Then would it not be better for a man to *view* my views, rather than just to hear my views?" asked Simple.

"Probably so," I said, "if visualization be possible."

"Then to that young white reporter I would say, 'Actions speak louder than words, so get down with the action, man.' I would tell him, 'Move to Harlem, man. At the same time, let me move downtown where you live. Change pads with me. You and your family take my apartment uptown, and let me and my family take your apartment downtown. Just for a month, we will swap places. Then after thirty days, you interview me and I will interview you. By that time you will have found out how much the difference is in the price of a pound of potatoes uptown and a pound of potatoes downtown, how much the difference is for what you pay for rent downtown and what I pay for rent uptown, how different cops look downtown from how cops look uptown, how much more often streets is cleaned downtown than they is uptown. All kinds of things you will see in Harlem, and not have to be told. After we swap pads, you would not need to interview me,' I would say, 'so let's change first and interview later.'"

"You would just be trying to make it hard for that young white reporter," I said. "You know he would have no time to make an investigation in depth of life in Harlem, so why not simply give him your summation in a few words?"

"I could do it in *one* word," said Simple, "but it would not be a word fit to print."

Simply Simple

"Almost nobody in this world ever does everything right," said Simple, "so everybody ought to have the right to do *some* things wrong—including Adam Powell. Powell is a Baptist. When I were a child in Virginia, the Baptists could do no wrong. Also, down South if you was *not* a Baptist, your soul were lost. Just to be sprinkled a Methodist, your soul was just not saved. You had to be dipped—with water in your ears Baptist-style—to be saved. When I were baptized, I was almost near drowned. That Sunday when I come up out of that holy water, the minister said, 'Jesse B. Semple, what have you to say?'

"I said, 'Reverend, you is trying to drown me.'

"Old Rev. said, 'Has the Spirit entered into your soul this morning?'

"I said, 'All I know is, I am full of water.'

"Rev. said, 'You are one of these hardened sinners. You must go and come again.'

"I went—but I have not been baptized again. But, since I have been having a toothache lately, I think I will be a Christian Scientist like my wife lately is. Joyce says a toothache is all mind."

"I thought you told me you loved gospel songs," I said. "There is no gospel singing in Christian Science churches."

"What?" asked Simple. "Then I will go to Bishop Child's temple where there is a fine choir. I was just trying to save dentist's bills and follow my wife's advice."

"Religion is designed to save your soul," I said, "not your teeth."

"Neither does religion help you on your income tax," said Simple. "Look at Adam Powell, pastor of the biggest Baptist church in the world, and they got him in the income-tax wringer. I asked Joyce what the Christian Scientists would say about that. Joyce said Science would say, 'Nothing is but thinking makes it so.'

"I said to my wife, 'If that be true, then what about our budget for food, house, and upkeep? Some weeks you tell me you cannot balance our budget unless I give you *all* my salary. Why don't you just *think* that I gave it all to you? Then our budget would be balanced and everything would be O.K.'

"Joyce said, 'Jess Semple,' and she shook her finger, 'don't be simple!'"

"I said, 'Baby, don't shake your finger in my face.' That is probably why Venus got her arms cut off—from shaking her fingers in some man's face once too often. And look at Mona Lisa smiling that sly little old smile, setting there thinking up ways to bedevil a man. I can tell by how she looks, Mona Lisa is up to no good purpose. If Mona Lisa was to come to life here in New York and take the A Train to Harlem, I would send her right back to France where she belongs. That woman would ruin a man—like Desdemona did Old Fellow."

"You mean Othello?" I said.

"Whoever that Negro were that was driv mad by a white handkerchief," said Simple.

"It was not Desdemona's fault," I explained. "It was Iago's."

"Whoever it were, Old Fellow had seen too many of them Mona Lisa smiles by that time to trust any woman," declared Simple. "Me, I trust nobody but my wife. She very seldom smiles. Joyce laughs—and when Joyce laughs, she's got a whole mouth full of teeth that flash like a house in the sea—I am telling you, man, I love to see Joyce laugh. But oh, my! When my wife gets mad, her eyes flash like lightning and her lips get thin as a buzz saw. That is when I leave the house and come here to the bar to get me a beer. Joyce never did smile no in-between smile like Mona Lisa."

"Did you go to the museum to see Mona Lisa?" I asked.

"I did not," said Simple, "but Joyce went and come back and told me what she looked like. I also seed Mona Lisa in all the papers. Even our Harlem *Amsterdam News* had her picture on the front page. That is why I thought Mona was colored. But my wife told me, no, she is not Afro American, she is white. I might have knowed in that case a man dare not say, 'Hi, baby!' to her for fear he will be put out of the museum.

"Joyce asked me why would I want to say, 'Hi, baby!' to Mona Lisa.

"I said, 'Just to see if she would laugh.'

"Joyce said, 'It is very crude of a man to speak to a strange woman you do not know.'

"I said, 'If I paid a dollar to look at Mona Lisa in a museum, I should at least have the privilege of saying hello to her. Even if she did come from France, she is no more than any other woman displaying herself in public, except that Mona is in a frame and you do not see much more than her head. I would like to see how Mona is built, myself.'

" 'Mona Lisa is a work of art. Her face reveals her all,' said Joyce. 'That single detail of her smile speaks mysteries.'

" 'Miseries,' I said, 'also hell and damnation for whoever were her husband.'

" 'How do you know she had a husband?' said Joyce.

" 'The *Amsterdam News* says Mona were pregnant. And when a thing is in the papers,' I said, 'everybody believes it.'

" 'The papers do not know anything about the private life of Mona Lisa,' said Joyce. 'Neither does anybody else. What does her smile mean? Who knows?'

" 'Maybe she is listening to a record by Dick Gregory,' I said."

Golden Gate

"If I was of mind to give a Christmas gift to the Devil," said Simple, leaning on the bar with an empty glass of beer, "I would give him Mississippi, the whole state of Mississippi, police dogs and all."

"You would be too generous with the Devil," I said, "giving him a whole state with all of those sinners in it to torture. He would have a lot of fun."

"I would not want the Devil to have fun with no present I gave him," said Simple. "No! So I better give something to bedevil him. Maybe I'd give him all the roughnecks in Harlem—garbage out the windows, pop bottles, and lighted cigarette butts. I would have the Devil hit on the head with a sack of garbage every time he switched down the streets of hell."

"I would go you one better. For Christmas I would turn the Devil black and let him find out what Jim Crow is like."

"Hell sure must be full of white folks," said Simple, "so if the Devil was black, he would be bound to have a hard time. Suppose he wanted to drive a train and be an engineer, the Railroad Brotherhoods in hell would not let him in the union. Suppose he wanted to get a cup of coffee driving on the highway between the Capital of hell and Baltimore, he would have a hard time. Suppose he wanted to play golf in Alabama, he would be burnt up. To turn him black would be a *real* Un-Merry Christmas for the Devil. But since I am not going to hell myself, why worry about it. I am wondering what it is gonna be like when I get to Glory. There must be white folks up there, too.

"You know," continued Simple. "Last night I dreamt I died and went to heaven and Old Governor of Mississippi, Alabama, or Georgia, or wherever he is from, had got there before me, and didn't want to let me in. He was standing at the Golden Gate, right beside Saint Peter, when I come ghosting up.

"He said, 'What are you doing here, Jess Semple? Don't you know you have to use the rear entrance?'

" 'What rear entrance?' I says.

" 'The COLORED ENTRANCE,' says Old Governor, 'around the back!'

"I said, 'I did not know heaven was located in the South. I thought it was *up* not *down*. Saint Peter, do you hear the man?'

"Saint Peter said, 'Heaven is so full of white folks now I have no control over it any more.'

"I said, 'How did so many white folks get to heaven, Saint?'

"Old Peter said, 'Jesse B. Semple, I do not know, but they are here.'

" 'I did not realize I was in hell,' I said. 'I thought when I riz through space from my dying bed, I had landed at the Gate of Heaven. Anyway, Peter, is not my sins washed whiter than snow? Am I not white now inside and out?'

"Whereupon, Old Down-home Governor spoke up and said, 'You have to bathe in the River of Life to be washed whiter than snow. The River of Life is in heaven. You are not inside yet, Simple. Therefore, you are still black. White is right, black get back! You are not coming in the front entrance.'

"I said, 'It is too bad I left my weapons down on earth. I am not a Freedom Rider, neither a sit-in kid. The two cheeks I have to turn have done been turned enough. They shall turn no more. You-all better get out of my way and lemme through this Golden Gate.'

"Saint Peter begun to wring his hands. He said, 'I will go call Gabriel. He is one of your folks. He can explain to you how things is up here since the white folks took over.'

"I said, 'Call Gabriel, nothing. If you gonna call anybody, call God!'

" 'God is busy with Vietnam, West Berlin, and NATO,' said Peter.

" 'I did not know God's name was Uncle Sam,' I said. 'Besides, I am as much angel as you, Peter. If you and Old Gov. there don't get out of my way and let me in this gate, I will take my left wing and slap you both down. Then I will take my right wing and whip you good.'

" 'Jesse B., we go in for nonviolence in heaven,' cried Peter.

" 'I am not in heaven, yet,' says I, 'only on the threshold. But if I don't get in, it won't be because I didn't try. Where is Old Governor gone at?'

" 'He has run to call his dogs,' said Peter.

" 'You mean to tell me, you let Southern white folks and their dogs both in heaven,' I asked. 'What is the sky coming to? Earth were bad enough. Maybe the Lord sent for me to clean up heaven. In which case, wait a minute. I will ghost back to earth and round up my boys from Harlem. I will ask them are you willing to die for your rights in heaven as on earth? If so, *die now*, make ghosts out of the Golden Gate. White folks have done got up there and made an American out of Saint Peter. They have set up a kennel of police dogs beside the River Jordan. They have put up WHITE ONLY signs at the milk-and-honey counter. Mens, do you intend to stand for this? Whereupon, from their stepladders on every corner in Harlem they will answer, "No!" Peter, I'll bet this Golden Gate will open then. We'll see. We'll see!'

"Whiz-zzz-zz-z! But when I ghosted back to earth, I woke up kicking and sweating, and found out that it were nothing but a dream. I were not dead at all—just having nightmares in my sleep. It is a good thing, because had my dream been real, I would of tore up that Golden Gate! Plumb up! White folks can run hell, if they want to, but they better not start no stuff with me in Glory Land."

Junkies

"Something is always happening to a man, especially if he is colored," said Simple at the bar. "The next atom bomb is liable to fall on me. Of course, the good thing about the bomb is that it will fall on a whole lot of other people, too—some of who deserves to be annihilated. I am perfectly willing to go myself, if my enemies in Mississippi are taken along with me. 'Greater love hath no man than that he lay down his life to get even.' "

"Where did you get that quote?" I asked. "It's not in the Bible."

"I made it up myself," said Simple. "An eye for an eye, a wig for a wig, and a tooth for a tooth. When both eyes are gone, all teeth are knocked out, and all wigs snatched, then let the bomb fall."

"Are you trying to say you are in favor of atomic warfare?"

"Air-raid shelters would do no good," said Simple, "because when you come out, your favorite bar would be blowed to hell and gone, your best barbershop would be missing, and your pastor dead from passive resistance. Passive resistance is not for me. I say, if die you must, let's die going down with the action."

"You are a fascist, a Birchite, an extreme rightest," I said.

"Is I?" said Simple. "Since the Republican Party seems to be going extreme right these days, I think colored folks ought to go extreme black. Since one end is pro and the other end is con, if you try to pro-test and con-test in between, you is sure to get hit. I sees no point in being the middleman. If I am all them names you just called me for being on the black side, O.K.—you be what you want to be and let me be, too. And buy me a beer for the sake of our friendship. If the bomb falls, I will let you come in my bomb shelter."

"How kind of you," I said. "But I don't believe in violence on an international or national scale."

"Between the violent and the nonviolent," said Simple, "it looks like to me neither one of them will win in the U.S.A., because if there was to be a race war, how is twenty million Negroes going to fight two hundred million white folks? And if Negroes was to pray-in and kneel-in and sing-in from now till Doom's Day and the white folks did not want to give us our civil rights, what more nonviolence could we do to make them stop twisting freedom's arm? Pray how? Picket who? Boycott what? March where?"

"Get the ballot," I said, "and use it. Vote! Vote in the South where we would have more than the balance of power. Vote in larger numbers and more intelligently in the North. Put more Negro representatives in political positions."

"Buy me a beer," said Simple, holding up his empty glass, "and let me tell you about Cousin Minnie. She hit the numbers last week for $116 clear cash after she had paid off her runner for being honest and bringing her her money."

"I declare!" I exclaimed.

"Minnie will declare nothing when income-tax time comes," said Simple. "It is a good thing Minnie is not famous like Adam Powell, else the government would get her. I would hate to be rich and famous, too."

"That's a remote eventuality," I said.

"A remote something," said Simple. "Almost as remote as my beer—which is gone. You are not setting us up tonight?"

"My bar money is low."

"Mine, too," sighed Simple. "My wife do not trust me with more than cigarette change from one day to another. And she allots nothing for beer. Joyce is a budget fiend. She loves to keep it balanced, but she hides the scales. Right now I needs a glass of cool keggie. Must I beggie?"

"Begging will do no good. I told you my funds are low."

"So you've got nothing to spend, and you won't spend that," said Simple.

"Oh, well, one for the road," I said.

"Whilst I tell you what I heard, which is an amazement," said Simple. "Every time I see Minnie, that cousin of mine has some new kind of tale to tell. Last night she was telling me about a junkie, the son of her neighbors next door. Minnie says that boy's mother is ashamed of him—a fine young man what turned out to be a junkie while still in his teen-age years. They are a respectable hard-working couple, his father being in the Post Office, and that boy is their only child. Minnie says they keep a nice home. But it seems lately their son-boy has been going from bad to worse on junk, using the hard stuff, and stealing things out of the house to support his habit—anything he can sell or pawn—their Chinese vase, the clock radio, the electric iron, the toaster, even to the bathroom scales.

"His mother has been trying to hide all these happenings from his father, this being their only son. She did not want the old man to know he took dope. Whenever the son would steal something, if Mama could find the pawn tickets in his dresser drawer, she would go and get the stuff back before Papa missed it. Almost every other day she had to go and get Papa's electric razor out of pawn. This went on all last summer. But seems like now the boy's habit has been getting worse and worser. One fix a day does not do him no more, neither two. Seems like he needs more and more money to feed the pushers. Do you know, that first cold snap one day last week, what his mother caught him doing?"

"No," I said.

"She caught him rummaging in her closet taking out her fur coat—her one and only fur coat that her husband worked hard to pay for. It were not a mink, but it was a good coat, and her son was about to steal it."

"What did she do?" I asked.

"Begged and pleaded with him not to take it. But he said, 'Mama, I got to have some cash.'

"She gave him what little money she had. But he just looked at them three or four dollars and hung onto the coat. 'I got to have more than that, Mama. *I got to have more.*' He started to the door, furs in hand.

"She said, 'Son, please!' But he paid her no mind. She tried to snatch the coat back, but her son hung on. She struggled and tussled with him. And finally she started crying, with the tears running all down her face.

"The boy did not want to hurt her, so he stopped tussling and said, 'All right, Mama,' and hung the coat back in the closet. He went out in the kitchen whilst his mother sunk down in an armchair to dry her tears. While she was wiping her eyes, that boy come out of the kitchen with a clothesline, sneaked up behind his mama, threw that rope around her, and tied her up in the chair—with the hard knots behind her back so there was no way for her to get loose. He took the coat and disappeared, her one and only fur coat taken by her one and only son! When the husband come home from work, there was Mama all trussed up and tied in the chair. The secret was out. She had to tell him their son was on dope."

"How sad!" I said.

"How sad is right," agreed Simple. "Somebody needs to do something about junk and junkies. How would any woman like to be tied up and robbed by her own son? It is like one of them horror strips in the comic books—only it ain't comic."

"It's not comic," I said.

Dog Days

"Added to all the other worriations she has in her life," said Simple, "my Cousin Minnie has now got another dog here in Harlem."

"What kind of dog?" I asked.

"A French poodle," said Simple.

"How on earth did Minnie get a French poodle?"

"From some old white lady for whom Minnie did some day's work. That old lady's poodle had poodles, and one of them puppy poodles became so attached to Minnie that the old lady asked Minnie if she had anywhere to keep a dog—if so, she could have it.

"Minnie said, 'I got a six-room apartment,' which were the biggest lie ever told, because Minnie has hardly got a six-foot room. Anyhow, the lady gave her the dog, and Minnie brought it home, all clipped and shaved with neck ruffs and leg ruffs like French poodles has when they is barbered right. But now that its hair is growing out again, that poodle looks like any other old dirty white rag-ball of a dog to me."

"A French poodle is an aristocratic kind of dog," I said, "which needs to be taken care of in high style, washed weekly, and clipped by experts. I doubt if Minnie has the time or money to give that dog the kind of care it needs to show off its pedigree properly."

"You may doubt it, but I *know* it, she hasn't," said Simple. "Minnie has already sung that dog its theme song, 'I Can't Give You Anything But Love.' She is fond of that dog, God knows, but my cousin has no business with a animal. There are too many dogs in Harlem as it is. She should have left that dog out on Long Island where it could run and romp with its own kind. A French poodle has no more business in a furnished room than a polar bear has in hell. Minnie cannot even afford to buy it dog food, let alone keep it trimmed and clipped. Why, that dog was even perfumed when she got it."

"What does Minnie feed it?" I asked.

"Scraps," said Simple, "on which it seems to thrive. Fact is, it is getting fat."

"French poodles are not supposed to get fat. They should be dieted so as to keep their figures long, slim, and trim."

"This poodle will soon be big as Minnie, I expect," said Simple, "also as dark, if she do not give it a bath soon."

"Poor thing!" I said. "What did Minnie name the dog?"

"Jane," said Simple.

"Why?" I asked.

"Because when Minnie first got it, it being a female, Minnie was always saying, 'That Jane sure is cute.' So she just named her Jane. Now, me, myself, I would not like to have no dog have a person's name. I would have called it Little Bits or Fluff or Snowball or Frenchie or Snoodles, something like that. How many dogs do you reckon there is in Harlem?"

"Certainly thousands," I said, "all over the place."

"I thought Harlem was going to the dogs," said Simple. "Anyhow, there are more dogs in the United States than there are Negroes."

"I did not know that," I said. "Where did you get hold of such a piece of information?"

"From the World Almanac which my wife buys every year," said Simple. "There are only about twenty million Negroes in America. But the World Almanac states there are twenty-two million dogs. Do you believe they count dogs more careful than they count Negroes?"

"It is easier to keep track of dogs because each dog has to have a license," I said. "Therefore most of them are registered."

"Negroes do not have to have a license," said Simple, "so it is not so easy to count us. Neither do we belong to anybody. But I'll bet back in slavery time every Negro was counted, and if one head were missing, the bloodhounds were sent after him. I would hate to be a slave chased by a bloodhound. In fact, I read somewhere once where in them days a good bloodhound was worth more than a good Negro, because a bloodhound were trained to keep the Negroes in line. If a bloodhound bit a Negro, nothing were done to the dog. In fact, Negroes were supposed to be bit."

"You can come up with the strangest information," I said.

"White folks do the strangest things," said Simple. "Imagine training a dog to chase Negroes! The kind of dog I would like to get acquainted with, me, myself, is that kind that walks around with a licker flask tied under his chin over there in them Swiss mountains, and if you need it, he will give you a drink."

"Saint Bernards," I said.

"Them dogs are saints," said Simple, "bearing drinks. I would like to have me a big dog like that, a dog that would not yip-yap-yip, but bark, BARK, BARK—I mean a real bass bark. I would like a dog-dog, not a play-dog, you know, a boxer, or a collie, or a nice old flop-eared hound. Not no poodle nor nothing like that. Neither no Doberman pinscher, which is too nervous a dog for me. And my dog would not have to own no pedigree. I do not want no dog finer than myself. But I sure would have me a dog if Joyce would let me."

"Your wife doesn't care for dogs?" I asked.

"She do, but not in a New York apartment," said Simple. "Joyce claims a dog should have a yard to run in and romp in, and also she has no time to be taking a dog out to walk on no leash mornings before she goes to work and evenings when it is time to cook dinner. Joyce says she knows I would not get up in time to do so, and when I come in from work I would be too tired, which is right. I reckon the real place for a dog is in the country where he could find a dogwood tree, and not have to depend on no fireplug. And speaking of dogwood trees, it were beneath one that I first found love in dog days in Virginia one August when the church had a picnic and that girl's grandma let me eat out of her picnic basket— since she thought I was hanging around because I wanted chicken. But what I really wanted was that girl, so we snuck off to the edge of the ravine and I kissed her beneath a dogwood tree."

"Why do you bring that up?" I asked.

"To revive my remembrance," said Simple. "Dog days and dogwood —dog-gone! And the chicken were good, too!"

Pose-outs

"Sit-ins and such, picketings and such, for civil rights has been so common," said Simple, "that they no longer attracts attention. A lot of demonstrations nowadays do not even get in the papers any more. There has been too many, so I thought up something new."

"What?" I asked.

"Pose-ins," said Simple, "or pose-outs."

"What do you mean, 'pose-outs'?"

"Statues is often naked, are they not?" said Simple.

"Yes."

"Well, by pose-outs," said Simple, "I mean Negroes undressing down to their bare skin and posing naked as statues for freedom's sake. Twenty million Negroes taking off every stitch—stepping out of pants, dress, and drawers in public places and posing in the nude until civil rights have come to pass."

"You are demented," I declared.

"No," said Simple. "Nothing would attract as much attention to segregation, integration, desegregation, and ratiocination than if every Negro in this American country would just stand naked until Jim Crow goes."

"Fantastic!" I said. "Mad! Completely absurd!"

"Yes," said Simple, "at a certain time on a certain day let even those Negroes that be in Congress—Dawson, Diggs, Adam Powell—like that first Adam in the Garden—rise naked to answer the roll call. Ordinary people, if at work in factories, foundries, offices, or homes, will establish a nude-in. If on the streets, a nude-out. Black waiters at the Union League Club, a nude-in. Colored boys pushing racks in the streets of the garment district, a nude-out. Black cooks could pose in white kitchens naked. Maids could pose dusting the parlor with nothing on but a dust cap. Pullman porters on trains in the raw. Redcaps at stations bare except for badge numbers. Ralph Bunche at the United Nations, naked as a bird. At home, a nude-in. On the street, a nude-out. Until all Negroes get our rights, we pose. You know that statue 'The Thinker'?"

"By Rodin," I said.

"Setting on a stone with nothing on in God's world—'The Thinker'— with his chin in his hand, just setting lost in thought. Imagine James

Farmer demonstrating for CORE at City Hall, posing at high noon naked, making like 'The Thinker,' chin in hand! Also on the same day at the same time Roy Wilkins upholding the NAACP, buck-naked between them two lions on the steps of the New York Public Library, with nothing on but his nose glasses. At the back of the library, on the terrace facing Bryant Park, Borough President Constance Baker Motley just as she came in this world, whilst at Fiftieth and Broadway where the theatres is, Miss Lena Horne, bare as Venus. Down the way a piece, in front of the Metropolitan Opera, Leontyne Price in all her glory on a podium, not a stitch to her name. The traffic tie-up on Broadway would be terrific. We would not need a stall-in. Nude-outs would be enough. In Central Park, Willie Mays, on Sugar Hill, Jackie Robinson. And uptown in Harlem at 125th and Lenox I would place on a pedestal Miss Pearl Bailey."

"Unclothed?"

"Except by nature," said Simple. "With Negroes posing like statues all over town, traffic would jam. On Wall Street tickers would stop running. In Washington at the sight of Adam Powell in his birthday suit, filibusters would cease to be. In Atlanta, Rev. Martin Luther King, with not even a wrist watch on, would preach his Sunday-morning sermon. In New York colored subway conductors would report for duty in the all-together. Every waitress in Chock Full o' Nuts would look like Eve before the Fall. In Harlem, Black Muslims would turn to Black Nudists. And at the Apollo, Jackie Mabley would break up the show. Oh, if every Negro in America, big and small, great and not so great, would just take his clothes off and keep them off for the sake of civil rights, America would be forced to scrutinize our cause."

"How shocking!" I said.

"Which is what we would mean it to be," declared Simple. "A nude-out to shock America into clothing us in the garments of equality, not the rags of segregation. And when Negroes got dressed again, we could vote in Mississippi."

"That would be when hell freezes over," I said. "Besides, by that time the Legion of Decency would have all of you in jail for indecent exposure."

"Not me," said Simple, "because I would be in Harlem. The colored cops in Harlem would be naked, too, so how would I know, without his uniform, that he were a cop?"

"Considering all the dangers involved, would you be the first to volunteer for a nude-out?" I asked.

"That honor I would leave to you," said Simple.

Soul Food

"Where is that pretty cousin of yours, Lynn Clarisse, these days?" I asked.

"She has moved to the Village," said Simple.

"Deserted Harlem? Gone looking for integration?"

"She wants to see if art is what it's painted," said Simple. "All the artists lives in Greenwich Village, white and colored, and the jazz peoples and the writers. Nobody but us lives in Harlem. If it wasn't for the Antheny Annie Arts Club, Joyce says Harlem would be a cultural desert."

"You mean the Anthenian Arts Club," I said.

"I do," said Simple. "But Joyce tells me that thirty years ago Harlem was blooming. Then Duke Ellington and everybody lived here. Books was writ all over the place, pictures painted, lindy hoppers hopping, jitterbugs jumping, a dance hall called the Savoy with fine big bands playing. No more! The only things Harlem is famous for now is Adam Powell, who seldom comes home, and the last riots. So Lynn Clarisse has moved to the Village. But we can always get on the subway and go down and fetch her."

"Or join her," I said.

"Or let her re-join me," said Simple. "Although I am not worried about Lynn Clarisse. She is colleged, like you, and smart, and can take care of herself in the Village—just like my Cousin Minnie can take care of herself in Harlem. Every fish to his own water, I say, and the devil take them that cannot swim. Lynn Clarisse can swim, and Minnie dead sure can float, whereas some folks can only dog-paddle. Now me, my specialty is to walk on water. I been treading on the sea of life all my life, and have not sunk yet. I refuses to sink. In spite of womens, white folks, landlords, landladies, cold waves, and riots, I am still here. Corns, bunions, and bad feet in general do not get me down. I intends to walk the water until dry land is in sight."

"What land?"

"The Promised Land," said Simple, "the land in which I, black as I am without one plea in my country 'tis of thee, can be *me*. America the beautiful come to itself again, where you can see by the dawn's early light what so proudly we hailed as civil rights."

"The very thought makes you wax poetic, heh?"

"It do," said Simple. "But Joyce thinks Lynn Clarisse should have moved to Park West Village, halfway between Harlem and downtown. Joyce thinks Greenwich Village is a fast place where colored are likely to forget race and marry white. My wife is opposed to intermarriage on the grounds of pride. Joyce says she is so proud of her African heritage she don't want nobody to touch it. But do you know what Lynn Clarisse says? She says, 'There is no color line in art.'

"My cousin and my wife was kind of cool to each one another on the surface that day Lynn Clarisse moved out of Harlem. But you know how easy womens get miffed over little things. I don't pay them no mind myself. The only thing that makes me mad is Cousin Minnie wanting to borrow five dollars, which is always once too often. Lynn Clarisse do not borrow. She came to New York with her own money."

"Are her parents well off?"

"Her daddy, my first cousin on my half-brother's side, owns one of the biggest undertaking parlors in Virginia. He makes his money putting Negroes in segregated coffins in segregated graveyards. He sent Lynn Clarisse to college, and now has give her money for 'a cultural visit' to the North. Young Negroes used to have to struggle to get anything or go anywhere. Nowadays some of them have parents who have already struggled for them, so can help them get through college, and get up North, and get more cultured and live in Greenwich Village where rents is higher than they is in Harlem. Thank God, my cousin's daddy is an undertaker."

"Morticians and barbers are almost the only Negro businessmen whose incomes have not yet been affected by integration," I said. "Certainly, restaurants and hotels in Harlem have suffered. Banquets that once were held at the Theresa are now held at the Hilton and the Americana or the New Yorker. And the Urban League's annual Beaux Arts Ball is at the Waldorf. Negro society has taken almost all its functions downtown."

"But as long as white undertakers refuse to bury black bodies, and white barbers will not cut Negro hair, colored folks still have the burying and barbering business in the bag."

"Except that here in New York, I suppose you know, some wealthy Negroes are now being buried from fashionable downtown funeral homes."

"Where the mourners dare not holler out loud like they do at funerals in Harlem," said Simple. "It is not polite to scream and carry on over coffins in front of white folks."

"Integration has its drawbacks," I said.

"It do," confirmed Simple. "You heard, didn't you, about that old colored lady in Washington who went downtown one day to a fine white restaurant to test out integration? Well, this old lady decided to see for herself if what she heard was true about these restaurants, and if white folks were really ready for democracy. So down on Pennsylvania Avenue she went and picked herself out this nice-looking used-to-be-all-white restaurant to go in and order herself a meal."

"Good for her," I said.

"But dig what happened when she set down," said Simple. "No trouble, everybody nice. When the white waiter come up to her table to take her order, the colored old lady says, 'Son, I'll have collard greens and ham hocks, if you please.'

" 'Sorry,' says the waiter. 'We don't have that on the menu.'

" 'Then how about black-eyed peas and pig tails?' says the old lady.

" 'That we don't have on the menu either,' says the white waiter.

" 'Then chitterlings,' says the old lady, 'just plain chitterlings.'

"The waiter said, 'Madam, I never heard of chitterlings.'

" 'Son,' said the old lady, 'ain't you got no kind of soul food at all?'

" 'Soul food? What is that?' asked the puzzled waiter.

" 'I knowed you-all wasn't ready for integration,' sighed the old lady sadly as she rose and headed toward the door. 'I just knowed you white folks wasn't ready.' "

"Most ethnic groups have their own special dishes," I said. "If you want French food, you go to a French restaurant. For Hungarian, you go to Hungarian places, and so on."

"But this was an American place," said Simple, "and they did not have soul food."

"The term 'soul food' is still not generally used in the white world," I said, "and the dishes that fall within its category are seldom found yet in any but colored restaurants, you know that. There's a place where jazzmen eat across from the Metropole that has it, and one or two places down in the Village, but those are the only ones I know in Manhattan outside of Harlem."

"It is too bad white folks deny themselves that pleasure," said Simple, "because there is nothing better than good old-fashioned, down-home, Southern Negro cooking. And there is not too many restaurants in Harlem that has it, or if they do, they spoil everything with steam tables, cooking up their whole menu early in the morning, then letting it steam till it gets soggy all day. But when a Negro fries a pork chop *fresh*, or a chicken *fresh*, or a fish *fresh*, I am telling you, it sure is good. There is a fish joint on Lenox Avenue with two women in it that can sure cook fish. But they is so evil about selling it to you. How come some of these Harlem eating places hire such evil-acting people to wait on customers? Them two ladies in this fish place stand behind the counter and look at you like they dare you to 'boo' or ask for anything. They both look mad no sooner than you enter."

"I'll bet they are two sisters who own the place," I said. "Usually by the time Negroes get enough money to own anything, they are so old they are evil. Those women are probably just mad because at their age they have to wait on anybody."

"Then they should not be in business," said Simple.

"I agree," I said. "But on the other hand, suppose they or their husbands have been skimping and saving for years. At last, at the age of forty or fifty they get a little business. What do you want them to do? Give it up just because they have got to the crabby age and should be retiring, before they have anything to retire on?"

"Then please don't take out their age on me when I come in to order a piece of fish," said Simple. "Why them two ladies never ask you what you want politely. They don't, in fact, hardly ask you at all. Them womens looks at customers like they want to say, 'Get out of here!' Then maybe one of them will come up to you and stand and look over the counter.

"You say, 'Have you got any catfish?' She will say, 'No!' And will not say what other kind she has or has not got.

"So you say, 'How about buffalo?' She will say, 'We had that yesterday.'

"Then you will say, 'Well, what have you got today?'

"She will say, 'What do you want?' I have already said twice what I wanted that they did not have. So now I say, 'How about butterfish?'

"She says, 'Sandwich or dinner?'

"I say, 'Dinner.'

"She says, 'We don't sell dinners after ten P.M.'

" 'Then why did you ask me if I wanted a dinner?' says I.

"She says, 'I was paying no attention to the time.'

"I said, 'You was paying no attention to me neither, lady, and I'm a customer. Gimme two sandwiches.'

" 'I am not here to be bawled out by you,' she says. 'If it's sandwiches you want, just say so, and no side remarks.'

" 'Could I please have a cup of coffee?'

" 'We got Pepsis and Cokes.'

" 'A Pepsi.'

"She rummages in the cooler. 'The Pepsis is out.'

" 'A Coke.'

"She comes up with a bottle that is not cold. Meanwhile the fish is frying, and it smells good, but it takes a while to wait, so I say, 'Gimme a quarter to play the jukebox.' Three records for a quarter.

"Don't you know that woman tells me, 'We is all out of quarters tonight.'

"So I say, trying to be friendly, 'I'll put in a dime and play just one then. What is your favorite record?'

"Old hussy says, 'There's nothing on there do I like, so just play for yourself.'

" 'Excuse me,' says I, 'I will play "Move to the Outskirts of Town," which is where I think you ought to be.'

" 'I wish my husband was here to hear your sass,' she says. 'Is your fish to eat here, or to go?'

" 'To go,' I says, 'because I am going before you bite my head off. What do I owe?'

" 'How much is two sandwiches to go?' she calls back to the other woman in the kitchen.

" 'Prices is gone up,' says the other hussy, 'so charge him eighty cents.'

" 'Eighty cents,' she says, 'and fifteen for the Pepsi.'

" 'I had a Coke,' I says.

" 'The same. You get a nickel change.'

" 'From a five-dollar bill?' I says.

" 'Oh, I did not notice you give me a five. Claybelle, have you got any change back there?'

" 'None.'

" 'Neither is I. Mister, you ought to have something smaller.'

" 'I do not carry small change around on payday,' says I. 'And what kind of restaurant is this, that can't even bust a five-dollar bill, neither change small change into a quarter for the record player? Don't you-all have nothing in the cash register? If you don't, no wonder, the way you treat a customer! Just gimme my five back and keep your fish.'

" 'Lemme look down in my stocking and see what I got there,' she says. And do you know, that woman went down in her stocking and pulled out enough money to buy Harry Belafonte. But she did not have a nickel change.

"So I said, 'Girl, you just keep that nickel for a tip.'

"If that woman owns the place, she ought to sell it. If she just works there, she ought to be fired. If she is the owner's girl friend, was she mine I would beat her behind, else feed her fish until a bone got stuck in her throat. I wonder how come some Harlem places have such evil help, especially in restaurants. Hateful help can spoil even soul food. Dear God, I pray, please change the hearts of hateful help!"

Flay or Pray?

"Tooth by tooth, before you can turn around, it is gone," said Simple sadly, leaning on the bar.

"What *it*?" I asked.

"Your youth-hood," said Simple. "With some mens, time goes hair by hair. I hope I never get bald-headed and toothless *both*."

"You probably will in due time," I said.

"Everytime the dentist pulls a tooth, ten years is gone," said Simple.

"That is hardly true," I said. "The average man has 32 teeth in his head. Ten times 32 equals 320 and nobody has that many years to live. Besides, some people keep all of their teeth until they die."

"Some live snaggled-toothed," said Simple. "And others keep just enough teeth to get in the way of a new plate."

"They are foolish," I said. "Bad teeth in the head are a health hazard and they ought to come out."

"There are plenty of things in a man's head that ought to come out," declared Simple, "like evil thoughts, and imaging you is more than you is and getting stuck-up and important. Also prejudice should come out."

"You can't pull prejudice out of a man's head like you can teeth. No dentist living can do that."

"Rev. Martin Luther King tries to pray prejudice out, but sometimes I think we are gonna have to flay it out," said Simple.

"Violence never solved anything," I contended. "You can't physically beat attitudes, racial or otherwise, out of people's heads. Deep-seated fixations are a matter for the psychiatrists and psychologists, not bully boys with clubs."

"Many a Negro's head has been flayed by a billy club, and many black souls on the way to the polls have been stopped by a cop who said, 'Stay away! Don't vote today!' Then the Negroes go back home, their minds changed about the ballot. Clubs have changed many Negroes' minds down South. How come they can't change white minds?"

"Brute force never changed any Negro minds at all. Negroes still hold the same thoughts silently in the face of intimidation. They just don't exercise their prerogatives."

"In other words, they don't vote in Mississippi. They are scared to vote. But it looks like to me," said Simple, "as many Negroes as there are in Mississippi, they would make the white folks scared to try to make so many Negroes scared. If all them down-home colored folks was to rise up in one mass, imagine!"

"You don't believe in Rev. King's policies of nonviolence, I gather."

"Only for the nonviolent," said Simple. "If I lived down South, I would lose my temper."

"Then you would lose your head," I said.

"I am afraid I would," said Simple. "I have been up here in the free North too long to go down to the unfree South. But I will contribute money."

"Sideline fighter," I said. "Talker at the big gate! Advocate of violence against your white brothers!"

"White brothers? The closest I could ever come to a white relative would be a twenty-second cousin on my Indian grandmother's side," said Simple.

"Your Indian grandmother?"

"Yes, they said in our family that grandma was descended from Pocahuntas. And Pocahuntus were married to Captain John Smith—and Smith were white."

"So?"

"So that would make his white brother's children's great-grandchildren my twenty-second cousins. But relatives or not, I would raise my hand against them, was them white cousins to segregate me."

"Flay, I take it would be your attitude, rather than pray."

"I have already prayed," said Simple.

Not Colored

"That man was too evil to be human," mumbled Simple, "both of them."

"What man?" I asked.

"That man in the back of my mind, my third Cousin, Tyson."

"I never heard of Tyson before. Is he another of your numerous relatives?"

"Tyson were too mean to buy his baby milk when his wife's breasts went dry," said Simple.

"And the other man you are talking about?"

"No relation. The other man were white and evil in a different kind of way—very nice to white folks, but evil to Negroes. It looked like his face would change from one mask to another when he seed a colored person."

"Did that man's path ever cross yours?" I asked.

"That is how come I thought about him," said Simple, "since I got a letter from my niece, Brendaleen. Brendaleen writ that that white man is still living right there in Virginia in the town where I were born but, thank God, not reared. Had that old man's paths and mine ever crossed after I got grown, I might of kilt him, I do believe. I know I sure would have been bound to kick him in his shins, like he kicked me once in mine. I were nothing but a child then, ten-eleven years old, going down the street by myself bouncing a ball, you know, like kids do. Right in front of the man Winclift's house, my ball bounced too high and landed up in a limb of his lilac bush at one corner of his front lawn. His lawn were green and pretty and his lilac bush smelt good and his house were beautiful and white with a fine veranda. Nothing like that house on the colored side of town. I liked to bounce my ball down that pretty street. But not no more, after it landed in his lilac bush—because when I went across a little tiny corner of his grass to reach up in that bush and get my ball, he yelled at me, 'Get off my lawn, boy!'

"I said, 'Yes, sir, soon as I get my ball.'

"With that he come running off his veranda like a charging bull, hollering like mad, 'Soon as *what* did you say?'

"I said, 'Soon as I get my ball,' and I did not move.

"That is when that grown white man hauled off and kicked me in my shins, not just one time, but twice, once on each one of my legs. Wow! You know how bad it hurts to get kicked on your shins? It hurted me so bad I could not cry and I could not run. So I just fell down and rolled myself off that grass onto the sidewalk. Then I sat up and reached down and held my legs until I could get up and walk away—without my ball.

"He said, 'I guess that will teach you little black bastards to get on my grass.'

"I did not say nothing. But then it was that tears come in my eyes, and they were not from bruises on my shins. When I got home and told the old folks about it, they just said Mr. Winclift were the meanest *young* white man in town. Now he is old, an old white man who I regret is not dead. I reckon he is just too mean to die. How come Brendaleen to mention him in her letter is that she says he just last week hauled off and slapped his colored cook for, as he claimed, burning up a pan of biscuit bread. This colored cook-lady went and got a warrant out for him. But you know and I know, nothing will come of a warrant in that little old Southern town. She will just stay slapped, that's all, like I stayed kicked. Which is one reason why them Japanese do not want no parts of Americans in their hearts. They remember Hiroshima."

"You can certainly make some unconnected circles in a conversation," I said. "That is what I call a *non sequitur* for true."

"Don't you see no connection between atom-bomb-dropping in Japan and shin-kicking in Virginia?" asked Simple.

"No direct connection," I said.

"Then you are not colored," said Simple.

Cracker Prayer

"Well," said Simple, "this other old cracker down in Virginia who acted like Mr. Winclift what kicked my shins, one night he were down on his knees praying. Since he were getting right ageable, he wanted to be straight with God before he departed this life and headed for the Kingdom. So he lifted his voice and said, 'Oh, Lord, help me to get right, do right, be right, and die right before I ascends to Thy sight. Help me to make my peace with Nigras, Lord, because I have hated them all my life. If I do not go to heaven, Lord, I certainly do not want to go to hell with all them Nigras down there waiting to meet me. I hear the Devil is in league with Nigras, and if the Devil associates with Nigras, he must be a Yankee who would not give me protection. Lord, take me to Thy Kingdom where I will not have to associate with a hell full of Nigras. Do You hear me, Lord?'

"The Lord answered and said, 'I hearest thee, Colonel Cushenberry. What else wilst thou have of me?'

"The old cracker prayed on, 'Lord, Lord, dear Lord, since I did not have a nice old colored mammy in my childhood, give me one in heaven, Lord. My family were too poor to afford a black mammy for any of my father's eight children. I were mammyless as a child. Give me a mammy in heaven, Lord. Also a nice old Nigress to polish my golden slippers and keep the dust off of my wings. But, Lord, if there be educated Nigras in heaven, keep them out of my sight. The only thing I hate worse than an educated Nigra is an integrated one. Do not let me meet no New York Nigras in heaven, Lord, nor none what ever flirted with the NAACP or Eleanor Roosevelt. As You is my Father, Lord, lead me not into black pastures, but deliver me from integration, for Thine is the power to make all men as white as snow. But I would still know a Nigra even though he were white, by the way he sings, also by certain other characteristics which I will not go into now because a prayer is no place to explain everything. But You understand as well as I do, Lord, why a Nigra is something special.

"'Lord, could I ask You one question? Did You make Nigras just to bedevil white folks? Was they put here on earth to be a trial and tribulation to the South? Did You create the NAACP to add fire to brimstone? You know, Lord, as soon as a Nigra gets an inch he wants an el. Give him an el, and he wants it ALL. Pretty soon a white man will not be able to sing "Come to Jesus" without a Nigra wanting to sing along with him. And you know Nigras can outsing us, Lord.

"'Lord, You know I think it would be a good idea if You would send Christ down to earth again. It is about time for the Second Coming, because I don't believe Christ knows what Nigras is up to in this modern day and age. They is up to devilment, Lord—riding in the same train coaches with us, setting beside us on busses, sending their little Nigra children to school with our little white children. Even talking about they do not like to be segregated in jail no more—that a jail is a public place for which they also pay taxes.

"'Lord, separate the black taxes from the white taxes, black sheep from white sheep, and Nigra soldiers from white soldiers before the next war comes around. I do not want my grandson atomized with no Nigra. Lord, dispatch Christ down here before it is too late. Great Lord God, Jehovah, Father, send Your Only Begotten Son in a Cloud of Fire to straighten out this world again and put Nigras back in their places before that last trumpet sounds. When I get ready to go to Glory, Lord, and put on my white robe and prepare to step into Thy chariot, I do not want no Nigras lined up telling me the Supreme Court has decreed integrated seats in the Celestial Chariot, too. If I hear tell of such, Lord, I elect to stay right here on earth where at least Faubus is on my side.'"

Rude Awakening

"I don't know why I keep on dreaming so much here of late," said Simple, "but I reckon it is because it dreams so good to imagine again in my sleep that I am the ruler of Dixie, me, colored and all my people, in charge of the state we Negroes helped to make so beautiful. It is beautiful in Virginia—and me setting on the wide veranda of my big old mansion with its white pillars, the living room just full of chandeliers, and a whole slew of white servants to wait on me, master of all I surveys, and black as I can be! Oh, it is fine! And dear old Mammy Faubus what raised me, bringing me my mint juleps in the cool of the evening on a silver tray. You Yankee Negroes up North don't know what you missed by never having a dear old white Mammy.

"The other day whilst I was setting fanning in my cane-bottomed rocker on my white veranda, who should come bowing around the corner of the yard but my dear old Mammy Faubus, shading her old blue eyes from the sun with her wrinkled white hand. She said, 'Mister Semple, sir, might I trouble to ask you to do me and mine a mite of Christian favor?'

"I said, 'What is it, Mammy Faubus?'

"She said, 'Excuse me, Sir, but a friend of mine from that little old Caucasian Christian Church down in Buckra Town has come to the kitchen door to ask us white servants for donations to her Organ Fund. We gave her what dimes and quarters we poor souls had. But she says she knows the Lawd would bless her if she could just speak to a rich Negro like you, Mister Semple. Do you reckon you could let that poor old sister just come around here to the front porch and tell you, "Howdy"?'

" 'Send her around here, Mammy Faubus, but tell her to be careful not to tread on my petunias.'

" 'Thank you, Mister Semple.'

"Around the corner of the house came a dear old white mammy who right away I know I knowed, because she had raised colored Colonel Washington's oldest boy. I said, 'Why good evening, Mammy Eastland.'

"You would of thought that old white sister was about to grin her head off. 'Good evening, God bless you!' she says. 'And thank you for letting me come into your presence. Mister Semple, you are a fine colored man!'

" 'Try to help all you white folks wherever I can,' I said, 'especially when you are a friend of Mammy Faubus, what nursed me. What can I do for you, Mammy Eastland?'

" 'I am begging for my church,' she said.

"Poor old soul, I thought, with hardly a rag to her back, yet begging for the Lord! White folks is truly religious! I were so moved I got up out of my rocker, reached down in my pants pocket, and give her a dollar. 'Take that, Mammy Eastland,' I said, 'and God bless you in your work. Are you still with my friend Colonel Washington?'

" 'I would not leave them good Negroes for nothing,' shouted Mammy Eastland. 'Him and his family are next to God in my book. Just like you and your family folks, quality folks! God never made better Negroes! Thank you, Mister Semple, thank you!'

" 'Just don't let me hear about none of your grandchildren trying to get into our colored schools, Mammy Eastland. And tell that educated son of yours to stop working with the NAAWP because it don't mean you white folks no good. I have no respect for uppity young crackers—talking about writing President Adam Powell at his Summer White House about how bad conditions is here in the South. You *old* crackers know your place. I believe in respect where respect is due. If your son asks you who I respects, tell him his mammy.'

" 'You's too kind, Mister Semple!'

" 'Not a-tall,' I said, waving her away with a wave of my black hand. 'Get on down the road to your work, Mammy Eastland, back to Colonel Washington's house, and don't spend more than half of that church dollar for snuff.'

" 'Lawd, Mister Semple!' she laughed, whaw-whawing till her old white shoulders shook. To tell the truth, I thought she was going to crack up at my little snuff joke. That Mammy Eastland! Oh, well, no white folks, no fun! But I don't mind helping poor white folks a little. And I never was a man to brag about what I do for others. Neither do I boast about what riches I possess. Some folks I know is too notoriety.

"Seems like since colored folks have taken over in the South all a lot of Negroes like to do is boast about their white mammies. It is beginning to be tiresome. Every time a bunch of colored society folks gather for a bridge game, or a planter's punch, or plantation brunch, somebody has got to brag about their old white mammy. To tell the truth, I do not believe every Negro that says he had a white mammy, had one. But me, of course, I was raised by Mammy Faubus. And colored Colonel Washington always had Mammy Eastland in his family for years. But we is aristocrats. Some of these other Negroes is new come by wealth, but the Semples and the Washingtons have had money so long we ignore it. That explains why my old white mansion is somewhat run-down—I am just too rich to have it fixed—but the tradition is still there.

"Just last week I give Mammy Faubus the money for a new dress. Now I could not see Mammy Faubus go without some new clothes to wear to the barbecue she tells me her church is giving next week, after which there is going to be a big camp meeting and singing. I just love to hear white folks sing!

"But I cannot understand their cracker children, neither their grand-children. Not knee high to a duck, some of these little blue-eyed crack-erninnies, yet they got the nerve to want to go to our colored schools! What is getting into white folks since Chief Justice Thurgood Marshall handed down that last decree from the Supreme Court bench granting everybody the right to file another suit to get their rights? Don't they want to go through the orderly process of the courts and sue and file until they get to be old men and womens?

"If at first you don't succeed, file and file again, I say. White folks, these things take time. Don't rush into integration without preparation. Just because a handful of old Negroes wearing robes in the Supreme Court says your rights are constitutional, it does not mean they are institutional. Our great institutions like the University of Jefferson Lee belong to us, and not even with all deliberate speed do we intend to constitutionalize the institutionalization of our institutions. In the dear and simple words of Mammy Faubus, 'Let things stay like they is.' Go slow on the status quo. Just stop to realize how folks like Mammy Faubus would suffer if times was to change. Who would she work for?

" 'Mister Jesse B., your family always was quality Nigras,' says Mammy Faubus, her old blue eyes flashing with pride. 'And I sure is a lucky white woman to be working for you-all all these years,' she tells me every day.

" 'The reward for service is more service,' I told her. 'You can serve us till you die, Mammy Faubus. Never will you want for a pot of victuals in Mister Semple's kitchen.'

" 'But it do look like,' says Mammy Faubus, 'since you Nigras taken over the South, the price of collard greens is doubled and grits gone sky-high.'

" 'That is because you white folks do not like to work like you ought to,' I said, 'and your white young upstarts wasting their time setting at counters downtown where they will never get served as long as I am black. Mammy Faubus, can't you talk to your grandchildren?'

" 'This is a headstrong generation, Mister Semple, white or black. Won't listen to reason! Colored Judge Johnson last week didn't fine them white sit-iners but five dollars, then give them a chance to pay they fines. But, no! Them young white varmints said they had ruther set in jail until they can eat in them fine black barbecue joints where white folks never been known to eat before. Why, when I were young . . .'

" 'I know, Mammy Faubus, when you was young things was different. But times do change. Now white folks all want to be black. You wouldn't want to be black, would you, Mammy Faubus?'

" 'Not in the Kingdom!' cried Mammy Faubus. 'All I want to do is save my soul. Let the Nigras take this world, just gimme Jesus!'

" 'Bless your sweet soul, Mammy Faubus!' I said. 'Bless your dear white soul! Now get back to your work. When you go out to the kitchen, fix me a fresh julep and slice off a few slices of that Smithfield ham with a biscuit to hold me till dinner. Fetch me my palm-leaf fan. It's right hot on this veranda today. After my snack I might just take a little nap, so hand me my footstool.'

"I did fall into a doze. But do you know," said Simple, "as soon as I went to sleep, I woke up—and found out it was all a dream. I mean I woke up for real. Negroes had not taken over the South. All I heard outside my window, which I drempt was a veranda, was them New York garbage trucks going by and the busses rumbling down Lenox Avenue.

"Some joker in the street was yelling, 'Hey, girl, wait for me!'

"And the girl yelled back, 'I can't wait! I'm late to work now!'

"It were daybreak in Harlem, and I woke up to the same old nightmare."

Miss Boss

"They pass like shadows," said Minnie. "Men, they pass like shadows in and out of a woman's life. Men pass like shadows. And the man I have got right now is about to go because I am going to put him out!"

"Cousin Minnie," said Simple, "the trouble with you is, you like to rule. You like, in the end, to *put an end* to all your men. As long as I have known you, it is *you* who always ends things when the ending time comes."

"I pay the rent on my place—with *his* money, naturally, if I can get it. I close the door to my place when the dough don't come no more. I change the lock when I can no longer stand his face—and his contribution to the pot is a disgrace. I rule! Yes, you right, I rule."

"That is the trouble, Miss Minnie. You rules. But a man should rule. When you get ageable, Minnie, you are going to be all by yourself. Why don't you find a good man and get married and give him the keys to your heart?"

"I don't believe the keys to my heart has been filed to fit my lock yet. They ain't made. If they is, no man has them."

"You are selfish, Miss Minnie. You got them keys to your heart in your drawer and you won't give them to nobody. Trouble with you is, you wants to domineer all the time. To *boss*, to have the *last* lick, and the *last* word. You is no fit mate for a man who wants a helpmeet. I tell you now, you want to share, but not care. It is a wonder some man has not blowed you down before now with a pistol, out of pure aggravation. You are my cousin, it is true, Minnie, but I would not fall in love with you. And if I had a good buddy who was to look upon you with a loving eye, I would tell him, 'No, don't—because she won't.' "

"Whatsoever you might tell your friend," said Minnie, "would do no good if I wanted him for mine. What I want, I get. Jess Semple, you know I got a way with men."

"It is a bad way," said Simple. "For the mens involved, bad. You are like a spider with a web—a long-term operator—in which operation I would hate to be your fly."

"You just do not go for my type," said Minnie. "Some men like to be taken. Some men is the kind of mules you can drive to water—*and they drink.* Oh, my, my, my! The shadows of the mules that I have driv to water—driv to the creek of love!"

"And then hauled off and hit them on the haunches with a singletree," said Simple. "Minnie, you is a bad mule driver. I myself have seen you aggravate and upset several mens since I been knowing you here in Harlem, married and single mens. You is no respecter of persons when it comes to pants. How you do it—and get away with it—I do not know. You is no Lena Horne, no picture in a frame, no New Year's advertising calendar with a pretty mama's photo over JANUARY. No, Minnie—yet and still, you make your way."

"I do not do too much talking with a man," says Minnie, "I let him jive."

"Yes, and when he gets through, he come out more dead than alive. You, Minnie, goes in for long-time action."

"Right now, I have nobody," said Minnie. "I am alone. My last and latest shadow has done passed. Down the steps and out my downstairs door, down the street and around the corner, Henry has gone his way. All them nights we was together, now I say, 'Baby, call it a day!' What few clothes he left behind, I have put them in the cleaners and sent him the ticket by mail. Henry departed."

"You first met him in this bar, did you not?"

"No, I met him in the Green Beacon. He followed me here. I met that other one, Luther, in the Green Beacon, too. Facts is, I met several good men in that bar—where you do not hang out."

"I never interferes with your 'Good evenings' to nobody, Minnie, even if you is my cousin."

"No, but the men see you, my cousin, around and they are afraid to come on strong—like asking me where do I live and if they can come home with me. They see you and get all formal, Jess. That is why sometimes I set at the opposite end of the bar from all relatives. And I do not like to be lectured, so just leave me be. Shut up."

"I will, Miss Boss, I will."

"Thank you," said Miss Minnie.

Dr. Sidesaddle

Dear Dr. Sidesaddle:

I, Jesse B. Semple, better known as Simple, take pen in hand to write you this letter. I have just read your article in *See-Saw Magazine* in which you writ about how you and your family have completely integrated, and that you-all have no problems whatsoever with your white neighbors and your white friends in your white house in your white neighborhood in the sideskirts of White Manors. First, Dr. Sidesaddle, I want to ask you how you can say yours is a white neighborhood if you are there? If one drop of black blood makes a white man black, you *colored* being in a white neighborhood must do something to that neighborhood that is not white.

Anyhow, dear Dr. Sidesaddle, your office is here in Harlem where I live. All of your patients is colored. You know that Harlem is not integrated and neither am I. But if you was to invite me up to your house in the suburbans, it would give me a chance to see what integration is like. But, of course, if I was to come up there, I expect no sooner had I arrived than somebody would say there was one Negro too many in the neighborhood. Of all the pictures I saw of you and your surroundings in that colored magazine last week, you and your wife and your children was the only colored in the pictures. All your friends and next-door neighbors are white.

The church you are going to in the pictures is white. I saw you and your wife setting in this pew. In front of you was white and behind you was white, and the minister was white. I did not even see a Negro in the choir—and you know Negroes can sing. Can't they have more than just two Negroes—you-all—in a integrated church? And when your children go to Sunday School do they ever see a black angel on their Sunday School cards? Do you-all ever sing any gospel songs? It looks like to me to be the kind of church in which a tambourine is never shook.

I went to a integrated church once with my wife, Joyce, downtown in New York City, in which, Joyce said, the members are all looking for the higher things. The minister read his sermon off of a paper, and I must say it was all I could do to keep from going to sleep. Nobody in the congregation even said, "Amen!" When the songs were sung, nobody clapped a hand. Joyce said, "This is a dignified church."

I said, "It is dull to me."

Joyce said, "You do not appreciate thoughts in religion. You want emotions."

I said, "I want something to keep me awake."

Dear Dr. Sidesaddle, in a integrated church does a minister *have* to *read* his sermon? Or do all white ministers read from a paper? How come they are not so full of the spirit that they can just spill out God's word without first writing it down and reading it from a paper? They just drone along and never raise their voices, even to say, "Hallelujah!" I do not see how they ever make converts. Was you converted in that white church, or did you just integrate on general principles? I bet you do not even dare to pat your foot during a song.

In the pictures in that magazine, it shows you and your family being served your dinner by a Japanese butler. Now, dear Dr. Sidesaddle, I has nothing against the Japanese. But as bad as Negroes need work, why not me for your butler? And, since I expect you grew up on collard greens and ham, I do not think you was eating Japanese food. But what I am trying to get at—and to which I expects from you an answer—is this: As you roll down here to Harlem every day to your office in your white Thunderbird to give out prescriptions to black patients and operate on black appendages, then drive home every night to your white house in your white neighborhood in the suburbans, do you draw the color line yourself? Or is it your intention to integrate me along with you up there in White Manors someday? Dear Dr. Saddleside—I mean, Sidesaddle— that is all I wants to know as I sign off—

> Yours sincerely truly,
> *Jesse B. Semple*

Wigs for Freedom

"You ought to of heard my Cousin Minnie last night telling about her part in the riots," said Simple, leaning on one of the unbroken bars on Lenox Avenue that summer, beer in hand. "After hearing three rebroadcasts of Mayor Wagner's speech after he flew back home from Europe, Minnie was so mad she wanted to start rioting again. She said old Wagner did not say one constructive thing. Anyhow, Minnie come in the bar with a big patch on the top of her head, otherwise she was O.K., talking about all the big excitement and how she was in the very middle of it.

"Cousin Minnie told me, 'Just as I was about to hit a cop, a bottle from on high hit me.' Then she described what happened to her.

" 'They taken me to Harlem Hospital and stitched up my head, which is O.K. now and thinking better than before,' Minnie said. 'But, you know, them first-aid doctors and nurses or somebody in Harlem Hospital took my forty-dollar wig and I have not seen it since. I went back to Harlem Hospital after the riots and asked for my wig, an orange-brown chestnut blonde for which I paid cash money. But they said it were not in the Lost and Found. They said my wig had blood on it, anyhow, so it got throwed away.

" 'I told them peoples in the Emergency Room, "Not just my wig, but my head had blood on it, too. I am glad you did not throw my head away." Whereupon one of them young doctors had the nerve to say, "Don't sass me!" But since he was colored, I did not cuss him out.

" 'I knowed that young doctor had been under a strain—so many busted heads to fix up—so I just let his remarks pass. All I said was, "I wish I had back my wig. That were a real-hair wig dyed to match my complexion and styled to compliment my cheekbones." Only thing I regret about them riots is, had it not been for me wanting to get even with white folks, I would still have my wig. My advice to all womens taking part in riots is to leave their wigs at home.'

"I said, 'Miss Minnie, you look good with your natural hair, African style. I did not like you with that blonde wig on, nohow. Fact is, I did not hardly know you the first time I run into you on 125th Street under that wig. Now you look natural again.'

" 'The reason I bought that wig is, I do not want to look natural,' said Miss Minnie. 'What woman wants to look her natural self? That is why powder and rouge and wigs is made, to make a woman look like Elizabeth Taylor or Lena Horne—and them stars do not look like natural-born womens at all. I paid forty dollars for my wig just to look *unnatural*. It were *fine* hair, too! All wigs should always be saved in hospitals, bloody or not, and given back to the patients after their heads is sewed up. Since I were unconscious from being hit with a bottle, also grief-stricken from little Jimmy Powell's pistol funeral, when they ambulancetized me and laid me out in the hospital, I did not even know they had taken my wig off.'

" 'Do you reckon you will be left with a scar in the top of your head?' I asked.

" 'If I do,' said Miss Minnie, 'I am proud of it. What is one little scar in the fight for freedom when some people lose their life? Medgar Evers lost his life in Mississippi. All I lost was my wig in Harlem Hospital. And I know that cop did not hit me. He was busy hitting somebody else when I started to hit him; he didn't see me. Some Negro on a roof aimed a bottle at that cop's head—but hit me by accident instead. Bullets, billy clubs, and bottles was flying every whichaway that Sunday night after that Powell boy's funeral. Lenox Avenue were a *sweet* battleground. But I would not have been in action myself had not I seen a cop hit an old man old enough to be his father. He were a young white cop and the man was an old black man who did not do nothing except not move fast enough when that cop spoke. That young cop whaled him. WHAM! WHAM! WHAM! I did not have no weapon with me but my purse, but I was going to wham that cop dead in the face with that—when a bottle whammed me on the head. God saved that cop from being slapped with a pocketbook full of knockout punches from poker chips to a bottle of Evening in Paradise, also a big bunch of keys which might of broke his nose.'

" 'Don't you believe in nonviolence?' I asked.

" 'Yes,' said Miss Minnie, 'when the other parties are nonviolent, too. But when I have just come out of a funeral parlor from looking at a little small black boy shot three times by a full-grown cop, I think it is about time I raised my pocketbook and strike at least one blow for freedom. I come up North ten years ago to find freedom, Jesse B. Semple. I did not come to Harlem to look a white army of white cops in the face and let them tell me I can't be free in my own black neighborhood on my own black street in the very year when the Civil Rights Bill says *you shall be free*. No, I didn't! It is a good thing that bottle struck me down, or I would of tore that cop's head every way but loose.'

" 'Then you might not of been here today,' I said.

" 'That is right,' agreed Miss Minnie, 'but my soul would go marching on. Was I to have gone to the morgue instead of Harlem Hospital, I would go crying, "*Freedom now*," and I would come back to haunt them that struck me low. The ghost of Miss Minnie would walk among white folks till their dying day and keep them scared to death. I would incite to riot every week-end in Harlem. I would lead black mobs—which is what the papers said we is—from Friday night to Monday morning. It would cost New York a million dollars a week to just try to keep us Negroes and *me* quiet. They would wonder downtown what got into Harlem. It would just be my spirit egging us on. I would gladly die for freedom and come back to haunt white folks. Yes, I would! Imagine me floating down Lenox Avenue, a white ghost with a blonde wig on!'

" 'I would hate to see you,' I said.

" 'I would hate to see myself,' said Miss Minnie. '*Freedom now!*' She raised her beer glass and I raised mine. Then Miss Minnie said, 'I might not of gave my head to the cause, but I gave my wig.'

"Peoples like to hear Cousin Minnie talk and sometimes when she gets an audience, she goes to town. It being kind of quiet in the bar last night, folks started listening at Minnie instead of playing the juke box, and Minnie proceeded to expostulate on the subject of riots and white and colored leaders advising Harlem to go slow and be cool. Says Minnie, 'When I was down South picking cotton, didn't a soul tell me to go slow and cool it. "Pick more! Pick more! Can't you pick a bale a day? What's wrong with you?" That's what they said. Did not a soul say, "Wait, don't over-pick yourself." Nobody said slow down in cotton-picking days. So what is this here now? When Negroes are trying to get something for themselves, I must wait, *don't demonstrate*? I'll tell them big shots, "How you sound?"

" 'Be cool?' asked Miss Minnie. 'Didn't a soul say, "Be cool," when I was out in that hot sun down South. I heard not nary a word about "be cool." So who is telling me to be cool now? I have not no air cooler in Harlem where I live, neither air conditioner. And you talking about be cool! How you sound?

" 'Get off the streets! Huh! Never did nobody say, "Get out of the fields," when I was down home picking cotton in them old cotton fields which I have *not* forgotten. In slavery times, I better not get out of no fields if I wanted to save my hide, or save my belly from meeting my backbone from hunger when freedom came. No! I better stay in them fields and work. But now that I got a street to stand on, how do you sound telling me to get off the street? Just because some little old disturbance come up and a few rocks is throwed in a riot, I am supposed to get off of my street in Harlem and leave it to the polices to rule? I am supposed to go home and be cool? Cool what, where, baby? How do you sound?

" ' "My name is Minnie and I lost my forty-dollar wig in the riots, so I am reduced to my natural hair," I'll tell them leaders. But what is one wig more or less to give for freedom? One wig not to go slow. One wig not to be cool. One wig not to get off the streets. When it is a long hot summer, where else but in the streets, fool, can I be cool? Uncontrollable? Who says I was uncontrollable? Huh! I knowed what I was doing. I did not lose my head because when I throwed a bottle, I knowed what I was throwing at. I were throwing at Jim Crow, Mr. K. K. Krow—at which I aimed my throw. How do you sound, telling me not to aim at Jim Crow?

" 'Did not a soul in slavery time tell old bull-whip marster not to aim his whip at me, at me—a woman. Did not a soul tell that mean old overseer not to hit Harriet Tubman (who is famous every Negro History Week), not to hit her in the head with a rock whilst she was a young girl. She were black, and a slave, and her head was made to be hit with a rock by her white overseer. Did not a soul tell that man who shot Medgar Evers in the back with a bullet to be cool. Did not a soul say to them hoodlums what slayed them three white and colored boys in Mississippi to cool it. Now they calling me hoodlums up here in Harlem for wanting to be free. Hoodlums? Me, a hoodlum? Not a soul said "hoodlums" about them night riders who ride through the South burning black churches and lighting white crosses. Not a soul said "hoodlums" when the bombs went off in Birmingham and blasted four little Sunday School girls to death, little black Sunday School girls. Not a soul said "hoodlums" when they tied an auto rim to Emmett Till's feet and throwed him in that Mississippi river, a kid just fourteen years old. But me, I am a hoodlum when I don't cool it, won't cool it, or lose my wig on a riot gig. They burnt down fourteen colored churches in Mississippi in one summer, yet, I'm supposed to be cool? Even our colored leaders telling Harlem to be cool! Well, I am my own leader, and I am not cool.

" 'Everywhere they herd my people in jail like cattle, and I am supposed to be cool. I read in one of our colored papers the other day where it has cost Mississippi four million dollars just to keep Negroes in jail. And Savannah, Georgia, spent eighteen thousand in one year feeding black boycotters in jail. One town in North Carolina spent twelve hundred dollars a day on beans for colored students they locked up for marching to be free. One paper said it cost the State of Maryland one hundred thousand dollars a month to send the militia to Cambridge to keep Negroes from getting a cup of coffee in them crumby little old white restaurants which has no decent coffee, nohow, but which everybody ought to have the right to go into on general principles. But me, I can't go in. Yet them that's supposed to be my leaders tell me, 'Give up! Don't demonstrate! Wait!' To tell the truth, I believe my own colored leaders is ashamed of me. So how are they going to lead anybody they are ashamed of? Telling me to be cool. Huh! I'm too hot to be cool—so I guess I will just have to lead my own self—which I dead sure will do. I will lead myself.' "

Concernment

"The NAACP and the unions is wrestling over color bars in employment," said Simple, "but there is no color bar in unemployment. When a man is unemployed and out of work, be he black or white, his pockets is *equally* empty. A white budget at home with nothing in it is just as budgetless as a black budget with nothing in it. If white wives is like my wife Joyce, when the family budget gets low a husband is liable to be up against some loud talking from his better half. She always claims she could do better if she was a man than her husband can. What makes womens so conceited, do you reckon?"

"I don't know," I said. "Maybe it stems from original sin."

"I know Eve figured she could have had two or three apples, instead of one, if Adam hadn't been so lazy and had gone to the tree and plucked them apples himself, instead of letting that serpent come creeping along with just one little old pippin which is what my old Aunt Lucy, who knowed her Bible, said was the beginning of original sin. And that lone fig leaf Eve wore everywhere she went—Adam could have cut her off enough new fig leaves to make a dress. He didn't. That is one reason Eve fussed at Adam so much."

"How do you know she fussed?" I asked.

"I know women," said Simple. "I bet Eve and Adam fussed and quarreled and hollered, then cussed so much, they should have been named Atom and Evil. Anyhow, if Adam had been out working somewhere, instead of lounging around in the Garden of Eden, he would have got along much better with his wife. Women do not like a man around just doing nothing. I am lucky to be working every day. That is why my wife is so glad to see me when I get home. Unemployment is no good, and it is too bad there is so much around these days.

"Everything is always worse for colored than for white, because we have less to begin with, so if we lose that little bit, where are we at?" asked Simple. "That is why a recession for white folks is a depression for us. But if the NAACP can open up the unions, maybe there will be a few more jobs around, at least."

"A great many more," I said.

"Except of course, if a Negro was ever to drive a train," said Simple, "I mean run a diesel engine on the Florida Express, the government would probably have to put a troop train in front and a troop train behind and B-29s overhead to get that train through Georgia. And the first Negro engineer on a New York-to-Jackson train would have to be protected like Meredith was at Ole Miss. If they also had colored conductors on that train, every coach would have to have soldiers in the vestibules and the FBI in the smoking rooms. It is no great big job for a conductor to collect tickets on a train, so why do you reckon them railroad unions will let a Negro *buy* a ticket but won't let him *collect* one? The railroads will let a Negro ride in a coach, but will not let him run an engine. In New York City, Negroes drive subway trains. They drive trucks. They run busses. Why cannot a Negro also run an American train on an American railroad in this American country?"

"Ha! Ha!" I laughed.

"Because a Negro is a Negro," said Simple. "I am telling you, we has so many problems, life is liable to kill us before death does. In the old days, you did not hear of Negroes committing suicide so much like you do now. Lately, we is getting just like white folks, taking sleeping pills by the handful, drinking poisons, jumping off George Washington bridges, driving Cadillacs into walls on purpose, also turning on gas and breathing our last instead of using that gas to cook dinner with. Crazy peoples are walking around talking to themselves, setting up in the subway muttering and mumbling all to their lonesome selves, whirling and twirling in the middle of the street in front of cars. Such things I did not see in the good old days when I first come to Harlem. Problems is driving colored folks crazy now, too, just like white folks."

"I think, my dear fellow," I said, "it is simply that as one grows older, one is more aware of the woes of the world. In your youth, when you were bright, optimistic, buoyant, self-centered, and young, your eyes were blind. Now you have more discernment."

"More concernment," said Simple, "which is what I wish the unions would have, too, because every man ought to have the right to work. Harlem is too full of hustlers these days. Fact is, in the opinion of some people I know who would like to be hipsters," said Simple, "work is the last refugee of a square, but hustling is an honorable hype."

"With which I totally disagree," I said. "Work saves the human race from sin, boredom, stagnation, and running amuck. Without work, what would you do with your day?"

"Waste it away," said Simple. "I could waste without haste. I could find plenty of ways to occupy my time, if I was not working. But I am not constituted to hustle."

"That I believe," I said. "You are no hypster. In fact, you cannot even lie with a straight face. But you certainly can con your friends out of beers. At this very bar, how many times have I treated you to drinks without any recompense whatsoever?"

"You know, me and Joyce have to balance our budget, and my wife does not count in beers," said Simple.

"I have to balance my budget, too," I said.

"Yes," said Simple, "but a woman balances different from a man. You are not married so, whenever you want to, you can shift your balance around—and pull a hype on yourself. But my wife wants our budget to come out even each and every week. A woman's voice is sweet to hear when it is full of love, but not when the budget don't balance. Joyce can figure backwards, count pennies down to the last Indian head, and don't mess with dollar bills! Every time I break a dollar, I think about what will happen at home. When I was a single man, I didn't care whichaway or where my dollars went."

"But your landlady did," I said. "I recall many a time you had to borrow from me to pay your rent."

"Bring up not such unpleasant subjects," said Simple. "That were far away and long ago. My wife keeps me and the landlord straight now. But, at least, I *borrowed* from you. I did not beg, neither steal, con, nor hype anybody out of a cent. I would not even take money from Zarita, who loved me, even if we had no legal ties. But, to be a decent bar girl, Zarita could lay down plenty of hypes herself—and still does, I reckon, wherever she may be. Zarita and my Cousin Minnie both knew how to get the ups on a man without giving in to him. Many a poor joker has sacrificed his week's wages to them womens just for a smile. Zarita was pretty, anyhow, but Minnie looks like come-what-may and worse today. Still and yet, that cousin of mine has got something that glues a man to a bar stool, if he is setting next to her. Without being a hustler, Minnie is one of the best lady hypsters since Eve hyped Adam. Some people, male or either female, just naturally have talent for laying down a hype. I don't, which is probably why I do not bother."

"You have a conscience," I said, "which in our day and time not everyone is born with. The typical hypster is what the psychology books term amoral, if not actually immoral—unconscious of sin, really, even though a sinner."

"I wish I could be unconscious of my budget," said Simple. "Say, brother—"

"I did not know we were related," I said, sensing what was coming.

"Well then, *friend*—listen," said Simple. "Before you embarrassed me, I was going to ask you another favor—as of old. Lend me a five."

"Until when?" I asked. "May Day, when you *may* pay?"

"Why be technical?" said Simple. "But if you did lend me a five, I was going to treat *you* to a beer."

"On such a rare occasion, I cannot resist," I said. "Here!"

"Bartender," cried Simple, "a beer—one for me and one for this un-budgeted steer! And now to get back on the subject of hypers, hypsters, and hustling. You know, peoples hustles in a lot of different ways. Some sell their bodies and some sell their souls. My feeling is, if you are gonna sell either, try to get a good price."

"Some people simply sell honest labor," I said.

"Yes, but they usually don't get anywhere," declared Simple lifting his beer. "The ones that has the fine houses and the fine cars and drinks the best whiskey is most in generally them that sells their souls. A few makes it to the upper brackets with their bodies—but they is mostly womens with the right telephone numbers."

"You mean, I suppose, kept women and call girls," I said, "because the poor bar-stool hustlers and street-walkers wouldn't be in bars and on corners if they made anything."

"I am also talking about womens who marry money *for money,*" said Simple, looking at his already empty glass on the bar. "But marrying money happens to very few colored womens. There are not enough colored men around with fortunes for many of our womens to make them their targets. Of course, a few colored folks in show business marry whites. But it is the colored celebrities that usually has the money, my wife says, and the whites marry them to get it."

"I think your wife is making a completely unjustified statement," I said. "A celebrity, white or colored, may marry for love just like anybody else."

"It is not necessary to marry to get love," said Simple, "so why confuse the issue? I am not opposed to intermarriage myself. But my wife, Joyce, blows her top at the very mention of it. Joyce says if we had a son what married white, she would put him out of the house.

"I said, 'Joyce, baby, he probably would not want to live in Harlem, nohow.'

"Joyce said, 'Let him go down to the Village then and live in sin.'

" 'What do you mean,' I asked her, 'live in sin, if they've got a marriage license?'

" 'To me,' said Joyce, 'it is living in sin for a colored man to marry any-body related to Talmadge, Eastland, Wallace, Sheriff Clark, and Satan—and all white folks bears kinship.'

"I did not argue with Joyce, because when she gets on that subject, we will not be moved. When my wife has a point, she likes to gnaw at it like a dog with a bone. When Joyce sees a mixed couple on the street, that gives her a point. It is one of her main concernments. But me, I do not understand how my wife can work for integration, give money to CORE, the NAACP, and all, yet get mad when she sees integration in action. Colored womens can be a contradiction. Am I right or wrong?"

"All women are contradictions," I said. "But contradictions are a part of their charm. 'Inconsistency, thy name is woman,' I quote. Or maybe it's 'inconstancy.' "

"Boyd, your diploma is worth every penny you paid for it," said Simple. "Only a man who is colleged could talk like that. Me, I speaks simpler, myself."

"Simplicity can sometimes be more devious than erudition," I said, "especially when it centers in an argumentative ego like yours."

"Of course," said Simple.

Statutes and Statues

"There were so many policemens uptown the week Malcolm X was buried that Harlem looked like a Cops Convention. And down in Selma, Alabama, that week the polices were so busy arresting Negroes that they had to swear in extra officers recruited from the Ku Klux Klan," said Simple. "It must have cost the City of New York a half million dollars to keep all them policemens up in Harlem all week long, what with overtime and all. And the State of Alabam' is almost gone broke arresting Negroes and feeding them in jail. It looks to me like it would be cheaper for white folks just to go ahead and give Negroes whatever it is they want, and stop having to spend so much money on polices, and jail bills, and court cases, and fat old judges making decrees that nobody pays any attention to. All this costs so much money!"

"Yes, it does," I said.

"But then the white folks have all the money," said Simple, "so they probably do not mind spending it. There is always more for them where that came from. But for Negroes the hardest thing is to try to get just three or four hundred dollars ahead. A black man has hardly got enough money to even get from Brooklyn to the Bronx, let alone a little extra change for a stopover in Harlem. We are a *broke* race of people. That is why I am all for trying to collect what is owed my great grandpa and grandma from slavery days for all that free labor my ancestries did in this American country!"

"The statute of limitations has long since passed," I said.

"Maybe that is why them dynamiters wanted to blow up that statue," said Simple.

"I am not talking about the Statue of Liberty," I said. "I am speaking of *limitations*."

"Which is about all we got," said Simple, "because the Statue of Liberty has her back turned toward Harlem."

"Liberty has always been looking out to sea," I said, "whence came the white Americans. But Africans arrived via the southern routes, mostly landing in Virginia and the Carolinas and places like that—long before Liberty lit her torch."

"Only Ku Klux Klan torches blazing," said Simple. "You know, as long as I have been in Harlem, I have not yet looked Liberty in the face, but I know she is beautiful on the postcards. And I hope she don't get blowed up before I see what she looks like. Where do you reckon folks is getting all these bombs and dynamite to blow things up these days when a child can't even buy a firecracker just for fun at Fourth of July time? Firecrackers is against the law. But it looks like almost anybody can get a stick of dynamite, a small bomb, a rifle, or a pistol if they want to do something wrong. But good people like me better not be caught by the polices with no kind of weapon, not even for protection in a self-service elevator.

"What can I carry to guard against the junkies who need thirty dollars for a fix? Junkies should be able to tell by looking at me that I do not have any money. But a junkie in need will steal even the widow's mite. The city ought to start a Junk Fund to take care of poor junkies and pay for their fixes, so they don't have to rob old ladies and stick up cabbies. The city used to have free Soup Stands during the Depression, so the city ought to set up free Junk Stands now."

"The English system amounts, in effect, to about what you are saying. Over there they have Dope Depots to supply the addict with his daily needs. Such a setup in New York could cut the rug out from under the heroin pushers and the big boys who make the million-dollar profits. Free Junk Stands would cut crime in half."

"I agree," said Simple "because then the junkies would not have to rob *me* to pay the pushers. So let the city stop spending so much money on cops to keep the ordinary Negroes in line, and spend some bread on free dope to keep the junkies in line. I think it is worse for a junkie to beat and rob an old woman in Queens than it is for a Negro to start a riot in Harlem. Them that participates in riots are usually big enough and ugly enough to take care of themselves. But an old lady of eighty-three, no. Or a lone man or lone woman caught in a self-service elevator by herself, no! Push-button elevators was made for stick-ups. There has not been an elevator man in most elevators in Harlem for years. The junkies *love* the elevator in our building. When a crazy junkie gets on at the second floor, what can you do? Or suppose you are a taxi driver in that front seat by his lonesome self in a lonesome neighborhood—and the guys in the back seat are desperate for dope money! I say let the city put into its new budget a big appropriation for Free Junk Stands—and give dope away."

"Your suggestion would be ridiculed at City Hall," I said.

"Maybe not by that new Borough President we got" said Simple. "That woman is good-looking and smart, too."

"Mrs. Motley is a handsome woman," I said.

"She looks like the Statue of Liberty to me," said Simple. "And her back is not turned to Harlem, because she lived in Harlem, and she knows what I am talking about. She knows we have got one million cops and a half million junkies and we need some free dope."

"Your figures are extremely in error," I said. "Besides you are confusing the issues."

"The issues are confusing me," said Simple. "But I hope that nice Motley lady does not live in a house with a self-service elevator. If she does, the city ought to take one of them parlays of cops off of one of our Harlem corners and give them to her for protection at night when she comes home from City Hall. With so many junkies around eying push-button elevators needing thirty-dollar-a-day fixes, I do not want anything to happen to my Statue of Liberty."

"You mean Constance Baker Motley?"

"I do," said Simple.

American Dilemma

"When I come around the corner last night here in Harlem," said Simple, "and nearly run into a white cop strolling around the corner from the other way, I almost said, 'Birmingham.'"

"Almost? What did you say instead?" I asked.

"Nothing," said Simple.

"What did the cop say?"

"Nothing, neither," said Simple. "If he had been a colored cop and I had bumped into him, I would have said, 'Excuse me.' But he being white, I did not say nothing. And what I thought was Birmingham."

"Seemingly then, you equate all white people with the brutalities of Birmingham, even whites in New York."

"I do," said Simple. "After dark, Harlem is black, except for cops. Here of lately, it looks like there is more white cops than ever strolling around our corners at night. They must be expecting more trouble."

"What 'they'?" I asked.

"The white folks downtown. If there was as many black cops downtown in New York as there is white cops uptown in Harlem, you would know something was wrong. I reckon it is Alabama and Mississippi making the white folks downtown afraid Harlem might get mad again and start breaking up things, like they did in the riots."

"I admit there is often tension in the air," I said. "But do you think it will reach riot proportions again?"

"All I know is, when I come around that corner last night off Lenox Avenue and run into that white cop, when he saw me he looked like he was scared. You know I am no dangerous man. I am what folks calls an ordinary citizen. Me, I work, pay my rent, and taxes, and try to get along. But that young white cop looked at me like he were afraid of me. I do not much blame him, up here in Harlem all by hisself at midnight A.M. in the middle of Negroes. Lenox Avenue can get real lonesome-looking late at night. When I saw that cop and thought about Birmingham, I bet he saw me and thought about riots.

"He were a young cop. Maybe he just recently got on the force. Maybe he needs to earn some steady money to take care of his wife and kids and buy hisself a house in some neighborhood where there is no Negroes.

None of these white cops here in Harlem ever live in Harlem. They say Harlem is the place where the Police Department puts rookies and green young cops to break them in. Or else they put old cops who has done wrong in some other part of New York, maybe taken graft that should have gone to the precinct captain, or something like that. So they put them up in Harlem for a punishment. Anyhow, the other night, here is this young white cop coming around the corner, and here is me coming around the corner. We almost bump. I pass, he passes, and nobody says nothing.

"In a way, I felt sorry for that young white cop. Was I not colored and he not white, I would have said, 'Good evening! It's kind of quiet tonight, ain't it?' And maybe he would have said, 'Good evening,' back. But neither one of us said nothing. I almost bumped into him. He almost bumped into me, curving that corner, and nobody even said, 'Good evening,' let alone, 'Excuse me.' All I thought about was Birmingham. What he thought I do not know."

"I gather then that there was no friendly word exchanged between you—you, citizen, and he, policeman, guardian of the law."

"No friendly word," said Simple.

Promulgations

"If I was setting in the High Court in Washington," said Simple, "where they do not give out no sentences for crimes, but where they gives out promulgations, I would promulgate. Up them long white steps behind them tall white pillars in that great big marble hall with the eagle of the U.S.A., where at I would bang my gavel and promulgate."

"Promulgate what?" I asked.

"Laws," said Simple. "After that I would promulgate the promulgations that would take place if people did not obey my laws. I see no sense in passing laws if nobody pays them any mind."

"What would happen if people did not obey your promulgations?" I asked.

"Woe be unto them," said Simple. "I would not be setting in that High Court paid a big salary just to read something off a paper. I would be there with a robe on to see that what I read was carried out. I would gird on my sword, like in the Bible, and prepare to do battle. For instant, 'Love thy neighbor as thyself.' The first man I caught who did not love his neighbor as hisself, I would make him change places with his neighbor—the rich with the poor, the white with the black, and Governor Faubus with me."

"I know you have lost your mind," I said. "How could you accomplish such an objective?"

"With education," said Simple, "which white folks favors. I would make Governor Faubus go to school again in Little Rock and study with them integrated students there and learn all over again the facts of life."

"You are telling me *what* you would do," I said, "not *how* you would do it. How could you make Faubus do anything?"

"I would say, 'Faubus! Faubus! Come out of that clothes closet or wherever you are hiding and face me. *Me*, Jesse B., who has promulgated your attendance in my presence! I decrees now and from here on out that you straighten up and fly right. Cast off your mask of ignorance and hate and go study your history. You have not yet learned that "taxation without representation is tyranny," which I learned in grade school. You have also not learned that "all men are created equal," which I learned before I quit school. Educate yourself, Faubus, so that you can better rule your state.' "

"Suppose he paid you no attention?" I said.

"Then I would whisper something in his ear," said Simple. "I would tell him that the secret records in the hands of my committee show that he has got colored blood. Whilst he was trying to recover from that shock, I would continue with some facts I made up.

" 'Governor Faubus, did you not know your great-great-grandfather were black?'

"He would say, 'What?'

"I would say, 'Look at me, Governor, I am your third cousin.' Whereupon Faubus would faint. Whilst he was fainted, I would pick him up and take him to a mixed school. When he come to, he would be integrated. That is the way I would work my promulgations," said Simple.

"I should think you would rapidly become a national figure," I said, "with your picture in *Time, Life, Newsweek, Ebony,* and *Jet.*"

"Yes," said Simple. "Then in my spare time I would take up the international situation. I would call a Summit Meeting and get together with all the big heads of state in the world."

"I gather you would drop your judgeship for the nonce and become a diplomat."

"A hip-to-mat," said Simple, "minding everybody's business but my own. I would call my valet to tell my confidential secretary to inform my aide to bring me my attaché case. I would put on my swallowtail coat, striped trousers, and high hat, get into my limousine, and ride to the Summit looking like an Englishman. But what would be different about me is I would be black. I would take my black face, black hands, and black demands right up to the top and set down and say, 'Gimme a microphone, turn on the TVs, and hook up the national hookups. I want the world to hear my message.' Then I would promulgate at large as I proceeded to chair the agenda."

"Proceed," I said.

"Which I would do," said Simple, "no sooner than the audience got settled, the diplomats got their earphones strapped on, and the translators got their dictionaries out, also the stenographers got their machines ready to take my message from Harlem down for the record. The press galleries would be full of reporters waiting to wire my words around the world, and I would be prepared to send them, Jack. I would be ready."

"Give forth," I said.

"Bread and meat come first," said Simple. " 'Gentlemens of the Summit, I want you-all to think how you can provide everybody in the world with bread and meat. Civil rights comes next. Let everybody have civil rights, white, black, yellow, brown, gray, grizzle, or green. No Jim-Crow-take-low can't go for anybody! Let Arabs go to Israel and Israels go to Egypt, Chinese come to America and Negroes live in Australia, if any be so foolish as to want to. Let Willie Mays live in Levittown and Casey Stengel live in Ghana if he so desires. And let me drink at the Stork Club if I get tired of Small's Paradise. Open house before open skies. After which comes peace, which you can't have nohow as long as peoples and nations is snatching and grabbing over pork chops and payola so as not to starve to death. No peace could be had nowhow with white nations against dark.

" 'You big countries of the world has got to wake up to the sense your leaders wasn't born with, and the peoples has got to reach out their hands to each others' over the leaders' heads, just like I am talking over your leaders' heads now, because so many leaders is in the game for payola and say-ola, not *do*-ola. But me, self-appointed, I am beholden to nobody. Right now I cannot do much, but I can say *all*.

" 'I therefore say to you, gentlemens of the Summit, you may not pay attention to me now, but some sweet day you will. I will get tired of your stuff and your bluff. I will take your own golf stick and wham the world so far up into orbit until you will be shaken off the surface of the earth and everybody will wonder where have all the white folks gone. Gentlemens of the Summit, you-all had better get together and straighten up and fly right—else in due time you will have to contend with what Harlem thinks. Do I hear some of you-all say, "It do not matter what Harlem thinks"?

" 'I regret to inform you, gentlemens of the Summit, that IT DO!' "

How Old Is Old?

"I looked in the mirror today and I saw my first gray hair," said Simple, "this morning."

"That's nothing," I said. "Some morning you will look in your mirror and see several gray hairs."

"Sometime I might look in the mirror and see *all* gray hairs," said Simple, "but I will not like it. The chicks will say I am old."

"Gray hair does not necessarily make a man old," I said. "Some folks become gray at quite an early age, others bald."

"I had rather be gray-headed than bald-headed," said Simple. "I never did want to look like Yul Brynner."

"Yul Brynner probably shaves his hair off."

"I want neither a razor nor nature nor tomorrow to take what little hair I own. Neither do I want to look like Uncle Mose before my time. I pulled out that gray hair I spotted in my head this morning."

"Little did I think you would be so vain, partner."

"Little did I think I was getting so old," said Simple. "But come right down to it, I have been in this world quite a while. I survived being born, being a child, being a man, and being married twice. I have also survived being an Afro-American, colored, and a so-called Negro.

"I have survived bad feet, a bad head the morning after, bad weather, and a bad back, also checks that bounce, landladies that bark, bite, and bifferate, plus a wife, Isabel, who did not understand me in my youthhood, neither I understood her.

"Oh, I have stood much in this world that I did not understand, and standed much that I did not understood, also undergone mistreatment from one billion white folks, one million colored folks, one hundred bosses, and one bartender who would not let me have a beer on credit.

"I have spent so much money in that place up the street that I ought to own that beer bar. I said to the barman up there last night, 'How come you come telling me the state liquor laws do not allow you to grant a customer credit? Why do them laws discriminate against me? You, the bartender, drink as much as you want to when the boss is not looking and do not pay a dime, not even credit. How come I cannot drink as much as I want and pay on time in *due* time?'

" 'It is the law of the License Commission,' says the bartender.

" 'Then you gimme one of them free drinks I see you sneaking into your mouth. I will sneak some change into your hand when I get paid.'

" 'Against the law,' says the bartender.

" 'Then treat me,' I says.

" 'Also illegal,' says the bartender. 'My boss does not budget no treats.'

" 'Then I will budget myself to another bar down the street,' says I, which I did, which is why I am in this new bar tonight and you could not find me until I hailed you passing by the window. Being my friend, unmarried, and without a budget, buy me a beer."

"I thought you were working around to something," I said. "O.K., since you are hard-up tonight—one beer for this gentleman, bartender!"

"Maybe two," said Simple, "because I still wish to argue with you on this subject of old age. How old is a man before he gets to be an old man? Forty, fifty, or sixty? Seventy-five I know is ageable, but am I old? I only been married twice."

Weight in Gold

"Like Billy Eckstine and Frank Sinatra's son, I wish I was rich enough to be kidnapped," said Simple, "because if I was, I would have done spent all my money before the kidnapping happened. I would never let them hold me for ransom, because the ransom money would be gone. I would just say, 'Boys, you have come too late. My pockets and my bank account is both now turned inside out. I have run through my million. Better to have had and spent than never to have had at all.'"

"My dear fellow," I countered, "if you ever possessed a great deal of money, say a million or so, you would find it next to impossible to spend it all. Besides, if you were sensible, you would invest the principal and live on the interest, like most rich people do."

"I would not be sensible," said Simple. "If I had money, I would go stark-raving mad and spend it! I could not stand being rich. There is so much I have wanted in past days, and so much I still want now—I would just spend it all, yes. And what I did not spend, I would give away to peoples I love. I would give Joyce, my wife, one hundred thousand dollars. I would look up Zarita, that old gal of mine, and, for old times' sake, I would give her fifty thousand dollars. To you, Boyd, my old beer buddy, I would give twenty-five thousand, and to my Cousin Minnie, ten, so she would not have to borrow from me any more. Also, I would present Minnie with a brand new wig, since she lost hers in the riots. And for every neighbor kid I know, I would buy a bicycle, because I think every boy—and girl, too, if they wants—should have a bicycle while young."

"In this New York traffic, as heavy as it is, you would give kids bicycles?"

"They can always ride in Central Park," said Simple. "When I were a kid, I always wanted a bicycle, and nobody ever bought me one. To tell the truth, if I was rich I would buy myself a bicycle right now. Then next month I would buy me a motorcycle. I always wanted one of them to make noise on. Then after riding around on my motorcycle for a couple of weeks, I would buy me a small car, just big enough for me and Joyce. After which I would buy a *big* car, then a Town and Country, then a station wagon. After that I would get a foreign sports car. I would do this gradual, not letting the world know all at once that I am rich. Also, I would not like to be kidnapped until *all* the money were spent. I would like to have my fun first, then be kidnapped with my name in the papers. 'JESSE B. SEMPLE NABBED BY MOB. *Held For Ransom. Harlem Shaken by the News.*'"

"You would be missed in this bar," I said.

"If I was rich, I would own this bar," said Simple. "I would buy up all the bars in Harlem and keep the present white proprietors employed as managers. I would not draw no color line. Of course, if the white mens quit and did not want to work under me, black, I would go to HARYOU and ask them to send me some bright young colored managers."[2]

"HARYOU?" I said. "HARYOU hardly supplies bartenders, does it?"

"I would not request bartenders," said Simple. "I would be employing colored *managers*. They tell me HARYOU is set up to give young Negroes a chance."

"Why, tell me, please, if you had money," I asked, "would you buy only bars? Why not restaurants, grocery stores, clothing shops, wiggeries?"

"Because bars has the quickest turnover," said Simple. "Besides, if I owned all the Harlem bars, I would have credit in each and every one of them. I would never have to ask anybody to buy me a beer. In fact, I would treat *you* every time we met. Oh, if I was rich, daddy-o, I would be a generous son-of-a-gun, specially with everybody I like. I not only like you, Boyd, but I admire you. You are colleged. You know, if I had money, I would send every young man and young woman in Harlem to college, that wanted to go. I would set up one of these offices that gives out money for education."

"You mean a Foundation for Fellowships," I said.

"And Girlships, too," declared Simple. "Womens and mens from Harlem would all be colleged by the time 1970 came. It do not take but four years to get colleged, do it?"

"That's right," I said, "depending on your application."

"I would tell all the boys and girls in Harlem to make their applications now," said Simple, "and I would see that they got through. White folks downtown would have no excuse any more to say we was not educated uptown, because I would pay for it."

"In other words, you would be Harlem's Ford Foundation," I said, "on a really big scale."

"Yes," said Simple, "because on my scales, every kid in Harlem is worth his weight in gold."

Sympathy

"Some people do not have no scars on their faces," said Simple, "but they has scars on their hearts. Some people have never been beat up, teeth knocked out, nose broke, shot, cut, not even so much as scratched in the face. But they have had their hearts broke, brains disturbed, their minds torn up, and the behinds of their souls kicked by the ones they love. It is not always your wife, husband, sweetheart, boy friend or girl friend, common-law mate—no, it might be your mother that kicks your soul around like a football. It might be your best friend that squeezes your heart dry like a lemon. It might be some ungrateful child you have looked forward to making something out of when it got grown, but who goes to the dogs and bites you on the way there. Oh, friend, your heart can be scarred in so many different ways it is not funny," said Simple.

"Why do you bring up such unpleasant subjects on a pleasant evening?" I asked. "We have got two nice cold glasses of beer sitting up here in front of us at the bar, and we could be talking about President Johnson and his budget problems."

"Or about Adam Powell and the lady they say he called an old bag-woman," said Simple.

"Or about who kidnapped Billy Eckstine and took the ransom out of his own pocket," I added.

"Else why Cassius Clay stuck by Elijah Muhammad instead of Malcolm X."

"Or why Malcolm X changed his name to Malik El Shabazz."

"Or how come, if you are a Black Muslim, a man can change his name any time he wants to," said Simple.

"We could even be talking about the weather," I said.

"Or the price of eggs," agreed Simple. "But I am talking about how a man's heart or a woman's is *not* an egg, and, broken though your heart may be, it is seldom busted. It is a good thing folks cannot crack the heart and drop the insides in a frying pan like an egg. It is a good thing a man cannot make an omelette out of your trouble. Your ticker may be battered, mistreat it as you might, but that old heart keeps on beating until you die *d-e-a-d* dead."

"Who did what to your heart, old man, that you keep on harping on the same subject this evening? Did your wife look at you cross-eyed when you came home from work tonight? Is Joyce on the rampage?"

"No," said Simple. "My subject has nothing to do with myself. I am standing here thinking about Cousin Minnie. In spite of her faults, Minnie is a good woman, although somewhat overweight, and inclined to borrow money from her relatives when she ought to get out and earn it herself. Last year, you know, Cousin Minnie thought she had found a good man who would neither beat her nor cheat her, kick or mistreat her, and would never go upside her head. This man did not do such heavy-handed things. But he did worse. Hainsworth lived a lie in Minnie's presence. He kept another woman around the corner with who he spent half the night. When Hainsworth come home to Minnie, it were almost time to get up and go to work. But this was not so bad. He told this other woman things on Minnie that a man should not tell God. He talked about Minnie like a dog outside the home, and this is what hurted Minnie the most—that this other woman should know more about her than she knowed about herself—and from Hainsworth."

"How did Minnie find out all this?" I asked.

"At the beauty shop," said Simple, "which is where womens exchange news, regardless of who is listening over the partitions. In Harlem the beauty shop booths is so close together, anybody is liable to hear anything. And Minnie overheard it from the horse's mouth—the other woman's—direct, herself—even as to what kind of skin lightener Minnie uses before she goes to bed. Also that Minnie has a strawberry birthmark on her left-hand thigh—which nobody could know to tell anybody except Hainsworth."

"I'll be dogged!" I said.

"Yes," said Simple, "that is what broke Minnie's heart."

"Temporarily, I hope."

"Minnie will recover," said Simple.

"Such little things," I said, "should hardly break a woman's heart."

"A small pin can puncture a big balloon," stated Simple. "Minnie's pride were like a big balloon and her love for Hainsworth were great—until she found out he had told this other woman all them things. She said to the whole beauty shop that Minnie could not even boil rice proper, neither fry fish crisp, that she made soggy bisquits and bitter coffee, and also Minnie looked like a pig in a poke when she come to bed."

"Great day!" I exclaimed. "What did Minnie say to Hainsworth?"

"She hit him in the head with a small hammer," said Simple.

"What? Where is he now?"

"In Harlem Hospital with a knot on his noggin like a hen's egg, also a split over his left eye which dead sure will leave a scar. But Minnie has a scar on her heart—which is worse," said Simple. "Also, Minnie has lost her faith in men, plus losing her meal ticket. Hainsworth were a good provider. Only trouble was, he were feeding two womens. Now both of them will suffer with him off the job. Had not that other girl blabbed so much in that beauty shop, both of them womens could have had a good dinner tonight."

"That's a shame," I said.

"Yes, it is a shame," said Simple. "To have a scar on your heart is bad enough, but to have nothing in your stomach is worse."

"That's bad," I agreed.

"Yes," affirmed Simple. "That *is* bad, especially since lately Minnie has not been feeling well. Do you know what she told me last night? Out of the clear blue sky in this bar Minnie said, 'Jess, the doctors say I have a tumor, and when they say that, you are liable to have cancer,' said Miss Minnie. 'I am going to the hospital on Monday, Jess Semple. Good-by.'

" 'Just like that, you say good-by tonight? And you are going home this early?'

" 'Yes,' said Miss Minnie. 'I did not tell you I was sick before, I do not tell you I am sick now. But I am. Monday I go to be prepared for the operation. Maybe it might not take like vaccination. If it do not take, I am gone to Glory. If I go to Glory, maybe you will remember me who set beside you once on this bar stool. And if not, or if so, anyhow, good-by.'

" 'Cousin, are you sure enough really sick? Are you telling me straight?'

" 'Yes, straight—and it's late. Good-by.'

" 'Late what?'

" 'Just late, that's all. Good-by.' And she left."

"She left?"

"Yes."

"Just like that?"

"Just like that. Minnie did not even tell me what hospital she would be in—Harlem, Bellevue, Medical Center, or where. She just left. Minnie would borrow money from me at the drop of a hat. Yes, she would. But I guess she doesn't want to borrow sympathy."

"No?"

"No," said Simple, "I guess she don't. She just up and left."

Uncle Sam

"Nobody is responsible for the relatives you is born with," said Simple. "You are only responsible for them which you yourself have taken unto yourself of your own free will. I have taken unto myself Joyce, my wife, and I love her. But I was born related to Minnie, that off-cousin who latched onto me since she come up North. Yet and still, God knows why, somehow I love her, although she can be a nuisance. Maybe because Cousin Minnie takes for granted she understands me, which I do her."

"By and large, you have the same interests," I said.

"By and large, we do," said Simple. "We both likes stools when they are in front of bars. Anyhow, after all, she is a relative, even though on the off-side, and I am sorry she is sick. My Uncle Sam is on the off-side, too. But I have never met Uncle Sam in the flesh."

"I did not know you had an uncle named Sam," I said.

"I have. You have, too. But we are not responsible for him. I am talking about the old man in the tight pants, the swallowtail coat, and the star-spangled hat who lives in the attic above the President at the top of the White House. Uncle Sam must have lost his wife, because I never hear of an Auntie Sam. Else he never married. But they say he is my uncle."

"On which side of the family?" I asked. "Your mother's?"

"Don't slip me in the dozens," said Simple, "or I will tell you on which side you are related yourself. There would have to be some crossbreeding somewhere. I am talking about the MAN, the American Man, the one with the pointed goatee. I mean the MAN on all the recruiting posters: UNCLE SAM WANTS YOU, pointing dead at me. When I was young enough to be drafted, Uncle Sam used to scare me half to death. But even then I had some questions for him. I said, 'Uncle Sam, if you is really my blood uncle, prove it. Before you draft me into any United States Army, prove your kinship. Are we *is*, or are we *ain't* related? If so, how come you are so white and I am so dark? Uncle Sam, explain myself.'"

"Did he ever answer you?" I asked.

"No," said Simple, "that is why I want to know if Uncle Sam *is* or *ain't*. He knows I am colored."

"So?"

"He is white."

"So?"

"So therefore Uncle Sam do not have to sue in the Supreme Court every time he wants to get a cup of coffee down South," said Simple. "Neither do Uncle Sam have to sue in Mississippi every time he wants to vote."

"Segregation will end and the ballot will come in due time," I said.

"So will death," said Simple.

"The Constitution, the government, the law are now all on the Negro's side."

"But is Uncle Sam?" asked Simple.

"As a symbol of the government, I would say *yes*—looking back, yes, Roosevelt, Kennedy, and today Johnson."

"Faubus, Barnett, Eastland," said Simple.

"I am not kidding." I frowned.

"Me, neither," said Simple. "They make a lot of star-spangled hats in Washington. I wants one for me."

"Why?"

"So I can be Uncle Sam," said Simple.

"You sound like Nipsey Russell. Fact is, with a star-spangled hat on, you would look like Nipsey."

"Nipsey I like on TV," said Simple, "so I could bear the resemblance. The government ought to make some great big subway posters of Nipsey as Uncle Sam. I say, there ought to be a *black* Uncle Sam."

"Chauvinist!" I said.

"If that word means what I think it do," cried Simple, "take it back."

"It does not mean that," I said, "so continue."

"What does it mean?" asked Simple.

"A man who is so full of racism that nobody else can stand him. Or another definition might be somebody like yourself who wants to make Uncle Sam black."

"Or at least brownskin," said Simple. "Or maybe Indian like the original Americans, or Chinese like Chinese-Americans, or Japanese like them Niseis in California. Since it is popular to integrate nowadays, how come Uncle Sam is never pictured as if maybe his mama had integrated before him?"

"Do you know what you are saying?" I asked. "You are speaking of miscegenation, not integration. The Uncle Sam you see on the signboards is, of course, of Nordic descent."

"I am tired of seeing my Uncle always of Nordic descent," said Simple. "I want to see him look like me—colored for once."

"Uncle Sam is a symbol, as I said. He is not meant to be of any one race or group. Symbols have no color."

"Then I want him to be a symbol of *me* once," said Simple. "I have never yet seen an Uncle Sam that looked like me."

"You seem to dwell in a world of fantasy," I said. "Suppose tomorrow all the newspapers were to picture Uncle Sam as colored, could you believe your eyes?"

"If I saw myself, *yes*. Adam Clayton Powell would also make a good-looking Uncle Sam," said Simple. "Or for a young version, Harry Belafonte would be handsome. But Sidney Poitier would be the stone-most! Star-spangled Uncle Sam! Or let's take Miss America with a sheet draped around her, looking like the Statue of Liberty. I have never yet seen her colored. If I was an artist, I would sometimes draw America looking like Marian Anderson, or Claudia McNeil who was in *Raisin in the Sun*. I do not see why Claudia would not make a knockout Miss America, full-bosomed as she is."

"Dream on," I said.

"Well, at least, they could make Miss America a Red Indian," said Simple. "Indians was the first Americans, but they got pushed back so much by the cowboys in the movies until now they is the *last* Americans. But in honor of the fact that they was once the first, there ought to be Indian Uncle Sams, too, and Indian Miss Americas."

"At least, their heads were once on a penny," I said.

"But no Negroes," said Simple. "Our heads have never even been on a penny. Neither on a dollar bill, nor on a five-dollar bill, nor a ten. And I have not seen a Negro on a postage stamp since Booker T. Washington."

"Frederick Douglass is lately on a stamp," I said. "However, Negroes are only about ten percent of the American population."

"But we raise ninety percent of the hell," said Simple, "so I want to see a Freedom Rider on a postage stamp, or else Martin Luther King, or me dressed like Uncle Sam. We have been mighty near one hundred years free. It is not easy by and large to live one hundred years in the Land of the Free, if black you be—so I deserves my head on a stamp."

"What kind of stamp?" I asked.

"The first space-stamp," said Simple, "designed to fly off into orbit—out of this world. Free! Uncle Sam *me*—on a letter to the moon!"

"Dream on, dreamer," I said, "dream on."

Uncollected Stories

Remembrances

"The first time I was in love," said Simple, "I was in love stone-dead-bad—because I had it, and it had me, and it was the most! Love! When I look back on it now, that girl couldn't have been good-looking. When I look back on it now, she couldn't have been straight. And when I look back on it now, I must have been simple—which I were. But then I did not know what I know today. At that time I had not been beat, betrayed, misled, and bled by womens. I thought then, if I just had that girl for mine and she had me for hers, heaven on earth would be."

"Why do you choose to recall all that tonight in this bar?" I asked.

"Because I am thinking on my youthhood," said Simple.

"How old exactly are you?"

"I am going into my something-or-other year," said Simple. "Tonight is nearly my birthday, and if you are my friend, you will buy me a drink."

"I have bought you so many drinks on nights which were not your birthday before! Anyhow, what'll it be—beer?"

"Same old thing," said Simple. "I do not want to go home to Joyce with whiskey on my breath. Gimme beer. Joyce is my wife, my life, my one and all, my first to last, and the last woman I intend to clasp! But sometimes I still think about that first little old girl I were really in love with down in Virginia when I were nothing but a boy. She were older than me, that girl, but only by a year. She were darker than me, too, if that be possible. And she were sweeter than a berry on the vine. My Aunt Lucy did not approve of her because her mama had been put out of church on account of sin. But I loved that girl! I'll tell the world I did!"

"I gather your romance came to naught," I said.

"Our romance came to naught, but she weights two hundred and ten pounds now, so I have heard, and has been married twice," said Simple. "But she were the first person except Aunt Lucy who made me feel like somebody wanted me in this world, relatives included. Everybody else was always telling me, 'I am your mother, but your father went off and left you on my hands!' Or else, 'I am your father, but your mother ain't no good!' Or, 'Your poor old aunt loves you, Jesse, but your papa nor mama ain't sent a dime here to feed you since last March.'

"But this girl ain't never said nothing like that. She just said, 'Jesse B., you was meant for me.'

"I said, 'Baby, let's get with it.' And we did, until the old folks broke it up.

"I had nothing, neither did she. So her mama said, 'Let my daughter be.'

"My Aunt Lucy allowed as how I were too young to be going steady, anyhow—that I must be getting too big for my britches, telling her I knew my own mind. About that time they sent me to stay with Uncle Tige out in the country, so I did not see Lorna Jean any more, until I were passing through Richmond on my way North, running away from where I ain't been back since. At which time, I were only interested in getting North. Now here I is this evening, tonight on my birthday eve, remembering a girl I have not seen in twenty-five years, but who were once my sputnik. I wonder do Lorna Jean ever think of me as I think of her, and do she have remembrances?

"Whilst I were living with Uncle Tige, I met another girl named Elroyce. I did not fall in love with her—just sort of liked her a little bit. She were fun to go around with. Once I took her to a dance, and when I took her home, her door were locked. In that day and time down in Virginia, nobody locked doors, there being no robbers then. But her mama had locked her door, lights out, house dark. It looked like nobody lived there, house empty, as if she did not have a daughter who had gone to a dance. It were embarrassing to that young girl to have to wake up them old folks to get in. Besides, it was not *that* late. That young girl's parents told her to be home at midnight. It were only just a little after one o'clock when we got there. That music was so good we forgot about time.

"It might maybe have been my fault we was late, because her mama told me I could take that girl out, but she said, 'Boy, you get my chile back home here by twelve o'clock. If you don't, it will be you and me!' The way things turned out, it were me and her. That old lady tried to ruin my life."

"The night of the dance?" I asked.

"No, not the night of the dance," said Simple; "nine months later."

"Oh!" I said.

"It were worse than 'oh,'" said Simple, "because I had not touched that girl. I were just a young teen-age boy myself. All I did was kiss Elroyce once or twice on the way home from that dance, from which we walked in the night in the springtime in the sweet and scented air. But the next week, I fell for another girl—you know how young folks is. Yet come that following fall, Elroyce's mama sent for me.

" 'Is you the father of her chile?'

" 'What child?'

" 'You see my daughter, don't you? Her chile.'

" 'No, ma'am.'

" 'Don't lie,' says Mama. 'Don't you lie to me about Elroyce!'

"I do not know why they always assumes the man is lying. It turned out that girl were secretly in love with me, so Elroyce told her mama I were the father of her child. Before God, I swear to this day I were not. I could not be. I had not touched her. But I left town. That is when I come North to Baltimore. It were not my offspring."

"Why bring up such unpleasant memories tonight?"

"Because her child would be twenty-five years old this year, and I wonder what he looks like."

"How do you know it was a boy?" I asked.

"It would have been a boy if I was its father," said Simple. "I would not know what to do with a girl—daughter—was I to have a girl—when she got teen-age. I would be afraid of springtime and dances and being out late for her, too, like that girl's parents was, if I was a father. But I would not never lock my door on no child of mine, no matter how late they come home. The *home* door, the door of home, should always be open always—else do not call it home. Rich folks' doors is locked. White folks' doors is locked. But the door to home should never be. If I had a child that stayed out all night and all day and the next day and all week, I would not lock my door against her—or him—be he boy or girl, I would not lock the door."

"Since you are not a parent, you are just theorizing," I said. "The hard realities of how to control teen-age children in this day and age baffle most people. I am sure they would baffle you."

"I baffles not easy," said Simple. "I remember how when I were in my teens, my folks did not so much lock their doors at night, but they locked their hearts. They did not try to understand me. Old folks in them days was a thousand miles and a thousand years away from their children, anyhow. I lived in the same house—but not *with* them, if you get what I mean. I do not believe, in this day and time, there is such a high wall between old and young. Do you think so?"

"Yes," I said, "I think there is—and always will be. Unfortunately, the gulf between the generations is a perennial one. Take rock and roll: the old folks hate it, the young folks love it."

"I must not be very old, then," said Simple. "I like rock and roll myself."

"Perhaps you are just retarded," I said.

"Which is better," said Simple, "than being discarded. I wish me and my wife had seven children."

"Why?" I said.

"So we could always keep an open door," said Simple.

Wigs, Women, and Falsies

"I wonder why peoples, when they have their pictures taken, always take their face? Some womens," said Simple, "have much better-looking parts elsewhere."

"You can pose the doggonedest questions," I said.

"Another thing I would like to know is why people's eyebrows do not grow longer, like their hair?" asked Simple.

"I do not know," I answered.

"But, come to think of it," said Simple, "some people's hair on their heads don't grow no longer than their eyebrows. In fact, some women's hair won't hardly grow an inch. Yet most mens have to go to the barber shop every two or three weeks. It should be men's hair that won't grow, not the women's. Why is that?"

"I am not a student of human hair, man, so I cannot tell."

"I knowed a girl once who was too lazy to comb her head," said Simple, "so she bought herself a wig. But she was too lazy to comb that. She would just put it on her head like a hat, and go on down the street."

"You have certainly known some strange people," I said.

"I have, daddy-o, but I have never seen nothing worse than a wet wig," said Simple.

"A wet wig?" I asked. "Where on earth did you ever see a wet wig?"

"On the beach," said Simple. "I seed a girl lose her wig in the water out at Coney Island. That woman had no business diving under the waves when she were in swimming, but she did. And off come her wig, which started riding the waves its own self. That girl were so embarrassed that she would not come out of the water until a lifeguard rowed out in a boat and got her wig, which, by that time, were headed for the open sea. She slapped the wig on her head. But it were a sight, tangled up like a hurrah's nest, and dripping like a wet dishrag. I never did see that woman go in swimming no more. In fact, I never took her to the beach again."

"How did you ever happen to get mixed up with a woman with a wig?" I asked.

"There is no telling who a man might get mixed up with at times," said Simple, "because in them days I were young and simple myself. Besides, she did not call it a wig. She called it a 'transformation.' I do not know why they call wigs 'transformations,' because I have seen some womens put on a wig and they were not transformed at all. Now, what I would recommend to some womens is that they get wigs for their faces—which, in some cases, needs to be hidden more than their heads. Some womens is homely, Jack! So if they gonna transform themselves, they ought to start in front instead of in the back."

"Some do," I said, "with falsies."

"Don't mention falsies to me," said Simple. "It's getting so nobody can tell how a woman is shaped any more, because they takes their shapes off when they get home. All those New Forms and Maiden Bras and Foam Rubber Shillouettes! I think there ought to be a law!"

"That would be a bit drastic," I said. "Don't you believe women have the right to make themselves more attractive? A little artifice here and there—lipstick, rouge, transformations, and such."

"And such too much is what some of them does," said Simple. "A wigless woman without her lipstick, rouge, and falsies would be another person. Impersonating herself, that's what! If it is wrong for a Negro to pass for white, it ought also to be wrong for any woman to pass for what she is not. Am not I right?"

"Every woman wants to put her best face forward," I said, "especially when she's out in public. At home, that's another matter. And you don't go home with every woman you see."

"I might try if my jive works," said Simple.

"You'd let yourself in for some rude shocks," I said.

"A man takes a chance these days and times," said Simple. "But then, men was born to take chances."

On Women Who Drink You Up

"Hello, stranger! Where have you been hiding?" I asked as Simple strolled into Paddy's Bar after a noticeable absence.

"I been busy resting," he said.

"In seclusion?" I asked.

"Naw," said Simple. "I just changed bars."

"What necessitated that change?" I asked.

"Because these women around here drink a man up," said Simple. "And after they have drunk you up, they will not act right."

"What do you mean by that?" I asked.

"You know what I mean," said Simple. "For instance, the other night I met an old girl in here, and she sat right there at that table and drunk six rum-colas—for which I paid. Also two beers for a friend of hers I had never seen before. Also a whiskey for a cousin who happened to pass by. You know, it being payday, I was free-hearted."

"Also high, I presume," I added.

"Not high," said Simple, "just feeling good. So when I walked that dame home, I said, 'Baby, lemme taste some lipstick.'

"She says, 'Oh, no! I do not kiss no strange men.'

"I said, 'What do you mean, *strange*—and I been knowing you since ten o'clock this evening?'

"She says, 'I knowed my husband six months before I kissed him.'

" 'Where is your husband now?' I said.

" 'In the army.'

" 'Do he come home often on furlough?' I inquired.

" 'He is in Texas,' she says, 'and that is too far.'

" 'Then lemme taste some lipstick,' I begged.

" 'I will not!' she hollers. 'How would you like it if you was in the army, and some wolf in sheep's clothing tried to lead your wife astray?'

" 'If my wife stayed out till three in the morning at a bar,' I says, 'I would think she wanted to be let astray. Also if she drunk six rum-colas, then asked for a zombie, I would know she wanted to be let astray.'

" 'You did not buy me the zombie,' she says.

" 'What is your name?' I asked her very quiet.

" 'Zarita,' she chirped. 'Why?'

" 'Because,' I said, 'if I ever hear anybody say "Zarita" again, I will run the other way—and I will not look back.'

" 'It do not matter to me,' she says, 'because I will be missing nothing.'

" 'You will never know what you missed, baby, till you miss me,' I said.

" 'If you are referring to them few drinks you bought,' she says, 'I thought you was just being a gentleman.'

" 'I was,' I said, 'but now I am being a man.'

" 'Excuse me,' she said. 'I do not like to be seen standing on the stoop talking to a strange man. Besides, it is chilly this evening.' And she went in and shut the door."

"I see! She left you standing in the cold," I said. "So you never did get to taste that lipstick?"

"I do not care nothing about that old broad," said Simple. "Nor any other old broad that drinks a man up that way."

"So that is why you changed bars?" I said. "Don't you realize there are women like that in every bar?"

"I do now," said Simple. "And I may buy one more drink for Zarita— but that is all."

"Leading army wives astray," I said, "is bad for morale."

"I reckon I am weak that way," said Simple. "Besides, if a woman wants to stray, I am here to help her. Look! Yonder comes Zarita now. Boy, lend me a couple of bucks till payday. You know, I'm kinder short."

"I thought you said you had turned away from women who drink a man dry. Haven't you learned your lesson yet?"

"I did not ask you for no sermon," said Simple. "I asked you for two bucks. It is a poor fool who cannot change his own mind . . . Take it easy, pal! . . . Good evening, Zarita!"

Hairdos

"Why is it," asked Simple, "you always hope you have good relatives, but you usually don't?"

"Don't what?" I asked.

"Don't have good ones," said Simple.

"I can't say I agree with you," I said. "Some of my relatives are fine people."

"A few of mine are," said Simple, "but I've got enough bad relatives to make up the difference. Take Cousin Minnie. She not only drinks but out-drinks me. Of the lady sex, too! And she makes no bones that her father, my uncle, were not married to my aunt, which makes her my cousin in name only. What you gonna do about relatives like that?"

"If she's a relative in name only, you certainly don't have to claim her."

"But she claims me," said Simple. "And she's as ugly as I are."

"In other words, you can spot the kinship."

"Spot it?" said Simple. "Minnie is not beautiful, I'm telling you. Minnie looks like me around the nose, but not around the head. These brownskin blondes and colored girls with yellow streaks through their hair, attracting attention to themselves with heads as God never gave them, look like nothing human to me, including Minnie."

"Some of them look very strange," I said.

"Have you seen them chicks whose hair is all black on top, but their ponytail is blond?" asked Simple. "That is the most. Then when they wear skin-tight toreador pants on the street to boot, and their behinds look like a beer barrel, I give up! At least my Cousin Minnie from Virginia does not wear no skin-tight pants in public."

"Has your Cousin Minnie got a yellow streak through her hair these days?"

"She has," said Simple, "which is one reason why I no longer speak to her when I see her in a bar. Cousin Minnie is too stout and too colored to be attracting attention to herself thataway. Everybody knows nature did not give Minnie no blond hair nowhere on her body. Yet she has done gone to the beauty parlor and had three inches of blondine put into her head. Do you think women are right bright?"

"They do strange things at times," I said. "Rings through their noses in India, saucers through their lips in Tanganyika, ivory splinters through their ears in Australia."

"And blond streaks in their heads in Harlem," said Simple. "You can never tell what a woman will think up. I said, 'Minnie, why did you do it?' "

"What did Cousin Minnie say?"

"Minnie said, 'I want to attract some attention to myself before I get too old to totter and dodder. I want the mens to notice me, that's why.' "

"I said, 'Girl, everybody has to turn around and look at you now, not once but twice. You look like nothing I ever saw in my natural life. You look like you belong in the sideshow at Coney Island.'

" 'If you was not my cousin by book, Jess Semple,' says Minnie, 'I would not take such remarks off you. You are trying to tell me I look like a freak?'

" 'I am,' I says, 'and you do! You was right nice-looking until you let them beauty-shop people put that yellow frizzle from your forehead down to the nape of your neck. Now you look like a stoplight before it changes to green—that in-between signal which is neither stop nor go. You don't look like a woman no more—and you don't look like nothing else either. Minnie, I will give you the money to go and have your hair put back like it was, if you will do so.'

" 'Gimme Five Dollars,' says Minnie, 'and I will think about it.'

" 'Oh, no,' I says, 'think about it is not what I meant. I do not want to see you again messed up like you is tonight. After all, we are related.'

" 'Didn't nobody else say they don't like my hair,' says Minnie. 'And this is the latest style.'

" 'I am glad your hair is not long enough for you to have a horsetail hanging down behind like Josephine Baker. If you did, I expect you would dye that yellow, too.'

" 'I am thinking of letting my hair grow long,' says Minnie.

" 'Baby, you would have to do some hard thinking,' I said without thinking. Knowing hair is a sensitive point with short-haired women, I did not mean to insult Minnie. But insulted she were.

" 'You do not need to hurt my feelings just because you do not like my new hairstyle. You have hurted me so bad now, being so critical, that I feel like crying. I am liable to break down right here on this bar stool if you do not buy me a Scotch and soda. Bartender, White Horse, please.'

"Do you know, I had to pay for that woman a drink! I could have bought myself six glasses of beer with the money her one Scotch cost, whilst the men was passing up and down the bar, looking from her head

to her haunches and back, whistling at her with their eyes. If I hadn't
been there, I expect Minnie would have been asked some very direct
questions, setting there with that Halloween streak down the middle of
her head! I wish she was no relation to me."

"Don't take it so hard," I said. "When the fad blows over, Minnie's
hair will go back to nature. Like two-tone cars, two-tone hair is just a
fad, and a rather amusing one, I think. At least it makes a man stop and
stare."

"Will you be so kind as to buy me a beer? Fact is, make it a whiskey.
A double, if you can stand it, daddy-o. I need something strong to take
my mind off of Cousin Minnie."

Cousin Minnie Wins

"It is better to be wore out from living than to be worn out from worry," said Simple. "Them that lives to the hilt and wears their worries like a loose garment lives the longest. I do believe my Cousin Minnie is going to live to be one hundred and ten. She worries about nothing, except sometimes wondering can she borrow Five Dollars from me. When I say no, she frowns up."

"I thought I heard you say lately you had put your Cousin Minnie down," I said.

"I did," said Simple. "I put her down, but she took me up again. I stopped going to the bars where I thought she went, but I find out that she goes to all bars. Every bar I go in in Harlem, in steps Minnie. That woman really makes the rounds, which is why our cousinship is going on the rocks these days. I do not like a woman that gets around to more places than I do. And since I been married to Joyce, I do not get around much any more. But my cousin, she is here, there, everywhere each and every night. I says to Minnie once, 'Don't you even take off Monday from gallivanting?'

"Do you know what Minnie says to me? She says, 'Monday? Why, Monday ain't even on my calendar. I call it *Hon*-day, meaning HONEY day—the day to catch up with all the sweet things you might have missed on Sunday. Monday is Honey-day, Jesse Semple. If I has nothing better to do, I come to call on you, my favorite cousin.'

" 'You are not *my* favorite cousin, Minnie,' I says, 'especially since you can out-drink me. Our cousinship has gone adrift on a sea of licker.'

" 'You talk as if you bought me all them drinks, old Simple Negro, whereas you has not spent hardly a dime on me at this bar all summer. You know I has friends who will treat me every time they greet me, wine me before they dine me, and dance whenever I want to prance.'

" 'Minnie,' says I, 'if you would work as much as you dance, you might have some money of your own in your pocketbook sometimes, and not have to depend on others for a treat.'

" 'Honey,' says Minnie, 'other folks' treats is most sweet. Besides, you know I told you, that last white lady for who I worked lived in a duplex apartment, and she had too many steps for me to be running up. Steps get me down.'

" 'How come dancing don't get you down, too? I have seen you dance all night and not pant a pant.'

" 'Dancing do not seem to tell on a body like climbing steps do,' said Minnie. 'I could dance all night, like the song says, without feeling it. But just let me climb up and down steps half a day, and my wind is gone. I were not that way in my youthhood. Do you think I am getting old?'

" 'You do look kinder ageable,' I said. 'But I am sure it is not from work, neither from worriation.'

" 'Work and worry will get a woman down,' said Minnie. 'I do not wish to go under. If I do, I had rather it be from a good time than from a good job. I have never yet had no job in the world I was willing to give my life to, no matter how good. Why, I worked for a rich old white lady once who paid me just to *be* there, since she were kind of invalidded like, and could not answer her own doorbell. But just being there bugged me. I got to thinking about all the other nice places I could be, and I quit. Facts is, Jess, I am not working nowhere now. Lend me Five.'

" 'I will not,' I says, 'because all you want money for is to live it up or drink it up. I can live up and drink up my own money.'

" 'Then let's drink up your Five together, Coz,' coos Minnie, 'and it won't be a worriation to either of us.' Facts is, that is just about what had already happened. Minnie had had three Scotches whilst we was talking, and I had had six beers.

" 'You wins, Min,' I said.

" 'I won, hon! I almost always wins with men,' she said. 'Lemme tell you how once I won. That were back in the days when I used to take care of men, instead of letting men take care of me. I were in love with that young stud—a dude named Luther McWilliams Warren—deep in love, money-spending, cooking-and-scrubbing, working-my-fingers-to-the-bone for his sake, crazy in love. He took me for a play toy. He went around telling folks I wasn't nothing but his rag doll till his china doll comes.

" 'When I heard that, I said to myself, "I better not catch you with no china doll, Luther McWilliams Warren! If I do, I will fix your wagon!"

" 'Misfortunately for him, I heard at the beauty shop about his other woman. I told him that night, "Baby, you better watch your step." Luther Warren did not believe me, so I just waited a few months till winter came—because I knowed Luther did not like the cold. I also knowed he did not like to be hungry, neither poorly dressed. Neither to be out of pocket change. In them days it was me who paid the gas bill, me who bought the food, and me who give him spending change, also new shirts, shoes, and suits. And him with a china doll at the other end of town all the time—a meriney hussy with a blond streak in her head what paid Five Dollars at the beauty shop to have that streak put in. Name of Dorinda. I found out who she was. But by that time I were tired of Luther Warren, anyhow. I thought to myself, let Dorinda *take care* of him awhile—which I knowed she wouldn't do, since she were the type who expected to reap, not *sow,* to take, not *put*—which, in later years, I have learned to do myself.

" 'Meantime, Luther sported with his china doll—endangering his life and laying himself liable, because she had a husband. I did not let him know how much I cared, or how jealous-hearted I were—beyond crying once in a while and twice pitching a boogie. But by fall, jealousy had died in me, and I had made my plans.

" 'On Thanksgiving, I fixed him a turkey—but I did not put no poison in the dressing. I wanted that man to *live* and suffer, not suffer and *die*. Time went by. Soon he come asking me what was I going to give him for Christmas. Would I buy him that new pinstripe suit he wanted? I said, *Um-hunnn-nn-n!* He thought when I purred like that, I meant yes, but I fooled that joker.

" 'The night before the day I pulled my trick, I were as sweet to him as sweet could be. I even give him Ten Dollars to go out with. I knowed where he went—Dorinda's. But I did not let on like I knowed. I had waited for the thermometer to drop. Radio said it would be zero come morning. I had already purchased my train ticket North. All I wanted were this real cold day to depart, and I was hoping he would not come home before afternoon. He didn't. He slept late—but elsewhere—not with me. I were glad. A well-prepared revenge is sweet.

" 'I called the gas man early that morning and had the gas turned off and the meter taken out. Electricity I had cut off, too. I told the grocery man I were canceling my bill. I called the phone man and had the phone, *not only cut off,* but removed. All of Luther's clothes in the closet I sold to the junk man. His hair oil I throwed in the garbage. His address books I tore up so he could not write nobody for help. I notified the rent man I were moving. I told that city goodbye and headed North to Freedomland. I always did want to come North, anyhow. So I came. I not only got rid of Luther, but rid of the South—all with one stone and a single ticket. I were not there when Luther McWilliams

Warren tore his self away from his china doll that day and come home. I were gone.

· " 'Home was not what it used to be to that joker, not no more. He liked to eat—but he found no meal. He liked heat—but he could strike a match to the gas burners all he wanted to—no blaze. He liked a hot bath. The tank was cold. I even pulled out the ball in the flush box so the toilet wouldn't flush. I also took out the light bulbs. Let him set there now and read the *Racing Form*! Luther Warren liked nice clothes. His clothes were sold, his drawers empty, his closet bare. He liked a bed to sleep on. I sold our bed to the second-hand store. He liked a roof over his head. Where we lived, rent was paid by the week, and the week was up. He liked company. Now not even me was around. Me, what he called his rag doll, had cut out, flew the coop, gone. And I did not even leave that man cigarette money—nothing but an empty house. Luther Warren was a picked chicken when I got through, with no hen house in which to find a roost, no yard in which to crow, and nothing to crow on. He must have been cold that day, too, in a cold house, in a cold world. I left him a note which said:

> " '*Your rag doll leaves you, daddy,*
> *Your rag doll is gone.*
> *Let your china doll feed you, daddy,*
> *From now on.*
> Signed: *Minnie—on my moving day.*'

" 'The last time I heard tell of Luther McWilliams Warren, he were poor as a church mouse. His sins had caught up with him. I *won*!' "

Riddles

"Until I met Joyce," said Simple, "I did not eat regular on a tablecloth. Now that we are married, each and every day we eat on a tablecloth, even if it does keep me running to the laundrymat—which I would only do for Joyce. Joyce says she will not eat her dinner on plastics. Breakfast, yes. Dinner, no! Joyce says she et on newspapers, linoleum, and so on, in rooming houses long enough. She says she did not marry me to go backwards.

"I said, when we first got married, 'Baby, you look good presiding over a nice table.'

"Joyce said, 'You look good, too, Jess, sitting over a plate. You are the apple of my eye, the cog in my wheel, the sugar in my tea. In fact, you are all in all to me.' "

"I believe you are a prevaricator," I said to Simple.

"Which means what?" he asked.

"A liar," I said.

"Don't talk so much truth, Boyd, you might offend me." Simple grinned. "Anyhow I was reading in an old paper I picked up to line the garbage pail where Einstein tackled the riddle of the universe and ended up with the atom bomb, which, says the paper, he did not aim to do. Einstein were trying to solve the riddle of the universe. Only thing is, them equations of Mr. Einstein's which they printed on the front page of the paper—everything down there equals zero, nothing, naught, I mean 0. Now, why is that?"

"Zero with Einstein was probably only a symbol for something else," I explained.

"For what?"

"Relativity," I said.

"Well, he put it all down to equal nothing, naught, o, zero—which may be true for relativity, but it dead sure ain't true for me."

"In the overall picture, his equations may all add up to nothing," I said, "since everything is relative."

"My relatives didn't have nothing," said Simple. "But in spite of that, I, me—my mother's boy, Jesse B.—I do not add up to nothing. Neither does my life, which is at least biscuits and gravy, corn bread and ham, whiskey and womens, daytime working, nighttime loving. That is my life—not no zero."

"Einstein's theory had no direct relation to you, my dear fellow. He was dealing in pure science, which relates to the basic sources of matter and material, the great principles of the universe, the paths of the stars, the vast whirl of the zodiac, and the mysteries of infinity. When Einstein wrote that *phi* over *psi* divided by *gamma* multiplied by the square root of *p* equals *naught*, he did not have you in mind. You are an infinitesimal unit in the great complexity of the cosmos."

"Um-huh!" said Simple. "Well, at the corner of 125th Street and Seventh Avenue in Harlem, U.S.A., also at 135th and Lenox, not to speak of in front of Paddy's Bar and Grill, I am my baby's favorite guy, and my, my, my! No lie! So I do not add up to zero. I think Einstein must have done got old when he put down that all that figuring equals nothing. Besides, them formulas he put on that paper ain't the riddles of the universe."

"Well, just what do you figure, then, is the riddle of the universe?" I asked.

"Womens," said Simple.

"Don't be absurd," I said. "Women have nothing to do with the vast complexities of the cosmos. They are not the riddle of the universe."

"Then it must be white folks," said Simple.

"Racist!" I said.

"My wife is colored," said Simple. "And to tell the truth, Boyd, I don't think womens is too much riddles, after all, especially if you be around them long. You know, when I was young I used to be always reaching for the moon," said Simple; "then I found Joyce—who is just a good wife and a good cook."

"Less than the moon, I presume."

"More," said Simple. "The moon is beyond a man's reach—but I got Joyce. She is a wonderful woman. Eve in the garden could not be no better, because Eve had no stove on which to cook. She lived under a tree. How do you reckon Adam got his meals?"

"An apple," I said.

"And that came from Satan raw. But my wife can cook fried apples real good. Do you know, I love that woman."

"You ought to," I said, "but I seem to remember you were married once before—with less fortunate results."

"Isabel—that chick in Baltimore!" cried Simple. "In them days I were reaching for the moon. I saw them pictures of them pretty stage girls

and colored models in the *Afro* and I thought I ought to marry one myself. So I hooked a waitress—the prettiest one on Pennsylvania Avenue—
which were the Lenox Avenue or South Parkway of Baltimore. I thought
I hooked her—but she hooked me. That Isabel were a lulu! A bodiddling! A rib out of Adam's wrong side. My first wife led me a dog's
life—which is why I say, don't reach for no moon. Take what you can
handle. If you be a normal man, try to find a normal woman. Not no
picture-book-stage-footlights-radio-TV famous chick. Such a broad will
drive you crazy. In the first place, how you gonna know how many millions of other mens is in love with her? How you gonna know who else
saw her picture in the papers? With so many mens to pick and choose
from, how do you know she is gonna like you, just you, for yourself
alone? Huh? I am asking?"

"Don't ask me," I said. "I have never been married."

"But you's colleged," said Simple. "You have studied on these things,
them things, and all kinds of things. Not only college, but you's psycol-
leged, so you told me."

"I have studied psychology," I said, "but I don't know everything.
And I did not specialize in sex and marriage."

"I am knowledged on both," said Simple, "including somewhatly the
riddle of the universe. Womens has been my pleasure in life. I works
for a living, but I loves for fun. When it comes to a woman, this is
what I would advise: Don't reach for the moon. Golden blondes is
out. Charcoal blondes is better. Color makes no difference, and hair
any beauty parlor can take care of. Rose Meta will see to the hair. Age
also is not so much of a difference. If a woman is too young, she will
be flighty. If she is too old, you will not marry her anyhow. Disposition,
that is important. If you cannot get along with her, love her and leave
her, but do not marry her. Cookery, a main item. Do she cook good?
Will she cook regular? Do she like to eat her own self, and is therefore
familiar with the kitchen? And do she, or don't she, lose all interest when
the meal is over? Will she also wash dishes, or will she say, 'Baby, now it
is your turn,' just when you are ready to take off your shoes and look at
TV? In other words, will she understand that a man is a man?

"If she understands, then that is the woman for me. I do not know
nothing about no woman in the moon, nor man in the moon neither.
And being no astronaught, I know I cannot reach no moon. If there
was a woman in the moon, anyhow, I would not want her. My choice is
Joyce. She is right here on earth, right here in Harlem—my complexion,
my size, all right, my delight! And I done got wise. Listen to me—I tells

all mens to stop reaching for the moon. Take what you can get, and in that way one and one make a better two. You know what Pearl Bailey sings? 'Takes Two to Tango.' Then get your partner not off no moon, man. Leave the moon alone. Reach where your arms can reach—then you can keep what your arms can hold. So says me, Jesse B.—Amen!"

Color of the Law

"Last Sunday I walked some thirty blocks down Seventh Avenue straight through Harlem, and in all them thirty blocks I did not see a single *white* person, other than cops—nothing but Negroes. Harlem is really a colored community. Of course, this were Sunday. Weekdays you see plenty of white folks in Harlem, since they own most of the stores, bars, banks, and number banks. But they do not live with us. On Saturday nights, these white folks take their money they have got from Negroes and go home to big apartments downtown, or nice houses with lawns out on Long Island—and leave me here in Harlem. They do not ever invite me to their homes for Sunday dinner—yet it's me what pays for their dinners. They make their money out of me. Then they want to tell me *not* to vote for Adam Powell or listen to Malcolm X because they raises too much hell! Do I tell them how to vote or who to listen to?

"The only white folks you see in Harlem on Sundays is cops, and of them you see plenty, two and three on every corner, and most of them white. They have some fine colored cops in New York, but where are they at? Off on Sundays? It looks like to me every day in Harlem they got white cops to spare. On Marcus Garvey Day they even had white cops on the roofs looking down on the Negroes—to keep us from running riot, I reckon. I guess they have not forgot the Harlem riots yet downtown. And now Negroes do get kind of evil.

"I feels evil myself when I sees a white cop talking smart to a colored woman, like I did the other day. A middle-aged brownskin lady had run through a red light on Lenox Avenue by accident, and this cop were glaring at her as if she had committed some kind of major crime. He was asking her what did she think the streets was for, to use for a speedway—as if twenty miles an hour were speeding. So I says to the cop, 'Would you talk that way to your mama?'

"He ignored me. And as good luck would have it, he did not know I had put him in the dozens. By that time quite a crowd had gathered around. When he saw all them black faces, he lowered his voice, in fact shut up altogether, and just wrote that old lady a ticket, since he did not see any colored cops nearby to call to protect him. In Harlem nowadays, when colored cops are around, they do all the loud talking, whilst the white cops just stand by—in case. Since the Harlem riots way back in the forties, white cops uptown ain't as rambunctious as they used to be—not unless they got six squad cars with them. Still and yet, they know the law is white, and *white* makes right insofar as the law goes—which is why I votes black. I will vote for Adam Powell as long as he claims to be colored.

"There were four white cops in the polling place where I went to vote. Right in the middle of Harlem, four white cops. Everybody else there were colored, voters all colored, officials all colored registering the books, only the cops white—to remind me of which color is the law. I went inside that voting booth and shut the door and stood there all by myself and put the biggest black mark I could make in front of every black name on the ballot. At least up North I can vote black. If enough of us votes black in Harlem, maybe someday we can change the color of the law. At any rate, I, Jesse B. Semple, have put down my vote."

Simple and the High Prices

"Listen," said Simple, "how am I going to live with prices getting higher and higher and my weekly wages staying just the same?"

"I do not know," I said. "What I am worried about is how am I going to live myself."

"Now, buddy-o," said Simple, "you know if I live, you live."

"I do not know any such thing," I said, "because if you can't live yourself, how could you help me?"

"I can always borrow a couple of bucks from Joyce," said Simple.

"Joyce's wages are not getting any higher, either, are they?" I asked.

"Womens always seems to manage to make out somehow," said Simple.

"If you can so easily borrow a few dollars from Joyce," I said, "why do you so regularly borrow from me when your own funds have run short—nearly every Thursday or Friday? Why don't you borrow from Joyce if it is so easy?"

"I did not say it was easy," said Simple. "What I said is, I *can* borrow from Joyce, but it is not easy. And she does not approve of my drinking. But if I was hungry, she would lend me. And if you was hungry, I would lend you. And if I was hungry, you would lend me."

"I have never known you to be hungry," I said. "I have only known you to be thirsty."

"Prices have never been so high before," said Simple. "I am liable to get hungry and thirsty, too, now. And I am a man who must always eat before I drink. Beer is bad on an empty stomach."

"Suppose you got to the point where you could not eat—what would you do then?" I asked.

"Just drink," said Simple.

"You mean you would let poverty drive you to drink?"

"I would not have to be driven," said Simple.

"What you ought to do is think," I said. "How do you expect the human race to get out of the hole we are in if folks do not think?"

"That is what I pay my congressman for," said Simple. "Also the President. They are the government. Let them think."

"In the final analysis," I said, "you are the government—and if each citizen does not think for himself . . ."

"I am not talking about no *final analysis*," said Simple. "I am talking about *high prices*. If I was to think all night, meat would not be one cent cheaper."

"That is where you are wrong," I said. "If you were to think constructively, and make plans, perhaps you could reduce the price of meat."

"I had rather think how to raise my wages," said Simple.

"That is one-sided," I said. "If you raise your wages, the producer will raise his prices. Then we have a vicious circle all around."

"With me in the middle," said Simple, "so I go down!"

"Naturally you go down," I said, "because you are caught in a dilemma."

"I don't know about the 'lemma," said Simple "but I sure am caught. Last week I went to buy a sport shirt for this warm weather coming up here, and the man said, 'Seven Fifty.' I said, 'Seven Fifty for what? I bought this shirt four years ago for Two Twenty-five.' The man said, 'Try and find it now.' I tried. At the next store, that self-same shirt was Eight. I said, 'Wait! Four years ago I bought . . . !' Before I could get it out good, the man said, 'You are four years too late.'"

"What did you do then?"

"I cut out, friend. And I did not buy the shirt."

"That is what makes depressions," I said. "You don't buy the shirt. The manufacturer can't pay his help. His help can't buy any shirts. No factories can pay anybody—and you end up out of work. That is the vicious circle."

"I am caught," said Simple.

"All of us are caught," I said.

"It sounds like W.P.A. to me," said Simple. "And if it is, I put my application in now."

"For relief?" I asked.

"For whatever they have to offer," said Simple.

Everybody's Difference

"I am a good-looking man, if I do say so myself," said Simple. "Sometimes I say to my wife, 'Joyce, baby, you have married a nice-looking joker.' And do you know what Joyce answers?"

"No," I said.

"Joyce says, 'You would be O.K. if you didn't act so simple.'"

"And why does she cast such an aspersion upon you?" I asked.

"Because sometimes I am simple," said Simple. "But it is not by intention. It is just the way God made me. But I am glad He did not make me bowlegged. I once knew a man who was so bowlegged he looked like a Japanese bridge. I also once knew a girl who was bench-legged. She looked like she was standing in two places at once. But if I was a girl I had rather be bench-legged than bowlegged—which for a woman, being bowlegged looks like such an open invitation.

"Now, take my Uncle Tige, he were so knock-kneed, and slue-footed, he looked like one foot was going left, and one foot was going right. Also he could of played golf with either foot and knock a ball *wham* and gone! Uncle Tige rolled like a sailor, too, when he walked."

"Uh! Uh! Uh!" I said.

"That's the way he navigated," continued Simple. "But talking about walking, you know my Cousin Minnie?"

"Of course," I said.

"Well, she has got what I call a bebop walk," said Simple. "When my Cousin Minnie walks down the street, one hip says BEE and the other hip says BOP—just like a seesaw, up, down—up, down! rock, roll—rock, roll. No wonder the mens turn around to look at Minnie. The Lord, I reckon, gave her them ball-bearing hips, but the Devil must of taught her how to use them. When Minnie turns into a bar, seven jokers follow her. And out of that seven, at least six will buy her a drink. Minnie has a way of leading men down the primrose path to poverty each and every payday. I have seen Minnie drink as many as seventeen drinks on a weekend night and not fall off the stool. As long as a man will buy, Minnie will try. Then get up and bebop on home *by herself*. Jokers turn their pockets inside out and say, 'I thought I had a dollar left.' But they do not even have bus fare home. By that time, Minnie has also done borrowed from each and every one of them, so she can take herself a taxi to her door. If nature is going to make a woman offbeat in the hips, it is not bad to be made like Minnie, who walks like jelly on a plate. If Minnie were as pretty as my old used-to-be, Zarita, she would be irresistible.

"I am married to the best woman in the world, but you know, the other day I saw Zarita and I could not help but cast a manly eye on her. I know I would be simple to take up with that woman again, and I won't. But sometimes your mind do not pay any attention to your judgment. Oh, well, the Lord made everybody different—some bowlegged, some knock-kneed, some pigeon-toed, some slue-footed, others bebop-hipped, and some on the simple side. But I reckon God knows what He was doing. He gives everybody their difference.

"God also made good and evil. And He made some people too evil for their own good. Take Cojo and Whitney, who are fighting souls. I hates to see two mens get hurted. But when they are as bad as Cojo and Whitney, I would not stop them from fighting each other. Let them go ahead and hurt themselves and hurt each other. That, I figure, is better than them hurting me if I come in between. Cojo and Whitney is fighting characters, both. Them boys has got so many scars on them that one more scar do not make no difference. They done lost so much blood in their time that either one of them could start a blood bank.

"Cojo and Whitney is the kind of Negroes who will back up integration and anything else to the last drop of blood. They do not care. They is the fighting forces of the race, the core of the last resort. They do not respect God, man, each other, nor white folks. Also they has no fear of razors, knives, guns, clubs, nor brass knucks. Now, take me. I had rather get shot than cut by a knife. To Cojo a knife is a play toy. To Whitney a razor amounts to no more than a rubber band in a child's slingshot. A bullet either one of them can duck. A baseball bat would just bounce off their heads. If Whitney and Cojo was due to be dead, they would have been died long ago. They is hard Negroes."

"I always thought they were friends," I said, "so why do they fight each other?"

"Is it not Saturday?" asked Simple. "Have they not 'over-indulged,' as says my wife, Joyce? And do they not feel playful? Therefore they fights."

"Those are slight provocations," I said; "in fact, no provocations at all."

"Sometimes just the sight of Whitney provokes Cojo," said Simple, "and the sight of Cojo provokes Whitney. Both is too evil for the other's good, even if they is friends. But you seen how tonight they done fit, fought, and re-fit. Is either one of them dead, kilt, grave wounded, or even sent to the hospital? No! Cojo is just gone around the corner to change his shirt, and Whitney is setting across the street in the fish joint ordering a catfish sandwich with his bleeding arm wrapped in the cook's dish towel. Was I to bleed so much, I would be in Harlem Hospital right now with Joyce sending for a minister to pray over my carcass, thinking I am about to die. They do not die of no little old things like a stab wound, a slit, or a cut. They bleeds, but they stops their own blood. They are hurt, but they do not groan, moan, or ask for sympathy.

"Looks like to me, with a blade flashing in his face, a man would be scared. Whitney do not even turn pale. Cojo do not tremble. Them kind of men have got the kind of steel in their souls, I reckon, which weapons do not touch, which no kind of afraidness can scratch, which an uppercut to the jaw do not faze, which can take a whole lot of punishment because their souls is unshootable, uncuttable, and unbeatable. Them is the kind of Negroes in slavery time who gave Old Master a Little Rock hangover—from which he has not recovered yet. Them is the kind of jokers who take no tea for the fever, who do not think now and *act* afterwards but acts then and there, when and where, sooner than soon and quicker than a rocket taking off for the moon. What the other man has got in the way of weapons makes no difference, and what you *say* you will do does not matter, because what Whitney and Cojo have *done* by the time you have *said* what you *will* do is IT. By the time you finish talking about what you *will* do, your mouth may have to place a long-distance call to your ear! But Whitney and Cojo are still here, all in one piece—even if one or two parts is bleeding. Which is why, if they go to fighting in my front parlor, I would not come between them."

"I see the wisdom of your position," I said. "But you said God made good and evil. All you have described with Cojo and Whitney is evil. What about the good?"

"The good is friends like you who might treat me to another cold beer," said Simple.

"In that case," I said, "the good will have to say, 'Good night.'"

Intermarriage

"I been reading in the papers about Sammy Davis turning himself into a Jew," said Simple, "but in his pictures, he still looks colored to me."

"Because a man changes his religion does not mean he changes his complexion, too," I said. "Sammy Davis is colored."

"But his race is now Jewish," said Simple.

"No," I said, "his *religion* is Jewish."

"I thought Jews were a race of people," said Simple.

"Judaism is a religion," I said, "and anybody can become a Jew in the religious sense by adopting the Hebrew faith—which is what Sammy Davis did."

"I think he made a mistake," said Simple.

"Why?" I asked.

"Because in a little while Jews are going to start trying to be colored," said Simple, "and Sammy Davis will just have to turn around and come back where he started from in order to be saved, because if the Jews are wise, they will not try to stick with the rest of the white folks from here on out. Instead they will come with us."

"What do you mean, 'come with us'?" I asked.

"I mean run WITH us—if they don't want to run FROM us like the white folks are doing in the Congo when they hear them Congo drums. There ain't but two ways to go tomorrow—ALONG WITH US or AWAY FROM us. Right now, most white folks is trying to run away from us, everywhere in the world—even when we are not chasing them. But we here in the U.S.A. is not chasing nobody when we buy a house next door to some white family. Yet and still, them white folks run like mad, be they Jewish or otherwise. Do you reckon if me and Joyce was to buy a house next door to Sammy Davis, he would run, too?"

"Sammy is probably a liberal Jew," I said.

"I am not talking about stingy," said Simple.

"I am not talking about being liberal with money, either," I explained. "I mean liberal in a racial and religious sense, accepting everyone equally."

"My wife is upset about Sammy marrying white," said Simple. "In fact, Joyce is mad."

"Your wife is like a great many other colored women. Their tolerance doesn't encompass interracial marriage," I said. "On that they take a rather narrow-minded view, especially when the male involved is a celebrity."

"And more so when that Negro is up in the money," said Simple. "Joyce says, 'Just let a Negro get a little money, he ups and marries a white woman—and his new wife is the one that wears furs and diamonds. Usually his first wife, colored, is left out in the cold when the money starts coming in,' says Joyce.

"The more Joyce talks, the madder she gets on that subject. Then she switches to colored women and white men. 'Lena Horne, Pearl Bailey, Katherine Dunham, Diahann Carroll, Dorothy Dandridge, Josephine Baker, Eartha Kitt—every last famous woman we got in show business almost—except Ethel Waters, who is rather old for wedding veils—has up and married white. So who shares all these rich colored women's money?'

"I said, 'Joyce, you are making me mad because I am not white—then I could marry me a well-off star.'

"That were a mistake which I should not have said, because then my wife got mad at me. Joyce yelled, 'I wouldn't put anything past you, Jess Simple. You just try to quit me for some blonde—and I will fix your little red wagon!' After that, she said some other things that were not nice at all. How come colored womens can't even talk calm about marrying white?"

Liberals Need a Mascot

"Just what is a liberal?" asked Simple.

"Well, as nearly as I can tell, a liberal is a nice man who acts decently toward people, talks democratically, and often is democratic in his personal life, but does not stand up very well in action when some real social issue like Jim Crow comes up."

"Like my boss," said Simple, "who is always telling me he believes in equal rights and I am the most intelligent Negro he ever saw—and I deserve a better job. I say, 'Why don't you give it to me, then?' And he says, 'Unfortunately, I don't have one for you.'

" 'But ever so often you hire new white men that ain't had the experience of me and I have to tell them what to do, though they are over me. How come that?'

" 'Well,' he says, 'the time just ain't ripe.' Is that what a liberal is?" asked Simple.

"That's just about what a liberal is," I said.

"Also a liberal sets back in them nice air-cooled streamlined coaches on the trains down South, while I ride up front in a hot old Jim Crow car," said Simple. "Am I right?"

"You are just about right," I said. "All the liberals I ever heard of ride with white folks when they go down South, not with us, yet they deplore Jim Crow."

"Do liberals have an animal?" asked Simple.

"What do you mean, do liberals have an animal?"

"The Republicans have an elephant, Democrats have a jackass," said Simple. "I mean, what does the liberals have?"

"I do not know," I said, "since they are not a political party. But if they were, what animal do you think they ought to have?"

"An ostrich," said Simple.

"Why an ostrich?" I demanded.

"Ain't you never seen an ostrich?" said Simple. "Old ostrich sticks his head in the sand whenever he don't want to look at anything. But he leaves his hind parts bare for anybody to kick him square in his caboose. An ostrich is just like nice white folks who can smile at me so sweet as long as I am working and sweating and don't ask for nothing. Soon as I want a promotion or a raise in pay, down go their heads in the sand and they cannot see their way clear. 'The time ain't ripe.' And if I insist, they will have the boss man put me dead out in the street so they can't see me. Is that what a liberal is?"

"Could be," I said, "except that an ostrich is a bird that does not sing, and a liberal can sing very sweetly."

"An elephant don't talk," said Simple, "but they are always making him talk in them cartoons where he represents the Republicans. So I do not see why an ostrich can't sing."

"I didn't mean sing literally," I said. "What I really meant was talk, use platitudes, make speeches."

"This ostrich of mine can make speeches," said Simple. "He can pull his head out of the sand and say, 'I see a new day ahead for America! I see the democratic dawn of equal rights for all! I see . . .'

"Whereupon, I will say, 'Can you see me?'"

"And that ostrich will say, 'Indeed, my dark friend, democracy cannot overlook you.'

"I will say, 'Then help me get an apartment in that city-built tax-free insurance project where nobody but white folks can live.'

"That ostrich will say, 'Excuse me!' And stick his head right back down in the sand. Then I will haul off and try to kick his daylights out. And Mr. Big Dog will say, 'Shame on you, trying to embarrass a friend of the Negro race.'

"I will say, 'Embarrass nothing! I am trying to break his carcass! Only thing, it is too high up for my foot to reach.' That is another trouble with liberals," said Simple. "They are always too high to reach."

"They're well-to-do, man. That's why liberals don't have to worry about colored folks."

"Then gimme an animal whose hips is closer to the ground," said Simple.

Serious Talk about the Atom Bomb

"I am tired of talking about race relations," said Simple.

"Me, too," I said. "Let's talk about human relations."

"The only trouble with that," said Simple, "is that we will not have no human relations left when we get through dropping that new atomical bomb on each other. The way it kills people for miles around, all my relations—and me, too—is liable to be wiped out in no time."

"Nobody is dropping that bomb on you," I said. "We are dropping it way over in Asia."

"And what is to keep Asia from dropping it back on us?" asked Simple.

"The Japanese probably do not have any atomic bombs to drop," I said.

"And how come we did not try them atomic bombs out on Germany?" demanded Simple.

"I do not know," I said. "Perhaps they were not perfected before V-E Day."

"Uh-umm! No, buddy-o," said Simple, "you know better than that. They just did not want to use them on white folks. Germans is white. So they wait until the war is all over in Europe to try them out on colored folks. Japs is colored."

"You are thinking evil now," I said. "Besides, it is your government and mine using those atomic bombs, so why do you say 'they'? Why don't you say 'we'? Huh?"

"I did not have nothing to do with them bombs," said Simple. "I see in the *News* where it cost Two Billion Dollars to develop them bombs, and get those atoms so they would split one another. If I had Two Billion Dollars, I would not spend it making something to kill off folks. I would spend it on things to make life better."

"For instance?" I said.

"For instance," said Simple, "I would take half of that Two Billion Dollars and build houses all over the country for poor folks to live in. I would get rid of these slums like Harlem full of cold-water flats and roaches. And I would make a playground in every block for kids to play on. And two bathrooms in every house so you could get in when you are in a hurry. Everywhere houses is old and falling down and too full of people, I would build a housing project with one of them Billion Dollars."

"You are making too much sense now," I said, "so I cannot argue with you."

"It is a wonder you did not bring up some technicality," said Simple, "because I do not see how it is they can spend all that money on warring and killing and in peacetime a man cannot even get Ten Dollars a week on W.P.A., but they can spend ten million times that much to blast somebody down."

"Don't keep on saying 'they,' " I said. "You are a voter, too, and this is your government. That Two Billion Dollars that made those atom bombs came out of your income tax."

"I hereby protest!" said Simple. "And if Adam Powell or Ben Davis or any of these Negroes or white folks either that I voted for last time start running on any Atom Bomb Ticket, they will not get my vote. Them atom bombs make me sick at the stomach! There is plenty we could do with Two Billion Dollars without turning it into double-barreled dynamite."

"What would you do with that other Billion left over after you build all those houses?" I asked.

"With that other One Billion," said Simple, "I would educate racist white folks."

"How?" I said.

"I would take and build schools all over Mississippi and all over the South, for white folks and Negroes, too. Because it is because they are so ignorant down there that they elect racist white folks to *our* Congress. I do not want racist white folks in *my* Congress. (You dig that *my*, don't you? Does my language suit you now, daddy-o?) *We* do not want no segregationist in *our* Congress drawing his salary from *my* income tax—concerning which I cannot vote if I live in Mississippi—and calling Jews and I-talians and me dirty names in the Senate Congress every day. So I would take that other One Billion Dollars and educate segregationist crackers like Bilbo. And my reason is, because if somebody don't educate them, they are liable to get hold of one of them atom bombs themselves—and blow us all off the map! Can you imagine Bilbo with an atom bomb? Then where would Harlem be?"

"Like the bear—nowhere," I said.

"You are being funny, and I am talking serious," said Simple.

Brainwashed

"That Minnie has put a touch on me again," said Simple.

"According to you," I said, "your Cousin Minnie has been up North for several years now. Yet every time you tell me about her, she is trying to borrow money from you. Hasn't Minnie got a foothold in the North yet?"

"It is very hard for a Negro to get a toeholt, let alone a footholt," said Simple, leaning on the bar. "I have been in the North longer than Minnie, yet if I was to lose my job tomorrow, I would be right back where I started from—at nothing. Negroes, by and large, do not make enough money to get a footholt. And a handholt I never expect to have."

"That is very pessimistic opinion for a man of your abilities to hold," I said. "How come you never expect to get any farther in life?"

"Because I started behind the eight-ball. Bad schools, half the time no schools, when I was a kid. Jim Crow all the way from Richmond to Washington to Baltimore to New York. High rents in Harlem, low-paid jobs downtown. Advancement for the white man on the job, stay-where-you-are for me. And added to that, I am married to a woman who lives black and thinks white nine times out of ten."

"What do you mean?" I asked. "I thought Joyce was a race-woman."

"She is," said Simple "in her heart, but sometimes I think her mind has been brainwashed."

"Why do you say that?"

"Joyce reads too many white papers and magazines—and *believes* half of what she reads in them. Me, I believe nothing they say. Joyce is also a fiend for culture. Whose culture? The white man's! Me, I love the blues. But Joyce, every time a Negro plays Show-pan at Town Hall, she wants me to spend $4.40 to go hear it. I just go to sleep on Show-pan."

"Chopin is everybody's music," I said. "It belongs to the world. It is too bad you can't stay awake when Chopin is being played. You have a sensitive wife whom you do not appreciate."

"I love Joyce," said Simple. "But that Atheniannie Art Club my wife belongs to has got me down—especially since they changed their name."

"The Anthenian Arts Club is one of Harlem's leading cultural organizations."

"But they used to be the Negro Art Club," said Simple. "Why did they have to go change their name to Atheniannie? 'It is time to encourage integration,' Joyce come telling me. Well, them women have got a integrated name for that club, but nary a white member as yet. Just like the Colored Golfing Association changed its name to the Associated Golfing Association—but I don't hear tell of no white players associated with them up to now. Them same Negroes are still playing golf with the same other Negroes as before. Suppose I was to change the name of my race from BLACK to BLUE, would I not still be black all over my black carcass? Who is fooling who with all this name changing lately, I want to know?"

"Somebody has to open the way to integration," I said.

"The Polish American Association had a big parade the other day and I did not read where they had changed their name to the Polite American Association. On St. Patrick's Day the Irish have big parades and I never hear tell of the Irish changing their names to anything but Irish. The Jews still celebrate Yom Kippur and close up every store in Harlem. But some Negroes are talking about we ought to change the name of Negro History Week to something *less* colored. Until I get a handholt, I refuse to call my toeholt a footholt because it is not and ain't, North or South, nothing but a *black* holt—of which my Cousin Minnie has less than me."

"Your wife, Joyce, at least, is reaching," I said.

"For Show-pan," yelled Simple.

"While you are reaching for a beer glass," I countered.

"Which now is empty," said Simple. "Set us up."

"I will contribute no further to your already wavering toehold," I said. "Good night."

"Then drop a dime in the juke box before you go," said Simple, "and play my favorite record one more time to liven up this bar."

Help, Mayor, Help!

"Well, if I was mayor of New York," said Simple, "the first thing I would do tomorrow morning would be to get me a Crazy Catcher's Wagon (like the Dogcatcher's Wagon) and go around New York gathering up all the crazy and half-crazy people on the loose from river to river. I would, to tell the truth, have me *two* Crazy Catcher Wagons, a Junior Wagon and a Senior Wagon. The Junior Wagon would be for the kids that cut up subway seats for no reason at all but to be slicing up something. It would also be for them that throws bricks through the windows of trains going up to Westchester when they come from Grand Central out of the underground on Park Avenue and into the Bronx. It would also be for little old young kids who get high on reefers and act wilder than teen-agers who get high on reefers, who in turn act wilder than grown-ups who get stoned. My Junior Crazy Catcher's Wagon would be full all the time from the Bronx to Harlem to Greenwich Village to Brownsville and Bedford-Stuyvesant to Far Rockaway. At Forty-second Street I would add a trailer to my Junior Wagon.

"My Senior Wagon, when it would not be busy being used for crazy-catching, I would use for wino-gathering. I would gather up all the winos drinking wine in public parks all day long and cluttering up the benches so mothers and children cannot set down, and cluttering up the air with bad language, and throwing wine bottles on the sidewalks in the parks so that they cut babies' feet. These old winos I would gather up in my Crazy Catcher's Wagon and take them away so the parks would be free for quiet folks to set down in again and catch a little fresh air whilst relaxing and enjoy the sunshine without hearing the loudest and baddest words in the world in front of children which they ought not hear. Was I the mayor of New York, I would clean the parks of winos, male and female winos, young and old winos. And I would hire me all the boats on the ocean for a month and ship all winos off to some far-off nice warm uninhabited island where they could have the whole island for a park—and drink wine all day to themselves if they wanted to, and have a wino convention and nominate themselves a wino Goldwater and wino Congress and a wino president and inaugurate themselves in wine, and put out a dictionary of bad language so that all wino-talking folks would be hep to the jive should new wino addicts arrive.

"Speaking of addicts, I would also (was I the mayor of New York) have me a Junkie Catcher's Wagon and go around New York gathering up all the junkies and getting them nice pads to cop a nod in—but far away from peoples who do not use junk, in someplace like Mississippi. Junkies would not mind being down in Mississippi because neither Jim Crow nor police dogs nor bombs bother dope addicts at all. A junkie does not care and is not bugged by anything in this world so long as he has his junk. Dear Mayor of New York, put all the junkies in Mississippi and let's clean up our town. Give all the junkies all the junk in Mississippi and put the pushers out of jobs in Harlem, in the Village, and also Times Square. City of New York, get some wagons. Take the junkies on a freedom ride. Free horse, free snow, free heroin, free coke—whatever they want in their new freedom land. Free goofballs and airplane glue to junior junkies. A bonus to all dope addicts who will get in the Junkie Wagon and go to Mississippi—award them an extra reefer, maybe a bag. Dear Mayor, if you do not hurry up and do this soon, you will never get New York cleaned up in time for the second year of the World's Fair, which is 1965. Hurry, Mayor, let's clean up New York.

"Dear Mayor, I would also get me a Hustling Beggars Wagon and collect all the fake beggars sitting in subway entrances with a fake bad leg collecting money. Else stumping through subway trains howling hymns with a cup marked BLIND—when they can see as well as I can. Or panhandling on Broadway claiming they do not have a subway token, so gimme fifteen cents—and making forty dollars a day begging fifteen cents. Get a Beggar Catcher's Wagon, Mayor.

"However, I would not want you to do anything wrong to any of these folks I mentioned, Mayor. Do not hurt them. Just get them out of New York City to where they can run wild in peace, be crazy, take dope, drink acid-raw stinking cheap lye-water wine, play blind in dark glasses and beg from each other to their heart's content. New York is a rich city, so let's maybe buy a reservation somewhere out in the Indian country, Arizona or somewhere like that, and put all teen-age subway seat-slashers, all grown-up dope takers, all middle-aged wino drinkers, all don't-give-a-damn-for-children-in-the-park cussers, all who beg as a profession, not as a need—put them all out West, else settle them in Alaska, else ship them to Puerto Rico and bring all the Puerto Ricans up here where Puerto Ricans want to be, and let them others I mention stop bugging me. Mayor, we now have a Litter Bug Campaign. Why not have a Human Bug Campaign? Put them in nice faraway places—all them that are too crazy to care, too hopped-up to care, too careless to care, or just naturally too mean and evil and nuisance-minded to give a damn. Mayor, let's care about them that don't care about us by giving them a separate state where they can care about each other.

"A Crazy Catcher's Wagon, Mayor, a Junkie Catcher's Wagon, a Professional Beggar Catcher's Wagon, a Wino Wagon, Mayor. Then take over for one week all the buses at the Port of Authority Terminal, and half the trains at Penn Station, and most of the boats in New York Harbor and fill them up with all these people who bug New York and bug themselves and get them all gone somewhere to some new cool wonderful spot out West, or to the Islands of the Sea, up North in Alaska, or anywhere but here. A reservation for the goofy, an island for the winos, a new land for the teen-age subway slashers—palm trees, wide-open spaces, nice happy places—for all the un-nice, upset, disturbed, hopped-up, wine-soaked people who cannot and do not and will not and *won't* act nice of their own accord in New York—and who is driving the rest of us crazy. Help, Mayor! Help! Help! Help!"

Little Klanny

" 'Listen, Little Klanny,' I said, 'in that picture of you in *Ebony* this month at the top of Reverend King's article about *Un-Christian Christians,* you don't look to be no more than five or six years old, standing beside your mama out in this field watching a fiery cross burn, and both of you got hoods and sheets on. At least, you got a part of a sheet on, cut down to your junior size. Little Klanny, your mama ought to be ashamed of herself, bringing you out in the damp of night to a Klan meeting to learn to hate somebody. The head Klansman is up there on a box talking about Negras and Catholics and Jews is no good. Who does he think discovered America? A Catholic—Columbus. And who does he think came next? The Negroes and the Jews. The Negroes is been here in this U.S.A. three hundred years. I don't have no record of the Jews, but I reckon they have been here almost as long. They are a people that get around.

" 'I expect your great-great-grandfather were Jewish, Little Klanny, and your manna don't know it. Or he might have been a big burly Negro. There was lots of mixing back in slavery days. You just happened to get bleached out white in time to join the John Birch Society when you get to be a little older. Little Klanny, you is too small now to know what hate is all about. You is practically a baby, and here your parents got you out there on Stoney Mountain with your robes and regalia flapping in the breeze when you had rather be home watching Donald Duck on TV. White folks must be out of their minds, bringing children to Klan rallies. And I must be out of my mind being present at one myself. But with me, it is all a dream, because I am at home in Harlem in my bed and *Ebony* just fell out of my hand when I dozed off.

" 'I am laying here tossing and turning, Little Klanny, dreaming that I am a reporter for *Time-Life-Ebony-Look* and the *Daily News,* who sent me to report on this rally of the Backwater Klan. I got my helmet on, also my bulletproof vest, and unlaced boots so I can step out of them and run if necessary. No use lying, I am scared. But I got mosquito netting all over my face so the Klansmen won't see how dark I am. Little Klanny, I am one of them folks you are supposed to hate. I am an Afro-American and I do not like nobody calling me *Negra* and worse, like your Kleagle up there on that box is doing. I am a *Negro* and I know, being dark, I have been due in the past to see dark days, but the days is passing. All the fiery crosses in the world is not going to scare me back into where I were before the Harlem riots, Martin Luther King, Adam Powell, and Malcolm X. Also, I might include that lady, Annie Lee Cooper, who hit Sheriff Clark in the eye in Alabama. When a Southern colored woman hits a Southern white sheriff in the eye in a public place like Selma, a new day has come.

" 'Little Klanny, you might as well tell your mammy and your pappy, too, to give up. There is not enough fiery crosses, hoods, and robes in the world to make me turn back now to segregation. The black man, Little Klanny, shall not be moved. I am telling you this because you, being a child, is young enough to understand. Your father and mother is fatheads with bone skulls in which the facts of life cannot penetrate. They don't believe in the United Nations, let alone a united America. They would like to put me back in the cotton fields forever so your daddy could be Old Marster, and you could be Young Marster, and your mammy could set on the veranda and study the beauty cream ads to get her Southern belleness back which were lost in her youthhood due to worrying about how to keep down Negras.

" 'Little Klanny, you know your folks could pronounce the *o* in *Negro* if they wanted to, and not say *Negra* all the time, which sounds too much like that other way of spelling it, with two *g*'s. Anyway, Little Klanny, you better not try to use neither one of them words. You might get your tongue twisted. You are only five years old now, I think, so just go home and learn your Mother Goose and don't bother with race problems until you get to be six. Seven or eight years is an even better age to take up the problem of Afro-Americans. At seven, study how we Negroes got here. At eight, study how we managed to stay here in America. And at nine, try to solve the problem of what are you-all going to do with us now. Or maybe the other way around. What is we going to do with you? Since you-all is, as *Ebony* says, *The White Problem.*

" 'When that problem is solved, Little Klanny, you can use your hood and robe for a play suit, and you can play with little colored children and have some fun, go next door to their house and eat soul food, beat the drums in the neighborhood combo with the hip cats, set up in Sunday School at the Sanctified Church, sing gospel songs, and in general have a good time. In fact, Little Klanny, you can be integrated into my race, the black race, without disgrace. Little Klanny, the day of American youthhood is coming when your parents can no more hold back young folks than they can hold back Negroes. Old Negroes and young white folks is going to own the world! Amen! And march together. I will be a preacher and a teacher going about the South teaching *old* white folks how to behave in the *new* age, since the color line is broke down.

" 'Little Klanny, I am dreaming up a breeze, ain't I, out here on Stoney Mountain? Rockaby, baby, on the tree top! When the wind blows, your cradle will rock. When the bough breaks, your cradle will fall, and down will come baby, cradle, and all. BAM! What's the matter with this dream? Am I falling, too? Me? Is my dream done turned into a nightmare? Has that Kleagle hit me in the head with a rock? Somebody just knocked me out of bed! Or did I fall out myself? I better stop dreaming, Little Klanny. But my last words to you is, "Pay your pappy and mammy in them white sheets no mind. Good night, baby! I'm gone." ' "

Simple's Psychosis

"I wonder why the human race won't behave itself?" I said.

"Because they don't want to," said Simple. "You are always wondering something foolish like that. You must be simple!"

"Whatever do you mean?" I said.

"Well, for instance," said Simple, "the other day I heard you say you wonder why white folks don't act right to Negroes."

"Why don't they?" I said.

"Because they don't want to," said Simple.

"That fails to explain their behavior," I said. "Why is it they don't want to? Why do American white folks fail to see it is to their own advantage to treat Negroes better?"

"Maybe they don't want that advantage," yawned Simple.

"Yes, they do! They want decent relations with the rest of the world, no more war, and all that. But if they don't change their attitude toward colored folks, they won't have a decent world," I said.

"Maybe they had rather have their attitude," said Simple.

"Well, I contend it will bring them to rack and ruin," I said.

"So what?" asked Simple.

"That would be too bad for them—and us, too," I said.

"How do you figger?" asked Simple.

"America would go to the dogs!" I said. "And if America went to the dogs, so would we."

"I had rather go to the dogs than to be a dog," said Simple. "And that is what I am now—as far as white folks are concerned—a dog!"

"You are only a dog if you think you are one," I said, "or if you let outside forces make you one."

"Then outside forces are hell," said Simple, "especially if they is white."

"You have got a white-complex," I said, "also a dog-psychosis. You need to be psychoanalyzed."

"For why?" said Simple.

"To change your mind," I said.

"It is not *my* mind that needs to be changed," said Simple. "It is them white folks."

"You are obsessed with the subject," I said. "You need to get it off your mind, else it will get you down. You have a white-folks fear-complex which psychoanalysis could remove."

"It is the white folks who are afraid of me," said Simple. "I sure ain't scared of them."

"You talk about them all the time," I said.

"Not as much as they talk about me," said Simple. "Besides, what is this psychoplexis you are talking about?"

"Well, it has to do with releasing your inner tensions," I said.

"Huh?" said Simple.

"In other words, it takes the weights of conflict off your mind," I explained.

"I have no waits, neither conflicts, in my mind," said Simple.

"Oh, but you have," I said. "White folks is one. You think about them night and day."

"I tell you it is them that thinks about me!" said Simple. "What I mainly thinks about is the good times I have had, not the bad—white folks or no white folks."

"You do seem to enjoy yourself," I said.

"I sure do enjoy myself," said Simple. "And when I get as old as Methuselah, I am going to get me a rocking chair. Every time I rock I am going to smile, I am going to remember the good times I have had—in spite of the white folks!"

"Then I guess you do not need to be psychoanalyzed," I said. "That is only for people who are not having a good time out of life."

"It must be for white folks," said Simple, "because they always talk like they are worried. Sometimes you talk like white folks yourself."

"Only when I am talking with you," I said. "Some of these arguments you hand out worry me. I have got to stop taking you seriously or else I will have complexes."

"Then let's us have a beer," said Simple. "That is very good for a man's complexions. Lend me a quarter and I will set you up. I am always kinder broke towards the end of the week."

"I am broke, too," I said.

"Then we will not have no beer," said Simple. "We will just keep on having complexions."

Pictures

"Since I saw them pictures a while back on the front page of *The New York Times* of that police dog in Birmingham biting a young black student in the stomach, I have ceased to like white folks," said Simple.

"As bad as Birmingham is," I said, "surely you do not blame white people in New York or Detroit or San Francisco for that Alabama dog."

"I do," said Simple, "because white folks is in the majority everywhere. They control the government in Washington, and if they let such doings go on in this American country, such as has been going on in Alabama and Mississippi, I blame them all. If white folks was bit by police dogs and prodded with electric rods, you can bet your bottom dollar something would be done about it—and quick—before you could say *Jackie Robinson*."

"You are no doubt right," I said, "but as long as they themselves are not bitten by dogs and prodded by electric rods and denied the right to march or to vote, most white folks in the North will do very little to help Southern Negroes."

"And I will do very little toward loving them," said Simple. "I am not Martin Luther King. Neither am I a young student or a child. I am a man, and I believe a man has a right to defend his self."

"Passive resistance is a technique designed as defense for the defenseless," I said, "a weapon for the poor and unarmed. I would like to see you standing up effectively to police dogs, clubs, and mobs. Except passively, how would you or could you compete?"

"I might die," said Simple, "but I would die fighting back."

"Then why do you not go down South and die? You are safe here in Harlem, New York City, talking so bravely now. Go South and see what happens to you, friend."

"I will not," said Simple. "That is why I left the South and come North when I was a young man, so I would not blow my top, get mad, fight, get beat, and die. I paid my own good fare to come up North. I figure the rest of those Negroes down South could do the same. What does anybody want to stay in Alabama, Mississippi, or Georgia for, as long as buses, trains, planes, or kiddy cars run and tickets are sold to get away? The Irish left Ireland when the going got rough. The Jews left Germany when Hitler turned on the gas ovens. The Hungarians run toward the Statue of Liberty some years back instead of staying in Hungary hungry. A lot of the white Cubans left Cuba when Castro let his beard grow. Why should not every black chick and child able to scrape up the fare *not* light out from there and say, 'Farewell, Mississippi! Farewell, Alabama! Farewell!' "

"I admit I do not know what makes anyone choose to stay in so unfriendly a land as the South seems to be," I said. "But I also am forced to admire—and *greatly* admire—those black men and women who do stay there and pray and march and demonstrate to make the South a better land."

"Which to happen, we will have to fight."

"What have Negroes got to fight white folks with?"

"God," said Simple.

"So you are going to drag God into the race problem," I protested.

"His eye is on the sparrow," said Simple, "so I know He watches white folks."

"And what means will God use to accomplish Civil Rights?" I asked.

"God works in a mysterious way," said Simple. "Maybe one of their own atom bombs will misfire, fall back to earth on Mississippi, and make cracker gravy out of every cracker down there. Maybe a moon rocket will circle the moon and drop on Birmingham and scare the Klansmen so bad they will tear their britches. Maybe the gold standard will drop out from under white folks and they will land in hell. Who knows what means God will take to straighten out this wicked world? But He will fix it."

"I did not know you are a man of faith," I said.

"Some days I am," said Simple. "Anyhow, God helps them that helps themselves. Ignited we stand, divided we fall."

"Meaning by that, what?"

"Meaning we of the colored race have got to stick together. In fact, I should say all the colored races of the world, including Africa, and elect either Adam Powell or Nkrumah leader."

"Your usual platform," I said. "Black Nationalism."

"Pure black," said Simple, "from Africa to Harlem. Ignited we stand!"

"You are ignited tonight," I said, "six beers—but I reckon you are speaking your sober mind."

"Sober as I can be in my mind," said Simple, "and my mind is most in generally clear. Besides, who can get high on just a little beer? And no matter how high I get, I am still colored, and still me, and still right here in Harlem by night, and working for white folks downtown by day.

Dark night, white day—but without white folks no pay. Harlem is run by white folks. And it has done got so a colored man cannot even write a few numbers and stay out of jail. And if he do write numbers, he sends the money downtown to the big white number bankers. It is them that controls us. Undertakers and barber shops is about the only businesses Negroes can own and control any more. And I even hear tell it is getting fashionable now for rich Negroes to have white undertakers. Do you reckon I will live to see the day when we have white barbers?"

"No telling what integration will bring," I said. "But I think it will be quite a while before white barbers take over Harlem shops, if ever. But surely, if you believe in democracy, you would not draw the color line on white barbers, would you?"

"So long as they did not draw their combs too hard through my head," said Simple.

Simple Arithmetic

"Next week is Negro History Week," said Simple. "And how much Negro history do you know?"

"Why should I know *Negro* history?" I replied. "I am an American."

"But you are also a black man," said Simple, "and you did not come over on the *Mayflower*—at least, not the same *Mayflower* as the rest."

"What rest?" I asked.

"The rest who make up the most," said Simple, "then write the history books and leave *us* out, or else put in the books nothing but prize fighters and ballplayers. Some folks think Negro history begins and ends with Jackie Robinson."

"Not quite," I said.

"Not quite is right," said Simple. "Before Jackie there was Du Bois and before him there was Booker T. Washington, and before him was Frederick Douglass and before Douglass the original Freedom Walker, Harriet Tubman, who were a lady. Before her was them great Freedom Fighters who started rebellions in the South long before the Civil War. By name they was Gabriel and Nat Turner and Denmark Vesey."

"When, how, and where did you get all that information at once?" I asked.

"From my wife, Joyce," said Simple. "Joyce is a fiend for history. She belongs to the Association for the Study of Negro Life and History. Also Joyce went to school down South. There colored teachers teach children about *our* history. It is not like up North where almost no teachers teach children anything about themselves and who they is and where they come from out of our great black past which were Africa in the old days."

"The days of Ashanti and Benin and the great trade routes in the Middle Ages, the great cities and great kings."

"Amen!" said Simple. "It might have been long ago, but we had black kings. It is from one of them kings that I am descended."

"You?" I exclaimed. "How so? After five hundred years it hardly seems possible that you can trace your ancestry back to an African king."

"Oh, but I can," said Simple. "It is only just a matter of simple arithmetic. Suppose great old King Ashanti in his middle ages had one son. And that one son had two sons. And them two sons each had three sons—and so on down the line, each bigger set of sons having bigger sets of children themselves. Why, the way them sons of kings and kings' sons multiplied, after five hundred years, every black man in the U.S.A. must be the son of one of them African king's grandsons' sons—including me. A matter of simple arithmetic—I am descended from a king."

"It is a good thing to think, anyhow," I said.

"Furthermore, I am descended from the people who built the pyramids, created the alphabets, first wrote words on stones, and first added up two and two."

"Who said all those wise men were colored?"

"Joyce, my wife—and I never doubts her word. She has been going to the Schomburg Collection all week reading books which she cannot take out and carry home because they is too valuable to the Negro people, so must be read in the library. In some places in Harlem a rat might chaw one of them books which is so old and so valuable nobody could put it back in the library. My wife says the Schomburg in Harlem is one of the greatest places in the world to find out about Negro history. Joyce tried to drag me there one day, but I said I had rather get my history from her after she has got it from what she calls the archives. Friend, what is an archive?"

"A place of recorded records, books, files, the materials in which history is preserved."

"They got a million archives in the Schomburg library," said Simple.

"By no stretch of the imagination could there be that many."

"Yes there is," said Simple. "Every word in there is an archive to the Negro people, and to me. I want to know about my kings, my past, my Africa, my history years that make me proud. I want to go back to the days when I did not have to knock and bang and beg at doors for the chance to do things like I do now. I want to go back to the days of my blackness and greatness when I were in my own land and were king and I invented arithmetic."

"The way you can multiply kings and produce yourself as a least common denominator, maybe you did invent arithmetic," I said.

"Maybe I did," said Simple.

Africa's Daughters

"You know," said Simple, "my wife kind of shook me up when she come telling me this morning, 'Us women is meeting in Africa next spring.' "

" 'What women?' I said.

" 'Colored women,' said Joyce. 'Us, Africa's daughters.'

" 'For what?'

" 'To discuss our problems,' says Joyce.

" 'What problems have colored womens got that mens have not?'

" 'Colored men,' said Joyce, 'are our problem.'

" 'No kidding,' I kidded.

" 'Jobs,' said Joyce. 'One of our problems also is jobs. All over the world, what kind of jobs are there for colored women? The world must think we are all cooks, servants, baby-sitters. Lots of white folks never heard of a colored stenographer, clerk, bookkeeper, woman doctor, scientist.'

" 'Then they don't read *Ebony*,' I said.

" 'One of our problems is to teach white people to know,' said Joyce.

" 'Know what?'

" 'Who we are,' said Joyce.

" 'But why meet in Africa to do that?'

" 'Africa is the fountainhead,' said Joyce. 'Africa is the new day. Africa will lead the way. Ethiopia shall stretch forth her hand.'

" 'And not draw back a nub,' I said. 'Anyhow, I agree with you, Joyce: Africa is up and coming, humming, done stopped drumming. But, Joyce, exactly what is you talking about, however?'

" 'I am talking about going to Africa,' said Joyce. 'If my club does not send me, I might not be able to go—in the flesh. But I will be there in spirit. An African conference of women, black, Jesse B., like me! From all over the world where there are black women—which is the U.S.A., also Cuba, Haiti, Jamaica, and Trinidad. Also Brazil, where they are black and beautiful like in that movie *Black Orpheus,* and all the West Indies, not to speak of Africa, full of beautiful black women! From everywhere the sisters of Africa are coming together next spring to meet to discuss how to get a good education for every child of every black woman. Also how to be sure husbands and fathers make a decent living anywhere in the world. Also that no woman has to be beholding to any man, white or black, for her living. And no woman needs to make her body a part of her job, like too many women have had to do in the past. I BELONG TO ME is the new slogan for black women. I SHALL BE FREE! the new slogan for black women. EQUAL JOBS AND EQUAL RIGHTS FOR MEN AND WOMEN, BLACK OR WHITE is our new slogan.'

" 'I am glad you include equal rights for mens, too.' I grinned.

" 'Keep on laughing,' said Joyce, 'but she who laughs last is always a woman.'

"I wiped that grin off my face, because I could see that Joyce was getting serious."

African Names

"Money is so hard for Negroes to make," complained Simple. "That is why we come North, to better ourselves. In recent years, so many Negroes have left Mississippi and Alabama that there is a shortage of labor in the cotton fields. So I hear that the white folks have proposed to bring in monkeys from Africa to help pick cotton. But they tell me one old Southern Senator is dead set against it. Do you know why? He says, 'Would you want your daughter to marry a monkey?' "

"Absurd," I said.

"Right," said Simple, "because how would he know if monkeys would be interested in them poor white Southern girls? On paydays the monkeys might head right straight for the colored parts of town. In Africa, monkeys is used to black faces. In America, white faces might scare them monkeys to death. I once heard about a pair of monkeys they brought from Africa for the Bronx Park Zoo that never would come out of their cages until they peeked through a hole and saw some colored folks standing in the crowd. Then they would come out and say, 'Howdy!' "

"You can really make up some far-out tales," I said.

"Animals have got plenty of sense. Them monkeys in that zoo knew that not a Negro in the U.S.A. would send way over to Africa for a pair of monkeys to put in a cage. Colored folks have neither the time nor the money for monkeys."

"Baw!" I said.

"Baw is right," said Simple. "That is what one sheep said to the other sheep one day: 'Baa!'

" 'Baa!' the second sheep replied.

" 'Whereupon, the first sheep answered, 'Moo!'

" 'Moo?' asked the second sheep. 'What does *moo* mean?'

" '*Baa* in a foreign language,' said the first sheep."

"I guess that sheep was majoring in French in school," I said.

"No," said Simple, "he were majoring in *bull*."

"Sometimes I think you must have majored in that yourself."

"You know I did not go far in school."

"Well, you can certainly tell some mighty tall tales," I said.

"Believe it or not," declared Simple, "my great-grandpa was so strong he could pull a plow without a mule. Fact is, his old white master sold his mule and kept Grandpa, and the plowing went on just the same. Just imagine, if Grandpa had of been plowing for his self, how rich we would have been today. The white Semples is a wealthy Virginia family what got rich off of plantations and slavery, but all they gave us Negroes was their name, *Semple*. And that I do not want. I would give Semple up for an African Mohammedan Ali Baba name any day."

"A black man with an African name would be colored in America just the same," I said.

"You has no race pride," stated Simple. "If I ever have a son, I am going to give him an African name."

"Roland Hayes has a daughter named Africa," I said.

"More power to him," said Simple. "Indian names is nice, too, but I do not know what my grandmother's great grandpa's name were, otherwise I might take it, long as it were not Black Foot."

"Maybe it was Red Wing," I said.

"Nice name," said Simple. "I wonder how my wife would like to be called Joyce Red Wing. I am going to ask her."

"Sitting Bull was also a famous Indian name," I said.

"No Bull," said Simple. "I do not think Joyce would like being Mrs. Bull."

"There was once a beautiful dancer named Maria Tallchief," I said.

"And a colored blues singer named Pine Top," added Simple. "But I reckon he was only part Indian, like me. If I was to find out my Indian name and add it to my African name in front of my Mohammedan name nobody would ever know I had been Jesse B. Semple before. I could put on my Social Security card a name out of this world. And when folks asked me my race, I could say, 'Just try to trace.'

"Suppose my name were Buffalo Horn Yusef Ali Congo, would it not have a noble sound? When Mr. and Mrs. Congo went out together, we would be solid gone. In there, like the bear! Me with my beard and Joyce with her Ashanti robe. And me, I would have on one of there fez caps like Dizzie Gillespie brought back from North Africa. And was I to run into Sammy Davis, who is Jewish, I would say, 'Shalom!' And Sammy would answer, 'Mazel tov!' "

"And what would Joyce say?" I inquired, getting quite intrigued with Simple's fantasy exchange.

"Joyce would say, 'Hallelujah!' " said Simple, "because it would be hard for her to get over her Baptist training."

Harems and Robes

"One nice thing about dogs," said Simple, "is that they are usually not stuck up. No matter how much pedigree a dog has got, it would just as leave belong to me as to Harry Belafonte. To a dog, a master by any other name smells just as sweet. Dogs is democratic. I love dogs."

"You're an old dog yourself," I said.

"I used to think about becoming a Mohammedan," declared Simple.

"A Mohammedan?" I said. "Why?"

"So I can stop being the least and look toward the East," said Simple, "grow a beard on my chin and give up gin, because you know Mohammedans do not drink. They think."

"An admirable ambition," I said, "if it would work with you. How about beer?"

"Have no fear. Were I to go on the Mohammedan side, I would abide by their laws and hymns. What I do, I do whole hog, once I *do* do. I been listening to the Muslims speak and I thirst for what they seek—to step beyond the *N* to the *M*."

"Meaning by that, what?" I asked.

"*N* stands for Negro, but *M* stands for *Man*. Also for Muslims. Muslims is colored, so I would just be joining hands with more colored, were I to become a Muslim. But my only drawback is Joyce. My wife is Baptist. Were I to come home one day renamed Alim, Joyce probably would holler out loud, demand that I shave off my chin whiskers, and drag me off to baptism. But I hear tell that Muslims can have four wives, so I could always hold a harem over her head."

"Four wives in Mohammedan countries, perhaps," I said, "but you live in the U.S.A., where the civil law prohibits plural marriages. In New York you can have only one wife. Besides, Joyce would hardly share you with *one* woman, let alone three. Also, how would you take care of *four* wives on your salary? Where would you put four wives in a Harlem kitchenette?"

"I would manage," said Simple. "Only thing that would worry me would be, how would I ever win an argument with four wives? But there is nothing in the Muslim religion that says a man *has* to marry four wives. I could just stay three-fourths single like I is. I would keep Joyce—and let the other three go. But I might buy myself a Muslim robe just so as to look different. With so many people in my neighborhood wearing robes, it is hard these days to tell real Africans from Harlem Africans. Folks are letting their hair go natural, jazz bands are playing African music, men are wearing Sékou Touré caps, womens are in Nigerian robes. I met a girl in a beautiful robe at a party on Lenox Avenue Saturday night.

"I said, 'Miss, what part of Africa are you from?'

"She said, 'Alabama.'

"I said, 'I reckon you can get served in a bus station down in Alabama, then.'

"She said, 'That is one reason I wear these robes. They help—even in New York—if you are black. Another reason I wear these African robes is because I am proud to be descended from Africa, proud of my ancestry, proud of my people, and proud of their robes.'

" 'Good,' I says. 'Sister, I am proud of you. Meet your brother.'

"On that we shook. But when I asked her for a dance, she said no, she was with her boy friend and he was six feet tall. So I went back to dancing with my wife.

"I said to my wife whilst dancing, 'Joyce, honey, let's get ourselves some African robes and see if they help us get our rights quicker.'

"Joyce said, 'Not I. Just as I would not pass for white, so I will not pass for African. I want my rights in the U.S.A. just as I am, black, without one plea.'

" 'Baby,' I said, 'you have to plea more than once with American white folks to get what rightfully is your rights. If a robe and turban help, why not?'

" 'I will stand up for my rights without a robe,' says Joyce. 'The black women of America have as much right to all rights as white women have without putting on any foreign robes to get them. I love Africa, but I was born in Florida, U.S.A., America. Of my African blood I am proud, but I want American rights. Of my black face I have no shame, therefore I have the right to want the right to show my face anyplace in America any other folks show their face. I say, no more segregation in the U.S.A. for Africans with robes or Negroes without robes. Rights should not depend on a robe.'

" 'Neither on a turban,' I said. 'But you remember how a Negro newspaper man few years ago put on a turban and went down South and got served from here to yonder and the Carolinas to Texas. Them stupid Southerners thought he was an A-rab.'

" 'An air-rab,' says Joyce.

" 'Some kind of foreigner, anyhow,' I said. 'So with a turban he was not Jim Crowed—yet he was black as me. Which goes to show there is no reason for prejudice. It do not make sense. Dress like me—segregated. Dress like a foreigner, take a foreign name, speak Spanish, and wear a turban—integrated. I see no harm in fooling white folks, myself.'

" 'It is so undignified to have to lie,' said Joyce. 'So undignified not to be *able* to be yourself, whoever you be. I want to be *me*—Mrs. Jesse B. Semple.'

" 'Good for you, Joyce,' I says.

" 'My Afro-American angel,' cooed Joyce, dancing with her head on my shoulder.

" 'Congo cutie,' I whispered in her ear.

" 'Lenox Avenue lion,' she purred to me.

" 'Whrrr-rr-er!' I roared. 'You're *mine!*' "

Money and Mice

"Now, you take my boss," said Simple. "I come to work earlier than he do, I work longer, and I leave later. But that white man makes one hundred times more money than I do. Why is that?"

"That is because he uses his brains, he can do what you can't do, and he knows more than you ever know," I said.

"That is no reason why he should get all *that much more* money—because if it wasn't for what I do, there wouldn't be no results coming from what he know. I turn out what he thinks out. Who does the work in the plant? Me, and mens like me. Old boss comes to work at 10 a.m. and before you can turn around, he has gone out to lunch again. He comes back from lunch at 3 p.m. and goes home at four-thirty before the traffic gets heavy, also so he can stop for a drink at the club. He takes a looo-oo-ong weekend, leaves the office of the plant on Thursday afternoon and don't come back no more until Tuesday morning. Yet I am there working all day long, each and every day during the week. But he gets the most pay, for the *least* hours, for doing the least."

"You have to realize, old man, that what your boss does, he does in his head."

"Yes, but what I do, I do on the job, and with hard labor at that. What he sells, I help to make. My boss can't turn out nothing just from his head that anybody can see and feel and buy. His head can't turn out no products."

"No, but his products start in his head," I said.

"But they end in my hands," said Simple. "So ain't my hands worth as much as his head?"

"Unfortunately, no," I said. "Smart heads are rare—but handy hands are common. Almost anybody can drive a nail or use a lathe. But not everybody can think up new furniture styles, for example. Your boss is an industrial designer, a planner, and a merchandiser."

"But I make the merchandise," insisted Simple. "I make it. I do not care who thinks it up—I MAKE it."

"But if somebody didn't think it up, what would you have to make?"

"I'd make something else," said Simple. "And I figure that MAKING is as important as THINKING. Besides, anybody can think quicker than they can do. I can think of all kinds of things in a minute that it would take me days to make. For one minute's thought, should I get ten days' pay?"

"If you think wisely and well enough, in a single minute, it is conceivable that you might merit more than ten days' pay. What a creative mind can conceive in a short time might be worth more than what many hands can do in a long time. For example, take Edison—when he thought up the electric light bulb, imagine what a gift of light he gave humanity. But the concept of a bulb, the original design, had to first come out of Edison's mind. Did he not deserve great monetary awards for thinking up such a boon to mankind as the electric light?"

"Edison might could think up one light, and make one light. But to make all the millions of bulbs used today, it takes factories full of men working all day long, and with their hands, like I work, and at machines, to make all them bulbs. And them mens deserves their awards, too. If they never think thoughts, their hands make things that thoughts have already thought up. And thoughts without hands would not account to a thing. All I am trying to say is, let me who makes the things get some of the money, too, and some of the short hours, too, and the long weekends, too. And don't let the man with the mind make a hundred times more a day than the man with the hands. I am the man with the hands."

"Friend," I said, "I have never heard you discuss any one subject so long before without bringing in race and color. When are you going to bring it all around to race?"

"I am not thinking about race today," said Simple. "What I am thinking about is how we is all caught in a trap, and how prices has gone up so high that a man, no matter what his race and color, needs to make more money to live. I am thinking about money, which is green, neither black nor white—money, which do not care who spends it; money, which don't feel as good to me in somebody else's pocket as it does in mine. Friend, I am thinking about money—which goes beyond race. If all the Negroes in the world had money, the color problem would be solved in the morning. In this American country, money makes a man a MAN, otherwise he is nothing but a mouse. To be men or miceses, that is the problem. And I sure would hate to be a mice."

"You would hate to be a mouse," I corrected.

"I mean a mouse," said Simple, "because I see in the papers where doctors and laboratories and such used up twenty million mice in the U.S.A. last year testing out new medicines and needles and things on them. I would hate to belong to any part of the mice family, white or otherwise, and be snatched up and vaccinated with some kind of needle to see if I am going to catch whatever it is they are testing for. I pity them poor animals—born to die with fevers and things before their time."

"Don't you think it is better mice serve some useful purpose than just getting caught in a trap baited with cheese and having their necks broken in the corner of somebody's kitchen? At least in the laboratory a mouse has a function. New drugs that cannot be tried out on human beings may be tested on mice, and their effects noted. Also diseases, by inoculating mice. Thus they serve the cause of science."

"If I was a mouse, I would hate to have my life cut short for science or anybody else," said Simple. "I had rather take my chances on the trap and the cheese. Let me pick my own trap and fall in it. Life ain't nothing but a trap, nohow, and inside the big trap is all kinds of little traps. But I don't want nobody to up and throw me in no trap just to see how I will react. That paper said the reactions of the mouses were being studied as to how they reacted when they are injected. A mice in a trap do not have to react, because his neck is broke. He is dead. I had rather be dead than stuck with a needle to see how I will react. And you would, too, wouldn't you?"

"I would hate to be a guinea pig," I agreed, "or a mouse in a laboratory. But then I would hate to be a mouse anyway."

"I would hate to be a man were I not already one," said Simple. "I have never heard of animals sticking another one with a needle to see how it would react, or putting him to sleep just to see if he will wake up again. Animals do not do no such things to each other. Only mens do such to animals."

"Your holier-than-thou attitude toward science is surprising," I said. "You eat pork chops, but a pig has to be killed to get those chops for you. You eat beefsteak, veal, lamb, chicken, and in all cases some animal has to face his end to feed your belly. So why this sudden compassion for mice—just because you happen to read a little article on medical research in the papers today?"

"Sometimes it do not take much to start me to thinking," said Simple. "Twenty million is an awful lot of mice. And now you have started me to thinking more. Every time I eat a piece of meat, some animal has died so that I might eat and live. You are right! Lord, come to think of it, when I die the worms will eat me. Chickens will eat the worms. Folks will eat the chickens. Then where will I be? What kind of trap is we all caught in, I ask you? And me with no money, neither!"

Population Explosion

"Now that winter has come and it is getting real cold on Lenox Avenue," said Simple, "some nights I just stay home and read the papers, in which I see a lots these days about the population explosion and how we ought to be doing something about it."

"What *we?*" I asked.

"We white folks," said Simple. "Did you not see in the papers last week where a blue-ribbon citizens' committee has propositioned to the White House that our American nation spend One Hundred Million Dollars on birth control? If that be so, we intends to go hog-wild. It looks like to me not One Hundred Million but just one *single* million would be enough to subsidize every drug store in the United States and buy ten times enough birth-control things for every man, woman, and child in the country."

"What things exactly do you mean?" I asked.

"I hear it is against the law to tell anybody what them things' names is because that would be birth control—which is only to be *did*—not spoken about. You know that?"

"I am afraid I am not an authority on birth control," I said, "not being a married man."

"You should be *authority the most,*" said Simple, "also the most careful. The way many a unmarried man has got hooked is by *not* being an authority. But I suppose you can learn, since a great deal of that One Hundred Million, the newspaper states, might be spent on education."

"Certainly a lot of people are unfamiliar with birth-control devices," I said.

"They should not be if they is over ten years old," declared Simple. "But a lot of education would have to be translated, anyhow."

"Translated?" I inquired.

"Yes," affirmed Simple, "for colored—into jive talk for Harlem, into Indian for Indians, Gypsy for Gypsies, and Chinese for China."

"Why are you naming just colored folks?" I inquired.

"Because that is who the white folks is aiming birth control at, is it not?" asked Simple. "They always talking about there is nine hundred million people in India and in another ten years there will be ten hundred million. And in China there is seven hundred million, which will be ten hundred million by 1992. Africa has got so many million Africans that white folks do not even count them, and many is too dark to see. Every so often our white folks hints at Harlem, too, but they do not dare come right out and say we has a population explosion on Lenox Avenue. They just say 90 percent of the free maternity wards in Manhattan is occupied by colored."

"I see in today's paper where the American Medical Association indicates favor of birth control, even of sterilization and abortion when advisable."

"They got all kinds of Health Wagons going up and down the streets of Harlem now, free X rays, free vaccine shots and things. But nobody has to take them. Suppose, though, they passed a birth-control law and the Supreme Court upheld the right of the city to cut down by law on the uptown population explosion and they sent a Sterilization Wagon to Harlem. Naturally, like they did with HAR-YOU-ACT, they would try it out on colored folks first, calling themselves being helpful to 'poor underprivileged Harlem,' curbing the population explosion. But you know and I know, Harlem do not want to be stopped from exploding. They better send that Sterilization Wagon to Vietnam, where they can gas the people into being caught and made prisoners and sterilized. Suppose we fought the whole war with Sterilization Wagons? That would be one way to wipe out all future Vietcongs for generations to come."

"But Suppose the Vietcong captured a lot of our Sterilization Wagons and then used them against American troops," I said.

"Negotiations for peace would begin at once," said Simple. "White folks are not thinking about being sterilized, neither in war nor in peace. It is India, China, Africa, and Harlem they is considering—One Hundred Million Dollars' worth of birth control for us! You know, I really do believe white folks always got something up their sleeve for colored folks. Yes, they has!"

Youthhood

"I wonder where," said Simple, "did I leave my youthhood?"

"And why such wonderment?" I asked.

"When I go upstairs now, I pants," said Simple, "out of breath."

"You go upstairs too fast," I said.

"I used to go upstairs and I did not pant," said Simple, "so I must be getting ageable."

"I trust nothing worse is happening to you than shortness of breath."

"Not yet," said Simple. "I still has all my functions—and hope to have until I get to my second childhood."

"I trust you are not one of these people who want to go back to their childhood: 'Oh, to be a child again just for tonight.' "

"Not I," said Simple. "I do not want to be no child again, especially at night. Nighttime is when I were the most lonesome, when I were a child. And I would be lonesome now was it not for Joyce. As for going back to my youthhood, not me! No, never! In my youthhood I did not have nothing I wanted, and it looked like I did not even know what I was looking for. No, I do not want to be young again, not me."

"I am glad to hear you say that," I said, "because it always seems sort of silly to me hearing grown-up folks say they would like to be children again—to avoid cares and responsibilities, I suppose. But it is such a futile wish."

"I say again, not me," said Simple. "I had more cares and responsibilities when I were a child than I have now. Grown-up peoples were a worriation to me. Every time I got attached to somebody I was living with I got shifted to somebody else. I were a passed-around child. The only relative that really wanted me, and loved me, were my old Aunt Lucy. And to tell the truth, she were nothing but a step-aunt. But Aunt Lucy tried to raise me right. She whipped me almost every day. She tried to rid me of my badness, but the only way she knowed was prayers and whippings. But I tried to do better, and I did better, and I growed up to be a man, all on account of Aunt Lucy. I give that old lady credit. But I would not want to be no child again. 'Spare the rod and spoil the child' was the motto in them days—and my behind is still sore."

"Were I to have a child, I do not believe I would lay nothing heavier on it than the palm of my hand, and I would go light on that. I would use psychology on a child—unless I lost my patience. In which case I would spank it just enough to make it scared. I might lose my patience again, but I would hate to really get mad and whip it. Grown-up peoples should not get mad with a child, even when they aggravate you. We is too much bigger and too much older than children to get mad at them. Children has nowhere else to live except with grown peoples and when you get mad with children, you make them feel like you do not want them any more.

"A little small child cannot take care of his self, neither can a teen-ager who has no experience in the world. So the worst thing you can do to a child or a teen-ager is to make him feel like you do not want him around. All them relatives of mine that made me feel that way in my youthhood is a stone in my heart right now. But Aunt Lucy never did make me feel like she did not want me around. Even when she whipped me, I knowed she loved me. Which makes all the difference in the world. But if I had a child, I do not believe I would ever even whip it."

"You would probably spoil it," I said. "You know, the psychologists say there is such a thing as too much love."

"I do not believe there ever is," said Simple.

Hail and Farewell

"I am practically gone," said Simple.

"Gone home tonight, you mean?" I asked.

"Further than home," declared Simple, "and longer than tonight."

"To Glory?" I said. "Or Vietnam?"

"Worse," said Simple. "I am going to the suburbans."

"To the suburbs? How come? Listen, what's happening, huh?"

"Joyce has saved enough money to make a down payment on a house, that's what's happening. You know my wife always wanted a house. She is now going to make a down payment," said Simple. "The first week of the first of the year 1966, my Joyce—who controls the budget and our Carver Savings Bank book—which is *not* a *joint* account—is having the cashier make out a certified check to this real estate agent who has done sold my wife a house so far away from Harlem you have to get off the train at the dead end of the subway, then take a bus to get to our street, then walk three blocks after that to reach this house which my wife is making me buy. I will be shoveling snow, stoking the furnace, and putting washers in sinks for the rest of my natural life."

Simple took a long drink from his beer glass; in fact, he drained it, then signaled the bartender for another.

"You don't sound too happy about it," I said.

"I am not," moaned Simple. "I had rather have a kitchenette in Harlem than a mansion on Long Island or a palace in Westchester. A lawn with grass to mow and leaves to rake is the *last* thing I want. And God knows I do not like to shovel snow. No, I do not like shoveling snow! *No!*"

"Maybe you can pay the little boy next door to shovel snow," I said.

"Suppose there is not a little boy next door," said Simple. "Or suppose he is white."

"Are not you-all moving into an integrated neighborhood?" I asked.

"Joyce says we will be the first Negroes in the block," said Simple. "That will also be a drag. I likes to be around my people. But Joyce says it is our duty to show white folks we can keep a house up as well as anybody else. I know Joyce will work me to death keeping that house spick-and-span inside and out, just to show white people Negroes are not tramps. Colored folks have always got to be worried about what white folks thinks. Joyce says they do not meet enough representative Negroes—whatever kind that is—so when we move we are going to show our neighbors a neighborhood do not run down just because colored peoples move in."

"Suppose your neighbors object to our presence, start throwing stones at your windows and things like that, then what?"

"They say our neighborhood is integrated, but the block is not. It is still an all-white block this week, but FOR SALE signs are up everywhere. It will be an all-colored block before you can say *Jackie Robinson*. Joyce and me will be breaking the ice in January—then the real estate agents will do the rest—selling houses to Negroes at twice the price. Me and Joyce will be 999 years paying off our mortgage—and I will be still sending back payments from the Golden Gates. To me there is not a suburb in the world worth the price they is charging us for our house. But Joyce always did say she wanted a house with trees and a big back yard, and a picture window in the front room. I told Joyce we liable to look out the window someday and see the Ku Klux Klan in hoods and robes standing there. I asked her is there any Deacons for Defense amongst our colored neighbors in the next block. But Joyce says the real estate man assured her there is not trouble in the offing. Just pay our money down and move in, he says. But, Boyd, I do not want to move out of Harlem. I will miss Harlem, Seventh Avenue, Lenox, the Apollo, and the Palms, also this little old bar in which I am now drinking. I will also miss my friends—and you."

"I'll come over some Sunday and pay you a call," I said. "In fact, I will come to your housewarming—if it is not in the wintertime."

"I do not blame you for not wanting to wade through snow from the end of the bus line," said Simple. "But if you really be's my friend, you will come over once in a while just to cheer me up. I will need it, way out yonder by my lonesome, without a juke box nowhere in earshot. And unless we build a playroom in our basement, there will not be a bar in sight—only a carton of beer from the supermarket, which I will have to fetch myself in case Joyce will break our budget to raise my beer allowance. Joyce will have to do something to keep me happy in the suburbans, I'm telling you. I been a Harlemite too long to be a suburbanite, even if I am getting a bit ageable. Joyce states we are old enough to settle down now, stop paying rent to landlords, and live like decent folks in our prime. What does she mean by *prime*?"

"Prime," I said, "means the time in life when the experiences of youth and the wisdom of maturity meet to give you a balanced viewpoint on living—the time when a man is really ready to live."

"If that be true, then," said Simple, "why leave the place where life is—to go live with the birds, the bees, and caterpillars and bats? Life to me is where *peoples* is at—not nature and snow and trees with falling leaves to rake all by yourself, and furnaces to stoke, and no landlords in earshot to holler at downstairs to keep the heat up, and no next-door neighbors on your floor to raise a ruckus Saturday nights, and no bad children drawing pictures on the walls in the halls, and nobody to drink a beer with at the corner bar—because that corner in the suburbans has nothing on it but a dim old lonesome street light on a cold old lonesome pole. And to get to Harlem from where you live you have to walk to a bus line, then ride to a subway line, then change at Times Square for the A train to Harlem. Friend, when I move to the suburbans, I am gone. So bye-bye-bye-bye! Goodbye! Yes, Jesse B. Semple is gone."

Notes

Simple Stakes a Claim

1. Gamal Abdel Nasser (1918–1970), president of Egypt from 1956 to 1970). Lawrence Eugene Doby (1924–), the first African American baseball player in the American League. Don Newcombe (1926–), a Brooklyn Dodgers pitcher who was a teammate of Jackie Robinson.

2. Miss Lucy is Arthurine Lucy, the black woman who integrated the University of Alabama in 1956.

3. John Kasper, an inflammatory racist who fought against the integration of schools in Charlotte, North Carolina.

Simple's Uncle Sam

1. Rev. Fred Shuttlesworth, a leader in the fight against segregation in Birmingham, Alabama, was one of the founders of the Southern Christian Leadership Conference and a frequent target of bombing attacks. See Andrew M. Manis, *A Fire You Can't Put Out: The Civil Rights Life of Birmingham's Reverend Fred Shuttlesworth* (Tuscaloosa: University of Alabama Press, 1999).

2. HARYOU is Harlem Youth Opportunities, Unlimited, a program developed in the 1960s to help young people in Harlem receive training, creative outlets, and other means to achieve respectable and productive lives.

Index of Titles